I0593138

STOLEN LOVE, FRACTURED LIVES

LYN BEHAN

PUBLISHED BY BEHANPUBLISHING, 2023

First published by AIA Publishing 2020

Paperback : ISBN 978-0-64565872-9

Cover design by K. Rose Kreative

CHAPTER 1

SYDNEY 1968

Dr Richard Broughton strode down Elizabeth Street, hunched against the bitter wind, his scarf wound around his neck, one hand in his coat pocket and the other holding a briefcase. He was glad he'd been wearing his thick tweed overcoat when he left England on that freezing day back in January. Even Big Ben had stopped due to the snow! One of his friends, another lecturer from his university, had driven him to the railway station with all his cases and bags.

'You won't need that thick coat in Australia,' he'd joked. 'Hot and sunny over there!'

Well, it had been sweltering when he'd arrived at Mascot Airport. He'd felt a bit foolish carrying a heavy coat and scarf over his arm as he waited outside for a taxi. But now, in August, he was glad to have it. He wished he was back in his flat, small and spartan as it was. His thoughts rambled on. And that woman, Marguerite somebody, had rung him at work and bulldozed him into giving this lecture.

'It's for charity,' she'd said. 'The Smith Family.' Whoever *they* were.

Apparently her nephew had been at one of his lectures about the fourth dimension and had raved about it. Who would bother coming out on a cold and miserable Saturday in August to listen to a lecture on advanced geometry?

A scruffy looking young woman was standing outside the hall as he approached.

'Excuse me,' he began.

At the same time, she looked up at him and said, 'Excuse me, do you have the time?'

He looked at his watch. 'Quarter past two.'

'Thanks. Are you going to the lecture?' She indicated a poster on one of the doors.

He turned and looked at it

Cubism and the Fourth Dimension.

Calling all Art and Mathematics Lovers.

Is There Common Ground?

Dr. Richard Broughton will give a fascinating talk.

Saturday 10th August.

He scowled. *Art lovers?* He knew nothing about art! This was going to be a farce. He made a snorting noise and was just thinking about writing *CANCELLED* in big letters across the poster and going back to his flat when a woman emerged from the hall.

She beamed at him. 'You must be Dr Broughton! I'm Marguerite Daley. We spoke on the telephone. I have the gallery just down the road. Now, we're all ready for you. Come in, come in. I'm expecting a big crowd.' She took his arm and started to draw him into the hall, then, noticing the woman standing behind him, half turned. 'Oh, hello, Sybilla dear, so pleased you managed to come.'

Inside the hall she turned to him. 'Do you need a microphone? Is this lectern suitable for you?'

'Yes, yes, it's fine, and I probably won't need a microphone if people would only sit up at the front, instead of huddling in the back rows.' He knew he sounded grumpy.

'Oh! Well, look, I won't make too many rows, and if more people come, I can put extra chairs out.'

He nodded. 'Yes, that's fine.' He gave a brief smile to make up for his bad humour. 'Thank you.' He looked around. 'I have slides. Do you have a projector and a screen?'

'Ah!' Marguerite looked contrite. 'Oh dear, no. I didn't think.'

'Well a flip chart will do. I have pens.'

'Oh! Sorry; I should have asked you what you needed. So sorry.' She bit her lip and put her hands together in a gesture of atonement.

Richard grimaced, then he shrugged and sighed. 'Well, I have a few copies of notes and diagrams. Perhaps you could pass them around, and the audience can share.' He put his briefcase on a chair and opened it. 'Yes, I think I have enough copies here. How many people are you expecting?'

'There's been a lot of interest, particularly from my friends in the art society,' Marguerite said, not answering his question. She brought a glass of water to the podium and took the copies he handed to her. 'Do you need anything else?'

'No thank you.' He removed his overcoat and put it on the back of a chair, then took out his notes from a lecture he'd given last semester and scanned them.

People drifted in. He noticed elegantly dressed women—*probably the Daley woman's arty crowd,* he thought scornfully—a few men and a lot of what were probably art students, judging by their eclectic garments.

He looked down and noticed the scruffy young woman sitting in the first row right in front of the podium. Probably down and out, judging by her clothes, just come to get in out of the cold. Then he remembered that Marguerite had spoken to her. He looked more closely at her.

She looked up at him and smiled.

Surprised, he smiled back.

At exactly 2.30 pm, Marguerite came up to the podium, spread wide her arms and started to talk. 'Welcome everyone. Today we are very lucky to have Dr Richard Broughton with us. He's going to talk about cubism and the fourth dimension, and I'm sure all the art lovers here are going to be enthralled to hear how Picasso and Braque came up with their ideas.'

Richard frowned. What did she mean, Picasso and Cubism? He hadn't mentioned anything about that in his lectures! And who on earth was this Braque person? He'd better try and simplify this talk.

She clapped her hands towards Richard, who glumly realised that his audience would be very disappointed not to hear about Picasso. He overheard a man whisper to the woman sitting next to him, 'I thought you said it was about nudism and Picass ...' before she nudged him with her elbow and shushed him.

'Thank you, Mrs Daley.' Richard nodded to her. 'And good afternoon, ladies and gentlemen. As Mrs Daley has mentioned, this talk is about the fourth dimension.' He took a breath. 'Now we all know what a two-dimensional image is; it's what we see in a drawing or painting. In mathematics, this is represented by an abscissa or x-axis and an ordinate or y-axis. To get the distance between a point on the x-axis and a point on the y-axis, as you all know, we use the Pythagorean Theorem, which states that in any right-angled triangle the square of the hypotenuse is equal to the sum of the squares on the other two sides.'

He looked around at the audience. A few people frowned and others nodded; some had blank looks on their faces. He continued, 'An artist tries to represent three-dimensional space in two-dimensional space on their canvas by providing an image or projection as viewed from a single viewpoint. In fact, that viewpoint is comprised of many 3D objects.

'Consider a cube, for example; viewed from one side, it's just a two-dimensional rectangle, but if we look at it from any other angle, it may comprise many cubes. Going back to our theorem of Pythagoras, if we now have another axis, which we will call the z-axis, and a point on this axis, as well as points on the x and y axes, then a distance in 3D space is thus the square root of the sum of the squares of these three co-ordinates.'

The eyelids of some of the audience started to close. *Better get them to do something.*

'Now if you would look at the notes that our kind hostess has handed out, you'll see in the first diagram a picture of a cube, then in the second diagram the cube opened out to form what is known as a hypercube ...'

The audience sat up as they rustled and examined the notes. Some of them looked at them upside down. *Not that it makes much difference*, Richard thought gloomily.

He carried on. Most of his audience had glazed expressions in their eyes, except for Down and Out right in front of him. She sat forward the whole time and appeared to be listening intently and studying the notes or fixing her gaze on him.

He struggled on, trying as best as he could to skip the more mathematical parts of his lecture. At last he was nearly finished. 'As you all know, time is considered to be the fourth dimension, and this is where, as I understand it, the concept of cubism in the art world comes in.' He glanced over at Marguerite, 'however, I'm a mathematician, not an artist, but I'm sure Mrs Daley could tell us more about the art aspect of cubism.' He raised his eyebrows and gave her a sideways look as he waved his hand to where she sat on his left.

Marguerite jumped up. 'Oh, Dr Broughton, that was such a fascinating talk, thank you. Now I'm sure you must all have lots of questions.' She smiled at the audience, who shuffled on their hard chairs and seemed to be making moves to go.

Down and Out put up her hand.

'Yes?' He looked down at her.

'You spoke about how to create a hypercube by starting with a cube in 3-D space, and then creating another cube at a certain distance, but when you spoke about a z-axis, I got a bit lost. I'm not even sure what an x-axis is ...' She frowned and looked at the diagram on her lap. 'I didn't quite follow it. Could you clarify it a bit more?'

'Well, I'd need a flip chart to explain fully.' Richard looked around.

Marguerite saved him. 'Dr Broughton doesn't really have time to go into such detail.' She smiled at the audience. They'd started fidgeting with their bags and getting to their feet. 'So I'd like to thank him for such a fascinating talk. I'm sure we now understand the origins of the art of cubism.' She bent down, picked up a brown carrier bag and held it out to him. 'Would you accept this as a token of our appreciation, Dr Broughton?'

He nodded. 'Thank you.'

'Now, can I ask you all to give a big hand to Dr Broughton.' She turned back to Richard and clapped enthusiastically.

The sound of scraping chairs and a desultory clapping came from the audience. They moved towards the exit, mostly appearing relieved that the lecture was over.

Richard thanked Marguerite and put the bag into his brief case. Out of the corner of his eye, he saw Down and Out coming towards him, holding the notes which she'd gone around and collected. The audience seemed happy to leave them behind.

'I thought you might need these,' she said, holding them out.

Marguerite turned to her. 'Thank you, Sybilla dear. I'm in a bit of a rush, so I'll come back later and sort out the chairs. Now I really must fly back to the gallery.' She picked up the donation box and with a wave of her hand was gone.

Richard took his overcoat from the back of the chair, put it on and wound his scarf around his neck. As he bent down to pick up his brief case he noticed Down and Out standing in front of him.

'I really want to know more about this subject,' she said earnestly. 'Do you give private lessons?'

'No, I don't.' Then, thinking he might have sounded a bit abrupt, he mumbled something about being too busy lecturing to give private tuition. He started down the steps of the podium to the exit.

She followed him. 'I really do need to know more. It's important for my work. I'm an artist. I need to learn about cubism. Please, will you teach me?' she spoke quickly and eagerly. 'I'll pay you, of course! Just tell me what you charge.'

'I told you. I don't—'

'At least, as soon as I sell a painting, I can pay you,' she interrupted, then paused. 'Wait! I've had an idea. Come with me to Marguerite's Gallery. You can pick any one of my paintings that are on display in exchange for teaching me.' She caught hold his sleeve, her eyes shining. 'Please!'

'Well, like I just said, I don't—'

'It's not far! Please?'

He groaned inwardly, but it seemed she wasn't going to let him go. 'Well, I ...'

'Won't take a minute; gallery's just around the corner. Oh, by the way, I'm Sybilla Cresswell.' She didn't let go of his sleeve, and he was too polite to shake her off.

He nodded and followed her as she clumped out of the hall and down the street to a plain-looking building that professed to be an art gallery.

'Here we are.' She pushed open the door.

Marguerite stood near the back with a client. Catching sight of them, she turned and waved.

Sybilla led him to a corner of the gallery. 'Look, all the paintings on this wall are mine. Pick the one you like best.'

He walked along, stopping at each painting for what he thought was an appropriate length of time and pretended to consider each one, but really, he couldn't make sense of any of them. At the last one he stopped, relieved to find it was what he considered a normal kind of painting. 'I think I like this one best, Miss Cresswell.'

Sybilla laughed. 'It's a self-portrait.'

He looked at it more closely, then looked at her. In the painting, her long, chestnut hair fell in waves over her bare breasts. *She's beautiful*. He nodded. 'Hmm.'

Sybilla clapped her hands. 'Wonderful! I'm so excited. I'll get a sticker from Marguerite.'

While he waited for her, Richard studied the painting. It was quite nice. Not that he knew anything about art. Then he suddenly realised what was happening, what he'd let himself in for—been tricked into! Panicking, he looked around, calculating that he still had time to casually walk out and escape while she was occupied with her sticker, whatever that was. Just as he thought this, she came hurrying back, smiling at him.

'I thought you might have done a runner. You looked like a trapped animal.' She grinned at him and stuck a small blue dot on a corner of the painting. 'I've told Marguerite I'll fix up her commission when I've sold my other paintings. I'm sorry, but you won't be able to take it home until the end of the exhibition.' She took him by the arm and led him out of the gallery. 'Now,' she said, 'when can I come for tuition? This evening?'

'Well, I ...' he began, but Sybilla hit her forehead with the heel of her hand.

'I'm so sorry,' she exclaimed, 'how thoughtless of me. Of course, it's a Saturday and you must want to spend the time with your wife and family. I got carried away. I'm sorry. Perhaps Monday?'

He thought quickly. The day was a wash out anyway. And it seemed he wasn't going to get rid of her very easily. 'No wife or family, and it might be a good idea for us to get this over with now. I live about twenty minutes' walk away; would it be all right if we go to my place?'

'Excellent!' Sybilla sounded jubilant. She picked up her bag and tried to keep pace with his long strides.

He noticed and adjusted his pace. 'Let me carry your bag.'

'It's heavy,' Sybilla said, 'and you have your briefcase to carry.'

He took her bag. 'You're right; it is heavy.'

'I can't leave it in my van; the doors don't lock.'

He made no comment at this, but a few moments later, he said, 'I hope you don't make a habit of going to the homes of strange men, Miss Cresswell.' He frowned at her disapprovingly as they walked along.

'No, Dr Broughton, I don't, but I could tell straight away that you are a man of principle and honour.'

'Hah! You mean I'm old enough to be your father.'

'No, I didn't think that.' She laughed, but when he looked down at her, he saw a slight blush on her cheeks.

His flat was on the top floor of a small block. He led the way up the dimly lit flight of stairs. It was now after four o'clock and nearly dark.

'Through here.' He opened the door and switched on the light, indicating a small living room. He moved into the room and turned on a table lamp. *At least that makes it look a bit cosier,* he thought, drawing the curtains.

Sybilla put her bag on the floor and looked around the spartan room. The kitchenette—a sink, stove and small counter—occupied one corner with a table and chairs nearby. Two ancient armchairs faced a small electric fire. Another wall held a shelf of books and the door to a bathroom. She bent to take off her boots.

Richard put his briefcase on the table. 'No need to take off your boots.' He frowned. They looked like old army boots.

'Oh, it's habit,' she replied, wriggling her toes.

He noticed a hole in one of her socks.

She took off her coat and, looking around for somewhere to hang it, peered through a half-open door to a neatly made bed.

Richard stepped forward, took her coat and hung it behind the entry door, then indicated the kitchen table. 'Please sit down,' he said, pulling out a chair for her. He opened his briefcase, took out the bag Marguerite had given him and took it into the kitchen. 'A bottle of wine,' he muttered to himself as he placed it on the bench, then he filled a kettle and put it on the gas stove. 'Would you like a cup of tea?'

'That would be lovely.' She took his notes from her bag and started to study them.

He looked at her as he made the tea. What a strange character, he thought. She didn't seem to have any dress sense or colour co-ordination. She wore a big bright-red-and-green baggy jumper over faded navy trousers that seemed too big for her. A multi-coloured scarf tied up her reddish coloured hair.

He poured the tea and indicated the cups on the kitchen bench. 'Milk and sugar are here; please help yourself.'

'Thanks.' Sybilla went into the kitchen. 'I like the cups,' she said as she stirred milk into the delicate bone china cup.

'I don't like drinking tea from thick china.' He placed his cup and saucer on the table. 'I'm a bit old-fashioned.'

Sybilla smiled, but said nothing.

'Right,' Richard said briskly. 'Now, let's start.' *And get it over with as quickly as possible.* He took his notes from his brief case and pulled out a chair and sat beside her. 'You were asking about Hypercubes; well, this is how it works ...'

She listened carefully for several minutes, then said, 'sorry, Dr Broughton, but I was hopeless at maths at school ... um, I'm a bit lost.'

'But you understand geometry, surely?'

'Maybe you could refresh my memory,' she said humbly.

'You would have learnt it at school,' he said, trying to hide his irritation.

'I left school when I was fifteen ...'

He blinked in surprise and frowned.

'And I missed a lot of school,' she continued. 'I had to look after my mother.'

He wanted to ask why she had to look after her mother—was there no-one else, and why didn't she stay on at school?—but he decided it would only prolong the session. Anyway, he wasn't really interested in her life history.

He started again, very slowly, making sure she understood each step. He drew a picture of a triangle with squares on each side and explained the theorem. Then he looked at her. She seemed to be studying his hands. Suddenly self-conscious, he moved them away, and, with a bit of a start, she looked up, then looked at the diagrams for a minute.

A smile lit up her face. 'I understand!' she announced. 'That's so clever! Now I understand squares.'

Richard couldn't help smiling. It always pleased him when someone comprehended something he'd been teaching.

Then her stomach rumbled.

He looked at his watch. 'Goodness, it's after six; you must be hungry. I know I am.' He didn't quite know what to do. If they stopped now, it would mean she'd have to come back again for another session. Best if they kept going, get it over with. Maybe he could rustle up something to eat. 'How about some bread and cheese?'

'Oh, I don't want to be a nuisance. I could leave now and come back tomorrow. Or any other time that suits you. I'm in Sydney for the rest of the week.'

He swore silently to himself; the last thing he wanted was her back again. 'Won't take me long.' He got up from the table.

'Can I help?' Sybilla offered.

'Not enough room in this kitchen for two. No, you sit and digest all I've been explaining. We've covered a lot this afternoon.'

She nodded. 'Um, is there a toilet I could use?'

'Oh, yes, through that door.' He indicated the door to the left of the book shelf, hoping the room was presentable. He considered himself a neat and tidy man, but sometimes he overlooked small things.

'Thanks.'

She came back a short while later and went to the bookshelf, her stomach rumbling again. 'You don't have many books ...'

'No. I only brought a few.'

'Oh?' She looked like she wanted to ask him more but, to his relief, closed her mouth without another word.

He moved their notes to one side and set plates, cheese, cutlery and a loaf of bread on the table. He found a dish and put a slab of butter on it, then asked, 'Another cup of tea or would you prefer wine?'

Sybilla looked around from studying a framed photo on the shelf between the books. 'I don't mind, whatever you're having.'

'Well, shall we try this bottle of wine that your friend gave me?'

Sybilla nodded. 'Yes, that would be lovely. And Marguerite isn't really my friend. She runs that gallery and likes to help young artists, so she holds exhibitions for those she thinks have promise. She saw some of my paintings last year and invited me to exhibit. And she sometimes gets people to lecture about art.'

'I don't know how on earth she heard about me,' Richard said, 'and I don't think I even mentioned Picasso. She completely misled me; she didn't mention Cubism or Picasso when she bull-dozed me into the talk.'

Sybilla laughed. 'No, you didn't mention Picasso at all, but I don't think anyone noticed. Oh, except for the man who thought he was going to a lecture about nudism, not Cubism! Apparently Marguerite is always trying to raise money for various charities and on the look-out for interesting speakers.'

'Gullible speakers, you mean.' He smiled, relieved to find a cork-screw in one of the drawers, and opened the wine. 'It's a red. Is that okay?'

'Lovely.'

'And who is this Smith Family anyway?'

As they ate, Sybilla explained the charity to him, and when he'd finished eating, she stood and took the plates to the kitchen. 'Thank you so much. I'll wash up.'

'No, please, I'll just stack them in the sink and do them later.' Anxious to get this session over, he cleared the table and moved their notes back to where they'd been.

Sybilla sat down again. Richard poured her another glass of wine, then got up and turned on the electric fire. 'It's got so cold. I'm sorry, your feet must be freezing.'

She laughed. 'Well, yes; they are a bit.'

Sometime later, Richard looked at his watch. 'I didn't realise there was so much you wanted to cover. It's getting late and we still haven't finished.'

'What time is it?' Sybilla jumped up, a worried look on her face. 'I didn't notice the time passing. I don't own a watch.'

'It's nine thirty.'

'Oh no! I'll be locked out!'

He frowned. 'Locked out?'

'I'm staying in a hostel, and they lock the doors at nine thirty. I won't be able to get in.' She must have noticed his anxious look because she tried to reassure him. 'It's all right; I'll sleep in my van.'

He stared at her. 'I can't let you do that! It's winter; you'll freeze, and not only that, it's also raining.'

They'd both been so absorbed that neither of them had noticed the rain. Now they could hear it beating against the kitchen window, but she was already putting on her boots. 'It's fine.' She smiled. 'I've got an old sleeping bag in the van.'

'That's ridiculous; you'll get soaked getting to your van. Anyway where is it?'

She frowned. 'I left it at the hostel, about half an hour's walk from the gallery. There was nowhere to park near the gallery. But please don't worry. I'll be fine.'

'No! Goodness me, I couldn't possibly let you walk all that way in the dark. I might be able to hail a taxi for you.' But he didn't fancy the idea of standing out in the rain waiting for a possible passing taxi. The block of apartments wasn't on a main road; it would take ages. He didn't have a telephone in the flat. The idea of walking with her to her van was equally unappealing.

She hesitated before saying, 'I don't have enough money for a taxi ...'

He didn't know what to say. 'Well, I could ...'

'Lend me the money? No, Dr Broughton, you've been so kind; I simply couldn't.' She took her trench coat and started to put it on.

'Look, I don't mind paying for a taxi ...' *Anything to get this over with and her gone.*

'No. Thank you, but no. I'll be fine.'

'Well then,' he said slowly. 'You'd better stay here. You can have my bed, and I'll sleep on the floor in here.'

She looked at him and shook her head.

'Please, Miss Cresswell. It's ridiculous to go out in that storm in the dark. Really. I don't mind in the least.'

Sybilla stopped buttoning her coat. A loud crack of thunder and lightning made the lights flicker, and she looked at them nervously. 'It's Sybilla.' After hesitating, she added, 'Well, okay, then, thank you, but I'll sleep on the floor.'

'I couldn't let you do that. It's bare linoleum, and cold. I'll put clean sheets on my bed for you.' He walked towards his sparsely furnished bedroom—just a double bed pushed against the wall, a wardrobe and chest of drawers.

Sybilla followed. Richard waved her away, but she surveyed the bedroom, then stared at the bed and frowned. 'There aren't enough blankets to make two separate beds.' She looked back at him. 'Dr Broughton, I don't mind if we share your bed. I'll wrap my coat around me and be quite cosy and you can wrap the blankets around you.' She gave a slight grin. 'I promise I won't accost you in the night!'

Colour flooded his face. He rubbed his chin. 'Perhaps I had too much wine to drink tonight; I'm not used to it. I think my judgement's a bit clouded, but if you feel safe with that, then ...' Somehow he didn't fancy the idea of that grubby trench coat on his bed. 'Maybe a cup of hot chocolate?' he suggested, heading towards the kitchen.

'Thank you.' She got a book from her bag, and they sat in the two old arm chairs in front of the electric fire, cups cradled in their hands. Sybilla curled her feet up under her, trying to hide the hole in her sock. She remained quiet for a while, the unopened book on her lap, then looked up. 'I noticed that photo on your bookshelf.'

Richard frowned. 'My wife.'

'Oh! I thought you said you weren't married. Is she still in England?'

'She was killed in an air raid in the war.'

'Oh! I'm so sorry.' Sybilla hesitated. 'Perhaps I shouldn't have mentioned the photo, but she looks so beautiful.'

'She was.' He sighed. 'It was in 1942. Twenty-six years ago.' The pain returned with the memory.

'That was the year I was born,' Sybilla said slowly. '1942.'

He stared at her. 'That's how old Brenda was when she was killed—twenty-six.'

Sybilla shivered.

He sat, lost in thought, then suddenly remembered his guest and looked at his watch. 'It's after ten. Perhaps you'd like to use the bathroom. I'll find a new toothbrush for you.'

'It's all right; I have one in my bag.' She got up, rummaged in her bag, produced a small toiletry bag and held it up. 'Also a towel, and my nightclothes.' She took them out of her bag and disappeared into the bathroom.

Richard boiled the kettle, made a hot-water bottle and put it in the bed, then started washing the dishes, wondering how on earth the day had turned out like this.

He'd finished drying the dishes when she emerged from the bathroom. Without the big jumper and loose pants, she seemed very thin.

'Oh, it's so good to have a hot shower! Your turn now,' she said.

He took his pyjamas and dressing gown into the bathroom.

The first thing he saw when he walked into the bathroom was a pair of wet, pink knickers and her towel draped over the shower rail. He shook his head. A few minutes later he came out, his dressing gown wrapped around him.

Sybilla, already in bed, looked up and smiled at him. 'Thank you for the hot water bottle. I won't need my coat on me. Goodnight, Dr Broughton. Thank you for everything. I'm sorry for messing up your evening.'

'Hmm.' He nodded, then got into the bed, still with his dressing gown on, and spread the blankets over both of them. She lay right up against the wall cuddled into the hot water bottle. He lay there for a while unable to relax, worried that he might roll over into the sagging middle of the bed in his sleep and touch her.

The next morning, he woke early to the sound of the rain pounding on the window. He felt constricted and had a sore neck. Why was he wearing his dressing gown in bed? Then he remembered. Slowly he turned his head. A mass of chestnut hair lay on his pillow, which Sybilla must have dragged over to her side of the bed. He grimaced. He must be crazy. At his age—fifty-five—sharing a bed with a beautiful young woman and lying chastely to one side. With a sigh, he slid out of the bed, crept out of the room and tried to close the door quietly.

***

Sybilla woke when Richard got out of bed. She lay there for a while until she heard the sound of the toilet flushing, then she got up, made the bed, ran her fingers through her hair and opened the door.

He looked up from where he stood in the kitchen. Tall and stern looking, dark hair carefully combed to one side, he seemed to fill the tiny space.

She smiled at him. 'Did you sleep okay? I did.'

He nodded. 'Yes, thank you. Now, I'm just making a pot of tea and some toast. Would you like some?'

'Love some. I'll just go to the bathroom first.'

While they sat eating breakfast, she stared into space, contemplating what he'd taught her. After a few minutes, she looked at him and met his gaze—he'd been watching her. 'I've been thinking about Hypercubes and Picasso,' she said. 'I know he and Braque tried to represent reality using cubism. Do you think they succeeded?'

'I've no idea,' he replied. 'I haven't looked into it. I know nothing about art.'

She stared at him. 'Really? The poster seemed to suggest you knew all about Picasso and art. Well, perhaps I can rectify that. When the rain stops, I'll take you to the art gallery.'

He opened his mouth, then closed it again, as if he didn't know what to say. She studied him. By the look on his face, perhaps trailing around an art gallery, looking at paintings wasn't his idea of a fun time.

She smiled. 'In the meantime, can we carry on with the fourth dimension?'

He nodded, and after clearing away the dishes, they got to work.

Time seemed to pass quickly. Apart from a short tea break, they kept going, stopping every so often for Sybilla to offer her take on how the fourth dimension might apply to cubism and art.

At midday Richard looked up and said, 'I'm hungry. I've got bacon rashers and eggs. Would you like some?'

Sybilla rubbed her eyes. 'Perfect. Can I help?'

He shook his head.

She frowned. 'Dr Broughton, I'm so sorry to have landed myself on you like this. As soon as the rain stops, I'll leave you in peace. What can I do to say thank you?'

'Nothing,' he said stiffly. 'I'm actually quite enjoying our little session; it passes the time on a wet Sunday.'

Sybilla watched him as he went to the kitchenette and started preparing the food. She took a sheet of plain paper and bent over the table, pencil in hand.

The smell of bacon soon pervaded the air, making Sybilla's mouth water, and Richard came out of the kitchen with bread, butter, knives and forks and two plates, which he placed on the table.

'Here we go.' He looked at her drawing. 'What's that you've been doing?'

She showed him her drawing of him in the kitchen.

'You've made me look quite young! Not like my passport photograph.'

She smiled, stuck her pencil through her hair, looked at the food, and said, 'this looks so good.'

He sat down opposite her, picked up his knife and fork, and waited for her to start eating. Then he followed suit. 'Cup of tea?' he asked when they'd finished.

'Yes, please.' She watched him as he got up and took their empty plates to the kitchenette. 'So you've always been interested in maths and physics?' she asked.

'Yes.' He frowned, remained silent for a moment, then looked out the kitchen window. 'Still pouring down. Hope there won't be floods.' His gaze returned to her. 'You might have to stay here another night.'

Sybilla shook her head. 'No, really, I can walk back to the hostel.'

'You mean wade or swim back. Look out the window.'

She got up and did as he suggested. The road was flooded. Cars moved slowly, and water washed over the pavement. 'I'd better go now, before it gets worse.'

'Miss Cresswell,' he said gently. 'You're welcome to stay here. It's no bother. Really.'

She smiled. 'You're so kind, Dr Broughton. I must say it's much more pleasant than the hostel.' She looked up at him. 'Thank you, but just until the rain stops.'

He nodded, but looked a little disappointed.

'Would you like me to tell you about Picasso and Braque and Cubism?' she ventured.

His eyes crinkled with amusement. 'It would make a change for me to be the student.' He stood looking out the window, then suddenly turned to her. 'How much do you have to pay at the hostel?'

'Not a lot; you sleep in a women's dormitory and bring your own sleeping bag.'

He rubbed his chin and looked down at the table. 'You could save that money and stay here, if you like. I'll be out all week; I have to go into work to prepare for the next semester, so you wouldn't be in my way.'

Sybilla doodled on her notepad. 'I couldn't possibly impose on you any longer.'

Richard picked up his empty cup and studied it. 'In the gallery, when you were getting that blue dot sticker, I noticed the price on the painting I chose. It's worth far more than just a few hours lecture from me.'

She shook her head. 'All this has been invaluable to me. It's been a fair exchange, and I can't wait to get home and start painting. I have so many ideas in my head now.'

He smiled. 'As you wish, but the offer stands. We managed all right last night.'

'Do you really mean that? I don't want to be a nuisance. I'm only here for a week, then I must head back up north, but I'd be able to buy more paints and canvasses with the money I'd save.'

Richard took the cups and saucers to the kitchenette and rinsed them. 'There's a spare key I can give you,' he said.

'I might run away with the china cups.' She smiled.

He grinned as he came back and sat in one of the arm chairs. 'Where's home?'

Sybilla laughed and sat opposite him. 'I live in a shack out in the bush near Gurunnuga; that's in northern New South Wales. The owner's been trying to sell the place for years, and he offered it to me rent free in exchange for looking after it. Keep the place tidy and in good repair. It suits me. There's a big shed I use as a studio, a few chooks wandering around, and I can find the odd egg. The shack is very basic, and there's an outside dunny.'

'Dunny?'

'Long drop.'

His brow furrowed. 'You've lost me.'

'Toilet.'

'Ahh. So you're there on your own?'

'Yes. It suits me. I'm a bit of a loner, and I can spend as much time as I like painting.'

'What about your parents? Don't they worry about you being in an isolated spot on your own?'

She looked down at her hands. 'My parents emigrated here from England before the war. My father joined up and was killed in the last few days of the war, so I don't remember him. Just have a few photos. And my mother had a stroke several years ago and died.'

'I'm sorry to hear that. Have you any other family?'

'No. Well, I suppose I have relatives in England, but my mother never kept in touch.' She paused, then looked up at him. 'What about you, Dr Broughton?'

***

Richard frowned, thinking of his widowed mother, now in her eighties and living with his sister in Edinburgh. He didn't feel like launching into his family history. 'Me? Well, I'm only here for twelve months, on a visiting lectureship.'

'So you don't live here permanently?

'No. I live and work in Bristol, in England.' He didn't mention that he'd been offered full-time, permanent tenure in Sydney. He hadn't made up his mind whether to accept.

After a moment of silence, Sybilla looked at him and said, 'Could we take a break, do you think? I have so much information going around in my head, and you must be tired from explaining so much to me.'

'I was thinking the same thing, and perhaps you can teach me about art another day?'

She grinned and fetched her book from her bag.

Richard turned on the electric fire, picked up the weekend paper and then watched her surreptitiously. She smiled at him, as she curled up on the other old chair.

'What are you reading?' he asked, curious because the book looked very slim.

'An anthology of poetry. I can't afford to buy books, and I love poetry. And I don't have room for many books.'

'Hmm.' He nodded. 'Not much of a poetry man, myself. Had to learn some at school, of course. Daffodils and clouds, that kind of thing, and some Shakespeare, of course. Don't remember much.' He smiled at her, shook out his paper and started to read.

When he got home from work the next day, Sybilla was in the flat. He'd half expected she would've disappeared, having changed her mind and gone to the hostel, instead of staying with an old fogey like him.

She got up from the chair, where she'd been reading, when he opened the door. The smell of something cooking greeted him. 'Hello, Dr Broughton, I'm sorry but I'm still here! I'm sure you were hoping I'd have changed my mind and you would have your home to yourself again.'

He gave a brief sharp, 'Hah!' and smiled. 'Quite the contrary.'

'Yeah, well, I walked to the hostel and got my old van and managed to find a parking space just outside here. I brought some food, home-grown vegetables from my garden, and I've made a stew for dinner. I hope you like stew?' she enquired anxiously.

'Yes, indeed. That sounds lovely.'

'And as Marguerite has sold one of my paintings, I was able to give her the commission from your painting and buy a bottle of wine to celebrate.' She grinned at him. 'Cheapie plonk, I'm afraid.'

'Well done. Congratulations.' He took off his overcoat and hung it behind the door. The room felt warm and welcoming, and the thought of not having to cook was appealing. Several sheets of paper covered in sketches lay on the table. 'May I?' He indicated the table.

'Of course.'

He looked at them and shook his head. 'They're beyond me. Sorry.'

'It's all right; they're only preliminary sketches, just trying out ideas ...' She gathered them up from the table. 'Dr Broughton?'

'Yes?'

'Could you call me Sybilla? It seems so formal to be Miss Cress-well.'

He frowned. 'If you wish and I suppose you may call me Richard.'

She hid a smile. 'Thank you, Richard.'

***

The next day when he got home and found the flat empty, Richard was surprised to experience a feeling of disappointment. She must have changed her mind and left. He took off his overcoat and hung it up, then went to the bathroom. An involuntary smile spread over his face when he saw her towel and a pair of knickers hanging over the shower rail. She must be coming back. Then he heard the main door open and close.

'Phew! Hello, Richard! I went to the art gallery and didn't realise the time.' She pulled off her trench coat, hung it up, then turned and smiled at him. 'I meant to get back and start to cook something for dinner.'

He wanted to think of something amusing to say, but nothing came to him. The best he could do was, 'How about fish and chips?'

'Oh, lovely!' Her eyes lit up, then clouded.

He guessed the reason and smiled. 'My treat! Are you hungry?' She always seemed to be hungry, he'd noticed. He suspected she didn't get enough to eat.

'A bit,' she admitted, then laughed. 'Are you? Will we go now?' She took her coat back from the door, unhooked his and handed it to him.

At the front of the block of flats, she took his arm, and walked briskly along beside him, chatting away about what she'd seen at the art gallery. At first, he was startled, but then enjoyed the feeling of her arm linked in his. A few passers-by glanced at them, and he wondered what they thought. They must present a very odd couple; a smartly dressed middle-aged man—at least he considered himself smartly dressed—and a young woman in big clumpy boots, a too-big old coat and that bright-chestnut hair tied up with the multi-coloured scarf. Perhaps they thought she was his daughter—that thought depressed him. He tried to concentrate on what she was saying about the art gallery. As they crossed the road, he automatically put his hand on her waist and steered her to the inside of the pavement.

'Why did you do that?' she asked.

'What?'

'Move me to your other side.'

He stared at her. 'Reflex action, I suppose.' He paused. 'Well, all Englishmen of my generation were brought up to do that.'

'Why?'

He laughed. 'To protect the woman from splashes from passing vehicles, horses and carts.'

She laughed. 'Oh, Richard, that's funny.' Then she grew thoughtful for a moment. 'But it's nice. Makes me feel protected.'

He looked down at her. The top of her head reached his shoulders. 'Don't your ears feel cold with your hair all tied up?'

She burst out laughing again. 'You're so funny, Richard!'

After buying the food, they sat on a nearby bench, opened the newspapers in which the fish and chips had been wrapped and began to eat.

'So how was your day,' she asked through a mouthful of fish.

'Interesting,' he replied.

'What were you doing? Meeting stuffy old Professors?'

'No.' He chuckled, 'working on setting up facilities to teach computer science.' He started telling her about his work.

She seemed to be listening intently, but then she frowned. 'I'd love to understand more, but really I've no idea about anything like that.'

'Like me with art.'

When they'd finished eating, he took the newspaper from her, screwed it up and put it in a nearby bin.

'Thank you, Richard. That was lovely.' She took his arm again. 'Shall we have a little walk before we go back?'

Surprised, he nodded, and they strolled around Victoria Park until Sybilla suddenly shivered. 'Okay, let's go back; it's getting cold.'

She spoke as he unlocked the door of his flat. 'Richard.'

He turned and looked at her.

'Thank you for everything. You've been so kind.'

He opened the door. 'It's been a pleasure,' he said, and realised they weren't idle words. He enjoyed her company.

***

A few days later as they finished eating breakfast, Sybilla looked at him and said, 'My last night here; I'm going home tomorrow, so you'll have peace and quiet in your life again.'

'I'll miss you.' It was true. He'd been so used to coming back to an empty home. His married life had been short. He'd met Brenda when they'd both been working at Bletchley Park. She'd been on a visit to her parents in London when she was killed. What would she be like now if she was still alive? They would've had children, had a family life, not the solitary existence which was his lot at the moment. He gave a deep sigh.

'Richard, would you like to come up to my place at some stage? The Christmas holidays, perhaps? You could have a look around the area, and I could repay your hospitality.' She must have heard the sigh and noticed the far-away look on his face. 'It's very basic,' she continued.

He looked up and blinked. 'I'm not sure; I'll think about it.'

She put her head on one side, studying him. 'Actually, I was wondering if you would sit for me.'

'Sit?'

'Yes, you have an interesting face. Very strong. In fact, I'd like you to model for me. You have a good body.'

He frowned. 'What on earth do you mean?'

'A life painting.'

He gave an embarrassed laugh. 'Strong? A good body? Don't be ridiculous; I'm an old man! Anyway, you haven't seen my body.' He stared at her, but she seemed to mean it. 'A life painting? If that means nude, then certainly not!' He got up from the table. To get away from the subject, he added, 'well, as tonight will be your last night, perhaps I could take you out to dinner.'

She burst out laughing. 'In these clothes! Oh Richard, I don't think so. But thank you for offering.'

He looked at her old clothes; she was right. He'd forgotten that his first impression of her had been of a down-and-out person.

***

That evening he came home with a bottle of champagne. He'd never bought a bottle of champagne before, but he felt they needed to mark the occasion. An appetizing smell greeted him on opening the door of the flat.

Sybilla jumped up from the table, where she'd been drawing. 'Guess what Richard?' She ran towards him and flung her arms around him. 'I've sold all my paintings except one! So I've cooked a special dinner and bought a bottle of wine to celebrate!'

'Congratulations!' Slightly embarrassed, he drew back from her embrace and held out the bottle of champagne. 'Put this in the fridge while I have a shower.'

'Champagne! Wow, you must be really celebrating me leaving.'

He grinned. He was beginning to appreciate her sense of humour.

'Absolutely.'

It was late by the time they'd finished eating—and finished the champagne and most of the bottle of wine Richard noticed. He rose unsteadily to his feet. 'I think it's time for bed.'

'Yes. I must be fresh for my long drive tomorrow.' She got to her feet and headed for the bathroom. 'I'm a little tipsy,' she giggled. A little later, she emerged. 'Your turn, Richard,' she said, as she made her way to the bedroom, 'Oh! I'm going to miss your lovely hot shower!' She yawned. 'I'm so tired.'

When Richard joined her in the bedroom, she lay in her usual position close to the wall. He climbed in beside her and pulled the blankets over them. 'Good night, Sybilla.'

She turned over. 'I'm cold. No hot water bottle.'

'Oh. I'm so sorry. I forgot. I'll get it now.' He made to get out of the bed.

'No, I'll get it.' She turned over and snuggled up to him. 'Oh, you're so nice and warm, Richard.'

His heart raced at the feel of her against him. 'Er, Sybilla.'

'Hmm?' She put her arms around him. 'I think I had too much to drink,' she murmured, then, her speech slightly slurred, added, 'but I just want to thank you for everything. I really like you, Richard.' She reached up to kiss him ...

***

Richard woke early next morning, his head pounding. He groaned and then realised that Sybilla was still cuddled up to him. He began to remember the previous night. 'Oh, no.' His voice was a croak. 'What did I do?'

She stirred and opened her eyes. 'Richard.' Then she drew his head towards her and kissed him.

'Stop!' He pushed her arms down. 'Sybilla, what have I done?'

She frowned and sat up in the bed, then realised she was naked and pulled the sheet up over her breasts.

'I'm so sorry,' Richard said. 'I don't know what came over me; I took advantage of you.'

'Nonsense; it takes two to tango.' She jumped up and started to dress. 'I'll make coffee.'

He watched her go, then groaned again and turned over in the bed.

A few minutes later, she returned. 'Here. Take these; make you feel better.' She handed him two aspirin and mug of black coffee. 'Sorry, it's a mug. Didn't think your lovely tea cups suitable.' She grinned at him, bent over him and ran a finger down the side of his face. 'It's okay, Richard,' she said softly. 'Please don't stress about it. Look, I'll be gone in a few minutes, and you can put me out of your mind. By the way, there's something of yours in the corner by the book shelf.'

He made to get up, but she pushed him back. 'Later. Look after I've gone.' She leaned over and kissed him full on the lips. 'Thank you, Richard. For everything.' Then she left, closing the door quietly behind her.

He dragged himself out of the bed, then realised he was naked. After hastily pulling on a pair of pants, he went to the corner by the bookshelves. A square, flat, brown-paper parcel leaned against the wall. He knew what it had to be. Slowly he unwrapped it and stared at the portrait of Sybilla.

***

Richard's life felt empty after she'd gone. He went around to Marguerite's gallery and looked for the painting Sybilla said she hadn't sold. It hung on the wall where her others had been, but now with different paintings beside it. He still didn't understand what the picture meant, and they'd never had time to go to the

NSW Art Gallery. He walked up to the counter. Luckily, it wasn't Marguerite there, but some young fellow.

'I'd like to buy the Sybilla Cresswell painting on the wall over there.' He gestured towards the far end of the gallery.

'Oh, hello, Dr Broughton,' the youth said. 'I was at your lectures last semester.'

Richard thought he looked vaguely familiar.

'Marguerite is my aunt,' the youth continued. 'I was telling her all about your lecture on the fourth dimension.'

So this is the oaf that got me into giving that lecture.

The youth wrapped the painting and handed it to Richard. 'It's one of my favourites,' he said. 'I'm surprised it didn't sell up 'til now. You've got good taste.' He nodded approvingly at Richard.

Back at the flat Richard propped it up on the book shelf. The colours were lovely. He turned it over. On the back Sybilla had written 'Sunset at the Dam.' Hmm. He put Sybilla's portrait beside it. Her eyes seemed to be looking right at him. He picked up the photograph of his wife and stared at it.

CHAPTER 2

Sybilla arrived back at the shack on a lovely sunny day. She stopped the engine and sat for a few minutes, then got out and stretched. It must have rained recently as everything looked lush and green. She thought of Yeats's poem, Inisfree: *And I shall have some peace there, for peace comes dropping slow.* Yes, happy to be back in the bush, she could feel the peace encircling her. She took several deep breaths. She had enough money from the sale of her paintings to last for a few months, then it would be spring and she'd be able to get some work on the local farms. She'd stopped at the village shop on the way and bought stuff: bacon, butter and a loaf of bread. One letter had arrived; the registration on the van was due. But she had enough money to cover that.

She opened the door of the shack—it had no lock—and went in. It felt chilly inside. First thing to do, light the stove, next check on the chooks, then take her new art purchases to the shed she called her studio.

The chooks came rushing out when they saw her. Poor things; they must be hungry. She'd bought some chook food, so threw a few handfuls to them and watched them scratching and pecking at it. She looked in the old water tank lying on its side where they liked to nest. Four eggs lay on the gum leaves that she'd gathered up and put inside for them.

That evening she fried bacon and eggs on the stove, all the time thinking about Richard, wondering if she was half in love with him. She loved his hands. Or was he a father figure? She'd never known her father. He'd been killed in the last year of the war. Her mum hadn't talked about him; well, she didn't talk about anything much. The only photo she had of him was a blurred one in his army uniform. Could have been anyone, really. They probably had a hard time when they came to Australia. The depression. She wondered if she looked like him—she didn't resemble her mother, except for the hair. She'd managed to find the exact colours for the self-portrait—burnt sienna with hints of red oxide. That sounded strange, but it turned out well. Would Richard like it? He said he liked the portrait in the gallery, but perhaps he was just relieved it was something he could understand ...

Her thoughts flitted all over the place. She missed Richard. Was he missing her? Probably not. Probably glad to have his bed to himself again. The bed. That last night ... being in his arms ... but he'd have no interest in her. He was clever and educated. She determined to write to him nearer Christmas and invite him to the shack. She'd memorized his address.

'Stop it, Sybilla,' she said out loud. With a sigh she lit the gas lamps and started to tidy up.

***

Everything went well until the morning she woke up and vomited. At first she thought it was a bug, but when it happened the next morning, an icy finger of fear slid down and settled in the pit of her stomach. She didn't usually pay much attention to her periods—they came pretty regularly—but now she realised it was some while since the last one.

Panicking, she tried to convince herself it was a false alarm. But a week later she was still being sick in the mornings and her breasts started to feel different.

The next time she went to town, she called into the share house where she used to live. One of the girls there was in a relationship with a married man, and he was well off. When Olive had become pregnant a couple of years before, he'd paid for her to go to Melbourne and have an abortion. Sybilla waited in the van until Olive got home from work, then she got out and followed her up the path.

'Hey, Sybilla,' Olive smiled at her. 'Haven't seen you for ages.'

Sybilla nodded then said all in a rush, 'I need an abortion. I hoped you'd be able to tell me ...' She trailed off.

'You poor darling,' Olive said, looking over her shoulder at Sybilla as she unlocked the door. 'Come in. I hope the father's rich; it's not cheap.'

Sybilla thought of Richard. 'I don't think he is.'

'Is he married?'

'No.'

'Well, get him to marry you.'

'I don't want to get married or have a baby.'

Olive shrugged. 'Like a cup of coffee?'

Sybilla shook her head. 'No thanks, makes me sick.'

'Okay, well, I'll give you a phone number. Ring them. You have to go to Melbourne. They'll tell you the procedure and how much it costs. But don't mention my name.'

Sybilla nodded. 'So how much is it?'

'Well, it was in pounds then.' Olive looked up at the ceiling, calculating. 'I guess it would be about three-hundred dollars now.'

Sybilla's mouth fell open.

Olive went to her bedroom, then came out with a card and copied the details onto a piece of paper. 'Good luck,' she said. 'And be more careful next time.'

'Thanks, Olive.' Sybilla turned to leave. There would never be a next time.

'And don't bother trying gin, or hot baths,' Olive said as they walked to the door. 'They don't work.'

Hah! Sybilla thought. She didn't have money for gin, and a hot bath at the shack? She had to boil all the water on the wood stove. By the time the second pot of water was hot, the first would be cold. 'Thanks again, Olive.'

But then Olive started to tell Sybilla about the procedure. Sybilla tried not to listen. It sounded appalling. She left quickly, went straight back to the shack and slumped down in the old swinging chair outside under the veranda. Where on earth would she get the money? She only knew one person who might be able to help.

CHAPTER 3

Richard thought about going to visit her at Christmas. She'd asked him to visit her, and he wanted to see her again. He knew he was far too old for her, but he hadn't felt this way about a woman since Brenda. Was he being stupid? What would she see in a crusty old widower like him? Her portrait was a constant reminder of her. Her eyes seemed to follow him. She'd said she didn't have a watch. He could buy her one for a Christmas present. He liked that idea. But when the days turned into weeks with no letter from her, he realised that it had all been a lovely dream, and anyway, why would a beautiful young girl be interested in an old man like him?

The weeks turned into months, and before he knew it, it was the end of the academic year, and he'd still heard nothing from her. As he'd surmised, she'd forgotten all about him. He didn't even have her address to send her a Christmas card.

Then, on the last day of the semester, he returned home to find a letter in his mail box.

Dear Richard.

I'm sorry to have to ask but I need $320 urgently. I don't know anyone else I can turn to.

I'll pay you back as soon as I can.

Can you send it as soon as possible please, registered, in cash, to:

Sybilla Cresswell, c/- The Post Office, Gurunnuga, NSW.
Yours sincerely
Sybilla.

He felt stunned. Over three-hundred dollars! That was more than his salary for two months. Whatever did she need it for? So ... she'd just been using him. He sat down for a moment and thought. No, that wasn't the Sybilla he'd known. He looked over at her portrait, looked at those lovely eyes watching him and drummed his fingers on the table, then he came to a decision. He remembered seeing a car-rental place down the road.

Half an hour later, he'd rented a car, paying an extra premium as it was the Christmas period.

'You're lucky; it's the last one,' the car rental man said as he filled in the paper work. 'How long do you want it for?'

Richard considered. He might as well have a look around the area while he was there. He hadn't seen much of Australia in the short time he'd been here. 'Three weeks, please.' Then he had another thought. 'Have you a map of New South Wales?'

The man poked around in one of his desk drawers and came up with an old motoring map. 'Here you go. It's a bit dusty so you can have it for nothing. Where are you heading?'

'Um, a place called Gurunnuga.'

'Never heard of it. Good luck. It's the green Holden outside. Here's the key; tank's full; return it full.' He handed Richard the keys and watched as Richard went out and stood fumbling with the key, trying to unlock the driver's door.

'It's not locked,' the car rental man shouted.

Back in his flat, the car parked outside, Richard took out the map and studied it. He found Gurunnuga; it was on the train line. But he still didn't have Sybilla's address.

I'll just have to go there and ask around. What was it she'd said about how long it would take to drive there? Seven hours? He looked at his watch. *I'll leave first thing in the morning. Better go out now and buy some summer clothes; shorts and sandals.*

***

It was a long drive up the New South Wales coast. Most of the little towns and villages he passed through all looked the same—dusty shops with concrete overhangs. He couldn't wait to get back to England. He'd been offered a permanent position at the university, but he'd turned it down. He was looking forward to the green hills and walking tracks of England, the Lake District, the Moors … and his friends. Somehow, he had the feeling his colleagues at the university in Sydney resented him. Now he looked forward to finishing his contract. Maybe he'd go to New Zealand for a week before he returned home. He was never likely to be in the Antipodes again. After Christmas he'd go to a travel agent and book his trips.

He arrived in Gurunnuga mid-afternoon, found the post office cum general store and asked the woman behind the counter if she knew a Sybilla Cresswell.

The postmistress nodded. 'Yes, Sybilla. She comes in here from time to time. I know roughly the road where she lives, but I don't know exactly where her place is.' She took a paper bag from the counter and a stub of pencil and drew a map. 'It's a bit isolated, might be hard to find. Follow this road and keep asking.'

He bought some mince pies she had on display.

'Home-made they are,' the woman said.

'They look delicious. Thank you for your help.' He smiled at her.

He spent over an hour driving down dirt tracks to isolated properties and getting conflicting directions, and then just at the point when he was about to give up, while driving slowly along yet another dirt track, he saw her old van and knew he'd arrived at the right place. He stopped behind the van and looked at the house. It was a shack all right. The rusty iron roof extended to a veranda around the small weatherboard building. He saw her lying on an old swinging chair under the veranda.

She looked up as the car stopped and got to her feet. When she saw him get out of the car, she rushed towards him and threw her arms around his chest. 'Oh, Richard! You came!' Then she burst into tears.

He held her close. 'Sybilla, what's happened? What kind of trouble are you in to need all that money?'

She raised her head and looked at him.

He took out a handkerchief and tenderly wiped her eyes. 'Come and sit down and tell me.' He led her to the swinging chair.

She sat back down and patted the space beside her. When he was seated, she frowned, and remained silent for several seconds, then said abruptly, 'I'm pregnant.' She took a deep breath. 'I have to do something about it.'

'Pregnant?' he echoed. 'Do something? What on earth do you mean, *do something*?' He stared at her in disbelief.

She stood up. 'Maybe I should make a cup of tea. I'll put the kettle on. I think there's enough gas.'

'Stop, Sybilla. Come here and tell me everything.' He took her hand and, reluctantly, she sank back beside him.

'I'm pregnant and there's no way I can keep it,' she said in one breath. 'I can only just manage as it is, and I have to take all kinds of jobs just to keep my head above water.'

'What about the father?' He could hardly bring himself to ask.

She stared at him. 'But you're the father, Richard. That last night I stayed with you. There's been no-one else.'

Stunned, it took him a few minutes to register this information, then disbelief swept through him. He shook his head. 'I don't believe it.'

Sybilla gave an exasperated sigh. 'Richard, I'm pregnant, and you're the father.' She stared at his baffled expression. 'You know, expecting a baby? A bun in the oven?' Tears came to her eyes. 'Richard, I swear, it's your child. I've been with no-one else.' She looked at him. 'Please. Believe me.'

'And I'm the father ...' he said, feeling a mixture of wonder and alarm. He blinked, smiled, then put his arms around her. 'You mean just from that one night? You're going to have a baby? And it's mine?'

She pushed his arms away. 'No. I'm not! It's impossible. I keep trying to tell you. I can't manage a baby.'

'Sybilla, I'll work something out. Give me a little time to think. It's been a shock, that's all.'

She shook her head. 'No! I can get an abortion. It's not legal, but I've got a phone number. I have to go to Melbourne. And it'll cost over $300.'

'Stop! Sybilla!' he almost shouted at her, then he put an arm around her and lowered his voice. 'You will not have an abortion. We'll just have to get married. It's the only honourable thing to do.'

She sniffed and blew her nose. 'Don't be ridiculous, Richard. You don't understand; it's impossible.'

He got up. 'Stay there and rest. I'll make a cup of tea. Are you hungry?'

She gave a watery smile. 'Yes, a bit.'

His head in a whirl, he went inside the shack and looked around. Whitewashed walls gave the impression of airiness. An old wood heater with a saucepan and kettle on it stood in the middle of one wall. A table and two chairs at one end and an old couch at the other end. A window on one side looked out onto lush greenery and spread filtered light onto a wooden dresser, which seemed to be used as a kitchen work top. Paintings lay propped against the walls. He frowned. 'You mentioned a gas ring,' he called out.

'It's out here, under the veranda. There's a box of matches on the top of the wood heater. I'm so tired, Richard. I've been sick and so worried, and the money I got from my paintings has run out, and I've not felt well enough to work for the local farmer here, picking fruit.'

He returned to the veranda, kettle in hand. 'Oh, Sybilla, why didn't you tell me before?'

'You were so kind to me; I didn't want to burden you with my problems. I thought at first it was a false alarm, but when I realised it wasn't, I didn't know what to do.'

'I can understand why you don't want this baby and why you might want to carry on with your life unencumbered and without the constant reminder of a ... a night when I,' he paused, 'well, when I forced myself on you.'

She sat up. 'Richard. It wasn't like that. You didn't force yourself on me.'

'Where do I get water?' He held out the kettle.

'Just over there.' She pointed. 'Look, there's a rain water tank with a tap.'

He filled the kettle, found the matches and lit the gas ring. 'Do you cook on this?'

'Sometimes. Usually I light the wood stove and cook on that, but it's been too hot the past few days and, anyway, I've got to split more timber for firewood.'

Inside he found two mugs and a tea pot on the dresser, and a packet of tea. He poked his head outside. 'Have you got milk?'

She shook her head. 'No. It's okay. I'll just have it black.'

He made a pot of tea, then remembered the mince pies he'd bought and got them from the car. 'Have a mince pie,' he said holding them out.

Sybilla tried to smile. 'Thanks. It must be Christmas.'

'I bought them at the post office in Gurunnuga.' He poured two mugs of tea, sat for a while thinking, then said, 'I hired the car for three weeks. I thought I'd have a look around this part of Australia while I was up here. Now things have changed, and we'll have to start making marriage arrangements.'

She interrupted him. 'Please, Richard. Stop it. I've made my decision.'

'As it seems you don't have much to eat here,' he continued, ignoring her exasperated tone of voice. 'I think I'd better go back to Gurunnuga to the post office and village shop and get some food and another bottle of gas. You stay here and rest. I can ask about places to stay around here. I think I can find my way there and back.'

She nodded and closed her eyes, then sat up. 'Richard, please don't ask about places to stay. That woman in the shop is so nosey; she'll want to know your life history. You can stay here. I can sleep in the studio, and you can have the sofa.'

'Right. We'll talk about that later. Is there anything else you need while I'm there?'

She shook her head.

Richard walked slowly to the car, his mind spinning. *Better concentrate on the road. Don't want to get lost again.*

The shop keeper at Gurunnuga seemed surprised to see him. 'Didn't you find her?' she asked.

'Yes, I found her.' Richard smiled. 'But I need groceries and gas.' He reviewed in his mind the food he usually bought for himself and doubled the quantities. But the woman stopped him.

'No good getting too much milk,' she said. 'I don't think she's got electricity, so there'd be no refrigerator, well, unless she has a gas refrigerator.'

He stared at her. 'Oh! Well, thank you for letting me know.'

'You'd best take a few tins of condensed milk or evaporated milk if you don't like it too sweet.'

He nodded. 'Thank you. What else should I take, do you think?'

'You her father?'

He started. 'No ... um ... I'm a colleague.' *Of course, every one would think that!*

He didn't reply to the rest of her enquiries. His purchases made, he drove carefully back to the shack, remembering various landmarks on his way. He was still stunned at Sybilla's news. A baby! It might be a boy. A son! Marriage! It all seemed unreal.

On his return he found her lying on the old swinging chair, sound asleep.

He brought the shopping inside, taking care not to wake her, then went out again and took in the surroundings. It was a beautiful place, surrounded by tall gum trees and behind the shack, what appeared to be a large paddock, somewhat overgrown.

He walked along a path, a few hens scattering at his approach, and reached a garden, fenced with odd bits of wire netting and a makeshift gate. It looked untended and neglected, as if it was mostly self-sown. Small, bright-red tomatoes flourished amid a riot of green stuff. He picked one and ate it, surprised at the sweet burst of flavour. He returned to the shack and found a bowl, then picked some of the tomatoes and what looked like a small marrow, or maybe it was a cucumber. He peered at it, then picked some leaves, which were possibly lettuce.

After rinsing it all at the rain-water tank tap, he went inside.

Sybilla stirred and sat up, then, seeing him inside the screen door, got up. 'I must have fallen asleep.'

He gazed at her. 'I was just going to make a salad with some ham I bought at the shop. I bought bacon and eggs, too. I thought they would keep for a few days.'

'There's a safe over there in that corner. I keep a wet towel over it with the ends in water. You can put the stuff in there.'

He walked over and opened the safe. 'Great idea. The evaporation keeps the food cool.'

She nodded. 'Not my idea; everyone does it.' Then she went back outside.

Through the window, Richard saw her fill a bowl with water and wash her hands and face, then she joined him inside. 'Thank you, Richard, for coming all this way.' She gave a tight smile. 'I really appreciate it. You don't have to stay here if you don't want to. I have the address and phone number of the place in Melbourne. I just need the cash.' She looked down. 'It was an accident, Richard. It doesn't have to ruin our lives.' She looked up, 'And marriage is out of the question; it would be a disaster.'

He took her hands. 'Sybilla, look at me. Do you really mean it? Really want to get rid of this baby?' he asked gently.

'I hate the thought. I'm terrified of operations and doctors, and this sounds appalling.' She paused. 'I got the phone number from a girl I know in town that had one. They tell you to go to a certain place in late evening, when it's dark, and to bring plenty of pain killers and sanitary towels. Then they meet you and blindfold you so you don't know where you're going. They put you on a table in a makeshift operating room and, and ...' She burst into tears. 'I'm terrified, Richard.'

He wrapped his arms around her and wiped her eyes. 'So why can't we get married, and I'll take care of you and the baby?'

She stared at him and shook her head. 'Richard, don't be ridiculous; we hardly know each other and, anyway, I don't want to get married. Domestic bliss is just not my thing. I want to be independent.'

He sighed. 'I wouldn't interfere with your independence.'

'Perhaps that would be your intention, but who would end up feeding the baby and washing nappies and getting up in the night? I'm an artist, Richard. I know, as an academic, you probably can't understand that all I want to do is paint. I do the minimum housework and stuff around the place just to keep myself clean and fed.'

Feeling certain that she'd think differently once the baby was born, he smiled. 'I can do all that, you know. I've looked after myself for years. I can do housework.'

'And go to work at the same time? I can just picture you, lecturing with a squalling baby over your shoulder ...' She tried to smile, then shook her head.

'I could get help.' He'd just realised something. 'I've got a sister in Scotland. She's a widow. Husband killed the first year of the war. She doesn't have children.' *Bloody war. If Brenda hadn't been killed by that bomb, they would've had children and he wouldn't be in this predicament now.* He frowned, lost in thought, then realised that Sybilla was watching him.

'So you'd take the baby to Scotland, and bring it up over there?'

Richard tried to picture his sister helping him look after a little baby. She was four years older than he, and lived with their elderly mother. Maybe she'd enjoy having a baby nephew. Of course, he'd have to find work in Scotland, possibly Edinburgh University. He liked Edinburgh ...

Her voice interrupted his thoughts. 'You're miles away again, Richard. What are you thinking?'

He came back to earth with a jolt. 'Sorry,' he said humbly. 'I don't know anything about babies, at what age would it be practical for us to take him to Scotland?'

'Him?' she raised her eyebrows, 'and us? Are you suggesting we'd go and live in Scotland?'

His face fell. 'We have to look at all the options,' he said defensively. 'I was offered full tenure at the university. I turned it down, but they said I could change my mind. If I did that, we could live in Sydney.'

'I don't want to move to Sydney. I like it here. In the bush.'

'We could find a place outside Sydney, and I could get the train into the city.'

'And leave me holding the baby.'

He frowned. 'So it would mean me moving here—If you're set on staying around this area.'

'What about your work?'

'I probably don't really need to work,' he said slowly. 'I've got investments and savings, and I'll get a pension later on.'

She laughed at that. Then her face fell. 'Richard, let's be realistic. It won't work. Sorry to have to ask, but how old are you?'

He flushed. 'Fifty-five.'

'Really? You don't look it.' She studied him, her eyes appraising. 'So, consider, when the child is a teenager, you'll be seventy.'

'I know a few lecturers my age at the university who have young children.'

'Do they have wives to look after the children?'

He had to admit that it seemed they did.

'Oh, Richard. The whole thing is impossible. Let's stop day-dreaming. And, anyway, it's nearly Christmas. I have to ring and make an appointment and then get to Melbourne ...' Tears filled her eyes. 'I don't think they'll be working over the Christmas and New Year.

He took a deep breath. 'Will you wait for two weeks? You can't do much until after the New Year, anyway.'

She bit her lower lip. 'I guess so. Seems I don't have much choice.'

'I promise, if we can't come to a decision by then, I'll go with you to Melbourne. I'll hold your hand, and they can blindfold me, too. Now, I'm hungry, how about we eat?'

After their meal, she got up from the table. 'I'll put the kettle on to wash up.'

'How do you wash the dishes here?'

She smiled, took him outside and showed him an extension to the shack—a small shed. It contained a big stone laundry tub on concrete blocks with draining boards on each side. An enamel bowl sat in the tub.

'Right, but come and sit down, Sybilla. I'm a bit tired.' He returned to the swinging chair, sat down and patted the seat beside him. 'I'll wash up in a minute.'

She joined him on the seat.

"Now, tell me,' he asked, 'when is he, I mean the baby, due?'

She shrugged. 'I don't really know. Work out nine months from that night at your place. Do you remember the date?'

'I think it was about the middle of August.'

She counted out nine months on her fingers. 'The middle of May. But it won't happen, Richard.'

He ignored her. 'Have you thought of adoption?'

'Yes, but I couldn't bear the idea of someone else bringing up my child. What if they were cruel to it?' She shook her head. 'No, termination is the only way to go. If I can't get the money, I'll have to try something else.'

'Sybilla!' He eyes widened in horror. 'Please don't even consider doing anything dangerous; I couldn't bear it if anything happened to you, and it would all be my fault.'

Sybilla sighed. 'I keep trying to tell you, there's only one way forward. Termination.'

'Um … what's the cut-off date?' Realising that his words were not the most sensitive, he hastened to add, 'I mean, when would be the latest you could have this … er … this procedure?'

'As soon as possible. I don't know really, but I think after sixteen weeks it would be too late.'

He lapsed into silence, then sat up. 'It's all my fault,' he repeated. 'I'm so sorry. I never intended to force myself on you. Too much alcohol that I'm not used to.'

'Richard stop it! Stop keeping on about it. You didn't force yourself on me.' She sounded irritated. 'Anyway, I think it was probably the other way around.'

'Well, if, as you say, I won't find anywhere to stay around here this close to Christmas, what do you suggest? Have you somewhere I can sleep? You mentioned a studio, maybe there?'

Sybilla frowned. 'What! Let you in amongst my artworks! No. Look, that old sofa in the shack actually opens out into a double bed. I don't usually open it up, that's one advantage of being small. I just lie down on it. But if you pull it out, it converts into a double bed.'

Richard looked at her dubiously. 'Are you sure?'

'Can't do much more damage, anyway. The horse has already bolted.'

He felt himself colouring. Seeing this, Sybilla laughed and took his hand. 'Relax, Richard, I didn't mean anything.'

To cover his confusion, he said, 'Right, so we've agreed that I will stay here for another three weeks, and think about all the options and then make a decision.' He raised his eyebrows, enquiringly.

She nodded. 'Okay.' Then she yawned. 'I'm so tired, Richard. Are you?'

He nodded. 'I am, a bit. It's been a long day.'

'I'll show you the dunny.'

'What? Oh, yes, you explained that to me ...'

She took him around the shack and pointed to a rickety looking corrugated iron hut and laughed. He followed her gaze.

'Yes. Right.'

They pulled out the bed settee, and his suspicions that it would be uncomfortable were confirmed when he lay down beside her. He was exhausted from the drive, plus trying to find her, then the bombshell of news that he might be a father. He lay awake, trying to assimilate all that had happened. It was hot. He wore only the bottom of his pyjamas but was still too hot. He tossed and turned on the old bed, his feet hanging out the end and a broken spring sticking into his back, until he eventually fell into a restless sleep and dreamed that Brenda was alive and they had a son.

Parrots squabbling in the trees outside woke him in the early morning. He lay for a few minutes remembering the previous day. Carefully he turned over. Sybilla still lay sound asleep, that lovely red hair spread over her pillow.

He sighed, cautiously got up, put on his sandals and went outside, found a tree and peed. The morning had dawned cool and quiet, apart from some raucous birds attacking a tree, which he thought might be a bottlebrush—he'd learnt the names of a few shrubs since coming to Australia. He saw her studio shed at the end of the garden, walked over to it, opened the door and went in. The smell of turpentine hit him. Paintings lay stacked up everywhere in the large space. He caught his breath when he saw several portraits which looked like him. Feeling that he was invading her privacy, he turned back towards the shack.

Under the veranda he found a pile of wood and an axe. *What had she said about being too tired to split timber for the fire?* He picked up the axe, turning it in his hands and feeling the weight of it, then put a block of wood on a bigger piece of wood and swung the axe. He split several blocks, feeling the satisfaction of performing physical work. Perspiration ran from him. The sun burst through the trees just as he became aware of her standing beside him, holding a kettle.

'What on earth are you doing, Richard?'

He put down the axe and turned to her with a smile. 'I thought you said you needed firewood.'

She put down the kettle, took his hands and examined them. 'You'll get splinters and blisters. Look, you already have the start of a blister.' She lifted his hand and touched his palm with her finger.

A small thrill went through him at her contact, but then she shook her head and dropped his hand abruptly. 'Sorry.' She turned away, picked up the kettle and went to the rain water tank to fill it. 'Cup of tea?' she asked, putting the kettle on the gas ring and lighting it.

'Thanks.'

'I'm feeling better this morning. No sickness,' she said. 'I'll be all right. No need for you to stay. I can travel to Melbourne on my own.'

He started to stack the split timber. 'We agreed I'd stay for three weeks. I'm going nowhere until we make a few decisions.'

'Decision already made. I'll get the money somehow.' She walked back inside and started making tea.

'I bought condensed milk yesterday.'

She nodded. 'Thanks.' A moment later, she came out and handed him the tin of milk and a tin opener.

Silently he opened the tin and spooned some milk into the two mugs she'd placed on a plank of wood which rested on two crates and supported the gas ring.

'Not bone china, I'm afraid,' she said, a smile hovering around her mouth. 'Did you say you'd bought bacon and eggs?'

'Yes.'

'Sausages?'

'Yes, and some mushrooms.' He smiled at her. 'Hungry?'

'A little bit ...'

'I think I get the hint. I'll get the breakfast on.'

After they'd eaten, Richard rubbed his chin. 'I need to shave. Have you got a mirror?'

'There's one in the studio. I had to buy it to do my self-portrait. Come in when you're ready.'

He gathered up the plates and cutlery. 'I'll wash these first.'

He found Sybilla in the studio in front of a large bench, bent over a painting, when he tapped on the door and cautiously entered. Wearing only a pair of shorts and feeling slightly ridiculous, he stood there with a towel over his arm, his shaving gear and a bowl of hot water in his hand.

She smiled. 'Come in, Richard. The mirror's over there.' She pointed to the opposite wall, then sat and watched him.

'You're making me self-conscious,' he said, turning around, his face covered in lather.

She just smiled.

'What are you smiling at?'

'The way your muscles move, your legs ...'

He made a spluttering noise. 'Now I've cut myself.'

***

That evening at dusk, she stood up and held out her hand. 'Come, I want to show you something.'

Surprised, he followed her. Out beyond the paddock, they followed a narrow path, Sybilla walking in front of him. He hadn't been this way before. Eventually the path widened to reveal a large dam. Richard gasped when he saw it. The sun was setting, the colours reflecting in the still water. 'Sunset at the Dam!'

Smiling, Sybilla turned to him.

'Now I understand.' He gave his head a little shake. 'You're so clever.'

After a few minutes, she took his hand and said, 'It's getting dark, better go back.'

***

The time seemed to fly past. Richard was surprised to find he was enjoying his break. He'd found some old tools in a shed behind the one Sybilla used as a studio and occupied himself with repairs and gardening. Sybilla disappeared into her studio behind the shack every morning, only appearing when he called her for meals.

He couldn't believe how happy and contented he felt in her company. She seemed to like peace and quiet just as he did. He'd driven into the nearest big town the day after his arrival and browsed some bookshops, coming back with a bag of books and enough food to last until after Christmas. He'd also gone to a jeweller and bought a watch.

He often reflected on her lifestyle. He could see how a baby would disrupt her painting. She was totally focused on her art; if he didn't call her for meals, she'd just keep working until it was dark. She had two gas lights in the shack, but they weren't really suitable to paint by.

On New Year's Eve, as they finished dinner, Sybilla put down her knife and fork. 'Richard, what's the date?'

'Thirty-first of December, 1968,' he replied.

'I thought it must be.' She hesitated, looked down at her plate and fiddled with her fork. 'The clinic will be back at work the day after tomorrow. We must drive to the post office and ring them. Um.' She looked up at Richard. 'You did bring the money, didn't you?'

'I've been doing a lot of thinking,' he replied, not answering her question. 'I can understand now I've seen you at work, that you couldn't manage a baby on your own.' He smiled. 'You'd be so absorbed in your painting that you'd probably forget all about him.' He leaned over and took her hand. 'I've got a few ideas.'

'Oh?'

'Yes. Let me clear the table, and we can look at them.'

After they'd taken the dishes away, he fetched a piece of paper from his bag and sat down opposite her. 'First of all, I'd like to say that I intend to help you in any way I can. Whatever you decide.' He put on his half-moon reading glasses and cleared his throat. 'Now, from my point of view I can think of nothing more exciting than having a son—I mean a child. And I want to be part of his growing up, so I have a suggestion ... I could find somewhere to live nearby and come here every day and while you work take care of him, and make your meals ... I notice you're not averse to my cooking.' He smiled, 'and perhaps do the garden or other jobs while he's sleeping. I understand from the books I've been reading, that babies sleep a lot.'

Sybilla stared at him and shook her head. 'What planet did you come from? How will you work? And there's nowhere close to here where you could live. You'd have to live in town.'

'Ah, well, that's all part of my plan. I'm not rich by any means, but I have very simple tastes, so most of my salary has been invested, and I get enough income from those investments to support me. Also, I have a house in England that I could sell and buy something here. And I could probably get some kind of part-time work later on when he goes to school.' Richard looked at her triumphantly; he'd been over and over his plan. It was foolproof.

Sybilla started to laugh. 'Have you any idea how much it costs to bring up a child? That whole plan sounds ridiculous to me.' She made to rise from the table. 'No, Richard.' She must have seen the disappointment in his face, because she added gently, 'Richard, babies aren't logical. They scream; they cry; they get sick and have dirty nappies. There's not even electricity here, nor a washing machine. How are *you* going to wash nappies and heat baby bottles and sterilize them or whatever you do with them? I can just picture you driving up here every morning, after I've been up all night with a teething baby and taking over, heating water and washing nappies by hand and cleaning and preparing my meals with a crying baby over your shoulder!' She sighed. 'I'm sorry Richard. It's been so nice having you here. We do seem to get on well together, but it's just not practical. And for another thing.

What if something happens to you? I'd be left holding the baby with nowhere to go and no support. If someone buys this place, then I have to leave. At the moment, I can pack everything into the van and sleep in it, if necessary, until I can find somewhere else to live. I couldn't do that with a baby.'

His face flushed and he sat looking at his hands, not saying anything. He frowned and stood up. 'I'm sorry, my dear. I'm being stupid. I suppose I got carried away. It's been so nice living here with you. The more I think about it, the more I like the idea of a child, and I'm desperately trying to think of ways to make it happen.'

She studied him. 'What exactly are you trying to say?' she said carefully.

He looked down at her. 'Sybilla, I'm old-fashioned. I got you into this mess, and it's my duty to take care of you and your child. Our child.'

Sybilla folded her arms on the table and mumbled something.

'What did you say?' Richard asked.

'I said, no one has ever taken care of me.'

'What do you mean? Come and sit down on this awful sofa and tell me. Surely your mother did?'

She gave a sardonic laugh as they sat down. 'I think my mother had a drinking problem. She was very clever at hiding the evidence because I never found any bottles, but she was always falling over and slurring her words. That's why I didn't go to school much, I had to stay home and look after her. Then she had a stroke and had to go to hospital. But she fell out of bed and broke her hip and then got pneumonia and shortly after died.'

He frowned. 'How old were you then?'

'Fifteen.'

'What ever did you do? How did you manage?'

She sighed. 'Well, I'd been working Saturdays in a small super-market. I used the money I earned to buy paints and art stuff. Drawing and painting were the only things I liked to do. I got friendly with the people who owned the local art shop, and they offered me a job when they saw some of the drawings and paintings I did. But after Mum died the welfare people came to see me and wanted me to go into a home. I refused, and when I went to work and the owner of the art shop found me crying, she asked what was up. I told her, and she said I could live in the back of the shop for a while, until I sorted myself out.'

Richard was appalled. 'You poor thing.' He took one of her hands in his.

'Anyway, after a few weeks, I found a share house with two other girls. So I moved there.'

'And?' he prompted.

'Well, I stayed with them for a couple of years, then I met this guy and moved in with him for a bit. He seemed nice in the beginning, but then he changed. He seemed to expect me to cook and clean and do everything for him. Then the owner of the art shop got sick and asked me to manage the shop for them. That was great as I got more money, and I could read all the art books when the shop wasn't busy.' She grinned. 'I left that guy and found a bedsit that I could just afford. I went to the markets and did sketches of people and sold them, and I displayed some of my paintings in the shop and they sold. Gradually, I saved enough to buy my van.

'Then Marguerite was in town one day, saw some of my paintings and took them to exhibit in Sydney. She got very excited and asked me to paint more and bring them down to Sydney.' Sybilla stopped and smiled at Richard. 'And while I was there, I met this really great looking guy ...'

A pang of jealousy swept through him, and he frowned.

'One of those academic types,' she continued, 'but very charming; in fact he charmed me into his bed and had his wicked way with me ...'

It took him a few moments to realise she jokingly referred to him. He kissed the top of her head and sighed. 'Well, I haven't been at all wicked since I came here.'

'That's true.' She rested her head on his chest. 'Oh, Richard, this is such a mess, but you do see that I can't possibly have this child.' She yawned.

'What if I bought this place and did it up? I noticed there's a power pole down the end of the driveway. It wouldn't take much to connect electricity. And if I sell my house in England, I'd be able to afford to make the place really nice.'

Sybilla looked at him. 'That still doesn't solve the problems. If anything happened to you, I wouldn't be able to cope. I can't afford a child.'

He remained silent for a moment, then looked at her. 'Marriage would solve that.'

She said nothing, just looked at her hands.

He continued, 'Lots of people do, you know, if they find they're expecting a baby. Of course, I know you don't love me, but I think we get on very well together, and if anything happens to me, well, then you would automatically inherit all my worldly goods, as they say. And I'd make a will, of course, leaving you everything.'

'No, Richard. You're clutching at straws.'

'Will you think about it, Sybilla? And tell me all the reasons why not.'

She nodded, yawning again. 'I've already told you. I'm not into the little wifey thing. What time is it?'

He looked at his watch. 'Nine twenty. You're tired. Go to bed.'

'I must wash up.'

'Your house boy will do it.' He grinned. 'I'm really quite practical.'

***

Early next morning, Sybilla woke him out of a deep sleep by grabbing his left hand. 'Quick, Richard, put your hand here!' She guided his hand to her belly, just above the mound of her pubic bone.

He frowned.

'Can you feel it moving?' she whispered.

'Feel what?' Actually, he could feel something else moving.

'It moved. I felt it move, like a little butterfly, fluttering.'

'Are you sure? Just there? Isn't that a bit low?' He turned on his side, propped himself up on his elbow and studied her face, trying not to look at the curve of her breasts under her t-shirt.

'Yes, I'm sure.' She turned to him. He could just make out her intense look in the early morning light. Then her face fell and she frowned. Tears filled her eyes. 'Oh, Richard, how can I do it? How?'

He took her into his arms and breathed in the scent of her.

She remained silent for a bit, sniffling and snuffling. Then she mumbled something.

'Sorry, what did you say?' He tilted her head to face him.

'I said, Richard, are you still prepared to marry me?'

His heart started to thump. He drew her to him and kissed her.

She broke away. 'I'll look after you when you get old, Richard. I promise.'

Suddenly his desire left him. He half sat up and frowned at her. A bedspring twanged. Groaning, he said, 'It's not like that, Sybilla.

It's not a contract; it's not, if I look after you now, you'll look after me in my dotage.'

She leaned forward and kissed him. 'But I want to, Richard. I want to be with you. I've never felt like this before.'

'What?' He demanded. 'Pregnant?'

She stared at him. 'I don't know. I just know it's nice being with you. I like feeling your arms around me. You make me feel special. And safe. I want you to stay with me. Always.'

As if in slow motion, he leaned towards her and kissed her ...

Sometime later, he asked, 'So you'll marry me?'

She sighed. 'I don't like the idea of marriage, but if you really mean it, then if it's what you really want, then yes. But Richard, what if we can't get along and decide to split up? Divorce?'

He frowned. 'Perhaps you think I'll be a burden on you in a few years' time, having to care for an old man. While you'd still be young.'

'No, I was thinking more that you'd get fed up with all the baby and child rearing stuff, and with me.'

He sighed. 'Sybilla, we can't see into the future. No one can. How about we get married, have the baby; I'll try and buy this place or something similar near here, and we review the situation every year? If you decide you want out, then I won't make it difficult for you. I promise you I'll always provide for you and the child. And I'd like to get married before the baby is born. I want to give him my name.' He gently removed his arms from where he'd been holding her, leaned over and kissed her. 'I'll get breakfast.' He slid out of the bed and went outside to wash.

Later, sitting at the breakfast table, Richard took Sybilla's hand.

'Where will you have the baby, Sybilla?' He asked. 'Where's the nearest hospital?'

'I don't like hospitals. I'll have it here.'

'Here? You don't mean actually *here*?' He spread his arms to indicate the surrounding bush.

She nodded.

'But there aren't any facilities here!'

'What facilities? Don't you know that women have been giving birth in the bush for quite a few years now.'

He stared at his hands. 'Yes. And some of them died.' He said quietly.

'Richard, I won't die. I'm young and fit.'

'But who will deliver it? Do you know a midwife?'

'I'll work something out.'

He had to be content with that.

He nodded and stood up, hoping she'd change her mind nearer the time. At least she was no longer talking of an abortion. He rubbed his hands together. 'Right, let's make a start.' He looked around at the shack. 'This place seems pretty well built. I must get the name and address of the owner from you. Do you know what he wants for the place?'

'No idea. All I know is that he moved to Perth for work. I'll get his address.' She got up, rummaged around in a drawer, and then came back and handed him a dusty, fly-blown postcard. 'Here's his name and address.' She clapped a hand to her mouth. 'Oh dear! This will be awkward.'

'What? I don't understand.'

'If you buy it, I'll have to move out.' She smiled.

'Ha! Think so? I'll let the air out of the tyres of that dreadful old van of yours!' He walked around the shack, appraising it. 'I think we could add more rooms to it quite easily. Have you got a tape measure?'

'Don't know. There might be one out in the back shed where all the old tools are.'

'Right. Well, I'll take measurements and work out what we need and draw up some plans. I think we'll have to get someone in to do most of the work.'

'Can you really afford all this, Richard?'

'Sybilla, I'm a frugal man; my wants and needs are simple. I might not get my pension for another ten years, but we'll have enough to live on until then. And I might get some part time work around here.'

She looked at him with admiration in her eyes. 'You're a man of many talents.' She paused, then said, 'How is it that you haven't remarried, Richard?'

He sighed. 'After Brenda was killed, I had no interest in remarrying, and somehow there weren't any women that attracted me. In my small circle of friends and colleagues, that is. No one seemed to come close to Brenda and what I felt for her. I don't know. It just didn't happen. Perhaps subconsciously, I didn't want to take the chance of another relationship.' He met her gaze. 'But how about you? A beautiful young woman like you? How come you aren't married with a devoted husband and children?'

She laughed. 'Like I said, I'm not interested in the little wifey thing, and having babies. Sounds very ostentatious, but I'm married to my art.'

***

The last week of his stay passed quickly. Richard measured and calculated, walked the boundaries of the property, split more timber, tidied up the garden and did various other odd jobs.

Sybilla asked him to sit for her in the shed. 'I really want to paint a portrait of you, Richard. Please sit for me.'

Reluctantly he agreed. 'But I'm not taking off my clothes!' He found it irksome having to sit still for her, but was flattered that she'd made so many sketches of him.

'Why me?' he asked.

She shrugged. 'Don't know.' Then she looked up and smiled. 'You're very sexy, you know ...'

He made to get up and kiss her but she shouted, 'Don't move!'

***

The day before he was due to leave, they agreed that he would get the train from Sydney to Gurunnuga at the end of January, when his year at the university was up.

'A month ago, I was all set to move back to England, and now my life has changed irrevocably. Are you sure you'll meet me at the station? You won't forget?'

'No, Richard. I won't forget.'

'Or change your mind.'

'No. I won't change my mind.'

He rummaged in his travel bag and drew out the little packet containing the watch. 'Look. I bought this for you. So that you'll know the time when you meet me.'

She opened it, and her eyes filled with tears. 'Thank you, I've never been given a present before,' she whispered. 'It's beautiful.'

***

Richard drove back to Sydney, hardly noticing the drive, his head so filled with plans. Lucky he hadn't booked the trip to New Zealand or the flight back to England.

After leaving his bag at the flat, he dropped the car off at the rental place and went straight to the biggest bookshop in Sydney. Instead of his usual haunts around the science shelves, he headed to the section on health. He selected a book called *Having a Baby Easily*, then one by a Dr Spock, a few others which sounded interesting and finally, one titled *Rearing the Healthy Child Naturally*. He thought Sybilla would like that one.

Still worried about her having a home birth, he went to the medical section and found an obstetrics manual. He flipped through it, then hastily closed it, but he took it, and the other books, to the counter.

The shop assistant stared at him as he made his purchases. *She probably thinks I'm buying these for a grandchild,* he thought ruefully.

Back at his flat, he wrote a list of things he must do: first, write to the owner of the shack, then to Sybilla; draw some sketches of his ideas for the house; write a letter of resignation to his university in England and to the university in Sydney; write to his mother and sister and tell them about his impending marriage—but he wouldn't mention the baby at this point. Then he had to think about selling the house in Bristol and how to get his books and records shipped to Australia. He sat back in his chair and marvelled at the way his life had been transformed. A child! Perhaps a son. He pictured himself playing cricket with him, and chess! He smiled to himself as he filled his pen with ink and started to write.

CHAPTER 4

Richard woke up gasping for breath, then realised that a small pair of arms was strangling him.

'Happy Birfday, Daddy.'

With a jolt he opened his eyes to see the two people he loved most in the world smiling at him.

'Look, Daddy, we have a birfday present for you! From bowf of us!' Jessica jumped up and down on his stomach.

'Ouf!' he gasped, then took her in his arms and covered her with kisses. 'Is it my birthday?' He looked at Sybilla who nodded.

'It's your sixtieth.'

'Really?'

Jessica bounced with excitement. 'Mummy, quick, give Daddy his present. It's from bowf of us.'

Sybilla handed him a rather large, flat, square parcel.

'Can you guess, Daddy? Guess?'

'Um, a book?'

Jessica burst out laughing. 'No, no, not a book! Guess again.' She clapped her hands together.

He took the parcel and looked at the smiling Sybilla. He guessed it was a painting, but of what? 'Um ...' He rolled his eyes up to the ceiling. 'Um, a chair?'

'No, Daddy, don't be silly,' she squealed. 'Open it; open it!'

Carefully he undid the wrapping paper and took out a painting of Jessica, sitting with a book in her lap. It was the same size as the self portrait of Sybilla from when they'd first met, which now hung in his study.

'It's beautiful,' he said, 'but who is that lovely little girl in the picture? Do I know her?'

'It's me, Daddy,' she screamed with excitement. 'It's me.'

'Oh, so it is!' He pretended to peer at the painting and then at Jessica. 'So it is! Thank you both, I love it.' He looked at Sybilla, who was gazing at him with such love in her eyes that he felt close to tears.

Knowing him, and seeing this, she said briskly, 'well, I think we need to make Daddy a special breakfast, don't you, Jessica?'

'Yes!' Jessica jumped off the bed and started towards the kitchen.

'Thank you darling, that's the most wonderful present.' He took Sybilla in his arms and kissed her. 'I'll hang it in my study, next to the portrait of you. My two beautiful girls.'

She smiled and stroked his face. 'It was hard for her to sit still for such a long time, not to mention keeping it as a surprise, but anything for her adored Daddy!' She moved from his arms.

'I can't believe I'm sixty,' he said with a grimace.

'You don't look it, and to me you're still that handsome young academic.' She smiled and moved away from his attempt to grab her. 'Better get up, Jessica's going to make you a special breakfast; prepare for lumpy porridge.' She disappeared out the door.

Slowly he got up and started to dress. He propped the painting against the dressing table. *Jessica's a miniature Sybilla. Same wavy chestnut hair and those eyes.* What had he ever done to deserve two such women in his life? The last five years had been the happiest of his life. He and Sybilla had settled down to married life and he thought she loved him as much as he'd come to love her. Every so often, she'd look at him appraisingly, shake her head, then make some kind of remark to the effect that she couldn't believe how lucky she was to be married to him.

He sighed. Sixty! He was an old man. Jessica would be five soon. He hated the thought of her going to school. He'd been the one who'd mostly looked after her all these years and he'd miss her.

He looked in the small mirror over their dressing table as he combed his hair. It was very grey now—Sybilla said it made him look distinguished. He smiled at the thought.

'Come on Daddy, bweckfast is ready!' Jessica called out to him.

He loved her lisp. *She'll lose that at school,* he thought wistfully.

A lumpy grey mess filled his bowl at the table. He stared at it, then smiled. 'Mmmh, this looks yummy. Isn't Mummy having any?' He winked at Sybilla.

'Not really hungry.' She smirked at him. 'Like some honey on it?'

'I'll get it!' Jessica ran to the pantry and came back with the honey jar.

He took a generous helping of honey and stirred it into the porridge. 'Mmm, it's lovely,' he said, spooning it into his mouth. 'Who made such lovely porridge? Was it you, Mummy?'

'No, it was me!' Jessica jumped up and down. 'And it will be my birfday soon.'

'Yes, you'll be five,' Sybilla said, 'and I was thinking that perhaps Daddy would like to teach you at home.'

'Home school her?' Richard stared at Sybilla, hope in his eyes. 'Could I? Would it be allowed?'

'Don't see why not; you've already taught her to read, and her times table and lots of other things. I think she'd probably be too advanced for the infant class anyway. She'd be bored.'

His mind raced. He'd order the appropriate books, find out what was required. What a lovely birthday present, having Jessica with him, teaching her maths, science ...

'And those lovely little teaching books you've written,' Sybilla continued. 'I think we should look into publishing them.'

Richard had written some simple arithmetic books for Jessica, and Sybilla had illustrated them. They were quite charming, and Jessica loved them. She'd soon learnt to add and subtract from looking at them. He hadn't thought of publishing them, but it might earn them a little money, and they could certainly use it. 'What a good idea,' he smiled at her, then turned to Jessica. 'That was a lovely birthday breakfast. Now I think I'll go and hang my present in my study.'

Jessica nodded. 'I'll help you when I've finished my jobs,' she said, as she started to clear the table.

Richard took the painting and hung it beside the one of Sybilla that he'd bought all those years ago. Well, not that many years, five to be exact.

He sat at his desk and admired the paintings, then looked around his study lined with shelves of books. He gazed out the window onto the garden.

What a lot we've achieved in just five years. They'd had two bedrooms, a study and bathroom built onto one side of the original shack, which didn't look like a shack anymore. He'd worked hard on making it comfortable and creating a vegetable garden, chook pen and small play area for Jessica. All the physical work had made him strong, and he was fitter now than he'd been in years. He felt blessed. They now had electricity. No telephone but that wasn't important—who would they be ringing anyway?

Jessica burst into the room as he was looking at the books he'd written for her. He'd made them by folding paper, stitching several sheets together along the fold, and then carefully writing his little stories in large letters. Sybilla had drawn pictures of numbers with tiny arms and legs joining together to make additions and then running away to be subtracted. Jessica loved them. Both he and Sybilla had enjoyed the process. Yes, he'd investigate publishing them. Perhaps write some more, for more advanced arithmetic. His mind raced, thinking of new ideas. He couldn't wait to start.

'Can we read one now, Daddy?'

'Of course, but I'm thinking about making another book for you, with multiplication and division.'

She jumped up and down, clapping her hands—a bit over excited.

He stood and caught one of her hands. 'How about we go for a walk and give the chooks some breakfast, then see what's grown in the garden that we can have for dinner tonight. After that we could drive into town and go to the library.' He might be able to find out more about home schooling at the library, and Jessica loved sitting on the floor of the children's section looking at pictures and reading.

***

Richard usually drove into town with Jessica once a week to shop, visit the library, and collect any mail from the post office. Often there was nothing of much importance, just a few bills, but one day in 1976 when Jessica was eight-years old, he was pleased to see one with a British stamp and his sister's writing on the envelope. He gave them to Jessica to hold.

'Looks like there's one from your Aunt Beryl,' he said to her. 'See the stamp with the picture of the Queen on it?'

Jessica peered at the stamp. 'I can see the Queen,' she said. 'Tell me again about my Aunt Beryl and when you were little.' She loved stories about the family in Scotland that she'd never met.

Back at the shack, Richard put the letters to one side while he started to prepare their dinner. Jessica went to feed the hens, collect the eggs and call her mother from her studio.

'I've got a letter from Beryl,' Richard told Sybilla as they finished their meal. 'I'll read it now.' Both Sybilla and Jessica liked to hear him read out Beryl's letters. She wrote amusing anecdotes about life in Edinburgh, where she lived with her and Richard's mother.

But when Richard opened the letter, the first sentence made him stop. He frowned and then, instead of reading it out aloud, silently read the rest of the letter. His eyes clouded. 'Oh dear,' he said. 'My mother died two weeks ago. Beryl couldn't ring me as we don't have a telephone, but she wrote straightaway. It was very peaceful; she just fell asleep ...' His voice caught, and his eyes filled with tears. 'I should have gone back to see her.'

Sybilla took his hand. 'I'm so sorry, darling.'

'I did go to see her before I left for Australia, but I thought I'd only be here for a year or two ...' His voice trailed off.

'My grandmother has died?' Jessica said, 'and I never even met her!'

He nodded.

Jessica looked from one to the other. Tears formed in her eyes. 'I never even met her!' she wailed.

Richard got up and took her in his arms. 'I'm sorry, Jessica, but we just didn't have the money to go to Scotland, and your Grandmother was too old and infirm to travel over here.'

'What about Aunt Beryl? She could come here?'

Richard thought about his sister—four years older than him, so nearly seventy. Somehow, he couldn't see her coming all the way to Australia to visit them. Anyway, she'd never leave her two Scottish Highland terriers.

A few months later, another letter arrived. Beryl wrote that she had received probate on their mother's estate and she enclosed a cheque for his share. *As you know, Mother didn't have much to leave but wanted it divided between her two children,* she wrote.

'I'm going into town to bank this cheque,' he said at breakfast the next day. 'Jessica, you'll have to stay home. I'll leave you school work to do. Will that be all right, Sybilla?'

Surprised, she looked up. 'Yes, of course, darling.'

When Jessica started to ask why couldn't she go, too, Sybilla looked at her. 'Jessica, Daddy needs to go alone. He doesn't often get time to himself.'

When Jessica started to complain, Sybilla glared at her. This happened so rarely that it silenced Jessica. Then she smiled at him. 'All right, Daddy.'

Richard drove the old van into town. He stopped at the bank and deposited his cheque, then went to the car dealers and wandered around the showroom looking at the cars.

A salesman, who'd been watching Richard, walked over to him and held out his hand. 'Jeff,' he said. 'Jeff Jones, looks like you're thinking of getting a new car?'

'Indeed, I am,' Richard said. 'I want a new van; a panel van I think you call them.'

The salesman's eyes lit up. 'Come with me; I've got just the vehicle for you. I'll show you the catalogue.' He beckoned Richard to his office. 'I don't have any in stock to show you; they go like hot cakes.'

Richard studied the glossy brochure for the Holden Sandman. 'Yes, it looks nice, but you see those seats?'

'Yes,' the salesman said, 'the very latest bucket seats.'

'No, no. I want one of those long seats, so my daughter can sit in the middle between my wife and I.'

'Oh, you mean a bench seat.' The salesman's face fell, then lit up. 'So your wife will be driving it, too?'

'Of course. This is to be a present for her.'

'Ah! Well, you'll want it fully optioned then.'

'Optioned?' Richard frowned, puzzled.

'Nice wheels, five litre, V8, power steering, aircon, all the trimmings etcetera, etcetera.' The salesman grew excited. 'And you'd best get an automatic; it would be easier for her to drive.'

'I don't know about that. She's used to a manual. Yes, best stick with a manual.'

The salesman frowned but nodded. 'Well, if you're sure. Now, what colour?' He pointed to the colours in the brochure.

Richard studied them. He had no idea which to select.

'The tangerine is very popular.'

'Tangerine looks nice.' Richard suddenly thought of Sybilla's old van. 'Will you take my van in part exchange?'

The salesman's gaze went to the van parked outside the showroom. 'Let's have a look.' He picked up a notebook and went outside. Richard followed him. The salesman walked around the old van and then tried to open the driver's door.

'Oh, sorry,' Richard said, 'that door is stuck. You have to get in the passenger door and slide over.'

The salesman grimaced. 'Sorry, mate, it's really not worth anything. Maybe just for parts. There's a scrapyard down the road. Perhaps take it there after you get your new one.'

Richard sighed. *It was worth a try.*

'Let's go back inside, and I'll do the paper work. You can put down a deposit, and I'll get the order in straightaway. There's a big demand for these vans, but I'll try and pull a few strings and get it for you in a few weeks.' He winked at Richard and rubbed his hands. 'I can ring you and let you know when it's ready.'

'Sorry, we don't have the phone. I'll just call in here in a couple of weeks and see if it's arrived.'

'Right.' The salesman held out his hand.

Richard shook it and went to take the brochure, then paused. Sybilla might see it and get suspicious. Best to leave it behind. No, take it and hide it in his study.

A few weeks later, the new van arrived.

'Just have a few checks to do to make sure it's all okay, register it, etcetera, etcetera,' the salesman announced when Richard called in while doing the weekly shopping. 'Come back for it tomorrow.'

The next day, at breakfast, Richard tapped a spoon on the side of his tea cup.

Sybilla and Jessica looked up.

'Important business in town today,' he said with a smile. 'You must both come with me; it's a surprise.'

'Oooh!' Jessica jumped up from the table and ran around the table. 'Come on, Daddy, let's go!'

Sybilla smiled. 'That sounds exciting; I'd better not start working, then.'

He drove them both into town to the car showroom. The new van was sitting out the front.

Richard pointed at it. 'Do you like that van?'

Sybilla took a quick look at his face. 'It looks very nice,' she said carefully.

Jessica clapped her hands and ran over to it just as the salesman came out of the office. 'Here it is all ready for you, Dr Broughton.' His eyes flickered over Sybilla and registered surprise. 'Mrs Broughton?' he queried.

'Yes,' Richard said with a smile—he was used to people's surprise when they realised this beautiful young woman was his wife.

'Well, just come in and sign a few forms, and it's yours to drive away.'

Richard went inside, leaving Sybilla and Jessica to inspect the van. A few minutes later, he returned with the keys, followed by the salesman. 'Sybilla, darling, meet your new chariot,' Richard said. 'Would you like to drive it home? I'll follow in the old van.'

'It's ours? Really? It's lovely!' She gave Richard a hug and a kiss, then turned to the salesman. 'I'll need to be shown everything first.' She smiled. 'Perhaps you can go over the essentials with me?'

'Good idea, Mrs Broughton.'

Fifteen minutes later, after a trial run around the car yard, Sybilla and Jessica took off. Richard heard Jessica saying, 'Can we call it Tangerine, Mum?' as they drove away. He watched the bright-orange van disappear out the gates, then turned to the salesman and held out his hand. 'Thank you.'

The salesman shook Richard's hand. 'Come back in three months' time for a service and check-up,' he said. 'Lovely to do business with you, mate.'

Richard got into the old van and slowly followed Sybilla, thrilled to have been able to give her something better in which to drive to Brisbane or Sydney with her paintings.

CHAPTER 5

Around the time of Jessica's twelfth birthday, Richard became aware of things not being quite right with Sybilla. Sometimes she slurred her speech. He thought she was probably just overtired from working so hard. He'd noticed that her fingers and toes had twitched sometimes—mainly at night in bed—but he'd thought nothing of it; made a joke of it, actually, laughing that she was twitching to get back in her studio and her latest art project.

Jessica had decided she wanted to go to school for her secondary education. Richard felt disappointed. He'd been looking forward to teaching her more advanced mathematics like calculus and applied mathematics. And physics. But he acknowledged that he didn't have the language skills to teach her French or German. Or the facilities for a chemistry class. Sybilla had tried to teach her art, but it seemed that Jessica had no aptitude in that direction.

'I can't believe that Jessica can't draw,' Sybilla said to him several times, shaking her head. 'It's so simple, you just look at something, then draw it.'

'Darling Sybilla, it's easy for you, but look at me; I can't draw for toffee.'

'Yes, but I'm her mother. She must have inherited something from me.'

'Beauty?' he'd suggested.

She laughed at that and hugged him. 'I love you, Richard Broughton.'

He often thought their life was idyllic. But on Jessica's twelfth birthday, doubts crept in. He noticed that lately Sybilla seemed a bit uncoordinated. If he didn't know better, he'd have thought she'd been drinking.

They were sitting around the table, eating Jessica's favourite meal, when Sybilla's hand suddenly jerked out and knocked over her glass of water.

'I'll mop it up, Mum.' Jessica jumped up, fetched a cloth and started to mop up the water.

'Shorry, darling,' Sybilla frowned. 'Don't know what happened there.'

'Just an accident,' Richard said, wondering if he'd misheard 'shorry' instead of 'sorry'.

But when Sybilla got up from the table to get the birthday cake she'd made, he noticed she walked somewhat jerkily.

The rest of the evening went off well, and Jessica was excited, talking about going to school. He and Sybilla had discussed it, thinking perhaps it would be good for Jessica to mix more with other children. They lived a very secluded life, so Jessica had no friends, and on the rare occasions when they'd been in a social situation, she'd been shy and uncommunicative.

When the first day of secondary school arrived, Richard drove her the two kilometres to catch the school bus. He gave her a kiss, watched her climb in, saw her sit by a window, and waved. He waited until the bus left before he drove home.

He found Sybilla in her studio.

'Jessica got on the bus okay,' he said, looking through the fly screen door at her.

Sybilla looked up from a canvas. 'That's great, darling.'

'Would you like a cup of coffee?'

'Not for me, thanks.' She'd already bent her head back over her painting.

He sighed and returned to the house. It seemed quiet and empty without Jessica. He went into his study, thinking he'd write to Beryl, then looked at his watch. Eight thirty. It would be hours before he could go to the bus stop and pick up Jessica.

He wandered around, tidying the place and doing some weeding, but the day seemed to drag. He couldn't concentrate on anything. It was the first day since she'd been born that they'd been apart.

The next morning at breakfast, Jessica announced that she would walk to the bus stop in future. 'You don't need to drive me, Daddy.'

'It's no problem. I'd like to.' He wondered if her request was because of the bright orange van. Maybe other parents had better vehicles. 'Is it the van?'

Jessica gave him a puzzled look. 'Tangy? Why? Is there something wrong with it?'

'Well, no. I just thought you might feel embarrassed in front of the other children. If they had nicer cars ...'

She shook her head. 'No, Dad. I'd just like to walk.' It seemed she wasn't going to tell him why.

Richard felt bereft when she set off forty-five minutes before the bus was scheduled to pick her up. He sat at the breakfast table twisting his knife in his hand. 'Like more coffee?' he asked Sybilla.

She tried to answer, but then started to choke.

He jumped up. 'Are you all right?'

She nodded.

'I'll get you some water.' He came back with a glass of water and held it to her lips, but she seemed to have difficulty swallowing. 'Some toast went the wrong way?' he said sympathetically.

Again, she nodded. 'Be all right in a minute,' she managed to say.

He watched her for a few minutes, then when she rose from the table, he started to clear the breakfast things.

'Studio,' she said on her way out the door.

But she walked strangely, lifting her knees and placing her feet, almost as if she were dancing.

A nagging thought came to him. When they'd first met, she'd told him her mother had died of a stroke. He hoped that wasn't what was happening.

But it went out of his mind when Jessica came home from school. She walked in the door and flung her school bag in a corner.

'Hello, sweetie, how was school?' he asked.

'Okay.'

'Have you made any friends yet?'

She gave him a scathing look. 'Give me a chance, Dad.'

He said nothing, just nodded.

'I'll change and go and do my jobs,' she muttered, going to her room,

He waited until, dressed in her old clothes, she'd disappeared out the door, then he gave her five minutes and followed her. He found her sitting in the chicken run, crying. He sat on the ground beside her and, without a word, put his arms around her.

'Oh, Daddy, everyone is whispering that I'm a swot and a know-it-all. No one wants to be friends with me. But I can't help it if I know all the answers in the maths and science classes.'

He hugged her. 'What do you think you'll do?'

'Dunno. Pretend I don't know the answers? Don't put my hand up when the teachers ask a question ...'

'You could stay home and I'll teach you,' he said, hope in his voice.

Jessica wiped her eyes and sat up straight. 'No, I won't let them beat me.' She stood. 'I'll feed the chooks and come and help you get dinner. Is Mum in the studio?'

He nodded. 'Yes.'

She blew her nose and tried to smile. 'Thanks, Dad.'

With a heavy heart, he got up and walked back to the house.

***

Richard didn't know what to do. As the days passed, Sybilla became more confused and distant, and the jerky movements increased. She stayed in her studio for hours; he had to call her several times for meals, and then she'd say she wasn't hungry and was busy. She'd always been absorbed in her painting. When she started on a new canvas, it'd always been hard to drag her away, but now, when he went to the studio, it seemed she hadn't made much progress since the day before.

He sighed. What with Jessica being moody with school and Sybilla being strange, he was at a loss. Was it a female thing? Early menopause with Sybilla, and just teenage hormones with Jessica? He resolved to consult his medical textbooks the next day. He'd bought enough of them over the years, starting with childbirth and going right through the baby stages and on to the teenage years.

He sat on his favourite swinging chair in the front of the house. When the old one had eventually fallen apart, he'd bought a new one, big enough to hold the three of them. He'd first seen Sybilla there after driving all that way from Sydney. He remembered the trauma of Jessica's birth. Sybilla had been adamant that she was going to have a home birth. She had some kind of horror of hospitals and doctors.

'I'm having the baby here,' she'd announced. 'You can deliver it, Richard; it's your child and your right.'

He'd been horrified. It was the last thing he wanted to do. Lucky he'd bought all those medical books in Sydney before he'd moved to the shack. He'd done everything he could to prepare for Sybilla's confinement. It'd been a nightmare, and now he shuddered at the memory. For two days Sybilla had been in labour; eventually, exhausted and crazed with pain, just as he was about to put her in the old van and drive to the nearest hospital, she'd given a terrible scream and the baby's head had appeared. A few minutes later, their daughter was born. He thought he'd carry that amazing memory to his dying day. His daughter! Their child! And she was beautiful. Trembling, he'd tied off the cord and cut it, wrapped her in the soft towel he'd prepared and tenderly put her in Sybilla's arms. But she'd been too exhausted to care.

'Is he all right?' she'd murmured.

'It's a beautiful baby girl,' he'd said.

Tears formed in his eyes as he swung in the chair, all the memories coming back to him. Such happy days. He'd been blessed with a beautiful, loving wife and an amazing daughter. They'd grown closer over the years, and he felt a deep love for Sybilla. He knew she felt the same way about him. The current discord was only a hiccup, he thought, trying to reassure himself. He tried to remember what Sybilla had told him about her parents. Her father had been killed in the last year of the war, when she'd been two. She had no memory of him, only a few photographs that her mother had kept. Was he, Richard, just a father figure for Sybilla? He dismissed the sudden thought. No, she loved him for what he was. But what had Sybilla said about her mother? He wracked his brain. Was it a stroke she'd had? He must ask her again. Had Sybilla had a minor stroke? He got up to go to his study and consult his medical dictionary.

***

Jessica changed from a happy-go-lucky little girl into a quiet, withdrawn teenager. Richard worried about her. He tried to talk to her, asked her about school, but she just shrugged and said it was okay.

In Jessica's last two years at school, he noticed an improvement in her moods. It seemed a lot of the students who'd made her life miserable had left after the results of the school certificate came out. And she'd become absorbed with maths and computing, declaring she wanted to study computer science. He felt delighted at that, and had already started on a text book aimed at computing for beginners.

But as Jessica's spirits lifted, Sybilla's sank. Her limbs seemed to have a life of their own, moving with random jerkiness almost as if her feet were dancing. A few times in the night, she'd kicked him violently, but quite unintentionally, and woken him. She wasn't sleeping. He'd heard her getting up and wandering around in the night, bumping into things. And she'd developed a disconcerting tic in her right cheek.

He'd tried to get her to see a doctor, but she was adamant in her refusal, until the morning he found her in her studio, staring at her hands.

'Are you all right Syb?'

She stared at him, then burst into tears. 'Oh, Richard, my hands won't work! I can't hold a brush steady; canst no longer paint!

Look what happened! My hand just jerked and ruined this painting.' He looked down at the canvas. A huge purple splodge of paint defaced the carefully detailed painting. 'Took long time do this one, now look!'

He was appalled. Art was her life. She'd been making a small, but steady income from the sale of her paintings, heading off periodically to Sydney or Brisbane in the van with paintings to exhibit, leaving him and Jessica for several days at a time without the pivot around which their lives revolved. It was strange, he often thought, that although Sybilla spent most of her time in the studio, leaving him to the day to day running of the house and garden and looking after Jessica, she was still the centre of his and Jessica's world. He'd been happy with this arrangement. He'd grown to love the bush, and often he and Jessica went for walks and tried to identify the different types of eucalypt trees. In the beginning, gum trees all looked the same to him, but now his eye was attuned to the different barks, leaves and flowers, and Jessica, who was like him in so many ways, enjoyed spotting birds or trees they hadn't seen before.

But now, knowing Sybilla so well, he knew that if she could no longer paint, she would feel that her life was ended.

'I think we need to see a doctor,' he told Sybilla.

Reluctantly she agreed.

'There might be some medication you can take,' he said, trying to inject a note of hope into his voice. 'We'll go now. I'll just change.' He hurried out the door of the studio to put on clean clothes, thinking it best to go while she was still in a fairly compliant frame of mind.

Sybilla remained silent all the way into town. He found a place to park close to the doctor's surgery, and when they got out of the car, Richard put his arm around her to help her walk. Her head and arms were jerking and her feet jiggling, making walking difficult.

The receptionist looked up as they walked in. 'Good morning. Name please?'

'Richard Broughton. I'm here for my wife.'

'Has she been before?' The receptionist looked through her files. 'No Mrs Broughton on our records.'

'No; I've been here before with our daughter, but not my wife. Sybilla Cresswell.' He indicated Sybilla, whose head was jerking uncontrollably, her face contorted in a grimace.

The receptionist frowned.

She probably thinks Syb is mentally retarded.

'All right. Fill out this form, please.' The receptionist handed him the form and a pen. She obviously thought Sybilla wouldn't be able to fill it out.

Two other people sat in the waiting room, and they studied Sybilla with interest. Then one of them went over to the desk, and in a loud whisper said, 'You can let this lady go before me; she looks like she's ... you know ...' He rolled his eyes.

Richard gritted his teeth at this and hoped Sybilla hadn't heard it. He took her hand and guided her to a seat, but she had difficulty placing her feet. It took several attempts for her to sit down. *This is awful.* He'd never seen her so bad. Perhaps it was the stress of coming to a doctor.

He filled out the form and, out of the corner of his eye, saw the other patient get up and whisper to the receptionist. After putting the form and the pen on the reception desk, he returned to his seat and took Sybilla's hands in his, to try and still the jerking.

The door marked 'Surgery' opened, and a woman with a young baby came out. The doctor followed and walked to the receptionist. She handed him Richard's form. The doctor looked at it, then peered over his glasses. 'Um, Sybilla Cresswell?'

Richard stood and helped Sybilla towards the surgery door.

'Dr Lachlan,' he introduced himself. 'Are you Mr Cresswell?' He raised his eyebrows at Richard.

'I'm Sybilla's husband, Richard Broughton.' Sybilla had kept her name when they married. 'I can't start signing my artwork with a different name,' she'd said. He'd registered Jessica as Jessica Cresswell-Broughton, but Jessica had dropped the Cresswell when she went to school.

'So what brings you here today?' Dr Lachlan indicated two chairs. 'Sit down.'

Richard stared at him. He thought it blindingly obvious why they were there.

Sybilla said nothing.

'Sybilla hasn't been well lately,' he replied when it appeared Sybilla wasn't going to answer. 'She's an artist and can no longer control holding a paintbrush to paint. She has these random jerky movements, and she has trouble sleeping.'

'How long has this been happening? Gradually over the past while or suddenly?'

'Gradually, I suppose,' Richard replied.

The doctor scribbled something, then stood up from behind his desk and went over to Sybilla. 'What's your name?' he asked in a surprisingly gentle voice.

'Shibla,' Sybilla slurred.

'Can I examine you, my dear?'

Sybilla bowed her head slightly in acknowledgement.

The doctor attempted to take her blood pressure. 'Can you hold her arm still, please?' He nodded towards Richard.

Dr Lachlan looked into her eyes, her mouth and asked her to walk along a line of tiles on the floor. She was unable to walk in a straight line and nearly fell. Dr Lachlan caught her. 'All right, my dear. Now, would you just put your arms straight up over your head?'

Sybilla did so, but her hands swayed as if she were doing some kind of erotic dance.

The doctor looked at Richard. 'Perhaps your wife could wait outside, Mr Broughton.'

'Shtay here,' Sybilla managed to say.

Richard stood; he didn't like the frown on the doctor's face. 'Come, darling. I'll just help you outside; I won't be long.' He hated the thought of having to subject her to the stares of the other people in the waiting room, so he turned to the doctor. 'Can you wait while I take my wife outside to the car?'

Dr Lachlan nodded.

A few minutes later, Richard returned to the doctor, who looked up at him with a frown. 'I'm afraid Sybilla has Huntington's Chorea, or Disease as it's now known,' he said. 'It used to be called St Vitus Dance, because of the dance-like movements. It's not very common and unfortunately, there is no cure.'

Richard stared at him. 'How can you be sure?'

'I saw a case of Huntington's when I was training, and the movements are unmistakable. I'm so sorry.' He sighed. 'I didn't want your wife to hear this, because there is a certain stigma attached to the disease. Most sufferers end up in mental institutions so their families tend to keep it quiet. It's hereditary. There's been a bit about the disease in the medical journals lately. A family in Venezuela. Mother with ten children. Very sad.' He looked down at his notes. 'Do you know which of Sybilla's parents suffered from it?'

Richard grimaced. 'Sybilla's father died in the war when she was only a baby. Her mother died fairly young from what Sybilla told me.' He sighed. 'As far as I know, she had some kind of fit or stroke, fell and then got pneumonia and never recovered.'

The doctor nodded. 'Hmm. It's probable that Sybilla's mother was the carrier.' He frowned as he looked up. 'Do you have children?'

Sudden fear gripped Richard. 'Yes, a daughter.'

'There's a 50/50 chance that she could also have the disease, I'm afraid.'

'You mean Jessica could get like this too?' His voice came out as a croak.

'Well, like I said, a 50/50 chance. You, as her father, don't appear to have it. Normally it presents between the ages of thirty and fifty. That's the problem. It doesn't present until after most people have had a family.' He studied Richard. 'At your age it's unlikely that you'll develop it. If you did, then she would certainly be affected.'

Richard heart started to pound. He suddenly hated this cool doctor. 'What can we do?' he managed to say through clenched teeth.

'Not a lot, I'm afraid. How old is your daughter?'

'Jessica is seventeen.'

'When she marries, she'll have to make hard decisions as to whether she should have children,' Dr Lachlan continued, not looking at Richard. 'There are no tests at the moment to determine if she is a carrier.'

Richard suddenly could take no more. He jumped to his feet. 'Thank you, doctor. You've given us a lot to think about.'

'Just a minute.'

Richard turned as he was about to open the door.

'You mentioned that your wife isn't sleeping well.' The doctor scribbled on a pad, tore off a page, then stood up and held it out to Richard. 'A prescription for sleeping tablets for Sybilla. It might help you both get some rest.' He walked to the door and held it open. 'I'm sorry to be the bearer of such bad news, Mr Broughton.'

Richard nodded and mumbled, 'Thanks.' He hadn't used the title doctor since moving to the bush. He'd been afraid local people would think him a bit arrogant. The phrase they used was 'up himself'.

Outside, he nodded to the receptionist, unsure if he had to pay for the consultation or not. He didn't stop to find out.

Sybilla raised her eyebrows at him as he got back to the van. 'What wrong me?' she asked.

'Don't worry, Sybilla darling,' he said, getting in. 'I'll take care of you.'

'What wrong me?' she insisted.

'It's something called Huntington's disease. It's hereditary.' He put his arms around her.

Sybilla remained silent for a while. Then she spoke, her voice a whisper, 'So my mother had this?'

'The doctor thinks so, yes.'

'I thought she had drink problem. Oh, Richard, I was so dismissive of her pain!' She started to cry.

'Oh, Syb, you weren't to know! She probably didn't know, either.' He started the engine. 'We'll work it out, darling, I'll do some research.'

***

Back home, Richard settled Sybilla on the swinging chair outside, then made tea and helped her drink it. 'Are you tired, darling?'

She nodded.

'Come and lie down, then.'

As soon as he thought she was sleeping, he went straight to his study and frantically searched through his medical books.

Here it is. St Vitus Dance. Huntington's Disease. Quickly he read the Symptoms.

Physical symptoms include:

Painful muscular spasms and cramps.

The body may also twist and contort and feet turn inwards.

Involuntary tremors, particularly of the head, which seems to rattle.

Cognitive symptoms include:

Short-term memory loss

Difficulties in concentrating and making plans.

Emotional symptoms include:

Depression

Behavioural problems

Mood swings, apathy and aggression.

Yes, Sybilla had the physical symptoms, except the cramps, thank goodness. Short term memory loss, yes. Difficulty concentrating? Well, he'd noticed that, too, just lately. Emotional symptoms? She did seem depressed and moody, not aggressive though ...

Some people with Huntington's disease become easily irritated. This can be partly caused by an inability to see things from another person's point of view. Some people with Huntington's disease may come across as self-centred and selfish.As the disease progresses, the parts of the brain that help control the muscles of the face, throat and tongue are increasingly affected. This can cause the person to have considerable speech difficulties and choking. The person may not initiate conversations either, as the sections of brain responsible for this are also impaired.

Richard slammed the medical book shut. Closing his eyes, he sat back in his chair. *No!* He screamed inwardly. *This cannot happen to my beautiful Sybilla.* Then the reality of what the doctor had said hit him. There was a 50/50 chance that Jessica would also develop this terrible disease. His world seemed to collapse around him.

***

Richard didn't want to worry Jessica with her mother's diagnosis, but a few days later as they prepared their evening meal, Jessica turned to him. 'Dad, do you think Mum is getting worse?'

He nodded. 'Yes.'

'Do you think we'd be able to persuade her to see a doctor?'

'Actually, we went on Monday,' he said.

'Oh?' Jessica said, startled. 'How did you manage to get her to agree?'

Sybilla had never made any secret of her antipathy towards any kind of medical treatment, doctors or hospitals.

Richard grimaced. 'She can't hold a paint brush steady.'

'Oh, no!' Jessica's hands flew to her face. 'What did the doctor say?'

'Sit down, Jess.'

Slowly Jessica sat down at the table, opposite him.

'Jessica, it's serious. The doctor thinks she has Huntington's Disease.'

'What's that? I've never heard of it.'

He told her what he'd found in the medical dictionary.

Her brows drew together. 'What does it mean, Dad?'

'She'll slowly get worse until ...' He put his head in his hands, then looked up at his daughter and continued, 'Apparently there's a wide variation in symptoms and how fast they develop. Now that I've read about it, all we can do is try and keep her calm, talk slowly, try and get her out for exercise ...'

'She'll go crazy if she can't paint.'

He nodded. 'I know.'

'Where is she now?'

'In the studio.'

Jessica stood. 'I'll go and fetch her. Dinner's nearly ready, anyway.'

Richard took a deep breath and went back to preparing their meal.

'Mum!' Jessica called out as she opened the studio door. 'You there, Mum?'

'Of coursh; where elsh would I be?' Sybilla spoke slowly with a bit of a slur and gave a crooked smile.

'What are you working on?'

'Nothing at the mome. Just sinking.'

'Dinner's ready.' Jessica went around the large draughtsman's table in the middle of the studio and put her hand out to her mother.

Initially, when anyone went to help her, Sybilla had insisted she could manage, but after a few falls, she'd become accustomed to accepting help.

***

Jessica decided she'd go to university in Sydney.

'Why not Newcastle?' Richard asked, when she opened her acceptance letter. She'd been nagging him every day since the results were out to go to the post office to collect their mail. 'Newcastle's closer.'

Jessica just shook her head and smiled.

Richard looked at his beautiful daughter. 'I need to talk to you.'

'Ah! I can feel a lecture coming up.' She hugged him.

'This is serious. I have to talk to you while Mum is resting.'

Jessica frowned. 'Has something happened that I haven't noticed?'

A year had passed since Sybilla's diagnosis; she seemed to have stabilized now that she was sleeping better and with Richard and Jessica taking care not to confuse her by talking too fast, or changing the subject without a long pause. They also took her for walks in the bush and Richard massaged her arms and legs nearly every day. The walks were agonizingly slow but seemed to benefit Sybilla.

'I don't suppose you've read the medical books about Huntington's Disease,' he said.

Jessica looked straight at him. 'Of course, I have, Dad.'

'Oh.' *Of course!* He thought. *She's my daughter; she would have done exactly what I did.* 'So you know you have a 50/50 chance of getting the disease?'

'Yes.'

'And that if you have children, and then went on to develop the disease, just like Mum, that those children would also have a 50/50 chance of inheriting it.'

She nodded.

'I just need to warn you to be careful of having unprotected sex. Just in case.'

She got up and hugged him.

'I understand, Dad. I won't be rushing into any relationships, don't worry. I'll be like Mum, wait for the right man to turn up.'

He held her in his arms and stroked her hair, unable to speak. 'I'll miss you,' he managed to mumble. He wanted to tell her that when she did meet the right man, she'd have to discuss with him what to do in regard to having children. But he couldn't bring himself to broach the subject. She would have thought about it; he was sure.

'I'll miss you too.' She paused. 'Well, I'd better finish sorting out my stuff.' She looked up, studying her father, who, at seventy-four, was still a handsome man, his hair now completely white, silver in some lights. 'I'm hoping I'll be able to get a part-time job near the campus,' she said.

He frowned. 'I'm sorry I can't do more to help financially; I hate the idea of not being able to drive you to Sydney, or even go on the train with you.'

'Dad, it's okay. You can't leave Mum, and there's no way she could go all that way in the train or even in the van. I'll be fine on the train.'

'Will you be able to come home for Easter?'

'Of course!'

'Do you think we should get the telephone installed, Jessica? I've been thinking of it; you could ring us, then, let us know how you're going.'

'It would be quite expensive for me to ring you, Dad. I'd have to find a call box. I'll write every week.' She hugged him again and went off to her room, leaving her father to check on Sybilla.

CHAPTER 6

Richard missed Jessica; he'd loved looking through her school work and offering advice. Probably useless advice, he thought now, but Jessica had always listened politely and either agreed or else they'd have a stimulating, to him anyway, discussion.

He sighed. He'd noticed that Sybilla seemed to be getting more depressed; she missed Jessica, too. He was getting old, and there was so much to do around the place. He often felt too tired to massage Sybilla's hands and legs.

He didn't know what to do. He thought he'd ask the doctor when he went for her prescription for sleeping tablets. But going to the doctor was a problem, too. He usually went on his own and got repeats for the scripts for the sleeping tablets while Jessica stayed with her mother. Now, he'd have to get Sybilla in the van and leave her in it while he went into the surgery. He didn't like leaving her for any length of time, and maybe it would be good for the doctor to check her over; it had been a while since Sybilla had been to see him.

He grimaced. That would be an ordeal. *Better face it.*

He got up and headed to the studio. Sybilla still liked to go there and look at her paintings and turn the pages of art books. He'd moved a comfortable chair in there for her, close to the window so she could look out at the bush.

'Sybilla, darling,' he called as he walked towards the studio. He'd found that he had to announce his arrival before opening the door so she wouldn't be startled.

She looked up as he came in, and he thought she was making an effort to smile.

He went over and took her hands. 'Darling, we need to go to the doctor to get a repeat prescription for your sleeping tablets.' He stopped to let her digest this, before continuing. 'Do you think you'll be up to coming in the van with me?'

She took a few seconds to think about it, then her head wobbled. 'If you shink so, Richd.'

He let out an inward sigh of relief. 'Now?' he asked. 'Well, in fifteen minutes?' He helped her to her feet. 'I'll just change and we can go slowly.' He led her back to the house.

Twenty minutes later, they were in the van, and he drove carefully into town.

He was relieved to see that Dr Lachlan was on duty—he just had to check that the sleeping tablets he'd been prescribing were still okay for her. Richard managed to get Sybilla into the surgery, reassuring her all the time that everything was all right. She complied meekly, but as they waited, the jerking in her limbs and head grew worse from anxiety. Luckily, they didn't have to wait long for their turn.

'Ah, Mrs Broughton,' Dr Lachlan said when they entered his room, 'please, sit down.' He read Sybilla's notes as he said this.

Once Sybilla was settled, he checked her blood pressure and gave her a brief examination. Then, speaking very slowly, said to Sybilla, 'My dear, do you think you could sit in the waiting room for a few minutes while I talk to your husband?'

Richard looked at her. 'Will that be all right, darling? I'll only be a few minutes.'

Sybilla frowned. 'Wash rong with Rich? He shick?' she managed to say. Her hands shook uncontrollably.

'Just routine,' the doctor reassured her.

'Why I not stay?' she asked.

'No reason, but I'd prefer you to sit quietly outside.' Dr Lachlan opened the surgery door.

'Come, dear. I'll only be a few minutes.' Richard glanced around and seeing that the waiting room happened to be empty, guided her out and sat her in a chair, then went back into the doctor's room.

Dr Lachlan looked up from studying his notes. 'I'll be brief, but I see Sybilla has deteriorated a lot since I last saw her. How is she generally?'

'She seems more depressed,' Richard replied, 'especially since our daughter left for university three months ago.'

'Still sleeping all right with those tablets?'

Richard shrugged. 'Not so well as initially. Perhaps she's getting used to them.'

The doctor appraised Richard. 'You're looking tired; I think I should examine you, too.'

'I'm fine, and there's really no need to examine me,' Richard said impatiently. 'I have to take Sybilla home before she gets overtired. I really came for another script for her sleeping tablets.'

Dr Lachlan nodded. 'You may have to think about getting her into a nursing home at some stage.'

'Impossible!' Richard said. 'I'll care for her.'

'Before long she'll need full-time care.'

Richard frowned. 'I can care for her.' He stood up.

Dr Lachlan wrote on his prescription pad and tore off the sheet. 'Here's a script for a stronger sleeping tablet. Just be careful with it. Make sure you keep them in a safe place away from your wife.'

Richard nodded. 'Thank you, Doctor.'

***

Richard waited at Gurunnuga station for the express train from Sydney. Jessica was on her way home for the Easter break. She'd found a job so could only stay a week. He paced up and down the platform, looking at his watch. Another ten minutes. At last the train stopped, and Jessica was the only person to get off.

His heart lifted at the sight of her. Swallowing hard, he brushed away tears. 'Jessica, darling!'

'Dad! Oh, it's so good to see you.'

He picked up her suitcase and held her arm as they walked out to the van.

'How's Mum?'

He shrugged. 'About the same. The doctor gave her different sleeping tablets. I think her body had got used to the others and weren't having the same effect.'

'How are you, Dad?'

He smiled. 'All the better for seeing you!'

'The big bad wolf, eh?' she teased.

They climbed into the van and drove home.

Jessica sighed. 'I so miss the bush.'

'Yes, it grows on you, all right.'

'I hope the next time I come home, I won't find you covered in moss and camouflaged as a bush!'

Richard laughed. 'I don't stay still long enough to grow moss!' It felt so good to have her back. 'I'm looking forward to hearing everything about university,' he said, driving carefully to avoid the ruts and potholes in the road.

'I love it,' Jessica said. 'The lectures are great, so interesting. The grounding you gave me in logic and statistics is really helping.'

Richard had left Sybilla in the swinging chair outside the house, telling her to stay there until they came back. When she saw the van coming, she struggled to get up. 'Jeshka!'

'Oh, Mum, how good to see you.' They hugged each other.

'Sit tell me evthing.' Sybilla managed to say and attempted to pat the cushion beside her. 'You met any nice lechers like Dad yet?' She said, looking at Richard.

He smiled. It was rare these days to hear Sybilla joking, then he realised it wasn't a joke. She was trying to say lecturers.

Jessica grinned. 'I'm looking, Mum, but none so far.'

The week flew past and soon it was time for Jessica to catch the train back to Sydney. Sybilla decided she'd come to the station with them.

'Are you sure it won't be too much for you, darling?' Richard asked.

'No. I go. I shtay van. You see her train. Park show I see her.'

Jessica looked at her father. They were pleased to see Sybilla so bright.

***

Jessica wrote that she wouldn't be coming home again until the Christmas break. She was working hard at her part time job to earn money to pay for her books and her expenses. She didn't want to be a burden to her parents, plus she was happy working in a book store at weekends, and the owners of the bookshop had asked her to coach their son in maths. That had led to other parents asking her to coach their children, so she was doing well. She was on top of her studies, too.

When Jessica came home that Christmas, she saw a marked deterioration in Sybilla, who could no longer turn the pages of a book to read. Richard had noticed this and now read to her every evening.

'Is this a new thing, reading to Mum?' Jessica asked, when her mother had gone to lie down for her afternoon nap.

'She can't control her hands enough to hold the book and turn the pages,' he replied. 'I didn't say it to her, just said, "How about we read a book together; I can read it to you." She seemed happy with that.'

Jessica noticed with alarm how much her father had aged, and now he had to do all the work around the place as well as care for her mother.

She spent her time at home cleaning windows, weeding and doing what housework she could without upsetting her father. She knew how proud he was, he would be mortified if he thought he wasn't keeping the place clean.

She read to her mother, too, wondering as she did so how much her mother actually comprehended.

Sybilla always smiled and thanked her. Her speech was slower these days and more slurred but she made herself understood.

***

When Jessica went back to Sydney for her second year, Richard and Sybilla missed her even more. Her bright and happy face around the place had put them in good spirits, and Richard felt Sybilla had made a great effort to be cheerful during the visit. But now Sybilla seemed to have lapsed into a deep depression, not wanting to do anything. When he read to her in the evenings, he could see she wasn't listening.

She suffered painful cramps which nothing seemed to alleviate, even when he massaged her legs. And the sleeping tablets no longer worked. She was restless and jerky in the night, which meant he didn't get any sleep, either. When the bottle was nearly empty, he decided to go and see the doctor again; there might be another sleeping tablet that she could take.

'Do you feel up to coming into town with me, Sybilla? I must see the doctor; he may be able to prescribe stronger sleeping tablets for you.'

'Not today.'

'Yes, it might be too uncomfortable for you, waiting in the van while I get the shopping. Will you be all right, darling? I'll leave everything in reach. You'll be all right sitting in your chair by the bed until I get back?'

She nodded. 'Of coursh, darling,' she managed to say.

'Do you want to go to the toilet before I leave?'

She nodded.

Richard helped her up. He knew she hated the indignity of being taken to the toilet. After washing his hands, he gently helped her back to the bedroom and sat her in the big old arm chair next to the bed.

She watched him as he changed his clothes. 'Rish Darling?'

He turned at her voice. 'Thank you for evthing. For suading me have Jessica. For give me such love 'n care.'

The words came out jerkily and not very well pronounced, but he understood and he could hardly bear it. He went over to the chair and took her in his arms. 'Sybilla, my darling,' he murmured. 'You're the love of my life. I want nothing more than to be with you. And our beautiful daughter, a gift you gave me.' He saw tears glittering in her eyes.

'You're so tired, darl Rishd. I too much for you.'

'Don't be silly; you're my life.' He kissed her. 'Just rest there until I get back. I've left water there.' He indicated a baby's drinking cup on a small table within her reach. She was able to hold it and sip from the lip without spilling the contents.

All the way into town, he worried; she had seemed so down.

He went to the doctor's first, and he fretted while he waited in a queue. At last his turn came.

'That last lot of sleeping pills should have knocked her out,' the doctor said after Richard had asked for something stronger. He looked puzzled. 'I'll give you another repeat, try them for a bit longer.'

Richard hurried out, went to the chemist and did the shopping while the script was being filled.

Back home, he went straight to their bedroom and was surprised to see Sybilla asleep in the old armchair. *That's good. The rest will do her good.* He was about to creep out of the room and leave her when he noticed the tipped up baby cup of water on the table and a few pills.

A sudden terror swept through him, and he hurried back to her. 'Sybilla ...' She wasn't breathing.

He shook her. 'Wake up, Sybilla! Oh my God, Sybilla! Wake up.' He felt for a pulse. Nothing. She felt cold. There was no sign of life. He threw himself down on his knees, put his head on her lap and sobbed. What had happened? He should never have taken so long in town. He looked at the two pills on the bedside table and frowned. They looked like the sleeping tablets.

A terrible realisation hit him. She must have only been pretending to take the sleeping tablets for the past few weeks, saving them up instead, and then she'd then taken them all as soon as he'd left. He'd kept the bottle of tablets hidden away, certain there was no way she could have found them.

What to do? Bitterly regretting not having the phone installed, he ran out to the van and drove the few kilometres to their nearest neighbour, Bill Yates, who had a telephone.

Bill was in his vegetable patch, weeding, when he heard the van screech to a halt. He looked surprised to see Richard in such a state. Though on good terms, they rarely saw each other.

'What's up, Richard?' he asked, leaning on his hoe.

'It's Sybilla,' Richard cried, jumping out of the van. 'I think she's taken an overdose. Please, ring the doctor, the ambulance; please, it's urgent.'

Bill nodded. 'No problem; I'll do it at once. Come in.'

But Richard climbed back in the van and drove at breakneck speed back down the dirt track.

Bill and his wife, Irene, turned up at the shack soon after. Irene came into the bedroom where Richard knelt holding Sybilla's hands and sobbing. At the sight of him, she shook her head and left the room. He heard her go to the kitchen and put the kettle on.

The ambulance arrived, and the paramedics rushed in and examined Sybilla. They soon finished. 'Sorry, mate,' one of them said, shaking his head, 'I'm afraid there's nothing we can do ...'

'The doctor is on his way,' Bill told them.

Richard was devastated. 'I should never have left her,' he kept repeating. 'It's my fault!'

He noticed the bottom sheet of the bed was hanging out, near her pillow. Without thinking, he went to tuck it in, and his hand felt something just under the mattress. He brought it out. To his horror it was a tablet. He felt again; several pills had been stashed there.

When Dr Lachlan arrived, he looked at the two pills on the bedside table, and Richard managed to gasp out his suspicions that Sybilla had been hoarding the tablets and hiding them under the mattress. The doctor nodded. 'She'd obviously been planning this for some time.' He took a small plastic bag from his pocket and put the pills in it. 'I thought it was strange that those sleeping tablets weren't working. I should have put two and two together ...'

'She told me she loved me; thanked me for everything before I left,' Richard sobbed, 'I should have been more aware, more ...' He broke down again, then lifted his head. 'Jessica! What will I tell Jessica?' he moaned. 'I killed her mother.'

Dr Lachlan patted Richard's shoulder. 'No, Richard. It was an accident.' He stared hard at Richard. 'It was an accident,' he repeated more loudly.

Irene looked at her husband and raised her eyebrows. 'Do you have a telephone number for Jessica?' she asked.

'Yes.' Richard stood and took a deep breath. 'May I use your phone to ring her?'

Irene nodded. 'Of course. But I'll do it if you like ...'

'No, I will.' He looked round wildly. 'What happens now?'

'Unfortunately, there'll have to be an autopsy,' Dr Lachlan said. 'I haven't seen Sybilla professionally for quite a while, otherwise I could have signed the death certificate. The ambulance will take her to the hospital.' He regarded Richard. 'Perhaps you'd better give me the bottle of sleeping tablets you got today.'

Richard stared at him. 'I'm not suicidal. I have Jessica to think of.'

The doctor nodded. 'All right.' He signalled to the ambulance men to take Sybilla.

Richard stood, mutely watching as they put Sybilla's body in the ambulance. The driveway was cluttered with vehicles.

'I'll have to go, to make room for the ambulance to leave.' Doctor Lachlan held out his hand. 'I'm so sorry, Richard.'

Richard shook his hand, fighting back the tears, then watched as the two vehicles reversed out and disappeared.

Irene held his hand. 'Come, Richard,' she said gently, 'we'll go back to our place and phone Jessica.'

However, Jessica wasn't at home. 'She's working,' said the person at the other end of the line. 'Can I ask her to call you?'

'Yes,' Richard said shakily. He gave her Irene and Bill's number, then sat down on the little telephone seat next to the phone.

'I'll make tea,' Irene said briskly. 'You must try and eat something, Richard.'

Bill hovered nearby, clearly uncertain what to do in these circumstances.

'Is it all right if I stay here until Jessica rings back?' Richard asked Bill.

'Of course, mate.'

Two hours later, the phone rang. Richard had moved to the lounge after Irene had gently suggested that it might be some time before Jessica rang. He'd just nodded, and she'd led him to a chair.

At the first ring, Richard jumped up and ran to the hall where the telephone was. 'Hello?'

'Is that you, Dad? What's wrong? What's happened?' Jessica's voice was filled with anxiety.

'It's Mum,' he managed to say.

'What? Mum? What's happened?'

Irene gently took the phone from Richard. 'Hello, Jessica, Irene here. Jessica, I'm sorry to have to tell you that there's been an accident. Somehow your mother took too many sleeping tablets ...'

'How could that happen? Dad is the one that gives them to her ...' They could hear the panic in Jessica's voice.

Richard snatched the phone from her. 'Jessica, Mum's gone ...'

'What do you mean, gone? Gone where?'

'She, she died, Jess.' He couldn't say the word dead. It was too final.

'Died?'

'Yes, they've taken her away ...'

'Away? Away where?'

Irene took the phone back from Richard. 'Jessica. I'm sorry. Your father is distraught. I think you'd best get up here as soon as you can. Ring here and let us know which train you'll be on. I'll come and meet you at the station.'

'You mean Mum is dead?'

'I'm so sorry, Jessica, but yes.'

'I'll be on the next train. I think there's one that leaves Sydney early in the morning.'

Irene ended the call and looked at Richard. 'Jessica's on her way.'

He looked back at her blankly.

'Jessica is on her way here, Richard. Would you like to stay here for tonight?'

He stared at her, then her words registered. 'No, no, I must go home. Sybilla needs me.' Then the reality hit him. Overwhelmed by the rawness of his pain, he looked at Irene for support, but she couldn't meet his gaze.

'Richard,' she said gently. 'Sybilla has gone to the hospital. Why don't you stay here until Jessica arrives?'

'No, no. I'll go home now. Where are my car keys?' He started to search through his pockets.

'Richard, Bill drove you here.' Irene looked at her husband. 'I'll drive you and Bill back to your place, then I'll come back here, and I'll go and meet Jessica at the station and bring her over to you.' She nodded at Bill. Reluctantly he nodded back. 'Bill will stay the night with you.' Bill grimaced.

The following afternoon, Irene met Jessica at the station and brought her back to The Shack.

'Dad!' Jessica rushed towards him and wrapped her arms around him.

Irene had told her what she knew about the awful events, and Jessica had remained stoic, until she saw her father, then she burst into tears.

'We'd better go,' Irene said, much to Bill's relief.

He'd had a sleepless night on the couch in the living room while Richard paced up and down for several hours. Eventually Bill had persuaded him to go and lie down by saying, 'You want to be rested for when Jessica comes.'

***

Jessica found it hard to leave her father after the funeral. He seemed to have shrunk within himself.

'Dad, I can stay longer,' she told him.

'No, dear. You must finish university. I'll be fine.' He gave her a hug.

'I'll come back at the end of this semester,' she murmured.

In the train back to Sydney, she went over and over in her mind the events of the past two weeks. It had been so hard. Her father had tried to be strong for her, and she'd tried to be strong for him.

The post mortem gave the verdict of accidental death, but Jessica knew it hadn't been an accident. Sybilla hated not being able to paint, hated being dependent, hated being a burden on her husband and child. It would have been anathema to her. *I suppose I'd feel the same way in her situation,* Jessica endeavoured to console herself. She tried to suppress the tears. Few people shared her carriage, but when it stopped in Newcastle, it suddenly filled with people.

'Anyone sitting here?' a voice said.

Without looking up, she shook her head. 'No.'

'Thanks.'

She looked out the train window, and then the reality hit. *I'll never see my mother again.* Sadness overwhelmed her.

Taking out her handkerchief, she blew her nose and tried to hide her tears, but her handkerchief quickly became sodden. A hand pushed a folded handkerchief towards her. She looked up and saw a young man, blue eyes and fair, tousled hair, looking at her with concern.

Seeing her look, he said softly. 'It's clean. I never use it.'

Somehow that sounded so ridiculous to her that she wanted to laugh. Laughing and crying at the same time caused her to hiccup. 'Sorry,' she mumbled and blew her nose loudly. Then she frowned at the handkerchief, a crisp linen one. 'Is that a monogram?' She mumbled as she indicated the embroidered JK on one corner.'

He gave an embarrassed laugh. 'Um, yes. My grandmother gave me three of them for my birthday. I have to keep one in my pocket to demonstrate that I use them. That's the first time it's been used,' he said, somewhat apologetically.

'Thank you.' Jessica looked at him through eyes still swimming with tears.

'I say, are you all right?'

Jessica nodded. 'I've just come from my mother's funeral.'

'Oh, I'm sorry; that's tough!' He shifted in his seat, then pulled out another handkerchief with the same monogram and handed it to her. After that he took a book out of his pocket, indicating he'd leave her alone in her grief, but she sensed him taking sideways looks at her from time to time. 'Do you live in Sydney?' he eventually asked.

She sniffed. 'I live near Gurunnuga, but I'm at uni in Sydney.' Trying to be polite, she asked him the same question.

'I'm from Newcastle,' he replied. 'But I've just started work at a school in Hornsby, teaching science.'

She nodded and fell silent.

As they approached Hornsby, she turned to him. 'Excuse me, JK, but how can I return your handkerchiefs to you? I'll wash them, of course.'

He smiled at her. 'I'll give you my address and telephone number. Perhaps we could meet somewhere?'

Jessica sniffed and blew her nose again. She must look awful with red rimmed eyes and red nose. 'That would be nice,' she snuffled. She had a good feeling about this man.

He took a notebook from his pocket. 'My name's Jason Kiernan, and this is my phone number. Please give me a ring; I'd love to meet you sometime when you're feeling better.'

She gave a watery smile. 'Jessica Broughton. I'm studying computer science. I don't have a phone number, but I'll give you my address.' She took the notebook from him and started to write.

'Hold on.' He smiled. 'Let me tear this page off for you.' He tore out the page he'd written his phone number on and gave it to her. 'Now write your name and address on this new page.'

The train stopped at Hornsby station, but Jason didn't move.

Jessica turned to him. 'Isn't this your stop?'

He smiled. 'Yes, it is, but I thought I'd carry on to Sydney. Make sure you're okay. Would you like a coffee? Something to eat?'

Jessica suddenly realised that she was hungry. Richard had made her sandwiches to take on the train, but she hadn't felt like eating. She gave a tremulous smile. 'That would be lovely.'

***

She and Jason met for coffee several times after that. They had a lot in common: Jason came from a village just outside Newcastle; they were both interested in science and loved bush walking.

He'd rented a small flat in Hornsby in a recently built tower block and was excited about the move. 'I have to get some furniture,' he told Jessica one Saturday when they met for coffee at Town Hall. He looked at her with admiration in his eyes. 'I was wondering if you'd help me? Choose furniture, that is.'

Jessica smiled. 'Love to! Shall we look at second hand places first? I love old furniture.'

He smiled with delight. 'So do I.' Then his smile faded. 'But I'll have to buy a new bed. I don't fancy sleeping on an antique mattress!'

'You're right; hadn't thought of that!'

'You'll help me choose a bed?'

'Of course.'

'Right, let's get the next train to Hornsby and look at beds.'

In the big department store, they headed to the bedding section. A salesman approached them with a smile. 'Ah! A lovely young couple looking for a nice queen-sized bed.' He winked at Jason.

Jason gave a little smile, and Jessica felt her cheeks redden.

'Look, here's one I'd recommend. Nice and firm. Take off your shoes and try it.'

Jessica giggled. And her face grew warmer. 'Um, actually it's not for me ...' she began, but Jason took her hand and blew her a kiss. 'Come on, darling! Take off your shoes!'

When she saw him taking off his shoes, she entered into the spirit of them being a married couple. They lay on the bed, then bounced up and down, while the salesman stood smiling.

After giving a short spiel on the differences between soft, medium and firm mattresses, he waved his hand towards the row of beds which seemed to be waiting invitingly. 'There are the other beds to try. See which one you like best. I'll just be over there, if you need to ask any questions.' He pointed to the other side of the floor, where he'd be able to keep an eye on them.

Jason eventually decided on a bed which wasn't the one they'd both preferred, but one within his budget. 'We'll be able to deliver it next Friday. Is that okay?' the salesman asked after Jason had given him a cheque.

'Great. Thank you.' He took Jessica's hand and winked.

***

Jessica graduated with honours, and her father came down for her graduation.

'Will you carry on and get a doctorate?' he asked, beaming at her.

Jessica hesitated. 'Not sure, Dad. I've already been offered a job with Minchin and Turner.' She saw his blank look and added, 'You know, the accounting people. It's a good opportunity.' She didn't like to say that all the software houses offered jobs to the top IT undergraduates before they'd even finished their studies.

Richard nodded. 'Well, done, my dear. Your mother would've been so proud.'

Jessica smiled. 'I know,' she whispered and gave him a hug. 'Thank you for coming, Dad. It was a bit of a journey for you.'

'I got the night train, so I'd be fresh for today. I've booked into a hotel near Central Station for the night. I thought I could take you out to dinner to celebrate.'

'That would be lovely, Dad.' However it created a dilemma. Jason had already booked a restaurant with the same idea of celebration. 'Um, a friend has already invited me to dinner, Dad, but I'm sure it will be okay for you to come, too.'

When Jason arrived to pick her up, she introduced her father. Jason's face registered surprise when he saw the old man, but he quickly recovered and smiled.

'I've heard a bit about you, Jason,' Richard said as they shook hands. 'I believe you teach science?'

Jason nodded. 'I've booked a table at a restaurant for tonight, Dr Broughton. It would be lovely if you could join us.'

Richard hesitated.

Jason looked at them both. 'Or perhaps you'd like some time alone with Jessica,' he said. 'I'm happy for you to take the booking ...'

'Why can't we all go? I'm sure the restaurant would fit us all in,' Richard suggested.

Jason nodded. 'Good idea.'

Jessica sighed with relief.

***

Jessica had been working for two years when Jason asked her to marry him. They'd been living together in Jason's rented flat since she'd started work. She caught the train into the city every morning.

He'd booked a nice restaurant for her birthday and ordered champagne. As they raised their glasses in a toast to each other, he smiled and looked into her eyes. 'Jess, darling, what do you think about us getting married?'

Jessica hesitated, and then frowned. 'Jason, I'd love to get married, but there's something you must know first.'

'What?'

She saw all kinds of ideas flitting across his face.

'I can't have children.'

'What do you mean?'

'My mother had Huntington's disease. It's horrible. I have a 50/50 chance of getting it, so I made the decision ages ago not to have children. It can show up at any time, usually between the ages of thirty or forty, and if I had it, then our children would have a 50/50 chance of having it. If you are also a carrier then they would definitely get it.' She raised her eyes and looked at him.

He sat with a horrified look on his face. 'How ... I mean what are the symptoms?'

She told him what had happened with her mother. He knew her mother had died, that was how they'd met, on her way back from the funeral, but he'd never queried what had caused her death. 'Look,' Jessica took his hand. 'Think about it. Think how important children are to you.'

'Is there no cure? Can you find out if you are a carrier?'

Jessica shook her head. 'Not at the moment. Perhaps with the genetic research that's happening at the moment it might be possible sometime in the future. Not at the present time, though. I'm sorry, Jason. I hope I haven't spoiled this romantic evening.'

He swallowed and managed a smile. 'Of course not. Happy birthday, darling Jess. I love you! Of course, I still want to marry you, even if we don't have children.'

'Think about it for a bit. It's a big decision,' Jessica said. 'There's no rush.'

He looked at her. 'Would you like to have children, Jess?'

'I'd love to have your child,' she whispered, tears in her eyes.

He took her hand, leaned across the table and kissed her. 'I love you, Jess. You mean everything to me. I can live without children as long as I have you. Please marry me.'

***

They drove up to Gurunnuga to tell Richard. It was his eightieth birthday, and Jessica wanted to celebrate it with her father. He'd been pleased when they'd phoned him to say they were coming up the following weekend for his birthday.

'Of course, I'd love to see you both, but no need to fuss over my birthday,' he'd shouted down the phone.

Jessica smiled as she held the phone away from her ear. Her father was getting a bit deaf and tended to shout.'We haven't been up for a while, and I want to see you.'

'That's lovely; looking forward to it. Everything all right down there?'

'Yes indeed, Dad.' She hugged her engagement to herself, wanting to tell him in person.

'Right then. I'll say goodbye. These telephone calls are so expensive.'

'Okay, Dad. Love you.'

'Love you, too, darling Jessica.'

***

Jessica frowned when she saw her father. He seemed to have lost weight, and the house wasn't as spick and span as he usually kept it.

'Happy Birthday, Dad. Look what I've brought you.'

'What is it?'

'Open it and see.'

Richard unwrapped the box and frowned. 'A telephone? I have a telephone.'

'This is a cordless phone, Dad; there are two handsets. You can have one in the bedroom and one in the kitchen, and you can walk around with it.'

He shook his head in amazement. 'Thank you, dear, and you, Jason.'

'So, Dad,' Jessica said slowly. 'You keep one by your bed. Just in case you get sick in the night or anything.'

He gave her a hug. 'It's lovely, dear.'

She'd tried to persuade him to sell the property and move into a retirement home near to where they lived, but he'd have none of it.

'What would I do all day in a retirement home?' he'd said, 'and anyway, it would probably take years to sell this place. With the way things are going, no-one wants to buy a place that's miles from anywhere and needs lots of maintenance. Also there's no work around here.'

He put the new phone on the table.

Jason said, 'Richard, I'll set the phone up for you, but first I need to ask you something.'

'Oh?'

'Yes, well, I'd like to marry Jessica. She's accepted, but I want to make sure it's all right with you.'

Richard looked at him, and then at Jessica. He raised his eyebrows at her.

She put her arm around her father's shoulders. 'Yes, Dad. Jason knows about Huntington's. I told him about Mum. We've decided not to have children.' She gave him a hug. 'Dad, I'm certain I don't have the Huntington gene,' she whispered to him. 'Please don't worry about me.'

Richard returned her hug, then held out his hand to Jason. 'Congratulations, couldn't wish for a better son-in-law.'

'Dad, why don't you come and stay with us for a bit,' Jessica suggested. 'We have a spare room you know.'

Her father shrugged. 'I'll think about it.'

She knew he never would. He was content at home with her mother's paintings to look at, and little things to remind him of her.

Jessica and Jason bought a town house in Hornsby, close to the bush, which they both loved, and Jessica happily walked to catch the early morning train to the city to work. Jason needed the car to carry all his books and markings to school. When it rained, he gave her a lift to the station.

They had a small wedding in Newcastle, close to Jason's family home, with just Jason's sister, his parents and grandparents and a few close friends. One of Jason's nieces, Kaila, was a flower girl. Richard travelled down on the train for the ceremony.

'She looks so sweet,' Jessica said to her father as they prepared to enter the church, Kaila dutifully walking behind.

'Mum would have been so thrilled,' Richard whispered to her as he took her down the aisle of the Catholic Church which Jason's parents attended regularly. 'She'd have her sketch pad out and be drawing you instead of listening to the ceremony.'

They didn't have a full ceremony, it was held at a side altar because Jessica refused to convert to Catholicism. Jason had said he didn't mind.

That afternoon they drove back to Hornsby, and the following day flew to Bali for their honeymoon.

CHAPTER 7

In 1993 a genetic test was developed for Huntington's disease. Jessica read about it in the newspaper on the train on her way to work.

Her heart started to thump. Perhaps she could get tested! She had a deep-down feeling that she didn't have the gene. She felt well and healthy, exercised, took vitamins, ate properly, didn't smoke and rarely drank. But she still couldn't take the risk of having a child. She did more research and found out that you had to have a lot of counselling before taking the test. Some people didn't want to know, especially if they'd watched a loved one suffer from the disease. Jason was all for her to go ahead and get tested.

It took several months by the time she had the counselling and travelled to Melbourne for the tests. She'd asked Jason to come with her for the final result, but he had a school trip and couldn't make it. Finally, the day came to get the results. She sat opposite the genetic counsellor, her heart in her mouth.

He studied her. 'Are you still sure you want to know?'

'Yes.'

'Right.' He opened the report, read it, then looked at her over his glasses. 'I'm sorry, my dear. The result is positive.'

There was a rushing in her ears. She sat motionless, feeling sick and dizzy, just looking at him.

He stood. 'I'm sorry, my dear. I know it's a big blow for you.'

She managed to stand up, shake his hand and mutter something, then left the consulting room and stumbled out of the building. She hailed a passing taxi and went to the airport to catch her flight back to Sydney. At the airport, she sat in a bar and ordered a drink. Her phone rang. It was Jason. 'How did it go?'

'Positive.'

After a silence, she heard him say, 'Shit, shit, shit. I'm so sorry, Jessica.'

She had the Huntington gene. She wished now that she hadn't gone through the months of hoping she'd be able to have a child. Now that she knew for certain she would end up like her mother, she'd be looking for the early signs all the time.

She threw herself into her work as a distraction, and soon headed a team of developers at Minchin and Turner. Often she had to travel interstate to attend meetings and demonstrate new suites of programs. On those occasions, Jason took the opportunity to visit his parents and catch up with old mates.

A lot of his friends had married and now had children, and they ribbed him playfully, asking when he and Jessica were going to start a family. His mother also kept making oblique references to having more grandchildren. He didn't want to explain their decision and all about Huntington's. He thought his family would be always studying Jessica and watching for signs. Better they didn't know. He'd researched the disease and agreed with Jessica that it would be selfish for them to have children. He loved his sister's two little girls. He was Kaila's godfather and travelled up to Newcastle every year on her birthday to take her out for the day and buy her presents.

Jessica often watched Jason and Kaila when they were together, thinking what a great father he would make. She thought about it a lot, especially when travelling, waiting at airports and seeing families together. When she got home one night from a week in Brisbane, having thought about it on the flight, she said to Jason as they finished dinner, 'Have you much marking to do tonight?'

Jason grimaced as he stood up. 'About the same as usual? Why?'

'I wanted to talk.'

'Oh? What about?' He sat back down.

'Well,' she hesitated, 'I was thinking, you know, we could have a baby using IVF with a donor egg.'

He frowned. 'How would that work for us?'

She explained, and saw his frown deepening.

'No way,' he exclaimed. 'I don't want to sit in a cubicle with a girly magazine and wank, then have some strange woman be the mother of my child.' He stood again. 'No. Forget about it. Even if you carried the baby and gave birth. No! Now, I'd better get on with my marking.' He went upstairs to their third bedroom which they'd turned into a study. She heard him shuffling papers, then slamming the door shut.

Jessica sighed. She'd love a child. Even if not biologically hers; the fact that it was Jason's would be enough. She'd mentioned adoption, but he'd been against that, too. But they were happy enough, she thought. They could afford nice holidays, and they'd nearly paid off the house. Jason seemed content working at his school. She thought their marriage was a good one.

***

Jessica felt guilty that she hadn't been to see her father for a while. Things were hectic at work, and then when she did get time off,

Jason wanted to go overseas for a break, or visit his parents in Newcastle. Gurunnuga was such a pain to get to. The train took forever, and if they drove, the journey was long and tiring.

The Easter break was coming up, and she planned to visit her father. Holiday flights and accommodation were very expensive during the school holidays, so Jason didn't mind driving to Gurunnuga. But two days before they were due to leave, they received a telephone call from Gurunnuga's local hospital. Jason was home for school holidays, and he rang her at work.

'Jess? It's your dad. The hospital just rang. He was admitted last night. Apparently, he had chest pains. He rang triple zero for the ambulance, but by the time they got to him, it was too late. I'm sorry, Jess.'

Jessica gasped. 'I'll get the next train home. Meet me at the station.' She told her team the bad news, and then left, frozen with shock.

She remained silent as Jason drove them north.

***

They buried Richard next to his beloved Sybilla. The funeral was well attended, considering he'd become a virtual recluse in the last few years.

Afterwards Jessica and Jason drove back to The Shack. Richard and Sybilla had always called it 'The Shack' even after it was no longer a shack but a pleasant rural property. Sybilla had painted a sign with the name on it which hung by the front door. Jessica looked around the place. It needed a good spring clean, and the garden was a mess. The paddock was overgrown and needed mowing. She sighed. She didn't have the energy or the will to do anything. She felt heartbroken at her father's death and berated herself for not seeing him more often.

'I suppose it's all yours now,' Jason said, scanning the property.

'I guess so.' Jessica walked into her mother's studio and sat and looked at all the canvasses stacked around the walls.

Jason followed her. 'These paintings might be worth something, do you think?' He looked at Jessica for a response.

She shrugged. 'Possibly, but there's no way I would sell them. Look, those must be early sketches and paintings of my father.' She pointed to them and started to cry. 'He was my last link with my childhood.' She sniffed. 'I've got no one else.'

Jason simply nodded. 'Come on, Jess. No point in hanging around here. Let's get back home.'

'Just a minute. I want to take some of these paintings home.'

Jason sighed. 'Okay, but we don't have room for many.'

'I'll have to come up again as soon as I can and sort things out.' She'd found the big tin box in his study where Richard had kept all important papers and his will. He'd left everything to her. She wasn't sure what she had to do to get the deeds and stuff transferred to her, but she'd sort it out later. At the moment she felt too upset and tired.

'But we'd better empty the fridge and turn it off,' Jason said, opening the door and looking inside. 'Not much here anyway. I'll just put everything in our esky, and we can sort it out at home. That okay?' He turned to Jessica who stood staring into the fridge.

What had her father been living on! There was nothing there except some mouldy cheese, butter and a few eggs. Guilt wracked her.

'I'll prop the door open with this tea towel, otherwise it'll go mouldy,' Jason continued. 'It'll defrost on its own, I guess, if we don't want to hang around to do it.' He sounded doubtful.

After dealing with the fridge, they made their way over to the shed which served as a garage, and opened the big sliding door.

'I'd better check if there's anything here we need to deal with,' Jason said. 'What about your Dad's van?' he asked as they went inside.

They looked at the old HJ Holden.

'I suppose we could try and sell it,' Jason said.

'It's been part of my life since I started secondary school,' Jessica said sadly. 'Tangerine. Tangy, I called it for short.'

'Hmm. It's still in pretty good nick.' Jason kicked one of the tyres. 'Probably got a very low mileage. I don't think your dad drove much the last few years.'

'No.' Jessica agreed.

'He must have been well into his eighties.'

'Eighty-six.'

'What if we take the van back to Sydney, get it serviced and a valet clean and put it up for sale?'

Jessica nodded.

'I'll drive it back, and you take the car,' Jason said.

Jason arrived first and parked the HJ in the double garage.

✳✳✳

Eventually Jessica sorted out the probate, but she hadn't got around to selling the van; somehow, she couldn't part with it. She hadn't been back to Gurunnuga since the funeral, and she'd had the telephone cut off. 'Waste of money keeping it connected,' Jason had said, and she'd followed his advice. She had all the mail redirected to Hornsby and resolved to go up for a week later on. She'd clean up the house and get it tidied up, and then put the place up for sale. However, a year later, she still hadn't returned.

It was 1999, and she was flat out at work with all the hype around the Year 2000 panic. Minchin and Turner had secured a contract with a government body in Sydney to update their legacy systems to be Year 2000 compliant. Jessica had a team of five programmers working on the system, together with four of the government permanent employees. She worked six days a week, often not finishing until late in the evening, trying to meet the deadline. Everything had to be in place; the conversion from the old system to the new one planned to run on the first weekend in December.

Now, at the end of November, the conversion programs were complete and the testing looked good. They planned to do the full conversion the following week, then her team could relax.

She looked forward to the Christmas break and to spending more time with Jason. She'd hardly been home in the last few months.

While on the train to work, she thought about the last time they'd been out together. It must have been Easter, and even that had been just a few days, and somehow not that great, now she thought about it. Jason had been very quiet lately. She must ask him about his work. Perhaps he was getting bored with teaching, needed to change jobs. But what? Teaching was hard to break out of. She sighed and focused on the problems at work.

When the train stopped at Central Station, she walked briskly to the block of offices where she worked. She rode the lift to the sixth floor, fumbled in her bag for her security pass at the main door to the office and inserted it. When the system rejected it, she tried again, but the door refused to open. Just then a security guard came over to her.

'I can't get the door to open for some reason,' she said to him.

'Excuse me, miss, but are you with Minchin and Turner?'

'Yes.' Jessica regarded him. 'The door isn't opening; is there a problem?'

'Well, yes, miss.' He consulted a folder in his hand, looking embarrassed. 'Name?'

'Jessica Broughton.' She'd kept her maiden name on marrying; it was easier since all her qualifications were in her maiden name.

'Hmm. Well, you see, the problem is that Minchin and Turner have gone into receivership. There's been some dodgy business deals, apparently, so we've been informed that none of their staff are allowed to work here anymore.'

'What? I don't understand.'

The security guard unlocked the office door. 'Come with me, miss, and show me your desk.'

Jessica led him to her work station.

'Just take your personal items and put them in that carrier bag, please.' He pointed to a bag on her desk. She looked at her team's workstations. A carrier bag sat on each of their desks.

'But I don't understand.'

'Sorry, miss. If you'd just open your drawers and remove only your personal belongings ...'

Jessica looked at the framed photo of Jason on her desk. She picked it up and put it in the bag, then opened the drawers of her desk.

'Just the personal stuff,' the security guard repeated. 'No, not that notebook.'

'But that's my personal notebook!' Jessica exclaimed.

'Sorry, miss,' he said, taking it from her.

Feeling her anger rising, Jessica took a pair of shoes, her bone-china coffee mug and a few other personal things and stuffed them in the bag. 'This is ridiculous,' she said, marching out of the office.

At the door she met one of her programmers trying to get in. 'A problem, Mary,' Jessica said. 'We're out of a job.'

Mary stared at her. 'I don't understand.'

'Neither do I. I'll ring head office.' Jessica indicated the security guard with her thumb as she headed to the lift. 'He'll explain.'

Once out of the building, she went into the coffee shop next door, asked for an espresso, then sat down at one of the tables and pulled out her mobile phone. She punched in the number of Minchin and Turner's head office. No reply. She tried several times as she waited for her coffee. Still no answer.

Two more of her team saw her inside and joined her.

'What's going on, Jess?' They each asked.

'Don't know, trying to find out,' she replied.

At last she received a response. 'Ah, Jessica.' It was one of the secretaries. 'I suppose you've heard?'

'No,' Jessica replied, 'I only know that we've been locked out of the office.'

'I'm afraid there's been a problem,' the secretary continued. 'Apparently, some of the directors have been found appropriating company money—some corruption issues. The company has gone into receivership ...'

'What does that mean for us programmers?'

'Well, your contracts have been suspended, and it means that you and your team are now out of work.'

'What? Won't we get paid? What about my team?' Horrified, Jessica's voice rose.

'Sorry, Jessica. It's the same for me. I'm only here to notify all the staff. I'm not getting paid either. Sorry, there's another call coming in. I have to go.' The line went dead.

By this time, the other members of her team had wandered in.

Jessica grimaced. 'Sorry, everyone; it looks like Minchin and Turner have gone bust. We're all out of a job.'

They stared at her, then one of the team said, 'What about our work?'

'Perfect timing,' Jessica said ruefully. 'You're all such good workers, we basically finished all the programming. Now the permanent staff of the department will be able to finish testing and making any minor changes.' She looked around at their sombre faces. 'I hope this won't be too hard on you all, especially coming up to Christmas. You're all great workers, and I'll give you good references. You should be able to get work fairly easily.'

Her words gave little solace, and they muttered over their coffee. Jessica felt sick.

'What will you do, Jess?' one of them asked.

'I haven't thought about it,' she replied. 'It's just been such a horrible shock. I guess I'll have to start looking for another job, too.' The thought depressed her. She'd been with Minchin and Turner since leaving university—what, six years ago now.

'What about getting paid for this month?' one of her team asked.

'I've no idea; I know no more than you do.' She looked around at them. 'You've been a great team; it's been a privilege to work with you.' Tears came to her eyes.

'We've liked working for you, Jess,' one of the team said. The others nodded in agreement.

Jessica tried to smile. 'I guess we'd better head back home now and start looking at the job ads. Thank you all again. I'm so sorry it's come to this.' Fighting back tears, she stood and shook hands with each of them, then made her way to the station and got the next train back to Hornsby.

CHAPTER 8

It felt strange to be on a train that was nearly empty, going against the tide of workers heading to the city. She sat in the carriage, wondering what to do next, staring out the window with unseeing eyes. She could afford to take some time off. She and Jason could do stuff together for a change— go for some bushwalks, take a picnic. They'd had no quality time together lately. *School holidays in a few weeks*. She could start looking for work, but nothing would be happening until after the New Year, and anyway, she needed a break. Thoughts jumbled around in her head. She tried to look on the bright side.

After getting out at Hornsby station, she walked home slowly, instead of her usual brisk pace. She frowned at the sight of a car parked in their driveway; Jason hadn't mentioned they were expecting visitors. She opened the front door and hearing voices, called out, 'Hello, Jason?'

Sudden silence descended, followed by a shuffling noise. Puzzled, she walked into the kitchen and found Jason half standing and a young woman sitting at the kitchen table.

'Oh,' Jessica said, looking at Jason and raising her eyebrows. When Jason just opened his mouth, then closed it, she smiled at him. 'Aren't you going to introduce me?'

The young woman started to get up from her seat, mumbling, 'I'd better go, Jase.'

Jason suddenly came to life. 'No, no. Stay please, Amy.' He put a hand on her shoulder to keep her from standing.

Jessica frowned. 'What's happening?'

'What are you doing at home? Why aren't you at work?' Jason asked.

'I've lost my job. Minchin and Turner have gone bust. Which means we'll be able to spend more time together, darling.' She smiled at Jason. 'And, why aren't you at school this morning?'

'Sit down, Jess. We need to talk.' He pulled out a chair.

Amy tried to stand up again. 'I'll go, and let you sort this out,' she said to Jason.

Jessica looked at Amy, who, judging by the bulge under her loose shirt, was obviously pregnant. A sudden feeling of unease crept over Jessica. She looked at Jason, who had reddened, then at Amy then back at Jason. 'About what? Talk about what?'

Jason opened his mouth, but nothing came out.

Then Amy spoke up. 'I'm pregnant with Jason's child,' she announced. 'We've been seeing each other for several months, but of course you wouldn't have noticed, as your work is more important than your husband.' She drew herself up to her full height and rested her hands on her belly.

Jessica closed her eyes. She felt sick and dizzy. This must be a bad dream, a nightmare. She caught the back of the chair to steady herself.

'I'll go,' Amy said. 'I'll see myself out. You two have a lot to discuss. I'll see you this evening, Jase. My place.' She walked out, and the front door closed behind her.

'Sit down, Jess,' Jason eventually said.

Jessica sat and stared at him.

'I'm sorry, Jess. I didn't mean for this to happen. It just did. I've been trying to tell you for ages. Amy teaches physical ed. At school. You remember the school trip we had away last July? Well, I gave her a lift home, and she invited me in for a coffee, and well, you were away working somewhere and ...'

Jessica took out a handkerchief and blew her nose. Losing her job was nothing compared to this. She loved Jason—he was the only man she'd ever been with. She blinked away tears. This was just a nightmare. She'd wake up and find Jason beside her and the alarm clock buzzing.

'But it's not your fault, Jess. Really. I didn't want to hurt you. I still love you, but I was lonely. You were away so much, working or interstate. I still love you, Jess.' He shrugged and looked at his hands, 'but now, well, it's a different situation.'

'And you always wanted a family.'

He said nothing.

'So what happens now? I suppose you want a divorce?'

He nodded, avoiding her eyes.

She stood up. 'I'm going for a walk. I can't take anymore.' She went out, slamming the front door, and started to walk in the direction of the bush, hardly noticing where she was going. Then she felt sick and dizzy again and reluctantly turned back. Her legs felt like jelly. She'd forgotten her key, so had to bang on the door and wait for Jason to open it.

When he saw her face, he tried to put his arms around her. 'I'm so sorry, Jess ...' he started to say, but she pushed him away and stumbled up the stairs to their bedroom.

She lay there for ages, her mind spinning, until there was a gentle knock on the door.

'Jess? I've brought you a cup of tea.'

The door slowly opened. Jason stood there, a picture of misery, with a cup of tea in his hand.

She stared at him, then nodded towards the bedside table. 'Thanks.'

'Jess, I still love you, you know ... Um, I have to go out now ...'

'To Amy, I suppose,' she said bitterly.

Jason nodded. 'Well, I just need some things from the wardrobe.'

'Take all your things; you can sleep in the spare bedroom from now on.' She turned her head away from him. After a brief pause, she heard the wardrobe and various drawers opening, then the bedroom door gently closing.

She waited until she heard the front door lock click and the car start, and then she got up. She needed a drink to calm herself.D ownstairs, she found a bottle of wine and started to drink.

***

The phone ringing roused her. She couldn't be bothered answering it, so the call went to the answering machine.

'Jess? Miriam here. Just ringing to chat, see how you're going after the bombshell this morning. Catch you later. Cheers'

Which bombshell? Jessica thought wearily. The loss of her job, or the loss of her husband?

The phone rang again. She glanced at the number. It was Jason. A feeling of hope went through her as she picked up. Maybe it had all been a nightmare. 'Yes?'

'Hi, Jess. Just checking if you're all right. Um, Jason here.'

She hung up.

She was lying on the couch in their lounge room. An empty bottle of wine sat on the coffee table, and a wineglass had tipped over on the carpet, leaving a red stain slowly spreading across the expensive wool pile. Reluctantly, she dragged herself up to get a wet cloth to try and prevent the stain from setting. While on her knees, scrubbing at the stain, she suddenly hurled the cloth across the room, picked up the wineglass and smashed it on the coffee table. Then she collapsed back on the couch, engulfed by sobs.

Well, at least Dad isn't alive to see the mess I've made of my life. She got up and started to collect the pieces of broken glass, managing to cut her hand in the process. Through a gaze clouded by alcohol, she picked up the cloth she'd been using to clean the carpet and wrapped it around her hand. Then she went to the kitchen, threw the broken pieces of glass into the bin, took another bottle of wine from the rack, found a clean glass and stumbled upstairs to the bedroom.

***

Some hours later, Jason shook her awake. 'Jessica, are you all right?'

She half opened her eyes. Everything started to swim. 'Sick ... Gon be sick.' She tried to get up.

Jason put his arms around her, took her to the toilet in their ensuite and held her while she vomited. When she'd finished, he found a towel and washed her face.

'Oh, Jason, I love you!' she slurred.

'Stop, Jess. Stop, please!'

Then it all came rushing back to her. Amy, a baby ... and she started to cry, great wracking sobs.

Jason helped her to the bed. 'I don't know what to say, Jess. Except I'm sorry. I really didn't mean to hurt you.'

'Just go away.'

'I've brought your phone up. Are you sure you'll be all right? Ring me if you need me.' He edged out the door.

Jessica lay swamped in grief, unable to sleep. Next morning, she dragged herself out of bed, showered, went downstairs and made a mug of strong coffee. Jason hadn't come home, she noticed.

Her phone rang. It was the Melbourne office. She picked up. 'Hello, Jessica,' her boss said. 'So sorry about what's happened. Can you get down here? We need to sort through some paperwork for the auditors and the administrators.' When he got no response, he continued, 'The flights will be paid for, of course.'

'Okay,' Jessica said, thinking that at least it would take her mind off Jason.

'There's a flight this afternoon, 4.15, think you can make it?'

'Yes.'

'Right, pick up the tickets at the airport. I'll book you into the usual hotel.'

'Okay.'

'You all right, Jess? You sound a bit strange.'

'Yes. I'm fine.' *What a lie.* She hung up and packed an overnight case, still feeling sick at Jason's betrayal. No need to let him know where she was. Then she thought better of it. He'd only panic if she wasn't home, and goodness knows what he'd do, call the police or something. She left a note. *Gone to Melbourne. Work.* And left it propped up against the coffee plunger.

During the flight, she thought of Amy's words. '*You were too busy to notice; your work was more important than your husband!*' Had that been the case? Yes, she'd been absorbed with work, working long hours; it was expected at every software house. She usually came home exhausted from working in airport lounges or in-flight, then fighting her way onto crowded trains.

Perhaps she hadn't been as loving as she should ... and Jason had said Amy was fun ...

***

The few days in Melbourne helped clear her head. Her boss was shocked when he met her at the airport. 'Have you been sick, Jess? You look so pale.'

She studied him. 'Pete, I'm fine. Well, not really. Marriage breakup.' She liked Pete; he was in his fifties and a gentle, kind soul—too gentle and kind for the cut-throat industry they were in.

'Oh, Jess. I'm so sorry to hear that. All you need with what's happened here.'

She shrugged. 'Could be worse. How about you, Pete? I guess you've lost your job, too.'

He sighed. 'Yes. Not good at my age, looking for a new job. And it won't look good on my CV that I've worked at Minchin and Turner for ten years. Not a good smell.'

Jessica hadn't thought of that aspect. She suddenly realised that the same would apply to her. It might be hard to find a new job. But at least she didn't have a family to support like Pete.

He turned to her. 'Jess, I'll give you a reference. I'll get some Minchin and Turner headed notepaper and write it for you. Least I can do. No chance of me getting a reference as it's my boss who's in the poo.'

'Oh, Pete, I'm so sorry. What'll you do?'

'Don't know.' He sighed. 'Well, we'd better get started; coffee first?'

***

On the flight back to Sydney, Jessica turned over options in her mind. Probably they would have to sell the house, and she'd have to find somewhere else to live. She didn't feel like staying in Hornsby—she couldn't face the possibility of bumping into Amy and Jason with a baby, but she'd have to move quickly workwise. In the IT world, you couldn't be out of the work force more than three months or your skills wouldn't be considered current. Software development evolved so fast it was a struggle to keep up to date. And now with the bad press from Minchin and Turner ...

She'd work on her CV as soon as she got home. Then she had another idea.

When she arrived at the town house, she found Jason in the kitchen filling the kettle.

He looked at her warily. 'How're things, Jess?'

'Fine,' she said brightly, resolved not to let him see how badly she'd been affected by his infidelity. 'Um, I was thinking, Jason ...'

'Hmm?'

'We could adopt Amy's baby. You said you still love me.'

He frowned and looked at the ground, then looked up at her, pity in his eyes. 'Jess,' he said gently, 'I do love you, but Amy won't give up this baby...'

'Ask her.'

'She wants us to get married.'

Anger flooded Jessica. She could see now that this had been Amy's plan—to trap Jason. Why couldn't she have found a single man instead of a happily married one? She felt like jumping up and punching Jason. Her fists clenched.

'Like a cup of tea?' Jason mumbled.

'No, thanks. I've got to do some work.'

'Right. Um, Jess?

'What?'

'Can we talk later?'

'Well, I have a lot to do. Can we do it now? And make it quick?' He indicated the kitchen table. 'Sit down, Jess.'

She pulled out a chair and sat looking at him, her back rigid.

'It's about getting a divorce. We have to live apart for twelve months in order to start divorce proceedings ...'

She nodded. 'I suppose you'll move out. Move in with this *Amy*.'

'Well, we've been thinking.'

'We?'

He looked down at his hands, not meeting her eyes. 'Um, well, we'll have to have a property settlement; sell this house and take half each.'

Jessica nodded. 'I suppose so.'

'And, well, I don't know how to say this, but Amy would like to live here; we both work in Hornsby and well,' he faltered, then looked at her. She remained silent. 'Well, I was thinking that I could buy out your share of this house.' His eyes slid away from her direct gaze.

'So, at thirty years of age, I lose my job, my marriage and my home all within the space of a week,' she said.

'You won't be homeless; you still have The Shack. Your parent's home, I mean. Your father left it to you.'

Jessica was speechless.

'Jess, you'll soon find someone else; you're still beautiful.' He looked at her, 'and clever and talented.'

'But that's not enough. Obviously.'

'Oh, Jess, I really didn't mean for this to happen. I do still love you. We made a good couple.'

'And only for the accident of a baby, I suppose we'd still be together?'

Jason said, avoiding her eyes again, 'and, well, anyway, you don't have to move out straight away,' he continued. 'I've had the place valued and been to the bank. I can get a loan for what would be your share. That's if you agree, of course.' He paused, then went on, 'But it would be the best thing for both of us. If we put the house up for sale, then we'll have to pay a real-estate agent's commission, and put up with open-house weekends and people coming to look around.'

'You've thought it all through, haven't you?'

Jason missed her sarcasm. He nodded. 'Well, Amy—'

Jessica interrupted. 'What if I want to stay here and buy your share?' Her voice came out sounding hard, but she couldn't believe what she'd just heard.

He stared at her for a few seconds, then said slowly, 'Jess, I don't think the bank would lend you money at the moment. You don't have a job.'

Bile rose in her throat. She bit her lip and clenched her fists under the table to try and stop the tears. 'I'll give it some thought and let you know,' she managed to say, then got up from the table, picked up her case and went up to the bedroom.

'By the way, I moved my stuff into the spare bedroom,' Jason called up the stairs after her.

Jessica paused and then continued up the stairs. She was determined to stay strong and not collapse into tears.

She had no-one to talk to who would understand. She didn't have any close girlfriends. The few times when she and Jason had gone out socially, it was mainly with his friends and their wives. But once those friends had started having families, somehow the get-togethers didn't happen so much. Now she thought about it, it had been ages, maybe a year since the last time. Probably because she and Jason didn't have much in common with them anymore.

The talk of babies, sleepless nights and the problems with getting baby sitters meant nothing to them. They'd nod and commiserate, and sit there, bored, as the conversation revolved around the best strollers, or car seats.

She'd always been a solitary kind of person. Probably from growing up fairly isolated and with older parents, well, an older father. Jason had been her life really. She'd felt he was her best friend and that she didn't need anyone else. The sense of betrayal, that she had trusted him absolutely, make her sick to her stomach.

***

Jessica updated her CV, but decided not to send it out to agencies. December wasn't a good time; nothing would be happening now until the end of January. Everyone would be on holiday. She'd wait a while. It would just get lost in amongst other emails.

After a few days at home in Hornsby, spending her time walking in the bush, or drinking, she came to a decision. She'd take the van and drive to The Shack—clean the place up. The work would be good for her. Then she'd put it up for sale and perhaps go overseas. England, maybe. Look up her father's family; try and get work there. A new start, a new direction. Buoyed by having made a decision, she looked around at what to take. Her mother's paintings to start with. She wouldn't need her office clothes in the bush. She carefully folded the suits and shirts and put them into a suitcase and her high-heeled shoes in a bag. It was lucky she'd kept the electricity connected, and she should be okay for gas, which was needed to heat the hot water and for cooking. Usually two big cylinders sat behind the laundry. One always kept for a spare.

When she heard Jason parking the car in the garage, she went down to the kitchen.

'Hello, Jess,' he said sheepishly. 'How're things?'

'Good,' she said briskly, her chin up. 'Jason, I've decided to move to The Shack. No point in staying here. Make a clean break. I'll take the van.'

Surprised, he nodded. 'Okay, yes. Right. Okay. When are you planning to leave?'

'First thing in the morning.'

He looked down at his hands. 'I'm so sorry, Jess, I wouldn't hurt you for the world.'

She snorted and gave a wry smile. 'Don't stress over it, Jason.' Then she went up to their study and started disconnecting the computer. Jason followed her upstairs. When he saw her packing the printer and PC, he exclaimed, 'Oh, you're taking our computer?'

'It's mine, actually,' she pointed out. 'If you remember, I had to buy it for work.'

He was standing leaning against the door frame, his hands in his pockets. 'Of course, of course, sorry. I'd forgotten. But you won't be able to use it at The Shack, will you? No internet there probably.'

'I'll work something out. I need to apply for jobs.'

'I'll move my school stuff out of your way,' he said.

'It's okay; it's not in my way.' She wrapped all the cables and connections around the printer and the PC ready to take them downstairs.

'I'll carry them for you.'

'I can manage, thanks.'

Jason was about to turn away when he remembered something. 'Oh, Jess, the bank rang me today. It looks like the loan has come through, and things will be ready to settle in a day or two.'

With nine days to go before Christmas, Jessica doubted anything would be happening with the house.

Getting no response, Jason turned and went downstairs. He came back soon after. 'Jess. We must talk about money.'

'And?'

'Well, we still have a joint account.'

When Jessica had first moved in with Jason to the rented flat, they'd opened the joint account, and each put a certain amount in it every month to pay for rent and other household expenses. They'd carried on this practice when they bought the townhouse, each putting equal shares towards the deposit. They just added more whenever they needed to make an extra purchase.

'And?' she said now.

'Well, I suppose we'd better close that account and divide the balance between us.'

Jessica nodded. 'Okay.'

'Umm, the car.' Jason shrugged. 'We each paid towards it. Shall I get it valued and give you half?'

'If you want. Oh, and take my name off the rego papers. I don't want to get any parking or speeding fines.' Her eyes narrowed. The words *by Amy*, hung between them.

'What about the stuff in the house—fridge, washing machine and furniture?' Jason continued.

'Don't worry about it. Keep them as a present from me.' She wouldn't need them. The Shack had everything, and she just couldn't be bothered.

'Okay. Thanks.' He turned and went downstairs.

She heard him on the telephone. Her stomach felt leaden. They'd hardly spoken except for the minimum to organise things. She saw their wedding album on the shelf of photo albums. Slowly she took it out, opened it, and stared at a photo of them kissing, then she snapped it shut. She'd leave it. She didn't want reminders. Amy could deal with it.

She started moving her stuff down to the garage, then packed everything in the van ready for an early start in the morning. She'd just finished when she heard Jason on the phone again, then a few minutes later, the car engine. She looked out the window and saw him driving out of the garage.

The word 'gutted' came to her; now she understood it. Automatically she went to the kitchen and the bottle of wine, then stopped. If she was to make an early start in the morning, she'd better not have anything to drink. Well, maybe just a glass. Or two …

She stopped after three glasses of wine, but then moved to the cupboard where they stored their wine, took out most of the bottles, put them in a cardboard box and made room in the van for it. Amy wouldn't be able to drink, being pregnant, and Jason wouldn't like to drink in front of her.

With everything packed, she went to bed. After tossing and turning for a while, she fell into a restless sleep.

Early next morning after a shower, she dressed in casual clothes and left. While driving up the freeway, she tried to put all thoughts of what had happened out of her mind. She stopped just past Newcastle for a coffee and again at Port Macquarie. Just as she was getting back in the car, her mobile phone rang. It was the solicitor for the house transfer.

'Oh, Ms Broughton,' a female voice said. 'We have all the papers ready to be signed for the transfer of the house to your husband

and a cheque for you. Do you think you could call round tomorrow to finalise things? If we don't do it now, then it will be the end of January before we can complete.'

Jessica thought quickly. In one way it would be good to get the whole affair over, but it would be so inconvenient—she only had a few more hours' drive to The Shack. Then she thought about the night train from Brisbane. She could catch it at Gurunnuga. At least she'd be able to sleep on the train.

'All right,' she said. 'I'll do my best.'

She stopped at Gurunnuga station to check the timetable. If she got the late-night train, then she'd be in Sydney early the next morning. She could do all the legal stuff, get her cheque and catch the afternoon train back. She'd arrive home about midnight, but that would be okay; at least it would be one thing settled. She rang the Country Link train company and booked her ticket to Sydney. She thought of getting a return but then changed her mind. She might be delayed, best to buy it at Central Station in Sydney on her way back.

At the village shop, she bought the essentials she'd need, then had a sudden thought. 'Do you know any handyman who could do some work?' she asked the woman serving at the counter, who looked vaguely familiar.

'I know you,' the woman replied, frowning in thought. 'Sybilla Broughton.'

'That was my mother. I'm her daughter, Jessica.' *I must have aged in the last few weeks if I look like my mother.*

'Of course, poor thing, she died. Took her own ... yes, well, indeed, you look just like her.'

Gently Jessica brought the conversation back to handymen. 'I need someone to do some work around the place, just wondered if you know anyone.'

The woman thought. 'Well, Rob Sullivan does a lot of handyman work. He can't take a full-time job because of his boys. Pity about what happened there, that dreadful Carly—'

Jessica interrupted before the woman could launch into a long story, 'Great, can you give me his number?'

'Just a minute, I'll have a look.' She rummaged behind the counter and came out with a card. 'He left a few of these cards with me. Here you go. Got his name and phone number on it.'

It was afternoon when she arrived at The Shack, and she felt even more tired and disheartened when she saw the state of the place. She hadn't realised things had got so run down. Luckily it was summer and the evenings were still light. She went in and tried a light switch and was relieved when the light came on. *First thing, turn on the fridge and put a bottle of white wine in it.*

At least she'd be able to use her computer. If she needed the internet, she could drive into town and go to the library—assuming the library had the internet. Taking a deep breath, she started to empty the van, dumping all the boxes and cases in the living room. She still had some sandwiches that she'd bought in Newcastle, but she wasn't hungry. She'd have just one glass of wine now and save the sandwiches to eat on the train that night.

It was dark when she arrived at Gurunnuga Station. She parked the van and waited on the platform, hoping the train driver would remember to stop. As it was an untended station, you had to state you wanted to be picked up there when you booked and inform the guard on the way back to be set down at Gurunnuga—otherwise it wouldn't stop.

She'd booked a sleeper, but sleep didn't come easily. She lay tossing and turning as much as the narrow bunk would allow. After arriving in Sydney just before seven in the morning, she went straight to the café in the station concourse and ordered a coffee.

She sat at a table watching the commuters scurrying around and wondered what she could do until the solicitors opened. *The handy man!* She'd ring him now while she had a signal. Better still, a text message with her address. She asked him to call round and give her a quote.

She bought a newspaper but couldn't seem to focus on the print. Still another two hours before the solicitors opened. She'd have time to walk to their offices and get some fresh air. She must look a mess, she thought, but she didn't care. As long as she saw none of her old colleagues. She decided it might be better to walk the long way around.

A few hours later, everything was settled. She'd signed away her share of the house and had time to bank the cheque. *Enough to keep me for a year or two if I can't get work.* She berated herself for the thought. Of course, she'd get work.

By the time she got on the train to return to Gurunnuga, she was exhausted. Her seat was at the back of the train, in the last carriage. She rested her head against the window and gave in to tears. Thirty years old. No husband, no job and no home. No, that wasn't strictly true. She had The Shack. But she couldn't isolate herself there. Her mind went around in circles.

Blankly she watched the passing scenery until dusk began to descend, then she got up and made her way to the refreshment bar. She bought a sandwich and two glasses of wine and walked back to her seat, carefully carrying the wine on a cardboard tray.

She dozed a bit and looked at her watch. Another hour.

She became aware of a woman standing over her with some kind of big padded carryall. 'Will you mind my baby while I go to the toilet?' the woman asked. 'There's nowhere to put her down.'

Jessica frowned as the woman put the carry all on the seat next to her. She could just see a baby's head. She nodded. 'Okay.' Just as she settled back to doze, she heard the train guard coming, asking for tickets, then the train jolted to a stop and the Tannoy speaker announced the name of the station, Nungai. The train started again as the guard opened the door of her carriage, and she got out her ticket.

'Stopping at Gurunnuga,' he said, examining it. 'Not long now.'

'Thanks.'

The guard glanced around the carriage—it seemed she was the only one in there—then he went back the way he'd come.

Jessica dozed off and jolted awake when she heard the announcement that the train was stopping at Gurunnuga. She jumped up and picked up her bag, then realised the baby was still next to her. *Shit, what to do?'*

Half dopey from the wine and the sleepless night, she grabbed the carryall and just managed to get off the train in time. She was the only passenger. *I'll hand the baby into lost property.* Then she remembered it was an unmanned station. It was in darkness except for an overhead light at the exit.

Shit, shit, shit, she thought as she walked to the van. It was after eleven o'clock. There was nowhere to go, and she couldn't remember if there was a Police Station in Gurunnuga. Reluctantly she put the carryall on the front seat of the van. Probably illegal, but what else could she do? The baby started to mewl, but the motion of the van lulled it back to sleep. Jessica felt anger rising in her. What a stupid woman; where did she disappear to? She suddenly remembered that the toilet was in the section the guard had come through, not at the back of the carriage she'd been in. Now she'd have to go back into town in the morning and hand the baby into the police station. It was all she needed. And what would she do with a baby all night? Her heart started to pound, and she felt a headache coming on. *Damn and blast!* It was all

Jason's fault. Her eyes welled with tears at the thought of Jason having a baby. What kind of god put her in this situation with an abandoned baby? How cruel could fate get?

Back at The Shack, Jessica took her bag and the carryall out of the van and went indoors. She switched on the light and put her bag on a chair and the baby carrier on the kitchen table. She gingerly picked up the baby and found a baby bottle at the bottom of the carrier. Well, that was something. It was probably hungry. But what to feed it? Lucky she'd bought milk yesterday. The baby started to whimper, so she picked up the empty baby bottle and tried to fight off her exhaustion and think. Could she just put milk in the bottle and warm it up? Suddenly she remembered her father's library of books—he might have some books on child care. She turned on the light in the study and looked around. Memories of her school days flooded back—the hours she had spent with him there ... She scanned the books. He'd been so methodical; surely... yes, she found a section on health and biology, and spotted a few relevant titles like *Having a Baby Easily* and next to it, one by Dr Spock. She put the baby over her shoulder and took out the first book. One chapter covered the baby's first month, and this baby looked very young. She didn't have much experience with babies, but this one seemed tiny. She found a chart of weight against age, then a chapter for mothers unable to breast feed. She looked at the charts and did a rapid calculation. First, weigh the baby to get its rough age. She hurried back to the kitchen with the book under her arm, patting the baby as she went. Kitchen scales ... lucky the ones in the kitchen were the old-fashioned kind with a big enamel dish and separate weights. When she put the baby on the big dish, it screamed. Quickly she added the weights to balance it. Okay, that would do.

Four-and-a-half kilograms. She looked at the chart. *Right, baby's about three or four weeks old. Now the milk.*

She looked up the section on emergency feeding. Evaporated milk, water and sugar. After her mother had died, her father always kept tins of evaporated milk in the pantry as he only went shopping every few weeks. Yes! She found three tins and didn't bother checking the best-by date— needs must ...

She put the baby back in the carryall and moved it to the couch while she concentrated on preparing the bottle. She boiled the kettle and swished the boiling water around in the bottle, then made up a jug of the milk mixture. After pouring some of the mixture into the bottle, she sat it in a bowl of cold water to try and cool it, then turned to the baby, who was red-faced from screaming non-stop.

She picked it up and rocked it up and down, then got a whiff of something smelly. *Oh God! A dirty nappy.* She found a towel and spread it on the couch, then lay the baby on it. Undoing the little jumpsuit revealed a sopping-wet, dirty, disposable nappy. She took it off—phew—gingerly picked it up and went to the laundry, where she dropped it into a plastic bag. She found some tissues and wet some, then wiped and cleaned the baby's bottom. *Oh, a little girl!* Her little legs kicked frantically as she emitted hiccupping sobs.

Jessica wrapped her in the towel and walked up and down until the milk had cooled—she tested it on her wrist as the book explained—then she sat to feed the little girl. The bottle empty, she put the baby over her shoulder and patted her back. After a loud burp, the baby's eyes closed and her little head rested on Jessica's shoulder. Jessica settled her on the couch, then rinsed out the bottle and put the rest of the milk in the fridge.

The unopened bottle of wine beckoned, so she took it out, poured a generous glassful and sank onto the couch next to the baby. *She's very cute,* she thought wistfully, then remembered the nappy she'd put in a plastic bag in the bin. The baby had nothing on except a little top and the towel wrapped around her. She'd better do something about it. She hauled herself up and searched the linen cupboard for an old towel. After finding one that would do, she located a sewing box with scissors and safety pins, then cut the towel into baby sized pieces. She wrapped one around the baby's bottom and pinned the makeshift nappy, then wrapped the baby in another towel. She washed her hands, then finished the wine and went to her old bedroom. *Shit.* Of course, the bed wasn't made. Only pillows and a doona. She fetched sheets and pillow cases and made the bed, but couldn't be bothered searching through her case to find her night clothes, so she undressed, then put her T-shirt back on. She picked up the baby, put her in the carryall and set it on the floor at the foot of her bed and collapsed onto the mattress. She was asleep in moments.

A whimper woke her.

With a jolt, it all came back to her. She looked at her watch. *Damn. Five o'clock.* She crawled out of bed and picked up the baby. Its nappy was wet, and she was obviously hungry. Jessica put the baby over her shoulder and with one hand filled the kettle and put it to boil. Then she filled the baby bottle with the milk she'd made the night before and stood it in a pan of boiling water to heat. By the time the milk was warm, the baby was ratcheting up its volume. Jessica sank onto the couch and plugged the bottle into the baby's mouth. Peace.

After she'd cut up more towels for nappies, burped and changed the baby, Jessica thought about making a cup of coffee, but decided to lie down for a bit instead. She felt so tired. The baby seemed content cuddled into her tummy. She had vague memories of reading of mothers who slept with their babies turning over and smothering them. But she was only resting, not sleeping ...

A loud knocking on the kitchen door woke her. She jumped up, disturbing the baby, who started to cry. Taking the baby, Jessica called out, 'Coming! Hold on,' as she hurried to the door and opened it.

A tall, good-looking man stood in the doorway, a smile spreading slowly across his face. She suddenly realised that she was dressed only in a T-shirt.

Heat rushed to her face. 'Just a minute,' she said and ran back to her bedroom. An old dressing gown hung behind the door; she grabbed it, lay the baby on the bed, put on the dressing gown, picked up the baby and returned to the door. 'Sorry about that,' she said to the man who still stood there, leaning against the door frame, one leg hooked behind the other, his hands in his pockets

'Rob Sullivan,' he said looking at her with slight grin. He straightened and offered her his hand.

Jessica shook it automatically, then became conscious of the state she was in, with her uncombed hair and rumpled appearance. Then the baby gave a grunt and a waft of dirty nappy came up like a miasma.

Now he really did grin. 'I got your message yesterday about work you wanted done around the place,' he said. 'I tried to ring you but couldn't get any reply. Sent a text but you probably didn't get that either.'

'Not yet; no signal here,' Jessica said.

'Well, this doesn't seem like a good time to call, but I'm happy to do any jobs you have. I charge by the hour if that's okay?' He named a figure.

Jessica nodded. 'That's fine. When can you start?'

'How about I come tomorrow morning and we see how we go? You look a bit tied up at the moment.' He looked at the baby. 'Cute baby. Little girl?'

Jessica nodded and said nothing.

'Right, be back tomorrow about nine. That okay?'

'Yes. Thanks. See you then, Rob.'

She was about the shut the door when he turned back. 'Love your HJ.' He smiled.

She nodded. 'Yes.' And closed the door. *HJ? Oh yes, the Holden van.*

Jessica fed the baby, cleaned her up, did her best with the pieces of towel for a nappy, then looked at the bucket into which she'd put the wet and dirty ones. *Deal with them later.* She showered and changed her clothes, then got ready to drive to Gurunnuga with the baby. She'd found her father's address book with the phone number of the police station, its address and opening hours. With the baby contented and asleep in the carryall, she settled it in the front seat of the van, got in and turned the key in the ignition. Nothing. *Shit, shit, shit! A flat battery!*

What to do? Jump leads? A battery charger? She took a look in the shed behind her mother's studio, but she didn't know what a battery charger looked like. And didn't you need another vehicle to use jump leads?

Here she was with no landline and no phone signal on her mobile. The nearest neighbours were Bill and Irene Yates, but their place was several kilometres away, and she'd have to carry the baby with her. Couldn't leave the little mite here on her own. And it was now eleven o'clock and with the sun beating down, it must be over thirty degrees. If she walked to the Yates's place, by the time she got there carrying a baby, it would be one or two o'clock, and the baby would probably be screaming. Even if

Bill was there and they came straight back and did the jump start thing, the police station would be closed by the time she got there.

The van was already getting hot. She wound down the windows a bit, took the carryall and went back into the house. She sank onto the couch. What to do? What else could go wrong? This was a living nightmare. Then she remembered the handyman. Rob said he'd be back at nine the next morning. She'd have to wait until then and hope he didn't have a problem with his boys or whatever the reason was why he wasn't able to work full time.

She looked at her watch. If she couldn't drive, she might as well have a glass of wine.

As she sat sipping her wine, she noticed the radio. Surely a missing baby would be on the news. She looked at her watch. Nearly twelve o'clock, news time. She turned on the radio, found a local station, refilled her glass, then sat back and listened. Nothing about a missing baby. She looked at the sleeping baby in the carryall. There might have been a note or something in it with a name. She'd examine it more carefully later, when the baby needed changing or feeding. She picked up one of the books she'd found in her father's collection, *Rearing the Healthy Child*, and started to read.

The next time she fed the baby, it looked up at Jessica and gave a little smile. Probably caused by wind, Jessica thought, since according to the book, they didn't smile until about six-weeks old; before then a smile-like grimace was usually caused by wind. But she looked so cute! Jessica cuddled the little girl to her. *I wish I could keep her!* The thought came to her unbidden. She sighed.

Nothing in the carry all gave a clue to who the baby was or where she'd come from.

The day passed, and between washing the towelling nappies, making feed and rocking the baby when she cried, Jessica only had enough time to unpack one of her cases and get out a change of clothes. She didn't have time to go around the house and garden and make notes about what needed doing.

When the baby woke at five next morning, Jessica fed her, then dressed and made her own breakfast. She'd be ready for Rob when he came. Fingers crossed that he'd come. She turned on the radio for the seven o'clock news. Still nothing about a missing baby.

At last she heard his ute pull up. Right on time. She walked out to meet him.

He jumped out of the ute while putting on a battered Akubra hat, and with a smile said, 'Hello, Mrs Broughton.'

The 'Mrs' startled her for a moment. 'Good morning, Rob, but please call me Jessica.'

'Okay. Shall we have a look around and make a list of what you want me to do?'

'Yes, but first, I have a problem with the van. It won't start. I think the battery's flat.'

'I've got jump leads somewhere in the ute. I'll get them, and we'll soon get her going.'

After ten minutes of trying to start the van, Rob shook his head and pronounced the battery clagged.

Jessica's heart sank. 'I think it must be pretty old. What should I do?'

Rob considered. 'Well, I can pick up a new one in the morning and bring it out with me if you like.'

'Thanks, that'd be great.' She didn't like to suggest he drive straight to town for one.

'Okay. No probs. It's a great van.' He smiled and put the jump leads back in his ute.

'Yes. My father was very particular about keeping it in good nick.' She could just remember when he'd bought it. He'd had a legacy from his mother, her English grandmother, whom she'd never met. He'd gone straight into town with the cheque and came back grinning from ear to ear. It was a few weeks later when he announced he had a surprise for them and took her and her mother into town. He'd been so happy. 'All the options,' he'd announced proudly. Jessica hadn't understood at the time what the options meant, but now she could picture the salesman saying, 'Your wife would love this.' And the deal would be clinched.

'Now, where shall we start?' Rob said, startling her out of her reverie. He pointed at the gutters. 'How about I start with those? Bad news if a bush fire comes through, and it's been pretty dry lately.'

Jessica followed his gaze and nodded. She could see plants growing out of the gutters. 'Yes, and in the meantime, I'll have a look around at what else needs doing.' He was already untying a ladder from the ute.

'Baby's crying,' he said.

Jessica blinked. 'Oh, yes!' She started towards the house. 'Let me know if you need anything.'

At half past ten, she put on the kettle and went outside just as Rob came around the corner of the house carrying two buckets of debris he'd cleaned out of the gutters.

'Want this lot in your compost bin?' he asked.

She nodded. 'Yes, please; if you can find it under all the weeds. I've just put the kettle on to make tea. Would you like tea or prefer coffee?'

'Tea, please. I'll just wash my hands and get my lunch bag.'

'How do you like it?'

'Milk, no sugar, and I'll have it out here please. Too grubby to come inside.'

Inside, Jessica took two cups out for the tea; she looked for bigger mugs but found none. Of course, her father always liked his tea in china cups. She smiled at the thought and prepared a tray with two cups and saucers, the teapot and a little jug for milk. From the kitchen window she saw Rob washing his hands under a tap near the garden.

When she took the morning tea onto the veranda, she found him sitting on the wooden floor, his back against the wall of the house with a lunch box and his hat beside him.

Jessica put the tray on a small table. 'Sit in one of the chairs,' she said.

He just smiled. 'Too grubby. Got covered in a lot of the gutter muck.' He picked up a cup. 'Hmm. Like your cups.'

Jessica smiled. 'My father always insisted on china cups for tea. For some reason he didn't like drinking out of thick cups. He was English.'

Rob laughed. 'That explains it.'

She looked at him. It did sound a bit funny in retrospect.

He took a greaseproof package from the lunch box and undid it, revealing two sandwiches. 'Like one?' he offered.

She shook her head. 'No thanks, but they do look nice.'

'Lovely place you've got here,' he said.

Jessica looked around. 'Yes, it is. It was my parents. My father did a lot of work on it. My mother was an artist. That was her studio. Over there.' She nodded towards it.

'So where are your parents now?' he asked. 'If it's not an impertinent question.'

'No, it's not. My mother died when I was twenty, and then my father just two years ago.' She sighed. 'I'm going to clean the place up and try and sell it.'

Rod nodded. 'Yes, it's hard to maintain a rural property if you're not living in it.'

'More tea?' Jessica held out the teapot.

'Thanks.'

He finished his tea, folded up the greaseproof wrapping and carefully put it in his lunch bag. 'Can reuse it tomorrow,' he said with a smile, putting the lunch bag down on the table. 'Now back to work.' He picked up his hat and put it on. 'What's the next most urgent thing? I did notice a cracked downpipe over there. You'll need to replace it. In a heavy downpour it will leak onto the weatherboards.'

She frowned. 'Oh.'

'I can bring a length tomorrow, if you like.'

'Thanks. Apart from that, the paddock is a mess; it needs slashing or something; It's too long for me to use the mower. And the garden is a riot of weeds.'

'Yes, and it's a lot to do when you have a young baby.'

'She's not mi ...' She was going to say, *I found her on the train*, but stopped. That sounded so stupid. And anyway, she didn't need to tell this man the story of her life. She picked up the tea tray instead. 'Perhaps the grass first?'

'Right, I noticed the grass yesterday, so brought my scythe.' He grinned and headed towards the ute, adding, 'I feel like the grim reaper when I use it.'

A good worker, Jessica noted with approval. She stood watching him, until the baby started to cry.

'We have a reprieve, little one,' she told the baby, rocking her in her arms. 'Thanks to the dud battery, but I'll miss you. We're alike, both abandoned.' She tenderly smoothed the baby's downy hair. How could anyone leave such a beautiful little girl, and what would happen to her when Jessica handed her in? Visions of an orphanage or foster home and cruel adoptive parents rushed through her mind.

She looked at her watch. Nearly twelve; news time. Still holding the baby, she stood up and turned on the radio. She could see Rob slashing, wiping his face with a handkerchief from time to time, and then drinking water from a flask. *He'll get sunstroke! And that old hat must be so hot.* Perhaps she should stop him. Find something else for him to do.

She lay the baby down in the carry all and went outside. 'Rob,' she called. 'I'm making tea; it's lunch time.'

He waved to her. 'I'll just finish this section. Ten minutes.'

She brought out the tea to the veranda when she saw him washing his hands. Once done, he came over and sat on the floor again.

'I do wish you'd sit on a chair,' she said.

'I'm fine.' He opened his lunch box, took out a big tub with salad in it and started to eat.

Jessica had found an unopened tin of biscuits in the pantry. She'd looked at the best-by date. It was last year. They'd do for her lunch with some cheese that she'd bought on her way up.

She opened the biscuit tin, took one out and cut a slice of cheese. 'Like some?'

He shook his head.

'Probably wise,' Jessica said. 'The biscuits are a bit soft. But I'm not hungry.' She nibbled on a piece of cheese and looked at the house. 'What do you think are the most important things to do, for selling the place?'

Rob considered her question for a moment. 'First impressions are really important, so the surrounds and the garden must look neat and tidy and look as if they're easy to maintain. Inside, you need to get rid of any clutter: photos, ornaments, that kind of thing. Maybe a coat of paint to freshen things up.'

His knowledge impressed Jessica, but it sounded like a lot of work. She sighed. 'Right, I'll make a list and prioritise the work.'

Rob looked at his watch. 'I allow half an hour for lunch,' he said. 'It's one now. I'll work for another hour, then I have to go. Pick up my boys. So that makes ... nine until two is five hours, minus half an hour each for lunch and morning tea, makes four hours. That okay?'

'Yes, of course.' Jessica felt suddenly embarrassed. 'Should I pay you now?'

'No, the end of the week is fine. I usually write the hours in my diary when I get home, but please would you do the same? So we both know where we stand?'

Jessica nodded. 'Sure. No problem.' She took the tea tray inside and started washing up. An hour later, while in the laundry trying to wash the nappies, a tap on the window startled her.

'Saw you in there,' he shouted. 'Leaving now. See you tomorrow.'

CHAPTER 9

Jessica listened to every news bulletin. Still no mention of a missing baby. Perhaps the woman had deliberately left her with Jessica, not wanting her anymore and thinking Jess looked a suitable person. That evening, after she'd wrapped the baby in clean towels and tucked her into the carry all, she sat down with a glass of wine and turned on the radio for the nine o'clock news. Still nothing about a baby.

Maybe I'm meant to keep her!

Could she adopt her if she handed her in? She recalled all the papers she'd got on adoption when she'd been trying to persuade Jason to adopt. The authorities wouldn't even consider a single parent, let alone an unemployed single parent. If she and Jason were still together, they might be able to adopt her. But Jason never wanted to adopt. The thought of Jason's betrayal hit her again. Her stomach churned. She refilled her wine glass and sighed. *You're getting maudlin, Jess.* Then unexpected tears filled her eyes and spilled over. Her life was such a mess. Where had she gone wrong? She'd always done the right thing; she wasn't a bad person, so how could all this have happened? In just a few weeks? She sniffed, blew her nose and fetched a new bottle of wine.

The next morning at nine o'clock, Rob's ute stopped behind the van. He jumped out and got the new battery from the back of the ute. When he saw her approach, he smiled. 'Got the battery,' he said. 'Here's the receipt.'

'Thanks, Rob. I'll get the money. Well, actually, I'll have to go into town to get cash.'

'That's okay, whenever. I trust you. Let's get the van going.'

He soon had the battery installed and the van's engine running smoothly, but he frowned as he got out. 'Looks like your petrol is very low.'

Jessica grimaced. 'I totally forgot about getting petrol on the way up.'

'These older cars suck up the juice,' Rob said. 'Look, I've got a jerry can of petrol in the ute. Should have enough in it to get you into town.'

'Thanks. Put the can in the back of the van and I'll refill it for you.'

'That's all right. Are you going in now?'

'Yes, as soon as I've fed and changed the baby.'

'You can leave her here if you like,' Rob indicated the veranda. 'I can keep an eye on her. I thought I'd make a start on the vegetable garden, so I'll only be weeding. I'll be able to see her from there, and hear her.'

Jessica hesitated. It made sense, except that the whole purpose of going into town was to hand the baby over to the police. Then she had an idea: maybe she could just go to the police station and ask if anyone had lost a baby, rather than just handing her over. Then she could leave her here with Rob. She felt certain she could trust him.

'If you're sure,' she said. 'I should only be a couple of hours.'

'I'll move the ute out of your way.'

An hour later she walked onto the veranda with the baby and put her in the carry all. It was so warm she left her dressed only in the towel nappy. Anyway, she had no other baby clothes. She'd washed the little jumpsuit, but it was too warm for her to wear. Carefully she placed the carry all in the shade on the outside table under the veranda.

Seeing her, Rob came over. 'She's cute; what's her name?'

Jessica panicked. Her gaze fell on a carrier bag just inside the door. A woman's clothes store. 'Katies. I mean Kate.'

'Hello, Kate,' Rob said softly, gently stroking one of the baby's cheeks. 'Great to see you using cloth nappies,' he said. 'Those disposables are so bad for the environment.'

Jessica nearly said, 'Are they?' then caught herself in time. 'Are you sure about minding her?

'Yes, anyway it wouldn't be good for her staying in the van in this heat.'

Of course. Jessica hadn't thought of that aspect. Plus carrying her around in the carry all while she did her shopping would be difficult and impractical in the heat.

***

Outside the Police station, Jessica hesitated. It would sound crazy to go in and ask if anyone had lost a baby. They'd think she was nuts. She walked up and down for five minutes, then decided to get petrol and the groceries and come back to the Police Station. She filled the van and Rob's jerry can, then drove to the shops and parked. Next to the supermarket was a charity shop. A big doll in the window, dressed in baby clothes, caught her attention, and she found herself going in and being irresistibly drawn to a corner full of baby clothes. *They're so cute*, she thought, picking up a little dress and some tiny pink jump suits. *I'll buy them and give them to the police when I take her in.*

In the supermarket, she found baby formula. *That's better than evaporated milk. Oh, and bottle sterilizing tablets. Oh and maybe a spare bottle.* She stopped at the shelves of disposable nappies, about to buy some, then thought of what Rob had said and paused. But why should she care what he thought? Even so she resisted buying them. Feeling more cheerful after her achievements, she returned to the van and put her shopping in the back.

What the hell am I doing?

With a sigh, she drove back to the police station. A sign hung in the window. Closed. With a phone number to ring for urgent help.

Relief flooded her. It was a sign! An omen! She was meant to keep Kate.

She drove back to the shack to find Rob sitting under the veranda, rocking Kate in his arms. 'She was a bit colicky,' he said when Jessica ran up the steps. 'It's okay sweetie, mamma's back,' he whispered to the baby, then smiled, stood up, and handed her to Jessica. 'Here you go, all good. Don't look so worried. She's fine.' He walked down the steps.

Jessica held the baby close to her and watched Rob return to the vegetable garden. Her head spun with ideas. First, see to the baby. She settled her back in the carry all and then got the shopping from the van. A glance at her watch told her it was one o'clock already. She'd better put the kettle on and make a pot of tea for Rob, and mix some of the new baby formula for Kate. Then she'd wash the baby clothes she'd bought. A sense of purpose filled her.

***

The next day, Rob arrived ready to replace the broken downpipe and finish digging the vegetable garden.

'I brought some seedlings I thought you might like,' he said. 'I always sow too many. And I hope you won't be offended, but I've also brought some of the boys' things from when they were babies. I've been meaning to give them away but hadn't got around to it. They might do you while you're here, save you buying new stuff just for however long it takes you to sort the place out. But I expect you're anxious to get back to your husband, and I'm sure he misses you and Kate.' He smiled at her.

Jessica looked at him. 'My husband and I are separated,' she said stiffly. 'I'll be here on my own until I manage to sell.'

'Oh!' His face fell. 'Sorry to hear that,' he muttered

Seeing his stricken face, she tried to smile. 'But thank you; anything you don't need will be very welcome.'

He took a bassinet and other things from the ute. 'Bottle warmer,' he said, handing them over, 'and baby carrier, and a few other things.'

'Thank you, Rob.' She turned away, her heart beating wildly. How could she backtrack now? She couldn't tell him the truth.

At three o'clock that afternoon, Rob came to the house and shouted through the door, 'I'm off now, Jessica.'

She came to the door. 'Right. Will I see you tomorrow?'

'Um, no, school holidays start today. Next Saturday is Christmas day.'

'Oh, right.' She'd forgotten all about Christmas.

'You doing anything for Christmas?' Rob asked.

'Hadn't really thought about it,' she replied, going to get her handbag. 'How much do I owe you, Rob?'

He handed her a piece of paper with his hours written on it and the amount.

'Thanks so much, Rob,' she said as she gave him the money. 'Will you be able to come back after Christmas? I think the outside needs painting.'

'Thanks, Jessica.' He tucked the money in his pocket and wrote her a receipt. 'I'll be able to come back to do the painting, but I'm not sure exactly when. Depends on the boys.' He frowned.

Jessica nodded. 'Well, whenever you can. Should I buy paint?'

Rob smiled. 'I can get it if you like. I can get a discount at the hardware shop. What colour?'

'I think the white looks nice; let's keep to that.'

'Fine; okay, then, see you in the new year. That's if the world hasn't been blown to bits by all this year-2000 computer stuff.' He made to go, then added, 'Happy Christmas, Jessica.'

'And to you.' Jessica stood and watched him as he strode towards his ute. Year 2000! She'd completely forgotten all the doomsday scenarios about aeroplanes falling out of the sky and the world in chaos. She'd known it had all been a fuss about very little. Her previous job and work seemed so far away now. She turned back inside. She had Kate to worry about now.

***

The Shack was so quiet. Jessica wondered why her parents had never had a television. She'd asked once when she was still at school. Everyone else had a television except them; it made her even more of an outsider and the butt of jokes. Some of her classmates delighted in talking about the latest sit com and asking her what she thought, knowing full well that she didn't have a television and wouldn't be able to answer, making her look stupid. 'Can we get a television?' she'd asked her father.

He'd looked surprised. 'What for? We have books.'

It was true. Books lined her father's study, and he drove into town every few weeks to the library and came back with an armful of books. Unless her mother was engrossed in a painting, they'd all sit reading in the evenings—Jessica, too—accompanied by her father's classical music records. At nine o'clock, Richard would look at his watch, turn on the radio for the news and say. 'Bedtime, Jessica.'

She wondered what he would make of her decision to keep baby Kate.

On Christmas day Jessica realised that she hadn't thought of Jason for days. She'd been so busy with Kate, and had at last started to unpack some of her stuff. After installing her PC and printer on the desk in her father's study, she suddenly thought that there was no point in sending off her CV. Who would look after Kate if she got a job overseas? Or even here. But she wouldn't be able to get a job around here. It would mean Brisbane or Sydney. Perhaps Newcastle. But that risked meeting Jason or his family. She'd been thinking of the UK, certain she'd be able to get a UK passport because of her father, and that would mean she could work there. She'd have to put Kate into day care, or whatever it was called. Take her before work and pick her up after work. But she'd need a passport for Kate if she went to the UK. And Kate would need a birth certificate to get a passport. *Birth certificate!* She hadn't thought that far ahead.

She poured herself a glass of wine and looked at it. She should have bought a bottle of champagne to celebrate Christmas and the baby. She smiled to herself. Then dragged her mind back to the matter of a birth certificate.

She found the telephone directory, looked up 'registry office' and found the address of the nearest one. After going over various scenarios in her head, she resolved to go in the very first day they reopened after the Christmas break and register Kate.

In the meantime, she was becoming besotted with her.

***

Her heart thumping, she opened the door of the registry office. She'd bought a baby carrier and wore it on her tummy, like a back pack, only on the front.

The woman behind the window smiled. 'Good morning, how may I help you?'

'I want to register my baby's birth.' Jessica smiled, thinking that at least the woman looked friendly.

'Have you filled out the form?'

'Um, no; is there a form?'

'Yes. But look, there's no-one in the queue, so we can do it together if you like.'

'Thanks. That'd be great.'

'Have you got ID? Driving licence?'

The woman looked at the licence Jess gave her, turned it over and looked at the address. 'This has a Sydney address.'

'I've moved.'

The woman frowned. 'You know you must notify the Road Traffic Authority of a change of address?'

'Yes. I've just had too much on my mind ...'

The woman nodded. 'All right, umm ...' She looked at the licence again. 'Mrs Jessica Broughton.' She wrote on the form.

'Actually, it's Ms, not Mrs,' Jessica said.

The woman looked up at her. 'Hmm, so what's your new address?'

Jessica told her and watched her writing it down.

Without looking up, the woman asked, 'name of baby's Father?'

Jessica paused and bowed her head. 'I don't know,' she whispered.

The woman's head shot up. She stared at Jessica, her pen poised over the form. 'Hmm,' she said again, her face registering disapproval.

Jessica saw her write 'Unknown' on the form.

'Sex?'

'Girl.'

'Address where she was born?'

'At home. The address I've just given you.'

'Not in hospital?'

'No.'

'Who was present? Midwife? Doctor's name?'

'No-one. She was early.'

The woman frowned again and gave a big sigh. 'You delivered yourself?'

'Yes.'

'You're supposed to have a signed affidavit from a witness to the birth.'

'I was on my own,' Jessica said softly and looked down. She pulled a handkerchief from her pocket and wiped her eyes and blew her nose.

The woman's expression softened. 'What about your family?'

'I don't have any; both my parents are dead.'

'Oh, dear. So you're all alone, then?'

Jessica nodded and sniffed.

'Have you seen a doctor since then? Been to a hospital, had the baby checked?'

'Not yet. I will, as soon as I've finished here.'

'Date of baby's birth?'

Jessica had thought that Kate had been about three or four weeks old when she'd found her. Two weeks had passed since then. So she'd be five or six weeks old. 'Fifth of December,' she stated firmly.

'Hmm.' The woman consulted a calendar. 'You're within the regulation six weeks. At least that's something.'

'Baby's name?'

'Kate Sybilla Broughton.'

Just then the baby stirred on Jessica's chest. 'Okay, sweetie,' Jessica whispered. 'Not long now.' She stroked Kate's downy head.

The woman gave a small smile. 'It's a bit irregular,' she said. 'But I can't see any reason not to issue a birth certificate. Sign here please.' She pushed the form and a pen towards Jessica.

'Could I have three copies please?' She'd need a copy for a passport for Kate, and it was always good to have a spare.

The woman looked surprised, but nodded, and filled out the certificates.

Jessica paid her and tucked them in her bag, then walked out with a spring in her step.

'Make sure you go to the doctor and get her checked out. And yourself.' The woman called after her.

Jessica nodded. 'Yes, I will,' she replied, with absolutely no intention of going to a doctor. They'd want to examine her, then they'd discover she'd never given birth.

'You're mine now, Katie, best Christmas present ever,' she crooned to the baby. 'Bugger Jason.' Now she could buy things. First, a baby car seat, then more bottles and baby formula.

CHAPTER 10

AD 2000. Jessica wondered about all the computer programs she'd worked on to make them compliant for the new century. Her work and its problems all seemed so remote now. She turned on the radio and listened to the news. Planes were still flying; life was going on as usual with the New Year's Day celebrations. The forecast big catastrophe hadn't happened, which she'd known all along would be the case.

A few days later, she heard a vehicle draw up and the toot of a horn. She suddenly panicked; what if it were Jason? Come to say sorry and it was all over with Amy. Her heart started to thump. How would she explain Kate? She ran to the window and looked out. Her breathing calmed when she saw Rob's ute in the driveway, and she hurried out to greet him, smiling with relief.

'Happy new year.' Rob smiled. 'I've got a glut of tomatoes in the garden, so I brought you some, and some lettuce.'

'Thanks! That's so kind of you. Will you come in and have a cup of tea? Or coffee?'

'No, thanks. I've got the boys in the ute; we're on our way to see their grandmother.' He indicated the front seat of the ute where two small boys sat strapped into the passenger seat, then opened the passenger door. 'Come and say hello to Mrs Broughton.'

Reluctantly the boys slid off the seat onto the ground.

'This is Andrew,' Rob said, 'He's seven. And that's Thomas. He's four.'

'Hello, boys.' Jessica smiled at them. 'Did you have a good Christmas?'

They both nodded. 'Yes, thank you,' Andrew said and nudged his brother, who nodded and mumbled, 'Yes.'

'Can we get back in the ute now, Dad?' Andrew asked.

'Yes.' Rob nodded then turned to Jessica. 'So you're okay then?'

She smiled. 'We're both fine, thanks. Nice quiet Christmas. Just the way I like it.'

'You still want me to come back and paint the outside of the house?'

'Yes please, Rob, whenever you have time.'

'End of the month. I'll buy the paint then. That okay?' He swung himself up into the ute.

She nodded. 'Happy new year, Rob.' And waved as he reversed up the dirt track.

She took the tomatoes and lettuce into the kitchen, thinking how kind it was of him to bring them.

The days seemed to pass quickly, between looking after Kate, giving the house a good clean, gardening and reading everything she could get her hands on about babies and bringing up children.

She checked the calendar that the local shop had given her. The end of January had arrived and no sign of Rob. Perhaps he'd changed his mind about coming to paint the house, but just when she had given up on him, she heard the ute coming up the track to the house.

'Sorry I couldn't get here before,' he said. 'Something came up. It might be a good idea for you to get the phone connected. I wanted to ring and let you know I couldn't make it.'

Jessica nodded. 'Yes. I probably should. Then I could get the internet connected, too.'

Rob looked at her. 'The internet?'

She nodded.

He stared at her for a few moments, then went off to get the paint and tools from the ute.

***

By Easter Jessica had the phone and internet connected; The Shack looked much better—freshly painted; the garden flourishing, and the lawns and paddock neat and trimmed.

Rob repaired a leak in the roof of Sybilla's studio, then joined Jessica on the veranda.

'Just finished,' he said, wiping his hands on an old cloth. 'Your mother's studio should be water tight now. Lucky none of the paintings and stuff in there were damaged.'

'Thanks, Rob.' Jessica sighed. 'I don't know what to do with all my mother's paints and canvases. I suppose the paint will be useless after all this time. But there's still all her paintings. I suppose I should sort them out, get them framed ...' Her heart felt heavy all of a sudden.

Rob nodded. 'Well, I guess you'll be putting the place up for sale now.'

'I don't know. I've been looking on the internet; there's lots of places around here that have been for sale for ages. It doesn't seem like a good time to sell. I'll wait until Spring and think about it then.'

'So you know all about the internet and computers, then?' Rob said casually as he started packing his tools into the back of the ute.

'Well, yes. It was my job. In fact, I must start looking for work very soon.'

He took off his Akubra, swatted at the flies and then scratched the side of his face. 'I was wondering if you'd teach me about them,' he said diffidently, looking down at his hat. 'Computers, I mean.'

Surprised, Jessica stared at him. 'What do you want to know?'

'Um, not sure, just how they work and programs and things. I was thinking of getting one. I heard that all the schools will be getting computers and I thought I should learn, too. Keep up with the boys.'

'That's a great idea,' Jessica exclaimed, 'and I'd be happy to teach you.'

Rob expression relaxed. 'What kind should I buy?'

Jessica smiled. 'I'll do some research and let you know. Now that I've got a phone, I can ring you.'

'Great! Bye for now, then,' and he swung himself up into the driver's seat and started the engine.

'What about the money I owe you?' She shouted, but he didn't hear her over the noise of the engine. He reversed out and disappeared down the track.

Pleased that she had something new to think about, Jessica went to the clothes line and took in the washing.

***

When Rob's computer arrived, he asked Jessica if she would come and get it set up for him the following Sunday. She hadn't been to his place before, knew only that it was about a twenty-minute drive from her place. She secured Kate, now seven months old, into the van.

Half an hour later, after following a few false tracks, she found his house. Apart from discussing what work had to be done at The Shack, she and Rob had never spoken of their personal circumstances. He'd arrived, worked and left. All she knew of his life was that he had the two boys, who she'd met just after Christmas, and that they had a grandmother. He'd never mentioned a wife, but she knew there'd been a woman in his life. What had the shop keeper called her? 'That awful someone ... Was it Chrissy? Carly? Something like that.' They hadn't even talked about what other work he did. Apart from the fact that she was separated from her husband and had a baby, she'd never mentioned her situation. He knew her mother had been an artist from going into the studio when he checked the leak in the roof.

The sign on the gate said, 'Sullivan. Please close the gate.' She stopped, opened the gate, drove through, stopped and closed the gate. A dog barking greeted her at the end of a long dirt track. Rob came out of the house, a simple weatherboard cottage with a veranda all around, and patted the dog, which looked like a kelpie.

'Hi, Jessica.' He smiled and indicated the dog, who wagged her tail. This is Kelly.'

Jessica bent down and patted her. 'Hello, Kelly; hello, Rob.'

'Is Kate in the van?'

Jessica nodded. 'Yes, I'll get her out.'

The two boys joined them. 'Hello, Mrs Broughton,' they chorused.

Jessica smiled; their father had obviously coached them.

'Come in,' Rob said. 'The computer's on the kitchen table. The boys are dying to open the boxes, but I said we must wait for you.'

Jessica carried Kate inside. It looked as if the house was one big room with some doors, which were closed, leading off it—probably to bedrooms. Two old couches flanked the other walls, facing a small television. A kitchen table and chairs stood in the middle of the room.

'Great. Now if I put a blanket on the floor, is it okay if I put Kate down on it?'

'Of course.' Rob moved some chairs to make space in front of an old Aga stove. 'It'll be warmer here. Boys, will you put away your Lego please? Or Kate might pick it up and swallow it.'

They quickly gathered up the pieces they'd been assembling.

Jessica surrounded Kate with some toys she'd brought, then turned to the boys. 'Will we open the boxes then?'

They nodded and eagerly helped tear off the packing tape. Once they'd taken everything out of the box, Jessica turned to Rob. 'Where are you going to be using it? Have you got a desk?'

'I've made a temporary desk in that corner.' He pointed to what looked like an old door resting on concrete blocks.

'Is there a power point close?'

'Yes, just next to it.'

'Okay, let's move everything over there.'

When the components were in place, Jessica started to connect all the cables, explaining the function of each one. All three Sullivans watched closely. 'There! All connected. Now we must load the software. That's the brains that make it work,' she explained to Andrew and Thomas., then turned to Rob. 'This will take a few minutes.' She inserted the CD's.

'Well how about a cup of tea while it's doing that?'

'Lovely.' Jessica smiled. 'Now, boys, you watch the screen and tell me when it stops and looks like it's waiting for something.'

Eventually she had the computer all set up. 'I've installed a word processor for you,' she told Rob, omitting to mention it was pirated from Minchin and Turner.

'Um. I don't know what that is.'

Of course, how silly of me. 'Okay, first lesson. If we sit down at the table, I can explain about creating files and storage. Then about creating documents.'

Rob frowned. 'I didn't realise it was so complicated.'

Jessica took out a notebook and explained, drawing diagrams as she drank her tea. The boys soon lost interest and wandered off outside.

'I think I'll need several lessons,' Rob said ruefully.

'That's fine. I can come over whenever you want.'

'But I have to pay you for your time and your petrol.'

Jessica studied him. 'Well, how about we do a deal? You come and work at my place and in exchange I come and give you computer lessons.'

'Great idea!'

'I need more firewood, and there's a fallen tree out the back of the block that needs cutting up and splitting.'

He grinned. 'Right, Missis Broughton,' he said in a little school-boy voice. 'I'll be over in the morning, after taking the boys to school.'

On her way home, Jessica realised that her visit to Rob had been her first social event since moving to The Shack. Over seven months ago! It had been nice having that interaction, even if it had been her doing all the talking. And she'd enjoyed setting up the PC. She missed the mental stimulation of work.

***

The next morning, after Rob had cut up the fallen tree and taken the logs back to the house in his ute, they sat outside enjoying the spring sunshine and having their morning tea. Jessica brought

Kate out and put her on the veranda in a rough playpen she'd constructed against the veranda railings.

Rob frowned when he saw what Jessica was doing. 'I'm sure that arrangement is illegal.'

Jessica looked up. 'What do you mean, illegal?'

'Well, see the veranda railings? They're too far apart. Kate could get her head stuck between them.'

Jessica cursed under her breath, snatched Kate back up and sat with her on her lap. Kate wailed until Rob took his keys out and jiggled them in front of her.

'You seem a bit down, Jessica.'

'Do I? Not really. It's only that I'm a bit worried about having to get a job.'

'Oh?'

'The problem is that I'd need to go to a major city to find work.'

'Sydney?'

God, no. The probability of meeting someone she knew there was too great. The IT world was small. She shook her head.

'Brisbane, then.'

'Yes, I thought of that. I'd have to find a place to rent and some kind of day care for Kate. But I don't like the idea of her being in day care for five days a week, and often in IT you have to work late to meet a deadline.' She frowned and sighed.

'What about teaching computing? I thought you were brilliant yesterday. You explained everything so clearly.'

Jessica smiled at him. 'Dunno. Don't you have to have a Diploma of Education to teach in a school?'

He said nothing for a while, just sat and ate his usual sandwich. Then he looked up. 'There's always TAFE, you know, the technical college. There's one in town. I don't think you need anything special to teach there.' He corrected himself. 'What I mean is that you need a trade qualification depending on what you teach, but not a teaching diploma. At least I don't think so.'

Jessica nodded. 'That's a possibility. I'd never have thought of that. Thanks, Rob.'

He packed up his lunch box and stood up. 'Ring them.'

'I will. I'll do it now.' She tucked Kate under one arm and picked up the tea tray with the other, precariously unbalanced.

Rob opened the screen door for her. 'Want me to mind Kate while you ring?'

'It's okay; I'll put her on a rug on the floor.'

Twenty minutes later she came out to find Rob splitting and stacking the firewood. At her approach, he rested on his axe and looked at her with raised eyebrows. 'Any luck?'

'Yes and no. There's a possibility of two evening classes a week teaching Introduction to Computer Science. I have to go in to-morrow for an interview, but I'd have to find someone to mind Kate those nights. The classes are six thirty until nine thirty. Do you know anyone that could mind Kate? Maybe somewhere in town? I don't think the day care places would be open in the evenings.'

Rob considered. 'No, can't think of anyone, but *I* could, Jess.'

'*You?*'

'Well, I do have child minding experience you know.' He grinned.

She frowned as she thought about it.

Rob studied her. 'What time do you have to go for the interview tomorrow?'

'Ten thirty.'

'Who were you planning on leaving Kate with?'

'Oh, goodness, I hadn't even thought that far ahead.' Jessica hit her head with her hand. 'How stupid of me. I'll have to ring back and say I won't be able to make it. I'll have to do a lot more investigation about all this.'

'Well, I don't have any other work planned for tomorrow. I can come over and mind her while you go.'

Her heart lifted. 'Would you?'

'Of course.'

'Thank you, Rob; and listen, payment as usual?'

He nodded. 'Thanks.'

Jessica had a feeling he didn't have much money and buying the computer would have made big inroads into his savings.

'Okay, see you tomorrow. Nine o'clock?' He picked up his tools and moved towards his ute.

'Thanks Rob. Appreciate it.'

It would be great to get back to computing, but she worried about Rob looking after Kate. She tried to convince herself she was being foolish. It would only be for a few hours.

As soon as she put Kate down for her morning nap, Jessica went to the tin box of her father's that she now used for important papers and took out all her qualifications and the reference from Pete. She found her briefcase and gave it a clean, then opened the case where she'd packed away all her work clothes. She selected a light-grey suit and white shirt, both of which needed ironing. She'd better do something with her hair as well.

Next morning, she was ready and waiting when Rob arrived.

He parked on the grass next to the van, jumped out of the ute and bounded up the veranda steps, but stopped when he saw her. 'Wow!' He gave a wolf whistle. 'You look amazing Jess!'

She reddened. 'Don't be silly; these are just my work clothes.' But she felt pleased, none the less. Then she realised that Rob had only ever seen her in daggy old clothes and her hair a tangled mess. Now, with her hair carefully brushed and falling in waves onto her shoulders, and wearing a smart suit and high-heeled shoes and with make up on, she hardly recognized herself.

Rob looked at her shoes. 'You'd better put your gumboots on and carry your shoes,' he said. 'You'll destroy them in the wet grass.'

She looked down. 'You're right.' She took off her shoes and put on the boots which stood upside down beside the screen door.

Rob laughed. 'That's more like the Jessica I know.'

'Kate's just inside on the floor, crawling about.' Jessica looked around to see Kate trying to haul herself up the screen door. 'She's had her breakfast, so should be good until I come back. I've left some lunch in the fridge for her in case I'm delayed.'

'Off you go then, good luck.' Rob walked towards the door. 'Just coming, Katie bub,' he called to Kate.

Jessica took a deep breath and walked towards the van while Rob gently opened the screen door and took Kate in his arms.

'Wave bye bye to mamma.' He took one of Kate's arms and waved it up and down, then he turned and went inside.

***

At twelve thirty Rob heard the van draw up outside. He walked out onto the veranda and, after a delay where she fiddled in the van, watched Jessica coming in. He studied her. He'd been attracted to her ever since he'd first seen her. Now he realised that he wanted this woman in his life.

She walked up to him in her gum boots, carrying her shoes and brief case.

'How's the career woman, then?' Rob leaned over the veranda rail, smiling at her.

She looked up at him. 'I've been offered two evening classes!' she said jubilantly. 'They seemed quite impressed with my CV and references.' She thought it fortunate that Pete had given her the reference. And it seemed the people interviewing her had never heard of Minchin and Turner. When they'd asked what she'd been doing for the past nine months, she just said she'd been on maternity leave.

'How's Kate?'

'A perfect dream. I gave her the lunch you left, and she went down for her nap about ten minutes ago.'

'Great! Thanks so much, Rob. I'll just get out of these clothes and tell you all about it. Oh, that's if you have time to stay? Have a glass of wine?'

He grinned and nodded. 'I'll come in, but no wine for me.'

'I start next term. That's only three weeks away!' she said as she went inside.

Rob followed her. 'You'll be able to practice on me again next Sunday.'

***

The following Sunday, they arranged that Jessica would take Kate over to Rob at five o'clock on the two evenings she would work and pick her up on the way home at about ten thirty.

'Are you sure that's not too late for me to come for her?' she asked when they discussed the arrangements.

'No, it'll be fine. I think I'll be able to stay awake.' Rob grinned. 'If Kate gets sleepy, I'll take her to bed with me.' Seeing Jessica frown, he added, hastily, 'and make sure she doesn't roll off!'

'Okay. Now we'd better get started on your lesson.'

Thomas and Andrew had been charged with entertaining the baby. They lay on the floor making faces and teasing Kate, who gurgled with delight.

Rob soon got the hang of creating folders and files, and using the word processor. But he was still very slow at typing, picking out the letters on the keyboard with his index fingers.

By the time she started at TAFE, with three more sessions with Rob under her belt, she felt more confident about teaching.

'I think you know enough now, you just need practice,' she said to Rob.

'Okay, Jess. But I'd like to get the internet. Would you be able to help me with that?'

'Of course, next Sunday?'

CHAPTER 11

A few months later, just days before Christmas, Jessica received divorce papers to sign. She and Jason had been living apart for twelve months. A year. What a lot had happened in that year. She'd been offered three days a week teaching for the start of the new academic year, and she still had her two night classes. Luckily, she'd found a day care place just around the corner from where she worked, and the woman who ran it offered to take Kate for the two nights she had classes. She felt blessed. A nice home, a part-time job, a beautiful healthy baby and no financial worries.

She wondered about Rob and the boys. Would it be a good idea to invite them over for Christmas lunch, or would Rob take the boys to their grandmother? She hadn't seen Rob for a couple of weeks since TAFE had closed for the Christmas break, and she hadn't needed a baby sitter.

She rang him one evening and, as she'd expected, Rob was taking the boys to his mother's place up the coast on Christmas Eve for a week, but he'd be delighted to bring the boys to Jessica's for New Year's Day.

***

Rob raised his glass of champagne. 'Happy new year, Jessica.'

Jessica smiled. 'Happy 2001, Rob.' They clinked glasses.

The boys were playing with their Christmas presents, and Kate, her face lit up with excitement, was standing and trying to walk. She waved her arms around and fell back on her bottom.

Rob leaned towards Jessica. 'Hope this will be a great year for you.' He gave her a kiss.

'And for you, Rob.' She moved back from the kiss, smiling at him. He was the only friend she'd made since moving to The Shack. She sensed he'd like their friendship to be more than that, but she didn't want to encourage him in a relationship that, as far as she was concerned, could go nowhere.

'You've achieved a lot in a year,' he said.

'Well, mostly due to you.' She took a sip of the champagne.

He gave her a questioning look. 'Jess, I was thinking about you and me and ...' but Thomas interrupted him by walking over to ask for his father's help with assembling a piece of Lego.

The moment passed, to Jessica's relief.

Her new working arrangements meant that she only saw Rob when she needed work doing at the property. They rang each other from time to time. Jessica liked Rob; in fact she found him very attractive, but she was afraid to take it any further. She couldn't go into a relationship without being upfront and honest and revealing the truth about Kate, and she couldn't possibly do that. Moreover, she had the Huntington gene. It wouldn't be fair to him. The thought of him having to go through what her father had gone through was too much. Funny, now she thought about it, but that aspect had never occurred to her with Jason.

But she enjoyed Rob's company. And, she admitted to herself, he was her only friend. She always invited him and the boys to Kate's birthday parties, and they went to Rob's for the boys' birthdays.

Just before Kate's fourth birthday, she rang him.

'Well, hello, stranger,' he answered when he picked up the phone. 'How are you?'

'Good, thanks, Rob. And you?'

'All good.'

'Just wondered if you'd like to come over next week for Kate's birthday and bring the boys.'

'Love to.'

'And have a look at my chook house; I think it's past it. I need a new one.'

'No probs. See you then.'

She put the phone down and smiled.

When he and the boys arrived for her birthday, Kate hurled herself at Rob. ''Lo Wob!' She shouted.

He grinned and swept her up in his arms. 'How's my gorgeous girl?'

'Where's Andwew and Thomas?'

'They're just here; look!' He put her down, and she ran towards the boys.

He nodded to Jessica who'd followed Kate out of the house, then turned back to Kate. 'Okay Kate, show me your chook house,' he called.

When Kate led him to the rickety old shed, he laughed. 'I can tell you now, no self-respecting hen would lay an egg in there!'

Jessica smiled. 'I'll leave you to plan a new one and buy the materials, just tell me what it costs. You and the boys and Kate work it out while I organise some lunch.'

Rob and the boys came over on the two following Saturdays, spending a few hours each time working on building the new chook house and run. The Saturday after they'd finished it, they all went into town to buy some chicks. The tiny fluffy birds enchanted Kate.

After introducing the chicks to their new home, Jessica went inside to prepare lunch, leaving Kate chatting to the chicks and deciding on names.

Rob followed her in. 'So what's been happening, Jess?'

'Not much, Rob. Just working, gardening, busy with Kate. You know how it is.'

He nodded. 'Just wondered, Jess, if you'd like to come on a ...'

Kate interrupted by yelling, 'Rob, Ginger's laying an egg!'

Rob sighed and turned to her. 'Kate, sweetie, I don't think Ginger's old enough to lay an egg. You'll have to wait a few more weeks for that.'

Sensing what Rob had been about to say, Jessica quickly turned the conversation to the topic of the recent bad weather and didn't give Rob a chance to finish his sentence.

***

When Kate started primary school, Jessica drove her to the school on the days she worked, otherwise she drove her to the bus stop—the same bus stop she'd used when she'd been at school. The experience was, however, very different for Kate than it had been for Jessica. Kate was such a lively, happy and bubbly little girl, everyone seemed to love her, and at the bus stop other children quickly surrounded her, all laughing and talking to her. Usually other mothers or fathers dropped their children at the stop as well. On the second day, one of the mothers came over to Jessica.

'You're Kate's mother,' she said. 'I'm Angela's mum.' She smiled. 'Jenny.' She raised her eyebrows at Jessica.

'Jessica Broughton.'

Jenny patted her stomach and grinned. 'Another one on the way. Thank goodness I'm over the morning sickness. It's horrible isn't it?'

'Um, yes.' Jessica didn't know what to say.

'I hope I won't have such a hard time with this one. How about you? With Kate?'

'Not too bad.' Jessica's heart thumped.

'Did you have an epidural?'

'No.' Jessica looked round for an escape as another woman with a young baby joined them. 'I'd better go,' she managed to say. 'Got someone coming this morning.' She rushed over to her van, leaving Jenny staring after her.

Jessica decided to avoid the other mothers in future. She couldn't chance being questioned about the merits of breastfeeding or her experience of childbirth.

Sometimes she saw Rob at the bus stop, dropping off his boys on his way to work. A few days before Kate's sixth birthday, she saw him and had time to invite him and the boys over for her party. She didn't notice the significant glances exchanged by the other parents.

Rob always seemed to introduce nice things to Kate when they came for her birthdays, and this one was no exception. After the celebrations, Kate took Thomas out to see the chooks. Andrew went out on the veranda with a book to read.

Rob stretched back in his chair and regarded her. 'Jess, did you ever think of getting a dog?'

'A dog! Well, I think we have enough with the chooks, and what would it do all day when I'm at work?'

'I just think it would be good. A dog would be some kind of protection for you.'

'Protection? I don't need protecting, Rob.'

'Well, you never know,' he said. 'A dog would warn you about snakes and prowlers.'

'Prowlers! What on earth do you mean?'

'Well, you never know. Sometimes people just take a chance and, well, you're a woman on your own. I worry about you.'

'That's sweet of you, Rob.' She smiled at him as she picked up the chopping board and tossed the tomatoes into a salad bowl. 'I'll think about it.'

'We could go to the pound next weekend, and I could help you pick out a nice dog.'

Jessica saw he was serious. 'It's nice of you to care about us, but ...'

He straightened, stood up and came towards her. 'I do care about you, Jess, in fact—'

But at that moment, Kate rushed in shouting, 'Ginger's escaped!'

Rob sighed and took her hand. 'Well, we'd better go and find her and put her back in the run before a fox gets her.'

They disappeared out the door.

Jessica watched them, then shook her head and went back to preparing the lunch. Perhaps Rob was right, a dog would make her feel more secure.

The following Saturday Rob's ute appeared in the driveway.

Kate stomped over to him. 'Look at my new boots, Rob!' she shouted, pointing to her new red gumboots.

'Lovely, Kate. Where's Mum?'

'She's here. Mum!' Kate shouted as Jessica appeared. 'Rob's here.'

Jessica smiled. 'Yes, I can see that.'

'Come to take you to the pound,' he said. 'Look in the back of the ute.'

He lifted Kate up.

'Looks like a dog kennel,' Jessica said. 'For us? But I'm not ready to get a dog.' She frowned. 'Really, Rob. This is too much.' She felt a bit annoyed and it sounded in her tone.

'A doggie!' Kate grinned with excitement. 'Yes, Mummy, please!'

Jessica sighed. 'Okay, two against one. I'll get changed.'

'Better take your van,' Rob said. 'There's room for three in the front seat.'

An hour later, they arrived at the pound to be greeted by the sound of yelping and barking dogs.

Rob picked up Kate. 'Now. We're just going to look at the dogs,' he told her. 'We won't say or do anything until the person who looks after the dogs tells us which one will be yours.'

Wide-eyed, Kate stayed quiet as they went along the rows of cages housing the dogs. Jessica followed silently behind.

Suddenly Kate whispered in Rob's ear. 'That one, Rob.' She pointed to a kelpie.

Rob smiled. The dog looked like Kelly, his kelpie. He nodded and said to the attendant, 'What about that one?'

'I'll get her out. Just a moment.' He opened the cage and clipped a lead onto the dog's collar. 'Nice young dog,' he said. 'Her owner, old guy, passed away and had no one to look after her.' He led the dog outside. 'Come and see how she reacts to you. She hasn't taken to anyone so far. Another few days and if no-one takes her, well, she'll ...'

The dog reluctantly followed the attendant out onto the grass. Rob put Kate down beside it. She held out her hand, and the dog immediately turned to her and licked her face.

'Ooh,' Kate said, 'she's giving me kisses.' She put her arms around the dog and hugged it.

Rob looked at Jessica. Her eyes were full of unshed tears. 'What's her name?' he asked the attendant.

'Lucky.'

Half an hour later, Rob, Jessica, Kate and Lucky were all in the van heading back to The Shack.

'We'd better stop and get dog food,' Jessica said. 'I've never had a dog before; I know nothing about them.'

Rob laughed. 'I'll give you a few instructions.'

Lucky was supposed to be an 'outside dog', but that only lasted a few hours. She and Kate became inseparable, and Lucky ended up sleeping on Kate's bed.

'A bad habit,' Jessica said to Rob a week later when he called round, ostensibly to check on Lucky.

He bent to pat the dog. 'Lucky will be great company for her.' Then he came round the kitchen bench where Jessica was chopping up basil to make pesto. 'Jess,' he said.

Her heart started to thump. 'Mmmh?' She lifted her head to look at him.

He raised a hand and touched her cheek. 'Jess, you must know how I feel about you, and I think you feel the same.'

She looked down, her heart racing, sensing what was coming and not knowing how to change the subject.

He put his arms around her and kissed her.

She couldn't resist and sank into his embrace. Then she suddenly broke away. 'Rob,' she said, her voice husky. 'I'm not in a position to start a relationship.' She sighed.

His hands fell to his sides. 'Why?'

'I can't explain. I'm fond of you, Rob. Your friendship means a lot to me, but I can't take it further than that.' She turned back to the chopping board.

'Sorry I spoke,' he said abruptly.

'Rob. It's not you, it's me!'

'Oh, that old chestnut,' he said bitterly. 'Of course, I'm just the handyman. I'll go and get Kate.' He turned on his heel and went out the door.

'Rob!' She called after him. 'There's a lot about me you don't know, and I can't explain.' But he was gone. *Now I've upset him*, she thought miserably, and the worst of it was that she actually wanted him, wanted to sleep with him, wanted him in her life.

Rob and Kate came back in, Kate chattering away. But Rob remained cool and soon left.

CHAPTER 12

On the few occasions when Jessica saw Rob at the school bus stop, she'd say hello, he'd nod and make a non-committal reply. He'd stopped ringing her for a chat or to check up on her, and when she'd rung to invite him and the boys to Kate's seventh birthday party, he'd made an excuse. Instead of a birthday party at home, Jessica took Kate to the cinema and for a birthday treat meal. When Kate had asked if Rob and the boys could come too, Jessica said they were busy. But she missed seeing Rob and chatting to him.

Now the fire season had started and the gutters needed cleaning, so one morning at the school bus, she asked him if he'd come and clean the gutters and bring some firewood ready for the next winter.

'No problem, Jess,' he replied. 'When?'

'The weekend? Saturday?'

'Okay. See you then, about nine.' He turned away, jumped into his ute and drove off.

Sadly, she watched him go.

When Saturday came, Jessica felt a bit anxious about meeting up again. He'd seemed so cool. It broke her heart. She desperately wanted to pull him into her arms and feel his mouth on hers. Perversely, she put on make-up and did her hair.

Lucky's barking announced his arrival—right on time. Thomas jumped out of the ute followed by Rob.

'Hi, Rob, Thomas,' she greeted them. 'Where's Andrew?'

'He's big now, wanted to stay home.' Business like, Rob took his ladder off the ute.

'Hello, Mrs Broughton,' Thomas said. 'Where's Kate?'

'She's inside; go in and see her.'

'Thomas, you're here to help me,' Rob said, starting on the gutters.

Thomas followed his father, but just then, Kate ran out. 'Hello, Thomas. Hello, Rob. Can I help you?'

Rob smiled at her. 'Hello, sweetie, of course you can. You can hold the bucket for me.'

Jessica left them to it.

At half-past ten, she went outside and called them in for smoko. 'I've made scones. Come inside.'

'We have our lunch,' Rob said.

But Thomas said, 'Yummy, come on, Dad. We can't miss this.'

They washed their hands at one of the rainwater tanks, then came over to the veranda. Rob and Thomas kicked off their boots. Kate copied them.

'So how's it been, Jessica?' Rob asked as he sat at the table.

'Okay. Just busy with work and day to day stuff here. Come on now, all of you, help yourselves to jam and cream.'

Kate took a scone, then stared at Rob. 'Mum, is Rob my Daddy?'

Jessica's heart seemed to stop. She bit her lip and looked at Rob for help.

He turned to Kate. 'Why do you ask, sweetie?'

'Cos my teacher said everyone has a mummy and a daddy, and Mary O'Keefe said she didn't have a daddy but had two mummies instead. Then I said I didn't have a daddy and only one mummy. Then one of the girls in my class said her mother said my daddy was Rob Sullivan.'

Rob stared hard at Jessica as he said, 'Well, no, I'm not, but actually, I'd really like to be your daddy and have a gorgeous little girl like you.'

Jessica choked. 'Sorry,' she gasped as Rob got up and thumped her on the back. 'Scone went the wrong way.'

'Not the only thing, apparently,' he replied.

Luckily, Thomas wasn't listening, too interested in helping himself to extra jam and cream.

Kate put a dollop of cream on her scone while she thought about it.

'Now Kate, tell me how your chooks are going. Do you get a lot of eggs?' Rob asked.

In her eagerness to tell him all about her hens, Kate forgot about her parentage.

When they'd finished eating, Kate took Thomas's hand and took him to see her chooks.

When Kate and Thomas had disappeared out the door, Rob turned to Jessica. 'You might have a bit of explaining to do there, Jess.' He gave a wry grin, then continued, 'um, Jess, I was wondering if you had any books on computers I could borrow. Andrew is really getting into this computing stuff, and I'm out of my depth ... um, well, I need to understand what he's talking about. He gets a bit impatient with me when I have no idea what he's on about.'

Jessica smiled. 'Of course. Delighted! Come into the study.'

'I'll finish the gutters and stack the firewood first. Thanks, Jess.'

She went into the study and began to look for suitable books. She loved this study. It'd been her father's, and she'd had her own little desk here where she used to study when her father home schooled her. She looked up at the portrait of him beside her mother's. The one of her when she'd been nearly five hung next to it. She'd taken them to Hornsby, then brought them back and replaced them in the study when she'd moved to The Shack.

She heard Rob at the front door. 'Come in, Rob. I'm in the study.'

He came and stood in the doorway, looking around the room. 'Lot of books.'

'Yes.' She couldn't remember him being in there before. 'Mostly reference and non-fiction. My father wasn't into fiction.' She smiled, remembering her father sitting at his desk, reading.

Rob looked at the portraits on the wall. 'That you?' he asked.

'No, that's my mother. It was a self-portrait.'

'You look very like her,' he said, turning to Jessica.

'My mother was very beautiful. That's me, there, when I was nearly five.'

Rob peered at it. 'Roughly the same age as Kate is now. She doesn't look a bit like you, Jess.' He paused. 'Must look like her father?'

Kate didn't reply, then pointed to the other portrait. 'That's *my* father.'

Rob nodded. 'Nice looking man.'

'Anyway,' Jessica said, 'I've found a few books that might help you.'

'Thanks.'

'And Rob,'

'Hmm?'

'I'm happy to help you, answer any questions, or explain anything to you.'

'Thanks, Jess. Appreciate it.' He picked up the books she'd put on the desk for him.

'Rob, bring the boys round sometime, would you?'

He just nodded, avoiding her eyes. 'Okay. See you.' He walked out of the room and left soon after.

***

When he returned the books a few weeks later, Kate ran out as he was about to leave. 'Rob! Can I talk to you?'

'Of course, sweetie.' He got back out of the ute.

'Come over to the chook house; I don't want Mum to see us.'

Mystified, Rob followed her.

'Rob, do you know who my father is?'

Rob thought hard before he said carefully, 'well, I always had the idea your father was the man your mum used to be married to. You do know your mum used to be married?' *Shit! He probably shouldn't have said that.*

'No. I didn't know.' Kate frowned. 'Mum never talks about anything like that. Was he a nice man? What did he look like?'

'Um, I never met him, but I'm sure that he must have been very nice and very good looking,' was all Rob could think to say.

She nodded gravely. 'Thank you, Rob. I just wanted to know. I've asked Mum, and she just says she'll explain later, when I'm older.'

'Well, then, that's the best thing to do. Just wait until you're older.' He looked at her. 'But I think he must have had dark curly hair and brown eyes, just like yours.'

Blast, Jessica. She should explain things to this worried little girl. In some ways Kate seemed more mature than most eight-year olds.

She smiled wistfully. 'I wish you were my daddy; I wish Mum would marry you.'

He sighed. 'Yes, I'd like that, too. But listen, Kate. You can pretend I'm your adopted daddy. We can keep it a secret between us.'

'Adopted daddy, like we adopted Lucky?'

Rob had a sudden vision of a row of cages containing eager men, all saying, 'Pick me; pick me' when a nice woman came past. He smiled at the thought, then bent down and took Kate's hand, 'and if you're ever worried about anything that you can't talk to Mum about, then ring me. Okay?' He gave her a hug.

Her eyes lit up with excitement. 'Can we have a secret signal?'

He laughed. 'Of course; what will it be?' He was delighted to see her smiling again.

She thought hard for a bit, then said, 'When I see you, I'll cough and scratch the side of my nose.'

'Which side?' he said gravely.

'Um ...' She looked at her hands. 'Which one is right?'

'Which one do you write with?'

She held up her right hand.

'Okay, that's your right hand, so put the other hand over your mouth and cough, and scratch the side of your nose with your right hand. Like this.' He demonstrated. 'You do it now.'

After a couple of attempts, she got it right.

'Thanks, Rob.' She skipped back to the house.

With a sigh Rob returned to his ute.

CHAPTER 13

A few days before her fortieth birthday, Jessica studied herself in the mirror. She had no-one with whom to celebrate the occasion. Well, except Kate, of course, but an eleven-year-old wasn't the same as close friends. She'd have liked to invite Rob, but that might start up the relationship issue again. That's if he'd even accept. She held her hands out in front of her. The twitching in her fingers and toes had started months ago and she could see a kind of nervous tic on one side of her face. She tried to remember when her mother had first shown signs of Huntington's. Was it when she, Jessica, had just started secondary school? Around that time, anyway. From what she'd read, the symptoms and the onset varied widely. Perhaps it would be just the twitching for a long time before the serious symptoms showed up. Well, she'd treat herself to a new hairdo, perhaps a completely different look, take her mind off things. The next day was a free day for her, so she made a hairdressing appointment. She'd get her hair done, then pick up Kate, and they could go for a meal. She'd get a bottle of champagne to drink that evening.

'Won't be long,' Mandy, the woman who usually trimmed Jessica's hair said the next afternoon. 'Here're some magazines to look at. Maybe fifteen minutes?'

Jessica nodded and picked up one of the dog-eared magazines. The headline on the front cover caught her attention.

Somebody Stole My Baby! the headline blazed above a picture of a woman. Frowning, Jessica turned to the page noted on the cover. It showed another picture of the woman, then her story.

'*Ten years ago, it happened*,' Melanie Barker*, told our reporter. (**not her real name.*)

'*I was living with a few other people, in the bush, kind of a commune. My partner was abusive, hit me around. He was on drugs. Well, a lot of the others were, too. Anyway, I got pregnant. He hit me, saying I was stupid to get pregnant. No one helped me. Except for one woman. When my time came, she helped me. It was a little girl. She was beautiful. I called her Celine, you know, after the singer. Well, when she was about two weeks old, my partner got really violent, said he didn't believe Celine was his baby and he'd get rid of her. This woman who'd helped me said I should leave. But I had nowhere to go. Anyway, the woman found a kind of carry all baby bed thing. I couldn't feed the baby; I was sick after she was born. But this woman had given me a baby bottle and told me I had to get away from the camp. She helped me.*

The following night, I waited for him to fall asleep, then I went through his pockets and took all the money he had from drug dealing and I left. I walked for hours, carrying the baby. I was exhausted. When I got to the main road, I got a lift from a truck. The driver was so kind. He couldn't believe I had a baby with me. I told him my story and he gave me food and asked where I was heading. I said I didn't know. He was going to Newcastle, so I said that was fine. He left me by the railway station.

I didn't know what to do. I went into the café there and got hot water for the baby's bottle and fed her. I came out and a train had just arrived. It was an XPT, an express, so I got in. I didn't know where it was going. I was tired and fell asleep. Then I woke up when I heard the ticket inspector coming, and an announcement that the train was stopping. I didn't have a ticket and I panicked. So I went the other way from him. I thought I'd get out the end of the train when it stopped and run to the front and get back on. But the baby carrier was a problem. There was a woman sitting on her own in the last carriage. I asked her if she'd mind the baby while I went to the toilet. She said okay. Then the train stopped and I got out. But it was one of those short platform stations, so when I got out, there was no platform and I fell and hurt myself. By the time I scrambled up, the train had gone. I was stunned and found out later that I'd broken my ankle.'

Jessica's heart seemed to stop, then started to thud. She felt sick, but read on:

'I crawled to the station, but it was one of those unattended ones. I lay on a bench all night and in the morning, someone found me and called an ambulance. But I never ever found my baby! I tried all sorts of things, went to the police station, but they said there was nothing they could do; no one had reported finding a baby. I don't think they believed me.

I told the police where I'd lived with the group, and they went there to check, but they told me that everyone in the group denied knowing me. I think they were scared to say anything to the police because of the drugs ...'

The article continued, saying Melanie had since found happiness with a new man and had two more children, but the memory of her first baby haunts her still ...

'I just want to know she's all right, and to see her,' she told our reporter. 'She'd be ten years old now ...'

Jessica started to shake. She looked around. No one was looking. Quickly she stuffed the magazine in her bag and stood up.

'I'm not feeling well,' she called to Mandy above the noise of the hairdryer.

Mandy looked round. 'Goodness, you're so pale!' She turned off the dryer. 'Would you like a glass of water?'

Jessica shook her head. 'No, it's all right, thanks. I'll just go home. I'll ring and make another appointment.'

'Okay, Jess,' Mandy watched her leave and then turned on the hairdryer. 'Lot of 'flu around at the moment,' she said to her client as Jessica staggered out onto the street.

***

Rob Sullivan drove into town. He had shopping to do before he went to the secondary school to pick up Thomas. He parked his ute, jumped out, and then saw Jessica's van. He grimaced. He hoped he wouldn't bump into her. If he saw her, he'd cross the road and pretend not to have noticed her. He still felt awkward about having declared himself. It had taken a lot of courage for him to ask her for books on computing. She'd been so nice then that he'd been close to bringing up the subject again, but remembering her previous rebuff, he'd decided not to chance it.

He started walking towards the shops and then saw her coming out of the hairdressers. He was about to turn around and go in a different direction when he paused. Something was wrong. Jessica had stopped, then started walking again, but it was more of a stagger. He frowned. He walked over to her, but she didn't even see him. 'Jessica! What's wrong?'

She looked up, and her eyes came into focus. 'Nothing,' she mumbled and tried to walk on past him.

'Jessica,' he said gently, taking her arm, 'you don't look well; you're as white as a sheet. I'll help you back to your van.' She was shaking so much that she could hardly stand. He put an arm around her. 'Come and sit down; look here's a bench. Tell me what's wrong.'

She looked at him, seemingly unable to form any words. 'I, I ...' she stuttered.

Rob sat with his arms around her until she calmed down. 'Whatever has happened?' he asked.

She just shook her head and started to cry in great choking sobs.

'Come, Jessica, people are looking at you. Let's sit in your van and you tell me what's wrong.' He guided her to the van. 'Where are the keys? In your bag?'

She nodded.

'Okay if I get them out?' Feeling uneasy, he kept his eyes on her as he bent to take her bag.

'I, I ...' She fumbled with the bag, trying to clutch it to her.

A magazine fell out onto the pavement. Rob bent to pick it up, but Jessica lunged to grab it. Surprised, something made him hold it up in the air, where she couldn't reach it. Then he saw the headline caption.

'Give it to me,' she screamed.

'Jessica,' he said, stuffing the magazine inside his jacket, 'people are staring at us. Get in the van. I'll give it to you then.' He took her arm.

She looked up. A couple of people were looking at them with interest.

He found the keys in her bag and unlocked the passenger door. 'Get in. Come on. Get in the passenger seat. I'll drive us somewhere more private.'

Momentarily silenced by the thought of people watching her, she did as he asked. Rob got in and started the engine. 'I'll drive to a place I know.' When he'd parked in a quiet street overlooking a reserve, he turned to her. 'Now. Tell me.'

She shook her head.

'It's something in this magazine, isn't it?' Rob said. 'Who's the woman on the front page? She looks familiar.'

'Just give it to me, Rob. I'm all right now.' But then she gave another shuddering sob.

He pulled out a handkerchief, glanced at it to make sure it was clean, then gave it to her. While she blew her nose, he flipped through the magazine. When it fell open at the page with the picture of the woman on it, he wound down the window and held the magazine out, away from Jessica's reach and read it. 'Why are you so upset about this article, Jess?'

She said nothing.

He frowned. 'Do you know this woman?'

She shook her head.

He thought back to when he'd first met Jessica. Now he considered it, she had acted a bit strangely with Kate, almost as if she didn't know quite what to do with a baby. His frown deepened. 'Is that baby your Kate?'

Dumbly, she nodded.

His mind whirled. *Jess, oh, Jess, what have you done?* 'You'd better tell me everything.'

She shook her head again.

He put an arm around her shoulder. 'Jess, my darling. Whatever you've done, we can work something out. Please tell me.' Gently he kissed the top of her head. 'Is this why you never wanted any kind of relationship with me?'

She nodded, 'and other stuff. Rob, promise you won't tell anyone? Not Kate, not anyone.'

Reluctantly he nodded. 'Okay.'

'Promise?'

'Yeah. I promise not to tell anyone.' He took a bottle of water from the door of the van and opened it. 'Drink some.'

Despite her shaking hands, she managed a few sips.

He put the bottle back, then took both her hands in his. 'Now. Tell me everything.'

Jessica told him, only pausing to blow her nose or hiccough.

Rob stared out the window at the gum trees in the park, listening carefully. 'I've never heard of this Huntington's Disease.' He interrupted her at one point.

'It used to be called St. Vitus Dance, because of all the jerkiness, like they were dancing.'

'Haven't heard of that either; go on ...'

When she'd finished, he remained silent for a while, then said, 'When will you tell Kate?'

'I don't know. I just don't know,' she wailed.

'A while ago she asked me if I knew who her father was,' he said slowly.

Jessica's head jerked up. 'What did you say?'

'I told her I'd always assumed your ex-husband was her father. I didn't tell her that I could never understand why he didn't visit her or contact her. I told her that he must be very kind and good looking as she must take after him. She doesn't get those brown eyes and dark, curly hair from you, Jessica. In fact, she looks nothing like you.' He turned to the magazine article. 'Actually, it seems she resembles her birth mother.'

'Rob, what shall I do?'

'You have to tell her the truth. You can't just wait for her to find out. That would be cruel.'

'Oh, Rob! How can I? Not yet, anyway. I thought it would be best to wait until she's older and would understand.'

He compressed his lips. 'The truth is often simpler in the end.'

Jessica heaved a sigh. 'What a mess I've made of my life.'

He took one of her hands. 'You did the best you could, Jess. Now, if you're all right to drive, I think you should go home. I'll pick up Kate from school and take her back to my place. Then, when you're more composed, come round and have something to eat with us and then take Kate back with you.'

'Thank you, Rob.' She reached up and kissed him. 'I feel calmer now. But I don't want Kate to see me like this.'

He got out of the car. 'Right, come on, then. Get in.' He held the driver's door for her and put the magazine back in her bag.

***

Kate was surprised to see Rob waiting for her outside the primary school. 'Hi Rob, where's Mum?'

'She was delayed. Asked me if I could pick you up,' he replied. 'Come on, jump in. I've got to pick up Thomas. He'll be waiting for me.'

Kate got in and remained silent while Rob drove around to the secondary school Thomas attended.

He blinked when he saw Kate in the ute. 'Hi, Kate! What's happened?'

'Nothing,' his father said. 'Jessica's been delayed, so she asked me to pick up Kate.'

'Shove over, Kate,' Thomas said, looking a little embarrassed at being so close to her. They hadn't seen each other for ages.

Thomas was Kate's favourite of the two boys. Andrew had always seemed a bit distant. 'I can't, there's no room.'

Rob took a quick glance at them. 'Thomas, put your arm around Kate and fasten the seat belt around both of you.'

'That's illegal, Dad.'

'I know.' He sighed, 'but we don't have anywhere else for one of you to sit.'

'What if you get stopped by the cops?' Thomas persisted.

Rob grimaced, then Kate piped up, 'We can say we're Siamese twins, joined at the hip.' She giggled.

By the time she and Thomas had stopped laughing, they'd reached 'Sullivan. Please close the gate'.

Jessica arrived two hours later. She looked pale, but composed. But when she saw Rob, her eyes filled with tears.

He put his arms around her. 'Kate's fine,' he whispered as Kate came rushing up.

'Mum, Rob picked me up at school,' she exclaimed. 'It's been ages since we were here. Come and listen to Thomas! He's got a guitar and he's *so* good!' She dragged her mother over to where Thomas sat in a corner, guitar under his arm.

'Hello, Mrs Broughton,' he said with a shy grin.

'I do wish you'd call me Jessica,' she said, taking a deep breath to steady herself. 'Okay, play something ...'

Thomas strummed a few bars, then stopped. 'I'm just learning.'

'Where's Andrew?' Jessica looked around.

'Oh, he's at uni, living in Brisbane now,' Thomas said.

Jessica's eyes widened. She'd missed so much of the boys' progress. She turned to Rob. 'What's he studying?'

'Computer Science. Thanks to you, mainly. You got him interested. Now come on guys, dinner's ready.' He turned to Jessica. 'Very simple, I'm afraid, vegetables from the garden and eggs from the chooks. I didn't have time to go shopping ...' He gave a rueful grin.

'Vegetable frittata, lovely!' She attempted to smile.

'Mum, can I get a guitar?' Kate asked Jessica. 'I'd love one! Thomas said he'll teach me.'

'We'll see ...'

***

Jessica enjoyed being at the table with Rob and the children. She tried to eat, but the thought of Kate's birth mother kept intruding. Her stomach churned every time she thought of the woman. How could she have believed it was OK to keep the baby? She'd convinced herself that Kate had been abandoned. Had she been so wrong to keep her? Rob brought her attention back by asking her if the food was all right, his face filled with concern.

'Lovely, thank you.' She gave a wobbly smile.

When they'd finished eating, Jessica stood up. 'Can I help clear up, Rob?'

'Not at all; sit down. I'll make coffee.'

'I'd better go; Kate will have homework.'

'Aw, Mum, no! Can't we stay longer? Thomas is going to teach me some chords.'

Jessica glanced at Rob. 'Perhaps you and Thomas can come over at the weekend? Thomas can bring his guitar.'

Kate jumped up and down. 'Yes, yes; please say yes, Rob!'

Rob smiled at Thomas, who had a broad grin on his face. 'All right. Sunday?'

'Yes, come for lunch.' Jessica looked around for her handbag. 'Come on, Kate, it's getting late. You have school tomorrow and I have work.'

Rob walked with them to the van. 'Try not to worry,' he said quietly to Jessica, then gave her a hug and a quick kiss.

Jessica felt herself sinking into his embrace. 'Thank you,' she whispered.

It was the turning point in her relationship with Rob.

A few months later, Kate rang Thomas to invite him to her twelfth birthday party.

'Mum's buying me a guitar,' she told him. 'I'm so excited! I was hoping some of my school friends would come, but it's too far out for their parents to drive, and they'd have to hang around here and there's nothing for them to do here except talk to mum.'

Jessica suspected most people considered her a bit stuck up and aloof, but luckily Kate was happy to just have Thomas and Rob celebrate her birthday.

On the day, Rob and Jessica sat watching the two budding guitarists. Thomas trying to teach Kate, and Kate desperately trying to follow his instructions.

'How are you, Jess?' Rob asked quietly.

She knew he meant after the magazine article. 'Fine. And you, Rob?'

He nodded. He never mentioned the subject again.

CHAPTER 14

The Shack needed repainting. Rob had bought the paint and was now washing and sanding the weatherboards. It was one of Jessica's free days and Kate was at school. Jessica had just turned on the washing machine when she heard the sound of a car stopping outside and Lucky barking and carrying on.

She walked out and stood on the veranda. She didn't recognize the car, but the driver's door opened, and a familiar figure got out and came towards her.

Alarmed, Jessica's heart flipped. She could only think one thing: *Thank God Kate is at school.*

'Jess!' Jason said. 'I didn't expect to see you here! I've been trying to find you. You're not in the phone book ...'

'What are you doing here, Jason?' She made her tone frigid, and took a deep breath to try and still her thumping heart. He'd put on weight and his face seemed puffy.

He grimaced. 'Um, I'm on long service leave. Was driving around the area and thought I'd drive by and see what The Shack looked like now.'

'Well, you've seen it, so please leave. Now.'

'Jess.' Jason put out a hand. 'I've always loved you, Jess.'

'Please leave.'

Lucky started to growl.

'Jess, Amy's left me ...' He swallowed. 'Taken our son ...' His eyes filled with tears.

Rob came round the side of the house. 'I thought I heard voices, and Lucky barking.' Seeing Jessica's stricken expression, he put an arm around her shoulders. 'What's happening, Jess?'

'Can we have a word in private, Jess?' Jason asked.

'No. Please leave; I don't want you here.'

Jason looked at her and then at Rob. His shoulders slumped. 'Your new man?'

'You heard her. Now go!' Rob said in a cold voice.

Jason glanced at Rob's clenched fists, then looked up at him. 'I just want a word with Jessica.'

Rob released Jessica and took a step forward. 'Go, before I throw you out,' he threatened. 'You're trespassing.'

Jason looked at Jessica. 'Please, Jess?'

She lifted her chin. 'I never want to see you again, Jason. If you come here again, I'll call the police.'

His posture drooped, and he turned and walked slowly back to his car.

Rob put his arms around Jessica. She felt drained. 'You okay, Jess?' He kissed the top of her head.

'That was my ex-husband,' she said, watching the car reversing down the driveway.

'I guessed as much. Stupid idiot,' Rob said. 'He was mad to let you go. Believe me, I'll never let you go.'

Jessica kissed him. 'Thank you, Rob.' She put her arms around him and rested her head on his chest. 'I love you, Rob.'

'Careful!' I've got paint on my hands!' He looked down at her. 'Go inside. I'll wash and make you a cup of tea.'

***

As time went by, Jessica managed to put the whole magazine article out of her mind. She had other things to concern her. One worry was that the twitching in her fingers and toes grew worse. She tried hard to control it, but without success. Her jerky movements, slurred speech and fatigue had become too noticeable.

'Mum, that's twice you've knocked over your water,' Kate said at dinner one night, 'and your head keeps kind of rattling. Do you need to get an eye test? You might need glasses ...'

'Good idea,' Jessica responded. 'Now, I'd better check your homework.'

Kate scowled. 'I haven't finished it.'

Kate had never been a scholar. Jessica spent hours trying to explain algebra and geometry; somehow, it didn't make any sense to Kate.

'I just don't like maths! I'm not like you. And I'm not like my grandmother either. I'm no good at art, or languages. I want to leave school as soon as I can.'

Jessica despaired. 'We'll see what we can do,' she said. 'But you must complete year ten; whatever career you choose, you'll need to be able to do arithmetic and write and spell.'

'I can just use my phone to do calculations. It's the twenty-first century, Mum.' She sounded scornful. 'It's 2014, you know. Get with the program, Mum.'

Jessica opened her mouth to say, 'don't be cheeky, Kate', then thought better of it. She'd bought Kate a simple mobile phone when she started secondary school. Mainly in case of emergencies. Instead she replied. 'Clear the table, and we'll look at your homework together.'

Kate scowled and started to doodle on her workbook. 'Sorry, Mum. Look, I'll do your hair to make up for being rude.'

Jessica smiled. 'All right, but no colouring, okay?'

'Aw, Mum, a few highlights would be amazing!'

The colour of Jessica's chestnut hair had begun fade but she still wore it in the same style, long and wavy.

'And you should get it cut, Mum. You'd look years younger.'

'Possibly. Now, how about I test you on those French verbs.'

Kate ran her fingers through her short curls and simply groaned. 'What shall we do for my fifteenth birthday?' she asked, trying to distract her mother from the verbs.

***

On the day of her birthday, Rob, Thomas, Jessica and Kate sat around the table eating Kate's favourite lunch that Jessica had prepared. Kate had shown them her new guitar and an ice-cream cake waited in the freezer.

'Happy Birthday, Kate!' Rob, Thomas and Jessica all sang to her.

Kate grinned with pleasure. She'd developed into a pretty, curvaceous girl. Thomas regarded her with admiration.

'Now!' She clapped her hands. 'I've got an announcement to make.'

Jessica's head jerked up; her stomach flipped.

'I've decided I'm going to leave school at the end of year ten!'

'You can't do that! You have to stay until you're at least seventeen,' Jessica managed to say.

'Yes, I can; I've researched it. If I can get an apprenticeship, I can leave at the end of year ten.'

'An apprenticeship?' Jessica had visions of Kate underneath a car, holding a spanner in one hand and an oily rag in the other. She glared at Thomas. He'd probably influenced her.

'Yes. You know your hairdresser, Mum, Mandy at Snippits?'

Jessica frowned, then nodded.

'Well, I went to see her yesterday. She said she'd take me on as an apprentice when I'm sixteen. In the meantime, I can work in her salon over the holidays and Saturday mornings!' She gave a triumphant grin.

Jessica just stared at her.

'Well done, Kate!' Rob got up from the table and gave her a hug. 'That's the spirit; I'm really impressed.'

Kate beamed at him. 'Thanks, Rob.' She scowled at her mother. 'At least someone thinks it's a good idea.'

'I think it's awesome!' Thomas said, blinking, and half getting up from his seat. He seemed to be wondering if he could take a chance and give Kate a hug too. After glancing at Jessica's face, he hurriedly sat back down.

Jessica thought quickly. Probably after a year of Saturdays in the salon, sweeping up hair and making cups of coffee, Kate would have tired of the notion and be ready to carry on at school. She turned to Kate. 'Well done, darling! That's very enterprising of you.' She tried to sound as if she meant it, then leaned over and kissed Kate's cheek.

'All the money I earn, I'll save towards getting a car. I'll need one. I don't expect you to drive me into town and back all the time, Mum.'

Well that's a good incentive for her to start saving, Jessica thought.

'I have to work Saturday mornings,' Thomas said. 'I can drive you into town.' He'd started an apprenticeship as a mechanic and had bought a battered old panel van. He spent all his free time tinkering with it.

Kate smiled at him. 'Perfect!' She clapped her hands. 'All organised then.'

'I think we need to celebrate all this good news.' Jessica stood up unsteadily. 'How about ice-cream cake?'

Jessica hadn't seen Kate look so happy for ages. Lately she'd been so moody. She'd put it down to teenage hormones.

After their meal, Kate said, 'shall I wash up, Mum?'

'No, thank you, darling; it's your birthday. I'll do it later.'

Kate smiled at her mother. 'Okay, so ...' She turned to Thomas. 'Come out on the veranda and we can practice.'

Jessica watched them walk out. She thought she heard Thomas mention something about starting a band. That would be another concern, if it happened.

Rob had heard it, too. 'Don't worry, Jess, I don't think there's any chance of them making a hit record.' He grinned, then took her hand. 'You know how I feel about you, Jess. I want to make our relationship open and permanent, not this clandestine love making.'

'Oh, Rob,' she sighed, 'please. You know it's impossible. I don't want to be a burden on you.' She kept her voice low, glancing anxiously at the screen door. Think of the logistics.'

'Logistics!' He snorted. 'What do you mean, logistics?'

She took a deep breath. 'How would it work? You come and live here? There's no spare room for Thomas, or Andrew. And the same at your place. There's no spare room for Kate. And I don't think Kelly would like Lucky around.'

He fell silent for a moment. 'I suppose we could both sell up and buy something together. Oh, Jess, I want to come home to you. I

want to fall asleep with you in my arms. I want to wake up to you.'
He rubbed his eyes.

'Rob. It's impossible. The Huntington's already started. I feel so
tired all the time, and my toes are twitching, and I can't seem to
concentrate anymore. And I know my speech is slurred sometimes. I can hear it myself.'

Rob leaned over and kissed her. 'Oh, Jess, I'd be able to look
after you,' he murmured.

The screen door suddenly slammed. 'Oh, sorry, didn't mean to
interrupt or anything.' Thomas smiled slyly as they jumped apart.
'Just getting some music from my case ...'

***

As the year passed, Jessica felt herself becoming more and more
confused. She found it difficult to concentrate, and the tic under
one eye became worse. While she deteriorated, Kate seemed
to bloom. Thomas drove her into town every Saturday morning
and dropped her off at Mandy's salon, then picked her up on
his way home. He'd wait outside until she'd finished. They were
inseparable, and Jessica worried about her when Thomas brought
her home late.

One Saturday when Rob was at The Shack repairing leaks, he
turned to her at lunch and said, 'Jessica, I know you're concerned
about Kate and Thomas.'

She looked up, startled.

'Don't worry too much. I've spoken to Thomas about sex and
birth control and told him that underage sex is illegal. He was a
bit embarrassed but just sighed and said patiently, 'Thanks, Dad.
I know all that".'

'I dread the day when Kate tells me she's going on the Pill.'
Jessica put her head in her hands.

Rob sighed. 'That's kids today. They think they know everything. I suppose we were the same when we were young.'

Jessica stared at him, realizing guiltily that she'd never been
interested in his past; or his ex-partner and how it had all ended.
She frowned. 'What happened to you, Rob? You must have had
Andrew when you were very young.'

He nodded and frowned. 'Yes. Too young.'

She looked at him enquiringly.

'Carly was very beautiful—blond hair, lovely figure. All my
mates were in love with her. I was elated when she agreed to go
out with me. I had a panel van like yours in those days.' He gave
a rueful grin. 'They were nicknamed Shagging Wagons back then.
Well, Carly got pregnant. Her mum wanted us to get married but
Carly didn't want to. I'd finished my apprenticeship as a carpenter
and had saved enough to buy a block of land. When Andrew was
born, we were living with her mother in town. I was working flat
out, trying to save enough to start building a house. I didn't know
at the time that Carly was leaving Andrew with her mum in the
evenings and going off out with her friends while I was spending
every spare moment out on the block, trying to build a house
for us. Then she got pregnant again.' His brow darkened. 'I've
sometimes wondered if Thomas is mine. I think she was playing
the field.'

Jessica took one of his hands, but said nothing, thinking about
Rob's sons. Andrew was the good looking one, the image of Rob.
Thomas was tall and ungainly—rasher thin, all knees and elbows,
hair like straw, fair skin, freckles and glasses. He looked nothing
like Rob. She squeezed his hand.

'Doesn't matter. I love him to bits. Like you with Kate,' he continued. Then he fell silent.

'Genetics doesn't have anything to do with love,' Jessica murmured.

Rob nodded. 'Well, I got the house to a liveable state, not like it is now, just basic, and we all moved in. I was working flat out, but Carly wanted more and more. She said she needed a car to get around, couldn't stay buried in the bush all day. I just couldn't afford a second car. So several times a week I dropped her and Andrew and Thomas off at her mother's place on my way to work, then picked them up on my way home.'

Jessica visualised Rob coming home with Carly and the two small boys and probably having to prepare their dinner. It didn't sound like Carly did a lot.

'Anyway, one afternoon after work I went round to collect her and found her gone. Her mother was all apologies. Apparently Carly just said she couldn't take it anymore. Her mother had asked her where she was going but Carly had just shrugged. She had a suitcase all packed, and then a station wagon stopped outside and she ran out and got in.'

'Well, Carly's mum couldn't look after the boys full time, and my parents had moved to Brisbane. I found a day nursery where I could leave them while I was at work, but I needed to be at work at 7 am, and the day nursery didn't open until eight. So I left my job and took on handyman work so I could organise my work around the day nursery hours.' He sat frowning, lost in thought. At last he looked up and smiled at Jessica. 'Then this gorgeous red head came into my life and knocked me for six! And broke my heart.' He leaned over and kissed her.

Jessica returned his kiss, then broke away from his embrace. 'You and Kate are the best things that ever happened in my life,' she said. He smiled and kissed her again.

The sound of a car horn announced the arrival of Thomas's van.

CHAPTER 15

Jessica spread a shirt over the ironing board and was about to start ironing when she heard Thomas's van pull up outside, a door slam and then the sound of the engine roaring off. Kate burst in the door. 'Mum! I'll be sixteen in a few months, then I'll be able to get my driving licence. Thomas said he'd teach me to drive. What do you think?'

Jessica looked at her beautiful daughter with her dark springy curls, tanned skin and lovely figure. Thomas was now twenty and in the last year of his apprenticeship in town. Jessica knew he was in love with Kate. It was obvious to everyone. Everyone, except Kate.

Kate frowned. 'Mum! Your hands are shaking so much, the iron is going all over the place! You'll scorch that shirt! Or burn yourself.' She ran over, took the iron from her mother's hand, turned off the switch and stood the iron up on end away from Jessica.

Jessica tried to smile. 'Just nerves, sweetie,' she said, 'probably at the thought of you driving ...'

'Aw, Mum! I'll be fine. Thomas has already shown me how to drive and let me have a go around their yard.' She looked anxiously at her mother. 'I haven't been able to save enough for a car yet.

Do you think you could lend me some money until I'm working full time at Mandy's?'

Jessica steadied herself against the ironing board. 'So you've definitely decided to leave school? Not thought about keeping going? Maybe learn chemistry, so you know what goes into the hair dye they use at the salon?' She tried to keep her voice casual.

'Chemistry! Come on, Mum, I don't understand it—those periodic tables or whatever they are and all the symbols. I know water is H_2O ...'

Jessica knew in her heart that Kate was never going to be an academic, but she was smart and cheerful and everyone loved her. Perhaps that was better than being clever and quiet and introverted like herself. No one could accuse Kate of being standoffish or up herself.

She smiled. 'Of course, darling. Maybe Thomas would keep an eye out for a nice little car.'

Kate beamed. 'He already is,' she exclaimed. 'Whoo, hoo!' She danced around the room, nearly tripping over the cord from the iron and soon after, Jessica heard her on the phone to Thomas. 'Mum said she'll lend me the money for a car! Tom, I'm getting wheels!'

'You have to pass your driving test first,' Jessica called out to her.

'I've got the form,' Kate replied.

At that moment, Jessica's feet started to jerk. Startled, she just made it to the couch and lay down.

'You okay, Mum?' Kate came out from her room. 'Tom's coming over after he's had his dinner. He's going to take me back to his place, so I can practice driving round the paddock. You look a bit pale. What's wrong with your feet? They're dancing up and down.'

'Nothing, Katie. Just wriggling my toes. Tired from standing at the ironing.'

'I could have done the ironing, Mum; why didn't you ask me?' She frowned and continued in a low voice, 'Do you think you're drinking too much, Mum?'

Jessica tried to smile. 'Um ... no, I don't think so. I only have one or two glasses of wine at night with my dinner.'

Kate gave her a hard look.

'Go and get ready for Thomas. I'm fine.' Jessica avoided meeting Kate's eyes.

Jessica was reluctant to get up from the couch in front of Kate; she was afraid her feet would still make that scary dancing movement. She breathed a sigh of relief when she heard Tom's van outside.

'Bye Mum!' Kate gave her mother a quick kiss and skipped out the door.

Jessica managed to get up and get a glass of wine. She sank back on the couch and took a sip. It seemed the moment she had been dreading had finally come. All these years she'd tried to push to the back of her mind the thought of becoming like her mother. It would be downhill from here. Tears of self-pity filled her eyes. She'd have to tell Kate before much longer. Then Kate would want to know if she had the Huntington gene, and then, and then... It was all too much. In one way she could understand her mother's decision to take her own life. But she, Jessica, hadn't been left alone at the time of her mother's suicide; she still had her father. But the situation was different now. Jessica took a gulp of wine. She was all Kate had. She couldn't do that to Kate. She remembered how she felt after Sybilla's funeral. She'd tried to understand but even now, after all these years she still felt the sense of loss that her own mother couldn't keep living for her child.

Jessica's mind went round in circles. In the not too distant future she'd need a permanent carer, then a nursing home. She hated the thought. Hated the idea of losing her independence, and where would that leave Kate? Kate must be her priority now. She'd try and talk to Rob about the situation; stop all this self-pity. She was lucky to have him. Dear Rob, why hadn't she told him everything years ago? She should have trusted him. She'd stuffed up her life. She'd have another glass of wine, then go and have a shower and try and pull herself together before Kate came home...

***

The Friday before Kate's sixteenth birthday, Thomas picked her up outside the school and brought her home. He'd been doing this for a while on the days that Jessica taught a night class.

Usually Thomas just dropped Kate home and then continued on to his place. He always had things to do at Sullivan's. He gave her a quick peck on the cheek goodbye. 'I'm looking forward to tomorrow night.' He smiled.

Kate smiled back. 'Me, too.'

Jessica had booked dinner in a restaurant in town to celebrate Kate's birthday for just Rob, Thomas, her and Kate. Andrew was away somewhere and Kate and her friends had organised an end-of-term party the following week for those students leaving after year ten.

Thomas drove off. Kate patted Lucky, walked inside and flung her school bag on the floor. Then, remembering, she returned to the bag, opened it and took out the Application for a Learner Driving Licence. She read the requirements for ID: something from List 1, and something from List 2.

Okay. A birth certificate for List 1—her mum would have that somewhere—but List 2 was more difficult. Ah, here was one she could use: 'Evidence of Enrolment at an Australian secondary school'. She read on to the next section: 'Witness to applicant's signature. Required when you cannot provide an acceptable proof of identity document that shows your signature.'

Curses. She'd have to get her mother to come to the motor registry with her. Anyway, she could get her birth certificate and hopefully find the form from when she'd started at secondary school. She knew her mother had an old tin box in the bottom of her wardrobe with those kinds of papers in it. She'd seen it when looking through her mother's clothes to see if there was anything decent she could wear. There hadn't been. She'd opened the box and seeing only the registration paper for the van and a few other papers that looked boring, she'd just closed it again.

Time for another look. She walked into her mother's bedroom, took the tin box from the wardrobe, and sat on the floor with her back against the bed and her legs stretched out. Then she riffled through the papers, looking for something that had 'Birth' on it. An old magazine lay on the bottom of the box. She took it out and put it on the floor to look at later. An envelope marked 'Birth Certs' looked like the right thing. She opened it and found her mother's, her grandparent's and her own birth certificate. Beauty! She picked it up and read:

Mother: Jessica Cresswell-Broughton. Father: Unknown. *Unknown! And Cresswell?*

Her mind went blank. She'd assumed her father was the man her mother had been married to years ago. After talking to Rob about it that time, she'd been reassured and had pushed it to the back of her mind. She couldn't image Jessica having a one-night stand with some stranger. It couldn't be true. Her mother would have to know who her father was. She sat back against the end of the bed, breathing hard. This was terrible.

Perhaps her mother had been raped! Her father a rapist! Or maybe she'd had an affair. Perhaps that's why their marriage broke up; her husband divorced her when he found out. Or maybe she was a test-tube baby? Perhaps Jessica had selected a male donor from a range of possible men.

'Yuk!' she said aloud.

Lucky came and sat beside her and licked Kate's face. Maybe Rob really was her father and her mother hadn't known who he was at the time ... no, that didn't make sense.

Kate decided she'd confront her mother as soon as she got home from work. Well, nothing she could do about that now. She put the birth certificate to one side, and looked for the evidence of enrolment at a secondary school. She examined every piece of paper but couldn't find it. She frowned; now she'd be delayed getting her licence. Perhaps they'd have a copy at school ...

She stuffed all the papers back into the tin, then picked up the magazine. The face on the front looked vaguely familiar. She read the headline, *'Somebody Stole my Baby!'* then idly turned to the article and started to read. But she grew impatient with the woman. She was a bit stupid to leave her baby on a train, asking some stranger to mind it. Kate was about to stuff the magazine back in the tin, when she paused, a frown wrinkling her brow. Why had her mother kept this magazine? It wasn't the kind of thing she would normally read. In fact, she never read magazines. Kate's mind somersaulted. A dull feeling settled in her stomach.

She got up and looked in the mirror then at the picture of the woman. The woman had said her daughter would've been ten now. Kate sighed with relief. Couldn't be her. She was fifteen. Then she looked at the cover of the magazine again. 2009! She'd been ten then. Shaking, she threw herself down on her mother's bed. Perhaps Jessica wasn't her mother! Maybe this woman in the magazine was her mother! What was her name? She jumped up and read the article again. Melanie Barker. She'd called her baby girl Celine. She should be Celine Barker. Not Kate Broughton!

She felt like she'd been hit by a truck. Like the ground had given way beneath her. She'd been living a lie; her mother had lied to her, deceived her, no *not* her mother! Jessica had been living a lie.

'Oh, Lucky, what should I do?' Lucky whimpered and Kate sat down on the floor and buried her face in Lucky's fur. Tom! He'd know! She ran to the telephone and rang his mobile number. When she heard his voice say, 'Hi, Kate,' she burst into tears.

'What's wrong, Kate?' He probably couldn't hear her reply through the sobs. 'Hold on, I'm on my way over.'

Thirty minutes later she heard the screech of brakes and ran out to him. 'Oh, Tom! Something terrible has happened.'

'What? What?' He put his arms around her as she sobbed.

'I'm Celine Barker! I'm not Kate Broughton!'

Thomas blinked. 'Of course you're Kate Broughton!'

'No, I'm not! Jessica isn't my mother! Look!' She showed him the magazine.

'Hold on, let's go inside. Let me sit down a minute.' They went into house and Tom sat down, took off his glasses and slowly read the article. 'This doesn't mean anything, Kate.'

'Of course it does! Look at my birth certificate. Father un-known!'

Tom frowned at it, then at Kate. His frown deepened as he thought. 'So Jessica must have had a ...' His voice faltered.

'Yes. A one-night stand. Unless I'm Celine.'

Tom shook his head. 'It doesn't make sense, and look, the article says the little girl would be ten now. You're nearly sixteen.'

'That article was written five years ago. Look at the date on the front of the magazine.' She paced around, while Thomas stared at her, trying to make sense of it all. 'Tom, I can't stay here. I can't face seeing my moth ... I mean Jessica. She's lied to me all my life! How could I ever trust her again? I hate her! Tom, can I come to your place?'

Though his eyes widened with shock at Kate's words, Tom nodded. 'Of course you can.'

'I'll get all my things.' She picked up her school bag and emptied it onto the floor, then found some carrier bags and stuffed them full of the clothes she dragged out of the drawers in her room. Next, the bathroom to get a few things.

'Don't forget your guitar, Kate.'

She picked it up and took it outside.

Thomas followed, lugging the rest of the bags.

Kate stopped when she saw Lucky at the door. 'Oh! Lucky! I've got to leave you.' She crouched down and put her arms around the dog's neck. 'I can't take you, Lucky, Kelly wouldn't like it.'

'Shouldn't you leave a note for your mum? I mean Jessica?' Thomas suggested. 'She'll be worried if you're not here when she gets home.'

Kate glared at him. 'Don't care! She can rot! I can't wait to get out of this house. This prison! I've been held a hostage for fifteen years!'

Thomas's eyebrows rose. "I say, Kate,' he stammered, 'that's um, well, um, I don't think she held you hostage...' He frowned.

'Don't care', she repeated and stalked towards Tom's van. He took the guitar and followed her.

***

When Rob got home, he found his house in complete disarray. Kate had emptied her school bag on the floor, and bulging carrier bags lay everywhere. She sprawled on the lounge, sniffing and sobbing, while Thomas hovered around, trying to get her to drink a cup of tea.

'What on earth's going on? What's all this stuff everywhere?' he asked.

'Kate's had some bad news,' Thomas said.

Rob frowned. 'What?' he demanded. 'What's happened? Is something wrong with Jessica?'

'Better not to mention her,' Thomas whispered in an aside to Rob.

'What's happened?' Rob was getting annoyed and anxious. 'Tell me. Has something happened to Jessica?'

'She's not Kate's mother.' Thomas indicated the magazine. 'You'd better read this.' He handed the magazine to his father.

Rob's heart sank when he saw it. He went over to Kate, who looked pale and exhausted, and bent over her. 'What's happened, sweetie?'

'Oh, Rob,' she wailed, 'Jessica isn't my mother! I was stolen as a baby! She pretended all along she was my mother. She's stolen my childhood!'

'Hold on a minute, Kate—' but he had no time to finish his sentence.

'I'm not Kate! I'm Celine!' Kate howled.

Rob sighed. 'Kate, Celine, whatever, I'm sure Jessica would have only done her best for you. Why don't we wait for her to get home from work and then we can talk it over? Perhaps wait until tomorrow? When we've all had time to digest this and see what's the best thing to do.'

'Did you know about this?' Kate sat up and stared at him. 'You must have!'

Rob looked away. 'No, I didn't know,' he said. 'At least not until a while ago.'

'So you've lied to me, too!' She jumped up. 'I can't stay here either! I can't trust anyone! Tom! Take me somewhere else.'

Thomas, his face a picture of misery, looked at his father.

Rob drew himself up to his full height and glared down at Kate. 'STOP IT, KATE!' he roared.

She stopped mid sob and stared at him.

'Just stop it,' he continued in a milder voice. 'You don't know the full story. Jessica has loved you and looked after you; given her life to you. Okay, perhaps she was wrong to keep you, but she didn't know what had happened to your birth mother. As far as she knew, you'd been abandoned. She did all she could to find out what had happened. Then ...' his voice softened, 'she just couldn't part with you. She loved you too much, Kate.'

Kate's mouth dropped open. 'You've always had the hots for her!' she growled. 'You'll find any excuse!'

Thomas started. 'Kate!'

'Now,' Rob said, ignoring her and looking at his watch. 'Jessica will be coming home from work soon, and she'll be worried sick when you're not there. I suggest we have something to eat, and you, Kate, can stay the night. You can sleep in Andrew's bedroom; in the morning, we'll discuss what to do.'

'I couldn't eat anything,' Kate declared.

'Perhaps not, but I've had a long day, and so has Thomas. There's some leftover stew in the fridge; we'll have that,' he glanced at Thomas. 'Could you heat it up please, Tom?' He turned to Kate. 'Then I'll go over to The Shack and wait for your mother.'

'She's not my moth—' Kate started to say, but Rob cut her short.

'She's been the best mother she could possibly be to you, Kate. I know this has been a shock, Katie love.' He kept his voice gentle. 'Let's all just try and calm down.' He went over to give her a hug but she turned away from him.

'I trusted you, Rob,' she said sulkily. 'You let me down.' She lay back on the lounge, then suddenly jumped up. 'I'm going to find her! Find my real mother. I've got a brother and a sister. I've always wanted a sister! Tom and Andrew are like my brothers, but I've always wanted a sister.'

Thomas's face fell when he heard that Kate considered him like a brother. 'Come and eat some stew, Kate,' he said, putting the pot on the table.

'Too upset to eat,' she replied.

'Well just come and sit up at the table and maybe have a tiny bit,' he coaxed, taking her hand.

Reluctantly she joined them at the table.

'How would I find my real mother, Rob? Her name's in the article, Melanie Barker. Should I write to them to get her address?'

'That was a fake name, Kate. It had a little star against it,' Tom said.

Rob sighed. 'First we must consider all the ramifications, Kate. It's possible Jessica could go to prison.'

'Prison!' Kate looked anxious, then frowned. 'Don't care. She stole me, she lied to me.'

'Just think about it for a day or two. Don't rush and do something rash that you'll regret.'

Rob stood up. 'I'm just going to have a shower and get cleaned up, then I'm going over to see Jessica. Kate, put clean sheets on Andrew's bed; Thomas will show you where they are, then try and sleep. Tomorrow is Saturday. Aren't you supposed to be working at Mandy's on Saturdays?'

Kate nodded, then scowled. 'But how can I go to work being so upset, and I probably look a mess.' She scrubbed her eyes with her handkerchief.

'Thomas can ring Mandy in the morning and say you're not well. You can stay here for a few days until we work out the best way forward.' He disappeared towards the bathroom.

It was ten o'clock by the time he arrived at The Shack. He reversed and parked so that he would face Jessica's van as she came in, then he sat and waited for her. When he saw her headlights coming down the driveway, he flashed his lights and got out of the ute.

'Rob! What are you doing here?' Jessica opened the door of the van, then glanced at the dark house—no lights on inside. 'Where's Kate? What's happened?' She bent down to pat the dog. 'Okay, Lucky; yes, I'm home.'

'Kate's fine, Jess. She's at my place. Come inside and I'll explain.'

Jessica grabbed her bag and followed him. She unlocked the door, turned on the light and walked inside. 'Come in, Rob.' After kicking off her shoes, she turned to him. 'Right; what's going on?'

'Sit down, Jess.'

She frowned but sat on the couch.

He sat in an armchair, facing her. 'Well, apparently, when Kate got home from school today, she decided to fill in her application form for a learner driving licence.' He sighed. 'She needed her birth certificate, so she went to look for it in a tin box in your wardrobe.' He paused at her sharp intake of breath. 'Then she found her birth certificate and the magazine with the article about the woman who lost her baby. She put two and two together.'

'Oh God!' Jessica covered her horrified face with her hands. 'Oh, my God, Rob,' she mumbled. 'What shall I do?' Her feet started to jerk uncontrollably.

Rob frowned and bent over and touched one of her feet. 'What's this, Jess?' he asked in a soft voice.

'It's the bloody Huntington's! It's getting worse. First my hands a few months ago, then it stopped, and I thought it was just a phase and now this. I won't be able to teach next year, Rob! I'll end up in a wheelchair.' She sobbed. 'And now Kate!'

He got up, sat beside her on the couch, put his arms around her and cradled her to him. 'Jess, darling, hush now; we'll work something out.'

'What did she say? How is she?'

'She rang Thomas, and he came and brought her to my place. She's there now. She's very distressed, saying she's going to find her birth mother, and that her name is Celine Barker not Kate Broughton.'

'What shall I do, Rob? Is it a crime to register a baby and lie about its parents?'

'Possibly.' He paused. 'Jess, we may have to get legal advice about all this.'

'Oh, Rob, I don't want to get you involved.'

'There were probably extenuating circumstances; the balance of your mind was disturbed after the death of your father, your marriage breakup and job loss. I'm sure you wouldn't go to prison.'

'Prison!' she exclaimed in horror. 'Oh, Rob!'

'Well, it depends on this Melanie's reaction.'

'I don't want to meet her; I couldn't!' Jessica collapsed into sobs. Her feet and legs jerked wildly. She looked up through the tears. 'Does she hate me? Kate, I mean.'

'Well, she's not too happy with you at the moment.'

'Oh, Rob! What shall I do?'

'Jess, darling, I think we all have to calm down and look at this rationally.'

'I've just spent the last sixteen years not thinking about it, pushing it to the back of my mind. Now it's payback time.'

'Look, I must go home now. But I'm worried about you being here all by yourself.' He stopped and thought. 'I'd stay here with you, but I don't like to leave Thomas and Kate on their own.' He sighed and studied her. 'But I think Thomas is pretty responsible. I'll ring him. Yes, I think it's best I stay with you,' he muttered to himself. Jessica looked so stricken and bereft; he took her hand. 'Listen, Jess. I'm going to ring Thomas and tell him to get Kate to go to bed in Andrew's room and for him to stay up until he's sure Kate is asleep. Then he can go to bed. I'll stay here.'

'I don't know, Rob; I just don't know anything anymore.' Her voice was a mere whisper.

'I'm going to get you a drink and put you to bed. Come on.' He got up, put one arm under her shoulders and the other under her knees and picked her up. Her feet were still jerking as he carried her to her bedroom.

'Can you get undressed?' he asked.

She nodded. 'I think so ... oh, Rob, I don't think I can; I'm shaking so much.'

Silently he helped her get undressed. He found her nightdress under her pillow and pulled back the doona and helped her into bed. 'I'm going to make hot milk with some whiskey in it,' he said. 'Do you have whiskey?'

'No; I can't stand it.'

In the kitchen, he found a bottle of Baileys, heated some milk and poured a generous slug of Baileys into it.

'Drink this, Jess.'

In spite of the warm December night, she lay shivering in the bed. He helped her sit up and held the cup to her lips. 'Come on, drink it,' he commanded.

Obediently Jessica sipped from the cup, spilling some of it, until it was all gone.

Back in the kitchen, he rinsed the cup then returned to the bedroom. He took off his outer clothes, then, still in his underpants and singlet, slid into the bed beside her. Slowly he took her into his arms and held her tight, trying to keep her hands from jerking. He trapped her legs between his to still the tremors. 'I never envisioned our first night together being like this,' he whispered into her hair.

'Oh, Rob, I'm so sorry, but now you know why a proper relationship between us is impossible.'

'Hush, Jess. Try and sleep. I have you safe.'

They lay like that for some time before Jessica eventually fell asleep. Rob stayed awake, wondering where the hell they would go from here.

***

Back at 'Sullivan. Please Close the Gate', Kate slouched on the couch, clutching a sodden bunch of tissues.

Thomas wracked his brains trying to think of something to cheer her up. 'I never knew my mother,' he eventually said.

Kate looked up with a frown. 'What happened to her?'

'When I asked Dad, when I was little, he said he and Mum didn't get on and she had to go away. Then Andrew told me later, when I was big, that she'd run off with another man.'

'Oh my God,' Kate exclaimed, then made a wry face. 'Well, I've got two mothers. You can have one of them. You can have Jessica.' Her face crumpled and she started to sob again. 'Sorry, Tom; that wasn't a nice thing to say.'

'It's okay, Kate. Actually, I used to pretend Jessica was my mother. She was always so nice and kind to me.'

Kate hiccoughed, 'and I used to pretend that Rob was my father. Oh, Tom, what will I do?'

'Dad said I was to make you go to bed,' he replied.

'Can't I come and sleep with you?' Kate sniffed. 'I don't want to be in a strange bed by myself.'

With difficulty, Thomas forced himself to say, 'no, Kate. It wouldn't be right. Anyway, I only have a single bed; there's not room for two.' He would've liked nothing better than have Kate in his bed, but his father's words on the phone to him earlier made him look at her with resolve. 'It wouldn't be right,' he repeated. 'Look, I've put clean sheets and pillow cases on Andrew's bed. In you go.'

Kate sniffed again and blew her nose.

Thomas had an idea. 'Maybe I should give you a drink to help you sleep.'

'Alcohol?' Kate's voice had a hopeful note.

'No, hot milk. Go on, get into bed, and I'll bring it in to you.' His heart pounding, Thomas heated up some milk and poured it into a mug. At the door of Andrew's room, he said, 'can I come in?'

He heard a mumble and opened the bedroom door. Kate was sitting up in bed with just a T-shirt on. He swallowed. 'Just brought the milk; I'll put it here.' He put the mug on the bedside table and bolted out, gently closing the door behind him. 'Goodnight, Kate.'

She muttered some reply.

**

Next morning Rob woke early. Jessica's legs and head were still jerking. He could hardly bear to look at her, to see her like this.

Then he thought of all the years they could've been together. If only she'd trusted him enough to confide in him. He slowly slid out of the bed, got dressed and headed to the kitchen. He heard her moving about in the bedroom, and she appeared just as he was making coffee.

'Sank you, Rob. For shtay with me.' She looked at him, her head twitching on her neck. Her feet turned as she walked towards him.

Her speech had got very bad. His heart sank. 'Come and sit down. What would you like for breakfast?'

'I'm not hungy, sanks.'

He poured them each a coffee, then sat down opposite her. 'What plans have you made for this situation, Jess?' he asked quietly.

She shook her head. 'None. I couldn't bear to sink I might get like my musser. I thought it would be different for me. Maybe they'd find a cure. Now I've dragged Kate into it. I should never have kept her, Rob. I was so wrong!'

He put his hand on hers. 'Jess, you did your best for her. She's angry and upset at the moment, but she'll come around.'

'If I go to prison, at least they'll have to look after me, and I won't be imposhing on anyone ...'

'Stop it, Jess. You won't go to prison.'

'Rob, you don't know what Huntington's ish like.' She spoke slowly, seeming to have difficulty getting out the words. 'It's pro- gressive. I'll gradually get worse, choking, unable to hold a book or a cup or speak properly. Change in personality, depression; it's a living death,' she paused and looked at the hand which Rob held. 'My mother took her own life,' she whispered, 'I can understand that now. She didn't want my father to wear himself out with her care, and she didn't want him to have to see her getting worse.'

She paused to drink some coffee, then managed to stand up. 'Rob, Kate is the important person now. What should I do? It's her birthday today. At least,' she hesitated, 'it's the date I figured out would be her birthday. Do you think she'll still want to go out and celebrate?'

He shook his head. 'I'll go home and ask her. I'll ring you.' He stood up and sighed. 'Dear, Jess, will you be okay if I go home now.'

'Yes Rob, I've got Lucky.' She tried to smile, unaware that it came out as a lopsided grimace.

Rob's heart nearly broke. He put his arms around her. 'Stay strong, Jess. I'll see what's happening at home and ring you. Try and rest a bit.' He kissed her and slowly let her go, the pain in his heart weighing him down. He picked up his keys and let himself out the door.

***

As he drove through the gate of Sullivan's, he saw Thomas's old van rattling towards him. He pulled over to the side of the track—the overhanging tree branches scraped the top of his ute—and lowered the driver's window when Thomas pulled up alongside him.

'Just going to work, Dad,' Thomas said, his head out of his window. 'I made breakfast for Kate, but she wouldn't eat anything.' He frowned. 'She's very upset, Dad. I didn't know what to do. I'll ring Mandy and tell her Kate's not well and won't be coming to work today.'

Rob nodded. 'Thanks, son.'

Thomas nodded, looking relieved to be out of the house away from Kate's misery.

'You're a good boy, Tom. I'm proud of you.'

Thomas's head jerked up in surprise—Rob supposed his compliments were rare—and he gave a half smile. 'Same here, Dad.'

They each drove their separate ways, Thomas looking more light-hearted, and Rob feeling the opposite.

After patting the latest Kelly who'd replaced the last kelpie, Rob opened the door and went in. Kate sat slumped on the old couch. She looked up as he came in.

'Hello, Kate. How are you feeling?'

Tears started to roll down her cheeks. 'I don't know, Rob,' she sniffled, wiping her eyes. 'I don't know who I am anymore. How could Jessica deceive me all these years? Lie to me?'

He sat down beside her and put an arm around her. 'Kate. Let me try and explain.'

'No; I don't want to hear excuses for her.'

'Kate! Just listen to me for a few minutes.' When she stayed quiet, he continued, 'at the time Jessica found you, her father had died the year before.'

Kate interrupted with an angry gesture. 'At least she knew who her father was!'

Rob caught her hand and continued as if she hadn't spoken. 'The company she worked for went bust, so she was out of a job; her marriage broke up when her husband got another woman pregnant and then they bought out her share of their house. Her mother suffered from an incurable, hereditary disease and committed suicide when Jess was only a couple of years older than you are now. Jess was on the train on her way to live in The Shack as she had nowhere else to go. Then this woman put a baby carrier down beside Jess and asked her to mind the baby while she went to the toilet; there was no-one else in the carriage.' He hesitated. 'However, the woman didn't come back. Jess couldn't just leave you there, so she got off at her stop meaning to hand you in to the station master, but the station was in darkness. So she decided to go to the police station with you in the morning. But next morning her van wouldn't start. I know, because that's when I first met her. And you.' He paused and looked at her, not knowing if she was actually listening to him.

'She'd sent me a text message the day before asking me to come and do some jobs. The landline wasn't connected, and there was no mobile signal at the house. She was completely isolated. When I turned up the day after to start work, she told me the van wouldn't start. I said I'd get a new battery the next day and bring it over. The following day when the van was going again, she went into town—I think to the police station. I minded you.'

'She could have taken me with her.'

'Actually, I told her not to. It was very hot; I thought you'd have been fried in the van. I didn't know it had air conditioning.' He sighed. 'You were so cute. Well, Jessica came back and seemed relieved. I didn't know it then, but apparently by the time she'd reached the police station, it was closed. And she'd listened to all the local news on the radio, and there had been no reports of a missing baby.' He squeezed her hand.

'Kate, Jess was absolutely certain that you'd been deliberately abandoned, and she hated to think of you going into foster care and maybe being adopted. She was lonely, felt unloved and had always wanted a child.'

'She could have got a dog ...' Kate muttered.

Rob stared at her, then slowly shook his head. 'Kate, oh Kate. Jess loved you from that moment on. She thought about adopting you but for one thing it would have taken ages, and probably you would've been put with foster parents. Even then, Jess thought, as a single woman and with no job, she'd have no hope of being allowed to adopt you. In desperation she pretended she'd given birth to you on your own in The Shack.'

Kate sniffed and blew her nose. 'That might be a reason, but it's not an excuse.'

Rob sighed. 'She's in a bad way, Kate. The disease that she's inherited from her mother has taken hold.'

'What disease?'

'It's called Huntington's Disease.'

Kate shrugged. 'Not my problem. She's not my mother.'

Rob wanted to slap her. Instead he got up from the couch and went to put the kettle on. 'I've got a few jobs to do around the place,' he said, then turned to her. 'Jess has organised a birthday dinner in town for you, just us and Tom. Do you want to go?'

Kate stared at him. 'No way. And it's probably not even my real birthday! Only my real mother knows that!'

Rob closed his eyes and took a deep breath. 'Okay, I'll ring Jess and tell her to cancel it.' He went to the phone and dialled the number. 'Hi, Jess. Best cancel the booking for tonight. You okay?' He nodded and put the phone down.

Kate slumped down on the couch and stared into space.

Rob cleaned the hen house. It gave him a chance to process all the things that had happened. Of course, Kate would be upset. He tried to imagine what it must be like for her, but he couldn't. Only someone who had experienced the same kind of issue would understand. Like the people who only found out when they were adults that they'd been adopted. Maybe counselling would help her. However that still left Jessica. As soon as he'd finished with the chooks, he'd go and look up on Google the penalties for giving false information on a birth certificate. He should probably have done that years ago. But it was more than that, he thought. Jessica had basically kidnapped Kate. He finished putting clean straw down in the hen house and emptied the bin of used straw onto the compost heap. When he'd refilled their food containers, he returned to the house.

Kate was still slumped on the couch. He washed his hands at the kitchen sink. 'Kate, my dear, I think you need help from someone who knows more than I do about all this.'

Kate raised her head. 'I just want to die. According to the magazine, my father was an abusive drug addict.'

Rob silently counted to ten. 'Kate! I love you. Jessica loves you. The boys love you. We want you in our lives. It doesn't matter what your biological father was or did. You are you. A separate person, made up of all different bits of your parents and grandparents and mixed together with a loving and nurturing upbringing.' He stopped, not sure where he was going with this. 'I'm not the person to help you, Kate, but you're a fine strong young woman; we have to think what your next steps will be. Why don't you go for a walk? Take the dog with you. Get some fresh air and try not to think about things too much?'

'Don't feel like walking anywhere.'

'Kate. I'm asking you to take the dog for a walk.'

Reluctantly she got off the couch. 'Can I have a shower first?'

He nodded.

'I don't have a towel.'

'In the laundry cupboard.'

As soon as he heard the shower running, he went to the PC. He wasn't reassured by what he discovered.

After taking the latest Kelly for a long walk, Kate returned, seemingly more composed, and ate the sandwich Rob had prepared. She said nothing until they had finished eating, then she thanked him, got up, cleared the table and washed up the dishes. When she'd finished, she turned to him.

'Rob, do you think I could stay here for a while? I have some money saved up to buy a car, but instead, I can pay my board with it. Just until I can earn enough to find somewhere nearer to my work that I can afford. I think Tom would give me a lift to work.' She looked at him, her eyes bright with tears, which she blinked away. 'I don't think I can face living with Jessica.' Her voice wobbled over the word Jessica.

Rob grimaced. 'Well, it's a bit cosy here. I don't know what plans Andrew has when he finishes uni, and of course he'll be home for Christmas ...'

'I'd like to try and contact my real mother,' Kate continued. 'Then I might be able to go and live with her. But perhaps I can sleep on the couch when Andrew's here.'

Rob sighed. 'Look, Kate dear. I know this has been a terrible shock for you, but I think it's best for you to go home, at least for a while, until you sort out what you want to do. I think Jessica would support you in whatever you decide.'

Kate wavered, then her bottom lip jutted out. 'I'm not ready to face her,' she said softly.

'Okay,' Rob got up from the table, 'but I want Jessica to come here on Christmas day. I don't like to think of her on her own. She has no one Kate, and I'm worried about how she's going to cope with this disease.' He didn't want to worry Kate with all that he'd found on the internet about Huntington's disease. She had enough to cope with at the moment.

Kate didn't reply. She got up from the table and cocked her head as if listening. 'I think I can hear Tom's van.'

Rob smiled. 'Not difficult. You can hear it coming miles away. Um Kate?'

'Yes?'

'I'm going over to see your moth ... Jessica now. If you'd like to prepare dinner, there's stuff in the fridge. See what you can come up with.' He thought that might take her mind off of her troubles.

'Okay.'

When he got to The Shack, he found Jessica trying to hang out washing, Lucky by her side. He watched her for a few moments. It seemed like she was moving in slow motion. He got out of the ute and joined her. 'Hi, Jess. How are you?'

'Fine, sanks, Rob.'

He studied her. She was obviously not fine. Deathly pale and seemed quite shaky. He finished hanging out the washing then turned to her. 'Can I give you a kiss?'

She nodded, a half smile on her lips. He took her in his arms, and she sank her head into his chest. 'Rob. I've made a few decisions. Come in.'

The cool inside the house made a welcome change from the December heat.

'Sit down.' She patted the couch.

'What have you decided?' He took one of her hands. The fingers were twitching.

Jessica took a deep breath. Slowly, trying not to slur her words, she managed to say, 'I've been researching care homes for people like me. There isn't much 'vailable; only options are aged-care homes.'

Rob frowned. 'That doesn't sound good for someone as young as you.'

She nodded. 'I know. I might be able to get home care, but it's unlikely as no one would want to drive all the way here to do a few hours work.' She looked down at her hands. 'The thing is, Rob, I don't think I'll be able to work anymore.'

His brows lifted in a silent query.

'I'm not able to think and reason properly anymore. I lose the thread. Computer theory is all about logic and reason, Rob. I can't answer my student's questions. I have to stop and try and understand what they're asking. Also, I've noticed lately that I have to take things really slowly, plan my steps, write things down. Even simple things. Put clothes in the washing machine. Put in washing powder. Turn the knob to mixed load. Hang washing on the line when machine beeps.' She looked up at him. 'I know. It sounds so stupid, but it's what I have to do now ...' Her eyes filled with tears. 'And I feel so tired and low, Rob.'

'Oh, Jess!' Rob held her close. 'I don't know what to say.'

'How's Kate? Is she very angry with me?'

He bent his head and frowned. 'I'm afraid so. I tried to explain how it all happened, but she doesn't want to know. Said I was just making excuses for you. Said I've always had the hots for you.'

She blinked. 'What!'

He gave a sheepish smile. 'She's right about that anyway.'

The colour rose in her cheeks. 'Oh, Rob, I'm sorry. I should have trusted you and told you years ago, instead of just brushing it under the carpet; hiding my head in the sand. I thought as long as I didn't verbalize it, then it wouldn't be true. Well, something like that. I tried to stop myself falling in love with you, Rob. It wouldn't have been fair. It's still not fair on you, especially now. See the mess I've made of my life.'

'We'll sort things out, Jess.' He got up. 'I'd better get back home, see how Kate is. Don't worry, things are never as bad as they seem.' Jessica smiled, but he thought it laced with irony. Perhaps with this disease things *were* as bad as they seemed. He hoped not. Anyway, he still had to try to keep her spirits up. He leaned over and kissed her. 'I'll come over tomorrow. Oh,' he paused, 'will you be okay to drive to work on Monday?'

Jessica nodded. 'Yes, no classes, just end of year stuff. Thanks.'
He took her twitching hands in his.

'I'm okay, Rob. Really.' Her smile seemed more genuine this time.

***

Sunday was quiet at the Sullivan's, and Kate felt sombre. She had so much to think about and plan, but how could she plan? She did her best to help around the house, in the afternoon half-heartedly offering to do some weeding in the garden.

'That would be good Kate, thank you,' Rob said. 'I'm going over to your mum's now. Would you like to come?'

She shook her head. 'No thanks, Rob. Have you got any gardening gloves?'

'Don't think so, at least, none that would fit you.'

She nodded. 'Okay. Perhaps I won't do weeding. I don't want to break my nails.'

'Good thinking.' Rob gave a half smile. 'All right, if you want something to do, there's a pile of ironing in the laundry.'

'Right.' She got slowly up from the old couch and then, dragging her feet, made for the laundry.

***

Thomas had to start work at 7.30 in the mornings, but Snippits didn't open until 8.30. 'Drop me at your work and I'll walk from there,' Kate said as she got into his van.

'Okay. I'll pick you up at five.'

'That means you have to hang around for an hour; don't you finish at four?'

'Yes, but the boss always stays late, and I'll just work a bit longer. I don't mind.' He smiled at her.

'Thanks, Tom. I really appreciate you giving me lifts.'

Thomas blushed. 'Anytime,' he mumbled.

When Kate arrived at Snippits, her boss, Mandy, was just opening up the salon. 'Good morning, Kate! You're nice and early. Did you have a good weekend?'

'Yes, thank you,' Kate replied.

'Do anything exciting?' Mandy paused. 'Hey, wasn't it your sixteenth birthday? Have a good time?'

'Yes, lovely.' Kate tried to inject a note of pleasure into her voice.

'So you'll be able to work every day now?'

'Yes, I've finished school.'

Mandy bustled around the salon, and Kate went to the appointments book, realizing that Mandy wasn't really listening. 'You've got Mrs Dymock for a shampoo and set first thing, Mandy,' she said.

'Oh, Kate, would you like to shampoo her?' Mandy called out from the little kitchen cum office out the back of the salon. 'You know how to do it, don't you? She's always early, and I just need to sort out a few orders.'

A small thrill went through Kate. This was the first time she'd been asked to actually touch a client. Her usual duties had been to sweep up cut hair, give the clients cups of coffee, take telephone calls and make appointments. Right on time Mrs Dymock arrived.

'Good morning love,' she said as Kate took her to one of the wash basins. 'Are you going to shampoo me today?'

'Yes, Mrs Dymock. Is that all right?'

'Of course.' She smiled.

Carefully Kate wrapped a towel around Mrs Dymock's shoulders and then a waterproof cover. She guided her head backwards to rest her neck against the bowl of the sink. Mrs Dymock's grey hair was getting thin.

'I'm thinking of getting a colour put in it today,' she told Kate.

'That'll be nice.'

'Yes, our daughter in Melbourne's youngest is graduating next week, for her degree you know, and I want to look nice.'

'Oh, you'll look lovely,' Kate murmured.

'The problem is my mother,' confided Mrs Dymock. 'I worry about her. She's eighty-five and lives on her own. I want her come and live with us, but she won't. And anyway, my husband's not keen; she gets on his nerves. She keeps telling the same stories over and over. He doesn't like that I spend so much time with her. Mind you, he's a good husband,' she hastened to add. 'I tried to get her to have home care, but she keeps saying she can manage and doesn't need anyone. She fell and broke her wrist a couple of months ago. I've been going round every evening after work, but now I don't know what to do. We'll be gone for three weeks. She insists she'll be all right—she has good neighbours—but she forgets things.' She sighed as Kate massaged her scalp. 'Oh, you're so good at that, Kate, dear.'

Kate suddenly had an idea. As she rinsed Mrs Dymock's hair and then wrapped a towel around her head, she whispered, 'Mrs Dymock, I was thinking. I have to move out of home. It's just too far for me to come to work every day now that I'm working full time with Mandy. I was just wondering, maybe I could stay with your mother while you're away.'

Mrs Dymock blinked and frowned. 'Well, I don't know, dear ... My mother can be a bit difficult.'

The other hairdressers arrived, and the small shop soon hummed with the sound of hair dryers and chat. Kate took Mrs

Dymock to a chair, ready for Mandy to style and set her hair. It seemed she'd forgotten about the colour rinse.

As Kate swept and tidied the salon, she overheard Mandy chatting to Mrs Dymock. Normally Kate tuned out this kind of small talk, but now she stopped sweeping and listened. Mrs Dymock was telling Mandy about her mother and the trip and Kate. She asked Mandy if she thought it would be a good idea for Kate to stay with her mother. Kate hurriedly resumed sweeping and moved slightly away.

'It's a problem, this elderly parent thing, isn't it, dear?' Kate heard Mandy say. Then she saw her lean over to Mrs Dymock and Kate just made out her next words: 'That's a great idea. Kate's a lovely girl, very quiet and trustworthy. I know it's a problem for her getting lifts to work.'

When Mrs Dymock was coiffed and happy, she came to the reception desk and handed Kate the money. 'Thank you, dear. I was thinking while I was under the hairdryer that it might work out you staying with Mum.'

Kate's heart flipped.

'How about I take you to meet her? I can ask Mandy if she could spare you for half an hour and we could pop over now, if you like.'

'That would be great,' Kate said. Mrs Dymock went over to Mandy, who was cutting another client's hair, and Kate saw her whispering to Mandy and Mandy nodding.

Mrs Dymock came back smiling. 'Come on love, Mandy's given you half an hour off. Oh, and please call me Dorothy. All this Mrs Dymocking!'

In the car, Dorothy explained about her mother. 'Sometimes she's very with it, and then the next day she can't remember stuff. I buy her frozen dinners that she can just put in the oven, but then a week later they're still in the freezer. I do my best, but my husband gets grumpy if I spend too much time with Mum.'

Kate just murmured. It seemed like this old lady could be a problem. Still it was only for a few weeks and would get her over Christmas, then Andrew would be gone, and she could move back with Rob and Thomas.

Dorothy's mother lived in the old part of the town not far from Snippits. Dorothy stopped the car outside a small weatherboard cottage. 'Here we are, Kate.' She rummaged in her handbag and found a set of keys.

Kate nodded, suddenly feeling nervous as they walked up the path. The garden was neat and tidy with grevilleas and other native shrubs along the border of a small lawn. Dorothy rang the bell, then tried the screen door and made tutting noises as it opened. Then she tried the front door, which also opened. 'I keep telling Mum to lock the doors! Come on in, Kate.' She led the way down the narrow hall. Kate heard the sound of shuffling, and a tiny white-haired woman appeared, leaning heavily on a walking stick.

'I thought I heard the door bell,' she said.

'Mum! I keep telling you to lock the front door! Anyone could come in.'

'I did lock it ...'

'Mum, this is Kate.' She gave her mother a quick peck on the cheek, then continued, 'her home is right out in the bush, and she's just started working full time for Mandy at Snippits the hair-dressers, and she hasn't anywhere to live in town. I was wondering if she could stay with you for a couple of weeks, just until after Christmas when she'll have time to look for somewhere else.' She turned to Kate. 'Oh, Kate, this is my mum, Mrs White.'

'Gladys,' said Mrs White. 'Call me Gladys.' She looked at Kate and smiled. 'Be lovely to have a young person around again. I miss Carolyn, now she's married.'

'Yes, Mum. So that's settled, then? Kate can sleep in the spare bedroom? Let's look at it now.' Dorothy moved past her mother and walked along the hall to the bedrooms.

'This is Mum's bedroom.' She indicated a door on the left. 'And this is the spare bedroom. It used to be mine. Many years ago.' She opened a door on the right, and they walked into a small, but neat and tidy, room. It smelt a bit musty, but Kate was delighted. Her problems solved for the next few weeks.

Dorothy walked over to the bed and pulled back the doona. 'Sheets and bed linen are in the linen cupboard, Kate.'

'It looks lovely, Dorothy,' she said. 'I'm so grateful.'

'It's not very modern, I'm afraid,' Dorothy continued, looking around. 'Mum and Dad moved here when they first got married when Dad came back from the war. There's been nothing done to the place since Dad died twenty years ago. Mum refused to change anything.' She sighed. 'Not even a coat of paint to freshen the place up.'

It did look very dingy, Kate thought. And the kitchen! Just a stone sink, an ancient gas cooker and a rickety looking table. At least the small fridge looked reasonably new.

Dorothy turned to her mother. 'If Kate helps you around the place instead of paying board, will that be all right, Mum?' Dorothy frowned at her mother. 'I think you've lost weight.' She turned to Kate. 'You can cook, can't you?'

'Yes, of course,' Kate replied. She wasn't any good at maths and school stuff, but she loved cooking.

Gladys Wright smiled. 'Lovely! It'll be nice to have company.' Then her face fell. 'You don't play that loud music, do you? What do they call it? Heavy something?'

'No, Gladys.'

'I'm sure you'll soon get used to things, Kate. How soon can you move in?' Dorothy asked.

'Um, I'm not sure, perhaps tomorrow? I can get a friend to bring me.'

Dorothy nodded; no doubt relieved that her problem had been resolved.

'Right, Mum. Kate will come tomorrow, after work. Now, make sure you lock the door after us.' She gave her mother another peck on the cheek and led the way out.

In the car, Dorothy started the engine and turned to Kate. 'I'm sure my mother isn't eating properly. I do a shop for her at weekends, and the food is still in the fridge a week later. I have to throw most of it out. I'll leave money with you to buy food for the two of you for next week. That okay? We can see how it's all going before I leave for Melbourne. Oh, and also, she can't see very well. She's waiting to have cataract surgery.'

'No probs. That'll be fine.'

'It's another week before we take off, so we can see if everything is working out okay before then,' she repeated. 'On both sides, of course.' She studied Kate. 'You look tired, Kate. Oh, I remember now, you've been celebrating your birthday, so Mandy said. Late nights I suppose.' She started to drive. 'No funny business at my mum's now, Kate!'

'Of course not!' Kate had a good idea what Dorothy meant by funny business. No boys or parties.

'So I'll meet you at Mum's tomorrow afternoon. About five? Did you note the address? Westland Terrace. Number seven.'

Back at work, Kate had a spring in her step. She couldn't wait to tell Tom when he came to pick her up.

Tom seemed surprised to see her so cheerful.

'Guess what?' she asked as she opened the creaky passenger door and got in beside him.

'Dunno. What?'

'I've got an extra job. Live in carer for an old lady. Just for a few weeks.'

Thomas started the engine. 'What does that mean?'

'I'm going to start tomorrow. You can take me to Gladys's house after work. It's not far. Oh, if that's okay with you, Tom?'

'Of course, Kate. Do anything for you.' He blushed.

'I'll pack all my stuff into your van tonight, ready for the morning.'

'Does that mean you won't be home for Christmas?'

'Yep! Problem solved. My m ... Jessica can go to your place, like your dad wants, and I won't have to meet her.'

Tom became silent. Kate chattered on about Mrs Dymock and Gladys. Eventually Tom said, 'So I won't get to see you as much, then.'

'Well, I'll be busy with work and carer stuff, but I'd still like to see you, Tom. You're my best friend after all, and it's only for a few weeks.'

He had to be satisfied with that.

CHAPTER 16

Rob relayed the news to Jessica. 'Kate's moving out,' he told her when he visited her that afternoon.

'Moving out? Moving where?'

'Apparently one of the clients where she works, Dorothy something, has an elderly mother, and Kate is going to move in with her, temporarily, while Dorothy is away for a few weeks.'

'Oh.' Jessica didn't know what to say.

'I think Kate just told her that she lived out in the bush and couldn't get a lift to work and needed to stay in town. I don't think she mentioned anything about the situation.'

Jessica nodded. 'Well, that's a relief. Come in, Rob. When is she moving out?'

'Tomorrow after work. She's put all her stuff in Tom's van already.' He followed her indoors. Lucky came in behind them.

Suddenly Jessica burst into tears. 'I can't bear it, Rob! I've stuffed up my life and Kate's, too.'

Rob put his arms around her. 'You won't do anything silly will you?'

'Like my muzzer, you mean?'

'Well, yes.' He hugged her tighter.

'No, not at moment, but I don't know how I'll feel in the future.'

'Jess, you know how much I love you. I'll always be here for you.'

'Oh, Rob, I don't serve you.' She rested her head against his chest.

'Come on, sit down,' Rob said, gently releasing her. 'I'll make a cup of tea. Have you eaten?'

'Not yet, not really hungy.'

'I'll make you an omelette. You must eat, Jess.'

Jessica sat at the kitchen table. 'I've decided to give in my notice. I can't go on working.'

'What!' He turned from the fridge where he'd been getting eggs and rummaging around looking for what else he could find to make an omelette.

'No! You can't do that, Jess. Take sick leave. How many sick days have you taken this year?'

'None. Never have. Always tried stay healthy.'

Rob sighed. 'Jess, I think you should see your doctor. Get sick leave. At least you'll still get paid. If you resign, that's the end.'

She shook her head. 'I can't do that, Rob.'

'Why not?'

'I'd have to tell her I have the Huntington's gene. She knows I have Kate. I've taken her when she's been sick or had her vaccinations ...'

'Well, you can go and see my doctor. If he asks if you have children, tell him you've never given birth.' He studied her. 'Please, Jess. You need help. They may have new drugs that can help you. I'll take you to my doctor.' He fixed his eyes on hers, until she dropped her gaze. 'I'll ring him now.'

Rob got his mobile phone, scrolled down his list of contacts and called his doctor. When the doctor's receptionist answered, he said, 'I'd like to make an appointment for Ms Jessica Broughton.' There was a pause. 'No, she hasn't been before. Right. Tomorrow at 2.30. Okay. Thanks.' He turned off his phone. 'I'll pick you up. No excuses, Jess.'

She sat with her head in her hands. 'Can't do this, Rob.'

'You must, Jess,' he said gently, taking her hands. She looked up at him, her eyes filled with tears as he continued, 'you can't go on like this.'

***

Next evening Thomas was waiting outside Snippits for Kate when she finished work.

She hurried out to the van. 'Hi, Tom; thanks so much. I'll show you the way; it's not far.'

Dorothy's car was parked outside when they arrived at Gladys's cottage, and as Kate got out, the front door opened and Dorothy appeared. 'Hello, Kate. Mum's all ready for you. Do you need a hand?'

'No, it's okay. This is my friend, Thomas.' She indicated Tom who was taking bags from the back of the van. 'Tom, this is Mrs Dymock - Dorothy.' She looked up and saw Gladys hobbling out the door just as Thomas took her guitar out of the van.

'Hello, dear.' She saw the guitar and turned to Kate with a frown. 'I hope you won't play that heavy music, dear. I don't like it.'

'Neither do I, Gladys, so I won't be playing it. Don't worry.'

Dorothy looked doubtfully at Tom in his mechanic's overalls and with a smear of grease on his cheek.

'Nice to meet you both.' Tom smiled at them and picked up some of the bags. 'I'll leave these by the front door. I won't take them inside; I'm a bit grubby.'

'Where do you work, Tom?' Dorothy enquired.

'At Olly's garage. I've nearly finished my apprenticeship.'

'Oh, right.'

'I'll be off now, Kate. If you need anything else, give me a ring.'

'Okay. Thanks a mill, Tom.'

Thomas got in the van and drove off.

Dorothy frowned. 'Is he your boyfriend, Kate?'

'No, he's like a brother to me, known him all my life.'

Dorothy's expression relaxed. 'Right, let's take all this stuff inside, and I'll show you things. Come on Mum, don't stand out in this heat.'

Dorothy gave Kate a long list of instructions: what her mother liked to eat; at what time; when to change the bed linen; where to shop; how the washing machine worked, until Kate's head was spinning.

'I've got to go now,' Dorothy said eventually. 'There's chops in the fridge for tonight—you won't have time to go shopping—and there's plenty of stuff in the freezer. Oh, before I forget, Kate, this is my mobile number in case you have to contact me or are worried about anything.'

Kate nodded. 'Thanks, Dorothy. I'm sure everything will be okay.'

Gladys, who'd been listening intently to all this, nodded and said, 'We'll be fine, Dot. You go now. We'll get on like a house on fire.'

Dorothy looked worried. 'There are smoke alarms and a fire blanket in the kitchen.'

'Go, Dot.' Gladys gave her daughter a nudge.

'Okay. I'll ring later on. Bye, Mum. Bye Kate.'

'Everything will be fine, Dorothy. I'll send you a text later,' Kate reassured her.

They waited until they heard the gate close and the car start, then stop as Dorothy got out, fumbled in her handbag and came back. 'Forgot to give you a spare key,' she said, handing one to Kate.

Kate nodded. 'Thanks.'

They watched Dorothy take off. Then Gladys turned to Kate and asked, 'do you like lamb chops, dear?'

'Yes.'

'Good, because I can't eat them. My teeth aren't that good, I keep telling Dot, but she won't listen, says I need to eat more meat.' Gladys sighed and shook her head. 'No, you cook them for yourself, dear. I'll just have a boiled egg.'

Kate frowned. 'Are you sure, Gladys? I can make something nice for you.'

'Maybe tomorrow, dear. I'm a little tired tonight—all this excitement of you coming.'

'I hope you'll be happy with me.' Kate bit her lip. 'I'll do whatever you say.'

'I know you will, dear. I could see right away that you were lovely and we'd get on fine. Now, you make yourself a nice dinner. Just a boiled egg for me. I'll sit and watch the telly for a spell.' Gladys smiled and sat down in front of the television.

Kate busied herself in the kitchen. She cooked the chops and some vegetables and was about to start the boiled egg when Gladys appeared. 'That smells nice, dear. Maybe I could try a chop after all.'

Kate smiled. 'Great!'

Gladys parked her stick and sat down at the table. 'Now, tell me all about yourself, dear.'

Kate stared at her plate. 'Not really much to tell.'

Gladys looked at her intently. 'Hmm,' was all she said, then changed the subject. 'Now, tell me about this guitar playing ...'

Kate explained chords and beats, until she saw Gladys's eyelids drooping. She looked at her watch. 'It's nine o'clock, Gladys. Do you mind if I go to bed?'

'Of course not, dear. I'm perfectly all right.'

'Shall I make you a hot drink?'

'That would be lovely, dear. I'll watch a bit of telly if that's all right.'

Kate felt so tired, she thought she'd sleep through the noise.

***

Next morning Kate got up early. Unsure what to do about Gladys, she showered and got her own breakfast. It was still too early to leave for work, so she looked in the fridge and the freezer to see what she could cook for their dinner that night. When she heard the toilet flush, she went to Gladys's bedroom and tapped on the door.

'Gladys, would you like a cup of tea?'

'Come in, dear.'

Kate opened the door and smiled. 'Good morning, Gladys. Would you like your breakfast before I leave for work?'

'Oh, that would be lovely, dear. Just some toast and marmalade and a cup of tea please.'

When Kate brought in the breakfast tray, Gladys was sitting up in bed, smiling. 'I feel like a queen; thank you dear.'

'I have to go to work soon. Will you be all right until I get back this evening?'

'Of course, dear. This is lovely. I'm looking forward to seeing you after work.'

'I'll lock the door behind me.'

'Right, dear. I'll be fine.' She smiled at Kate and started on her breakfast.

***

At one o'clock that same day, Rob drove up to The Shack, jumped out of his ute and called through the front door, 'Jess, are you ready?'

'Not going.' She appeared in the doorway. 'Canst go.'

Tight lipped, he looked at her. 'Jess. You're going. Even if I have to man handle you into the ute. I thought this would happen; that's why I'm early.'

He pushed past her into the living room. 'Come on, Jess. Get changed.' She was still in her dressing gown.

'I didn't sleep last night. I'm tired.'

'Yes, well apparently that's one of the symptoms. The doctor will give you a script for sleeping tablets.'

'Won't take drugs.'

His jaw tightened. 'Jess. Get dressed. I'll help you. Otherwise, I'll just pick you up and take you in your dressing gown.' He gently pushed her towards her bedroom.

All the strength seemed to go out of her, and she let herself be led to the bedroom. 'Where are your clean undies?' He pulled open a drawer, 'here?'

Jessica gave a small laugh. 'Yes.'

He handed them to her then opened a wardrobe door, surveyed the clothes on the hangers, took down a shirt and a pair of jeans. 'Put these on.'

Meekly Jess obeyed.

'Right.' He looked around, found a comb on the dressing table and picked it up.

'Rob! I can comb my own hair!'

He smiled, took her in his arms and, with one hand, tenderly combed the tangled mass of hair back from her face. Then he kissed her. 'You look beautiful, darling Jess. Now, shoes. Okay those sandals will do. Where's your Medicare card?'

'In my bag.'

'Right. We're ready.'

Half an hour later, they arrived at Rob's doctor's surgery. The receptionist took Jessica's Medicare card and gave her a form to fill out.

'What do I put on it?' she whispered to Rob.

'Just answer the questions. I'm coming in with you.'

'No!'

'Yes.'

When Jessica's name was called, Rob followed her in.

'Ms Broughton?' the doctor asked.

'Yes.'

'And this is Mr Broughton?' He looked at Rob with a frown.

'No, I'm Jess's partner, Rob Sullivan.'

'Oh, yes, you're one of my patients. I've seen your boys.'

'Yes,' Rob nodded.

'So Ms Broughton wants you to be here for this consultation?' Dr Bailey asked.

'Yes,' Rob answered firmly before Jessica had a chance to say anything.

'Hmm. So, Mrs Broughton, or may I call you ...' He looked at the form. 'Jessica?'

'Jesshca is fine.'

The doctor looked intently at Jessica. 'So what brings you here today?'

'Um. Nothing. I just, um ... wan a chess up.'

'Doctor,' Rob intervened. 'Jessica's mother had Huntington's Disease. Jessica was tested and she also has the gene.'

Dr Bailey looked at Jessica. 'Is that so, my dear?'

She nodded, tears coming to her eyes.

'Tell me what's been happening,' he said gently.

When Jessica seemed unable to speak, Dr Bailey turned to Rob and raised his eyebrows.

'Jess has had twitching fingers, and sometimes difficulty getting words out. She's not sleeping properly, and I think she's suffering from depression. Oh, and her movements are often unco-ordinated.'

Dr Bailey nodded. 'Stand up, my dear.'

Jessica stumbled as she tried to stand.

'See the tiles on the floor? Do you think you could walk along this line of tiles?' He stood to one side of her. 'Take it slowly.'

'I've never seen her as bad as this,' Rob said quietly in an aside to the doctor.

'Probably the stress of coming here,' Dr Bailey replied.

Jessica managed three steps, then her right arm flew out and hit the doctor in the chest, and she faltered.

He caught his breath. 'I don't think you intended to hit me, did you?' he said as he grasped her arm before she lurched and nearly fell. Rob jumped up and helped her back to the chair.

'Shorry, didn't mean ...'

'It's all right, Jessica. Just sit down again.' He regarded her kindly. 'Well, my dear, you would have seen the progression of Huntington's with your mother.' He looked down and frowned, then studied her for a few moments. 'Do you have children, Jessica?'

She shook her head.

'Well, that's good. I expect you made that decision after your mother's diagnosis?'

She nodded.

He turned back to his computer. 'I'd like you to have some blood tests, and I'll give you a script for sleeping tablets.' The printer whirred, and he took the printout and signed it, then sighed. 'I'm sorry, my dear.' He picked up his pen and turned it over, then put it back on his desk. 'There is one other thing,' he frowned. 'Driving.' He turned to her. 'I'm afraid I'll have to take your driving licence from you. Do you have it with you?'

'Lishense?' Jessica stared at him.

'I'm terribly sorry. I hate having to do this to you, but it's no longer safe for you to drive.'

'But Jessica lives out in the bush, nearly thirty minutes' drive from town, how will she cope?' Rob asked.

Dr Bailey pursed his lips. 'The next time you come, after I get the blood test results, we can discuss options and ways to help.'

'Like what?' Rob demanded.

'Home visits, various therapies—speech and physical therapies for example. There are drugs to relieve symptoms, but of course they have side-effects. We'll have to consider each one on its merits'

Jessica shook her head. 'Canst drive.'

Rob put a hand on her arm. 'I can drive you.'

Dr Bailey held out his hand. 'Do you have your driving licence with you, Jessica?'

She nodded and fumbled in her handbag. Rob tried to restrain himself from taking it from her and finding it. Eventually she took out a small wallet and offered it to Rob. He opened the cover, took out her licence and silently handed it to the doctor.

'I'm so sorry that I have to do this, Jessica.'

Rob stood. 'Can you give Jessica a sick note, Doctor?'

'Oh, of course.' He scribbled on a pad, tore it off and handed it to Rob.

'Thanks.'

'I'm sorry to give you this bad news, my dear,' Dr Bailey said to Jessica.

She nodded. Rob took her arm and led her out the surgery door.

'I'll take you for the blood tests tomorrow,' he said as they reached his ute and he helped her in. He looked at the printout. 'Fasting blood tests. I'll pick you up first thing in the morning. And I'll drop this medical certificate into TAFE on our way home.'

Unless Jessica insisted, he decided not to get the prescription for the sleeping tablets filled. She'd been depressed for some time, and he knew her mother had taken an overdose of sleeping tablets.

Jessica remained silent on the drive back to The Shack. Rob glanced at her from time to time. Eventually he said, 'Bummer, Jess. We'll have to think what to do next. Do you want to come to my place for tonight instead of going home?'

She shook her head. 'No, you have shtuff to do. I be right.' She kept staring straight ahead.

CHAPTER 17

That evening when Kate returned to Glady's cottage, she unlocked the front door and called out, 'Hello, Gladys! It's me, Kate.' Over the sound of the television blasting, she heard a murmur from the living room.

She found Gladys sitting in front of the television with the remote in her hand. 'These people don't speak clearly, dear. I can't hear them properly but now you're here and that's lovely. What was your name again?'

'Kate.'

'Of course. I knew that.'

With the help of her stick, Gladys got up from her armchair.

'I bought some mince on the way home. I thought I'd make a Bolognese for dinner, Gladys. Would you like that?'

'Just a boiled egg would be fine for me, dear. I'm not hungry.'

'I'll put the kettle on and make you a cup of tea, while I start the dinner.' Kate smiled at Gladys, who followed her to the kitchen.

Kate set a cup and saucer on the table in front of Gladys. 'What did you have for lunch?'

Gladys looked vague. 'Um ... A boiled egg?' She shook her head. 'Or maybe a sandwich.'

Kate saw no sign of any food having been prepared. Either Gladys hadn't eaten since breakfast, or she was very neat and tidy and had cleared everything away.

'Right, well I won't be long making dinner. Is there anything you'd like help with?'

'I'll just sit here and watch you, dear, if that's all right? You tell me about your day.'

Kate chatted away about her day as she prepared the food, and soon an appetizing smell filled the little kitchen.

'Mmmh, that smells nice, dear. Perhaps I'll have some after all.'

Kate smiled at her. She'd become a good cook lately since her moth ... Jessica, hadn't seemed able to get her act together for cooking. Either she forgot what she was doing and went off and did something else in the middle or dropped stuff. Also, it looked like she'd been hitting the bottle. Kate wondered how she was coping without her.

Gladys ate all her dinner. 'That was lovely, dear. How about we sit in the lounge room for a bit now?'

'You go and sit down. I'll just tidy up here and join you.'

When Kate had finished washing up and cleaning the kitchen, she put the kettle on and joined Gladys in the lounge room. The old woman sat in front of the television with her eyes closed. 'Gladys, would you like a cup of tea?'

'That would be lovely, dear.' Gladys sat up and turned off the television. 'I don't know, there's nothing on the telly, these days, dear. Oh, this is so nice, having you here. Tell me, dear, do you read much?'

Kate looked around at the shelves of books and hesitated, 'Not really.'

'You're welcome to read any of my books, you know. I used to read a lot, but I can't see so well these days. I'm waiting to get my cataracts done ...' She paused.

'Oh! Well, thank you, Gladys.' Then she suddenly got the unspoken message. 'Would you like me to read to you?'

'Really? Would you? Oh, yes please, that would be lovely!' Gladys beamed.

'No probs!' Kate tried to sound enthusiastic, but the truth was she rarely read books. 'I'll bring your tea and you pick a book.'

Gladys looked thrilled. When Kate came back with the tea, she had a book all ready and handed it to her.

'Pride and Prejudice,' Kate read. Her heart sank. Oh no, one of those old-fashioned books! 'Okay, ready?' She looked at Gladys, who sat expectantly with a smile on her wrinkled face.

'It is a truth universally acknowledged, that a man in possession of a good fortune must be in want of a wife.' Kate read out loud. *What crap*, she thought, but continued reading as Gladys sat, seemingly enthralled. To Kate's relief, the doorbell and the sound of the front door being unlocked interrupted the reading. She stopped.

Gladys frowned.

'Only me!' Dorothy trilled.

'Oh, knickers!' Gladys exclaimed, then clapped a hand over her mouth. 'Sorry, pet, but I was so enjoying you reading.'

'We're in the lounge,' Kate called out.

Dorothy entered. 'Just checking that everything's all right,' she said, breathlessly.

'It's wonderful!' Gladys said. 'What's her name here is just reading to me. We've had a lovely dinner, and she's so good at reading.'

'Would you like a cup of tea, Dorothy?' Kate made to rise, but Gladys stopped her. 'No, no, please keep reading, um, dear.'

Dorothy took a quick glance around the lounge room. 'So everything's okay?' she asked Kate.

'Yes, all good. Gladys ate a big dinner, now we're just reading *Pride and Prejudice.*' Kate held up the book.

'Oh, right.' Dorothy sounded surprised.

'Yes, keep going, dear,' Gladys poked Kate. 'I love this book. Have you read it Dorothy?'

'Some time ago.' Dorothy looked at Kate. 'Can I have a quick word in the kitchen, Kate?'

'Of course.' Kate put the book down. 'I won't be a minute, Gladys, and then we'll keep reading. Would you like another cup of tea?'

'That would be lovely, dear.'

Kate picked up Gladys's cup and saucer and followed Dorothy to the kitchen.

Dorothy turned to her. 'So it's all going well, then?'

'I think so, Gladys ate all her dinner last night—chops—and then her breakfast this morning, and tonight she ate a big plate of spaghetti bolognese.'

Dorothy looked startled. 'Well, that's good. Right; well if you're sure you're coping, I'll leave you to it and call in again in another couple of days.'

Kate smiled. 'Gladys is lovely. I'm happy looking after her.'

'Good, good, Well, I'll be off, then. I'll just say goodbye to Mum. Ring me if you've any problems, or send a text.' She hurried out of the kitchen, and Kate heard her telling her mother to take care and to ask Kate if she needed anything.

'I don't know, dear, my daughter fusses so,' Gladys said as Kate went back to the living room, 'but I suppose that's what daughters do. I expect you worry about your mother. You'll have to tell me about your family. Um, dear.'

Kate was taken aback. No, she wasn't worried about Jessica. And her birth mother? How could she worry about a family of which she had no knowledge?

'Now, dear.' Gladys took a sip of her tea. 'We can have a lovely time with you reading to me. Thank you for the tea; it's just the way I like it.'

Kate picked up the book. She was actually quite enjoying it.

She'd had a few text messages from Tom asking how she was getting on, and when they could practice guitar. She'd replied that she'd ask if he could come to Gladys's.

***

Christmas Day was on a Friday. Snippits had been extra busy all week, and Kate felt tired. On Christmas Eve, they all finished work at noon, and Mandy gave each of them an envelope. Kate's contained a Christmas card and her normal weekly wages, plus a fifty-dollar bonus.

'Thank you, Mandy.' Kate smiled. She hadn't expected this.

Everyone was happy and rushing to get out and finish their last-minute shopping. Kate suddenly thought of Gladys and Tom. She should buy them presents! But what? A pot plant for Gladys? A T-shirt for Tom? And she'd better get extra food. She hurried to the shopping centre.

Kate had been surprised to get a text from Dorothy on Christmas Day, wishing her happy Christmas and telling her to look in the tea caddy on the top shelf of the kitchen dresser. It contained an envelope with a fifty-dollar note and a thankyou card. Kate burst into tears.

'What's the matter, dear?' Gladys just happened to come into the kitchen at that moment.

'Everyone is so kind, Gladys. I don't deserve it!'

'Oh, sweetie, you deserve all the good things!' Gladys smiled at her.

'This is for you, Gladys. Happy Christmas!' Kate whisked the pot plant from where she had hidden it in the laundry.

'Oh, I love those poinsettias! Thank you, dear. But I didn't get you anything.!'

'It's all right, Gladys, just being here with you is a lovely Christmas present.' And Kate thought it was true. How could she have stayed at Rob's with Jessica there?

Kate cooked a turkey breast and roast vegetables for their dinner. For once Gladys didn't mention having a boiled egg instead. In the afternoon Tom called round. He had a bunch of flowers for Gladys and a little box for Kate.

'For me?' Surprised, Kate opened the box. Inside, a silver chain with a little silver guitar on it sat on a tiny velvet cushion.

'It's lovely, Tom!' She put it around her neck. 'Can you do it up for me, please?'

Holding his breath, he fumbled with the clasp. 'There,' he said finally.

She went over to a small china cabinet which had a mirrored back, bent down and admired the chain. 'Thank you, Tom,' she said and gave him a kiss on his cheek. Luckily, she'd thought to buy him something, and he seemed pleased with his T-shirt, which had a guitar design on it.

'Seems to be a theme going, here.' Kate smiled.

Gladys was thrilled with her bouquet. 'Such a nice young man, that Tom,' she told Kate after he'd left.

But Christmas day was hard for Kate. She lay in bed that night, thinking of previous Christmases when she'd been innocent and happy. She wondered what her real mother was doing. Was she thinking of her? Her stolen baby, Celine?' The tears rolled down Kate's cheeks. She suddenly felt so alone and adrift.

***

Christmas Day at Sullivan's was also low-key. Andrew had arrived on Christmas Eve. Thomas had been keeping him up to date via text messages about the situation with Kate. He'd hung Christmas decorations in the kitchen and tried to make the place look festive.

Rob went to The Shack and brought Jessica back for lunch. 'Come on in, Jess,' he said. 'Boys, Jessica is here.'

'Hi, Jessica,' Andrew gave her a hug and a kiss on the cheek. 'Haven't seen you for ages.'

Thomas looked up from laying the table. 'Hi, Jessica. Happy Christmas.' He also gave her a hug.

Rob checked the small turkey with all the trimmings he had in the oven. 'How about drinks, boys?'

Andrew opened a bottle of wine. 'Beer or wine, Tom?'

'Beer please.' Thomas nodded.

'Wine, Jessica?'

She shook her head. 'Not for me shanks.'

Andrew stared at her, then looked at Thomas, who gave a brief nod.

They think I'm drunk, Jessica thought, and didn't know what to say. The boys knew nothing about her disease; she'd asked Rob not to tell anyone.

Unlike the boys, neither Rob nor Jessica had much appetite. Jessica managed to knock her glass of water over. Thomas jumped up and got a cloth to wipe the table.

'Shanks, Tom,' Jessica said and put down her fork. She'd tried to get some food into her mouth and missed, and she couldn't bear being the object of pity and censure. 'Shorry, not very hungry today. Love meal, Rob.'

Rob leaned over and took her hand. 'That's okay, Jess. I know you're a bit upset about not having Kate here.' He glared at the boys.

They looked at their plates.

'Yes, it's not the same without Kate,' Tom mumbled.

***

Although Christmas lunch wasn't the same without Kate, in fact Tom was relieved she hadn't been there. It was a while since Andrew had been home and Kate had seen him. Tom brooded over the fact that Andrew had been blessed with all the good looks, none left for me, he thought ruefully. Andrew had always been a chick magnet, and he worried that Kate might fall for him, especially when she saw the two brothers together. He sighed. Kate was so beautiful; he didn't stand a chance against Andrew.

He called in to see her on Boxing Day, thinking it might relieve the monotony a bit for her.

'Hi, Tom,' she greeted him when she opened the front door. Before he had chance to say anything beyond a mumbled 'Hi', she continued, 'I wish Gladys had the internet. I've found information about the Hairdressing Certificate III using my phone, but I need to print off the details.' She led him into the kitchen, calling out 'Tom's here, Gladys.' When there was no reply, she smiled at Tom.

'Probably having a nap. Now, do you think you could print off this stuff if I send you the link?' She asked. 'I might be accepted at TAFE. It's a full-time course, three days a week for thirty-six weeks. So I'd still be able to work at Mandy's ...'

'Of course.' He was delighted at the prospect; it would mean he had a reason to visit her. 'How was Christmas?' Kate asked.

'Okay. Your mum, I mean, Jessica, came for Christmas lunch.'

'And?'

'Well, she was a bit strange. Knocked over her water and slurring her words.' He frowned. 'Don't like to say this, but do you think she has a drinking problem?'

'Yeah, I've noticed it for some time. Your dad told me she had some kind of disease. I don't remember exactly what it was. Isn't Alcoholism a disease?' Kate's brows drew together. 'I said it to her, and she got all upset and started to cry. I told her to go to Alcoholics Anonymous.'

'What did she say?'

'Nothing, just staggered off to her bedroom.'

'Hmm. When does Gladys's daughter get back?'

'January the third.' Kate slumped back on the kitchen chair. 'Oh, I'm so fed up with the TV noise; Gladys has it so loud, and it's crap programs. She falls asleep half the time, anyway.' She grimaced.

'What will you do when Dorothy's back, and you have to leave? Come back to our place?' Tom looked at her hopefully.

Kate sighed. 'Dunno. It's a bit of an imposition on your Dad.'

'He won't mind.'

'Hmm.'

'Come on, Kate, cheer up.'

'I keep thinking about my real mother and how to get in touch with her.'

'Did you write to the magazine?'

'Not yet. I'll maybe do it now. Send them an email.'

When she bent over her phone and started tapping at it, he got up. 'Okay, I'll head off. See you tomorrow?'

'Yeah, okay. I've just sent you the link to the TAFE stuff. Perhaps you can bring the printouts tomorrow. Bye then.' She got up and saw him to the front door and locked it after him.

***

Kate was glad when New Year was over and Snippits opened after the holidays. She'd had lots of texts from her friends asking when they could catch up, but she couldn't face them since finding out about her parentage. She didn't feel like laughing and joking. She didn't know who she was anymore. She was afraid she'd burst into tears and tell all. Anyway, they all had parents and brothers and sisters - real family. She was alone in the world, not knowing where she belonged. She just gave evasive replies, saying she was busy working, having a great time, hope they were, too, and stuff like that.

She waited a day before approaching Mandy with her TAFE forms. 'I'm not sure about how to fill these in, Mandy. Do you think you could help me?'

'Of course, dear. I did the same for Sandra a couple of years ago. No probs!'

Kate gave a sigh of relief. *One problem solved.*

When she got back to Gladys's cottage that afternoon, Dorothy was already there.

'Hello, Kate, dear! Thank you so much for looking after Mum.'

'A pleasure.' Kate smiled. 'Did you have a good time in Melbourne?'

'Yes, it was great. Now, dear, I need to talk with you. There's a bit of a problem.'

Kate's heart sank. She stared at Dorothy in alarm. 'What?' she managed to stammer.

'Well, when I told Gladys that you'd be wanting to move out soon she started to cry. Something about you having expectations, and she wants you to stay. Now, dear, I don't know what kind of expectations you have; my mother's just a pensioner you know.' She frowned at Kate. 'She doesn't have anything to leave, but she obviously loves having you here.'

Kate laughed. 'Oh, I've been reading *Great Expectations* to her; that's what she means!'

Dorothy looked relieved, then smiled and said, 'Well, you've been wonderful with her, and it's certainly a great relief to me, she looks so much better.' She hesitated. 'I don't know what your plans are ...'

Kate blinked. 'What do you mean?'

'Well, I was wondering if you'd like to stay on here and continue looking after Mum.' Seeing Kate's startled look, she hastened to add, 'Of course, we'd have to come to an arrangement moneywise; I wouldn't expect you to do it for nothing.'

Kate's heart lifted. 'That would be fine, Dorothy.' She tried to keep her voice cool and business like but inwardly she was thinking, *YES, YES!*

Gladys interrupted them by coming out into the hall. 'There she is, Dot! Please don't make her go!'

Kate gave her a hug. 'I'm staying with you Gladys, dear.'

'Ooh lovely. See, Dot, I knew she'd want to carry on with *Expectations*.'

Dorothy smiled. 'Hope you like Dickens, Kate. She's got a whole shelf of them.'

Kate opened her mouth, for some reason about to say, *she's like a grandmother I never had,* and then a rush of emotion overcame her. She gave Gladys another hug to hide the tears that came to her eyes, then blew her nose. 'All good, Gladys! How about a nice pasta dish for dinner tonight?'

'Just a boiled egg for me, dear.'

Dorothy winked at Kate and whispered, 'Mum and her boiled eggs!' Then in a louder voice, 'Such a relief! We'll talk about money next time, Kate. Have you enough for everything for the next few days? I have to rush now; look here's a hundred dollars to keep you going.' She opened her handbag and took out two fifty-dollar notes. 'Thank you so much. Bye now, Mum.' She gave Gladys a peck on the cheek and left.

Gladys smiled at Kate. 'Oh, I was so worried, dear; I thought we wouldn't be able to finish the book.'

'All good, Gladys. Now come into the kitchen and I'll make us a cup of tea, and I can start preparing dinner.'

Two problems solved!

As Kate went into the kitchen with a spring in her step, her mobile phone buzzed; an email. She put away the groceries she'd bought on her way back from work and then put the kettle on. 'Sit down, Gladys; excuse me just a minute while I check this email.'

When she saw the sender, her heart skipped a beat.

Dear Kate

Thank you for your email. When the article you refer to was first published, we received a number of letters from girls thinking they were the stolen baby. We passed them on to the lady in the article, but we don't know the outcome. I don't know if she still lives at the same address, as it's been several years since that item was published. But I will print out your details and mail them to her. Please let us know your address, and telephone number, in case the lady would like to contact you. We don't have a mobile phone number for her. I would be most grateful that in the event of a happy outcome you would inform us.

Regards

Joyce Weaver, Assistant Editor.

'Kettle's boiled, dear.' Glady's voice broke into Kate's thoughts.

Three good things in one day! Perhaps I should buy a lottery ticket!

'Right, Gladys, I'll make the tea now. I'll just send a message to Thomas.' Her fingers shaking, Kate quickly typed a text: *Hi Tom, Heard from mag. They want my address. Can I use urs? I can't use The Shack, and can't use this address as won't be here long.*

She'd just poured out two cups of tea when her phone pinged. *Sure.*

CHAPTER 18

Life settled into a routine for Kate. Three days a week at TAFE, studying hairdressing, two days and Saturday mornings at Snippits, as well as looking after Gladys, kept her busy. Too busy to think about Jessica and her real mother. She'd managed to save enough to buy an iPad so she now had the internet. She replied to the email from the magazine giving them the details they requested, but she heard nothing back.

By Easter she was getting impatient.

Tom was sympathetic. 'What about Facebook?' He suggested.

'I don't know her name.' Kate felt glum.

'What about sending a photo of you to the magazine? They'll be able to see that you look like the woman in the article. They might tell you her real name and then you can search.'

Kate brightened up. 'That's an idea! Will you take a photo of me, Tom?'

'Course.'

'Use my phone and I can email it to them and tell them a few more things about myself. Surely, they'd give me her real name, even if she's moved and they don't have an address.'

'Right.'

'Or perhaps they'd search for her themselves, if they think there's a story in it!'

Tom looked at her in admiration. 'You're awesome, Kate!' Then he hesitated. 'But they'd want to know about Jessica. Do you want that to happen?'

'Yes! No! Oh, I don't know, Tom. Have you seen her lately?' She thought about Jessica sometimes, wondered how she was, but she didn't feel she would ever be able to trust her again. Didn't think she could face seeing her. But all the same she missed her. They'd been so close all her life. She tried to push those thoughts away; they only made her start to cry.

Tom didn't answer, instead he took her phone. 'Come on, then; I'll take your photo now.'

'I must fix my hair first.'

'Looks fine to me.'

He'd successfully drawn Kate's attention away from Jessica, saving him from having to tell her that he'd seen Jessica a few days before and she hadn't looked good. To him it looked as if her drinking problem had got worse.

***

Rob had stopped at The Shack every day on his way home from work. It was a detour, but he'd been more worried than ever about Jessica since her visit to the doctor. She seemed to have deteriorated.

He'd brought her to his place for Easter Sunday lunch, but it hadn't been a success. Jessica had refused to eat, afraid that the boys would be disgusted at how often she spilled her food—if she could even get it onto her fork. Only after Andrew had left to go back to Brisbane where he worked and Thomas had disappeared outside to tinker with his van did she seem to relax.

'Darling, Jess, why won't you let me explain to the boys about Huntington's?' He couldn't understand why she was so stubborn about not telling anyone.

'Look down on me.' She eventually managed to say.

'That's nonsense! Of course people won't look down on you, or judge you. And, anyway, you refuse to go out, except for the doctor, and I have to drag you there, so how can people look down on you?'

'They pity me,' she mumbled.

Rob shook his head. They still sat at the kitchen table, and he took one of her hands in his. 'Do you think you could eat something now? A little bit of lamb? Some salad?'

She shook her head. 'Not hungry.'

'You must eat, Jess; you've got so thin lately.'

He studied her in silence for a while, then said, 'Jess, we have to talk about the future. You can't stay at The Shack for much longer. You're not coping.' He'd noticed how run down the place had become. Although he'd tried to keep the garden and yard tidy and mow the paddock, the house itself needed a good clean, and he couldn't do that. Jessica would be devastated.

'Made decision,' Jessica muttered. 'Gun sell up. Move into home. You help me sell, Rob?'

He started. 'When did you decide this?'

She tried to shrug, but it set her head jerking.

'Of course, I'll help you to sell, but where will you go?'

'You help me find place?'

He nodded. 'Yes.'

A tear trickled down her cheek. 'Sanks, Rob.'

He was overwhelmed with grief to see this beautiful, independent and clever woman so helpless. He got up from the table and lifted her into his arms, dismayed at how little she weighed. Then he took her to the couch and sat with her in his arms and held her while she cried.

'Rob. When it's too much, you help me end it all?'

He froze. 'What do you mean?'

'When can't take it anymore. Like my mother. End it.'

'Jessica! You can't do that! You mean, take your own life!'

'Yesh. Can't face it. Read about it.'

'Jessica,' he said softly. 'You just can't do that. Think of Kate! She'd be devastated.'

'She hates me.'

'No, she's young; she'll come round. If you did that, she'd always blame herself. Please, believe me.'

Jessica let out a sob. 'I'm not brave. I don't think I can face the future.'

'Jess, I love you. Please don't think that way.' He held her tight.

'Oh, Rob, you're so good. I've loved you for so long, but I was afraid.'

'Shh. I understand. Now. No more of this talk. Come, I'll take you home and we'll see what options there are for you in care.'

'Lucky's not well. She's not eating. I think she's pining for Kate. Will you look at her?'

He nodded. 'Of course.'

But when they got back to The Shack, they found Lucky lying lifeless in her bed.

'Oh, Lucky! Lucky!' Jessica's eyes filled with tears as she bent over the little dog. She gently stroked Lucky's head. 'What will I tell Kate? She'll be distraught.'

Rob put his arm around her. 'I'll bury her and make a little cross.'

***

Rob was surprised The Shack sold so quickly. 'Tree changers' was the new buzz phrase, people wanting to escape from the city and be self-sufficient. He'd found someone to come and clean the house and he'd spent two weekends working on the outside. Then he'd gone to a solicitor, the firm that Jessica told him had dealt with all the paperwork when her father died, explained the situation and got the contract drawn up and signed by Jessica. Her signature was a scrawl, but it sufficed. He'd found a real -estate agent in town, and one of their reps had come out and photographed the place. The second person to view made an offer. Rob advised Jessica to think about it for a day or two. When the prospective buyer came back with a slightly higher offer. Jessica accepted it straight away.

The sixty-day settlement gave Jessica, with the help of Dr Bailey, time to find accommodation in an aged-care facility just outside of town.

Dr Bailey looked at Jessica over his glasses. 'I'm sorry but there's nowhere else I can find for you at the moment. You'll be in there with people mostly in their seventies or eighties, and you're only what ...' He looked at her notes. 'Forty-six ... It won't be easy for you.'

She tried to nod. 'Sokay. Swot I serve.'

Rob could just make out that she was trying to say it was what she deserved. He stared at her. 'No, Jess, it's not what you deserve.'

Dr Bailey looked puzzled for a few moments. 'Well, in future, I'll see you in Oakley House, Jessica, when I do my monthly calls on the residents.' He stood up.

Rob helped her up and carefully guided her out of the consulting room.

'What do you want to do with the van? Tangy?' he asked as they made their way slowly to his ute.

'Kate,' she replied. 'For Kate. Tom drive to your place.'

He nodded. 'Okay, I think she's got her L plates now.'

Jessica made a choking noise, so he stopped. 'Are you okay, Jess?' Then he saw the tears in her eyes.

'Miss her,' she managed to say.

***

A week later, Rob told Thomas that Jessica was selling up and moving.

Tom frowned. 'Where?'

'Somewhere on the other side of town. Um, she's not taking the HJ, she wants Kate to have it, so asked if we'd keep it here until Kate passes her driving test.'

'Right.' Thomas nodded. 'When?'

'The weekend okay with you? Jessica's given me the keys.'

'Shall I tell Kate? I mean, tell her that Jessica's moving and given the van to her?' Thomas asked.

'Dunno. You know how feisty Kate is; she might refuse to have it. I'll keep it registered, and we'll wait and see what happens. We can put it in the shed; it's in great nick.'

The following Sunday at lunch, Rob said to Thomas, 'shall we go and get Jessica's van this arvo?'

Thomas nodded and mumbled, 'Okay,' through a mouthful of food.

'Have you told Kate about The Shack being sold?'

'No, I didn't know how to tell her, so I said nothing. She never asks about Jessica now. She's very stubborn. She said she'd never talk to Jessica again, and I don't think she feels she can go back on her word.'

'Well, best not to tell her anything. She's had a lot to deal with, and it might make her feel a bit lost. She doesn't need that.'

'Hmm,' Tom said. 'Kate's changed, Dad. You know how she was always kind of bubbly and jolly? Life of the party? Now she seems much quieter, and I don't think she sees her friends anymore. She's either working or at TAFE or looking after Gladys. It's only when I take her out for a driving lesson that I see her.'

Rob grimaced. 'I think she needs to see some kind of counsellor or psychologist. How's her driving going?'

'Okay; she's saving up for a small car.' Tom sighed. 'I think it will be a long time before she can afford one, the insurance especially.'

'Yes, and she won't be able to insure under Jessica's insurance, which now I think about it, I'll have to look into.'

When they arrived at The Shack, Rob said, 'You drive my ute and I'll drive the Holden.'

'Oh, really? I was hoping to get to drive the Holden.'

'Well, maybe we'll both just look at it and check it out first; it hasn't been driven for months, now.' Rob glanced at his son. 'I guess you can drive it back, and maybe keep it in good nick, Tom? Take it for a spin occasionally?'

Tom's face lit up. 'Thanks, Dad. Awesome.'

Rob smiled. 'You're a good boy, Tom.'

Tom returned his smile.

'I'll just pop in and see Jess.' Rob moved towards the house. As he walked up the steps of the veranda, he could hear scuffling noises inside. 'It's me, Jess,' he called.

He heard her shuffling to the door. She opened it, gave a lop-sided smile and put out a hand.

He took it. 'Tom and I have come to take the HJ back to our place. What are you up to?'

'Packing. Shorting stuff.'

'Need some help?'

She nodded. Rob stepped inside and looked around. The place was in disarray—piles of clothes on the floor, and books stacked against the walls.

'What I do with stuff, Rob?'

He gave a sigh. 'I don't know, Jess. I wish Kate was here to help you. Perhaps I can get some packing boxes and pack things she might need later and take them over to my place. Store them in the shed. Things like your mother's paintings, other little things that she grew up with.'

Jess's eyes lit up, and she nodded. 'Yesh, please. Good idea.'

'Maybe we'll take one room at a time. I'll get the packing boxes tomorrow and come round after work.'

***

Kate finished her Certificate III in Hairdressing and was thrilled when Mandy gave her a pay-rise. She now did trims for new clients—she'd practiced on Gladys, much to Gladys's joy.

'Can you give me a colour, dear?' Gladys had asked.

Kate had been dubious, especially when Gladys decided on mauve. 'Your hair is lovely the colour it is,' she'd replied. 'I'll just trim it and give you a wash and blow dry.'

Dorothy had been impressed when she'd seen Gladys's new style. 'You could do mine, too, dear,' she'd said.

'I'm still training,' Kate had replied. 'I need to practice on people, so that would be great, if you don't mind. But once I've finished my training, you'll have to come into Snippits.'

'Of course, dear. I quite understand.'

***

'Do you think Mum's getting more doddery?' Dorothy asked one day, a year later, as she was getting ready to leave after her weekly visit to Gladys.

'Um, well, yes, she's getting quite confused lately. Gets up in the night and comes into my room and asks why am I still in bed, I'll be late for work.'

'Oh dear, how often does that happen?'

Kate sighed. 'It's getting more and more frequent. Also ...' She hesitated. 'I've had to buy her incontinence pants.'

Dorothy paled. 'My goodness, dear. I'll have to take her to the doctor. It's getting too much for you.'

'She doesn't want to go out at all lately. I've tried to get her to go for little walks around the neighbourhood, but she just puts it off or says she has a cold coming.'

'You're so good to her, dear. But I think you need a break. Easter is coming; don't you want to be with your family or have a holiday? Go somewhere nice?'

Kate shrugged. 'It's okay, Dorothy; I really like being here with Gladys. And I'm saving for a car, so I can't afford to go away.' She didn't mention that when the time came for her to move, she'd have to find other accommodation, which with the bond and rent in advance would probably be expensive. At the moment she was saving what little money she earned at Snippits and most of the generous allowance Dorothy gave her. 'I'm very fond of Gladys,'

Kate continued. 'She's just the loveliest person. It's a shame her memory is getting so bad.'

'I'll make an appointment with the doctor.' Dorothy picked up her handbag. 'Right. Bye dear.'

A few weeks later, Kate came back from work, unlocked the front door and called, 'Hello Gladys, it's me, Kate!' as she usually did. Then she heard a low moan coming from the kitchen. She ran in and found Gladys lying on the kitchen floor. 'Gladys! What happened?' She bent down to take one of Gladys's hands, smoothed back the old woman's hair and saw a purple bruise.

'I can't move, dear. I think I hit my head on the table. It's very sore.'

'You'll be all right now I'm here. Let me get a blanket and cover you up to stay warm. I'll ring for an ambulance.'

'No, dear, I don't want to go to hospital. Ring Dot, she'll come.'

Kate fetched a blanket from her bed and a pillow to put under Gladys's head, and covered her up. Then she went into her bedroom and first rang triple 0, then Dorothy.

The ambulance and Dorothy arrived at the same time. Before she knew what had happened, Gladys was on a stretcher being put in an ambulance. 'I'll follow the ambulance, Kate,' Dorothy said. 'Would you pack a few things for her, please, dear? I think she might have to stay in hospital for a bit.'

'Of course, Dorothy.' Kate closed the front door, walked into the kitchen and rang Thomas. 'Gladys was so frightened, Tom,' she said, and then started to cry.

'I've just got home. I'll get changed and come over.' Tom hung up before Kate could protest.

Kate dried her eyes, went into Gladys's bedroom, found a clean nightdress, dressing gown, and toiletries and put them in a shopping bag.

When she heard Tom's van, she ran out with the bag. 'Can we go to the hospital please, with Gladys's stuff?' she asked him.

'Of course!' He leaned over and opened the passenger door.

They found Dorothy just coming out of the emergency section of the hospital. 'Oh, Kate, you've brought her stuff. She'll be so pleased. It looks like she's broken her hip, so they'll probably operate on her tomorrow. I'll take this into her now. Best not to come in; they've given her some pain medication and she's a bit woozy.' She turned and headed back into the hospital.

Kate started to cry again. 'Poor Gladys; she was so frightened about going into hospital.'

'She's in the best place now.' Tom opened the passenger door of his van. 'Jump in; I'll take you home.'

At Gladys's cottage, Tom stopped his van and waited, hoping Kate would invite him in, but she just leaned across and kissed his cheek. 'Thanks, Tom. You're the best.' She got out and walked up the path.

He waited until he saw her open the door and disappear inside. Then he put his hand on his cheek and smiled.

***

Rob went to Oakley House every weekend to visit Jessica. She had difficulty swallowing and needed spoon feeding. Rob could see her gradually deteriorating. He bumped into Dr Bailey one day as he went in and stopped him and asked how Jessica was going.

Dr Bailey shook his head and grimaced. 'Well, there's never good news with Huntington's, but she's as comfortable as we can make her. Of course, it's not ideal that she isn't somewhere with people her own age, but there are just so few facilities for younger people with disabilities.' He sighed and frowned, then continued, 'by the way, you might think that Jessica doesn't understand what's being said, but mostly she does. She's just not capable of giving a coherent reply.'

Rob nodded.

'We've got her on anti-depressant medication,' the doctor continued. 'Depression is a symptom of Huntington's and I think she's been depressed for quite some time.'

Ever since Kate left, Rob thought. He sighed and went into the big lounge. Several very old people, some in wheelchairs, sat watching an enormous television. He spotted Jessica in a wheelchair by the window. When she saw him, her eyes lit up and he could see her trying to smile.

'Low,' she managed to say.

'How about we go outside, take a turn around the garden,' he suggested, bending down to kiss her.

'Lovey.'

'Do you need anything, Jess? Look I've got a new cardigan for you.' He held up a bag. 'I think it will fit you. I can take it back if it's not right.'

Jessica's eyes filled with tears. 'You so good,' she slurred.

Rob felt a momentary flash of anger. *Kate should be doing this! Buying Jess new clothes and seeing that she had what she needed.* He took a deep breath and reminded himself that Kate didn't know that Jessica was in a nursing home. *But she could have asked Tom how she was. But then, when Tom had asked him how was Jessica, he'd just said ok. Jessica had been adamant no one was to know she was in a nursing home.*

He sighed and pushed Jessica's wheel chair out into the garden. After half an hour he wheeled her up the ramp into the entrance hall.

'Time for tea,' he said, spotting a tea trolley being trundled from the kitchen into the lounge. 'I'll stay a while and help you.' He took the non-spill cup and a biscuit from the trolley and wheeled her to a quiet corner. Patiently he helped her eat and drink. Then he gave her a kiss. 'I'd better be off, Jess. I'll see you next weekend.'

She watched him going out the big doors and sighed, seeming to shrink into the wheelchair.

***

Gladys had a hip replacement but wasn't strong enough to come home afterwards.

'I think we might have to start looking for an aged-care home for her,' Dorothy told Kate when she met her and Thomas coming out of the hospital after visiting Gladys.

'Oh dear.' Kate frowned.

Yes, apparently, she's been assessed by the hospital. It seems she has dementia.'

'Hmm, I wondered about that,' Kate replied. 'So I guess you'll be putting the cottage up for sale.'

'Yes, dear, not for a while though. We'd like you to stay on for a bit 'til we see what happens. That's if you don't mind. Keep the place tidy and aired ...'

'Of course, Dorothy. That'll be fine. I'll see you later.' Her heart sank as they walked away.

'Bummer,' Thomas said. 'Oh! I nearly forgot, Kate. A letter came for you at our place. It's in the van.'

'Thanks, Tom.'

Tom opened the passenger door for her. 'It's in the glove box. Lucky I remembered.'

Kate opened the glove box. She didn't recognize the writing on the envelope, but when she opened it, her heart gave a flip. 'Tom! It's from the magazine! They had a letter from Melanie; she'd moved, and my photo and details only reached her a few days ago. They're forwarding her letter.' She pulled out an envelope. 'Oh, my God, Tom!' She started to shake. 'Wait! What'll I do?'

'Open the letter, of course.' Tom started the engine.

'Wait, Tom. Stop! Don't drive yet. Let me read the letter.'

Obediently, Thomas turned off the engine and watched her as she opened the envelope. 'What does she say?'

'Hold on ... Okay, she says that I look like she used to when she was young. She wants to meet me! Oh, Tom! Oh, and her name is Wanda Lane. Melanie Baxter was just the false name they gave her in the magazine.' Kate turned to him; her hands shook and her voice came out in stutters. 'What will I do?'

'Meet her, I suppose. Where does she live?'

Kate looked at the letter again. 'Wollongong.'

'Wollongong! That's miles away.'

'Will you drive me, Tom?'

He remained silent for a few minutes.

'Please, Tom!'

'It's a long way. Why don't you get the train? I'll come with you, but not until I get time off.'

'Next weekend? We could get the train on Friday night and come back on Saturday night. Please, Tom!'

He hesitated. 'It might not be convenient for her.'

'She's put her mobile number in the letter; I'll text her now.'

Tom's heart sank. The last thing he wanted was to go chasing round the country and meeting strange people and seeing Kate being disappointed.

'I'm going anyway,' Kate said.

Tom looked at her. He loved her. He couldn't let her go off on her own. 'Okay, I'll come with you.'

Kate grinned. 'Thanks, Tom. You're a pal.'

He turned away and looked out the window of the van. That's how Kate thought of him—as a brother, a pal. 'We'd better head off,' he said. 'It's only one-hour parking here.' He put the van into gear and said brusquely, 'put your seat belt on.'

Absentmindedly, Kate fastened her seat belt, her eyes still on her phone, waiting for a reply.

***

In the end Thomas decided to drive her. When he checked on Google maps, he found that Kate's mother's address was nowhere near the train station. 'We'll leave first thing Saturday morning. Should be there by midday. It's about a seven-hour drive,' he told Kate. 'Give you time to see your mother. We can leave by two o'clock and be back here before it's dark.' He studied her. 'Think that'll be enough time for a first meeting?'

'Yes, possibly. She might want us to stay the night.'

When he stopped outside Gladys's cottage at five o'clock on the Saturday morning, Kate was already waiting at the gate. 'I told Mandy, I wouldn't be able to work this morning,' she said to him as she jumped into the passenger seat. She looked at his pale face. 'Thanks, Tom. I really appreciate this. Do you know the way?'

'Think so. Got Google maps on my phone.'

They settled down to the long journey and stopped in Newcastle for breakfast. Tom was starving, but Kate felt too excited to eat. She watched Tom wolf down his eggs, bacon and sausage, while she tried to drink her coffee. 'What if she's horrible, Tom?'

'Don't be daft. She'll be like you. Gorgeous,' he mumbled through a mouthful of food, then blushed and cast his eyes down to the sausage on the end of his fork.

Kate looked at him. He was just trying to cheer her up. She sighed. 'Maybe.'

When they reached Wollongong, Kate sent Wanda a text. *'Just reached Wollongong. Shouldn't be long now.'*

She got a thumbs-up sign in reply.

At last the GPS woman announced, 'you have reached your destination on the left.'

Kate looked at the house. An old car, perched on concrete blocks, sat in the driveway with weeds growing beneath it. On the straggly lawn stood a broken trampoline, and the front gate swung open at a drunken angle. Her heart sank.

'That looks like an old Chrysler Charger.' Thomas brightened as he indicated the old car. He turned from looking at the car to her. 'You getting out? What's wrong?'

Kate seemed frozen, then the front door of the house opened and a short, plump woman appeared in the doorway. Kate opened the passenger door, climbed out, fumbled for her bag and took a deep breath. 'You coming, Tom?'

Reluctantly he got out. 'I'll hang around outside. Your mother and all that. Emotional time ...' When he saw her start to shake, he put an arm around her shoulders.

The woman started down the path towards them and stopped at the gate. 'Celine?' she asked cautiously.

Kate nodded. 'I think so, except I'm called Kate now.'

The woman nodded. 'Yes, so you said.'

Tom looked from one to the other. They were obviously mother and daughter. He swallowed and tried to think of something to say. 'Um, do you think I could use your bathroom?' Both women stared at him.

The woman seemed to shake herself. 'Of course. Are you her boyfriend?'

Tom held his breath, waiting for Kate to say something. When she remained silent, he nodded. 'Kind of.' He took his arm from where he'd been holding Kate and put out his hand to Wanda. 'Tom Sullivan.'

Though still looking at Kate, she took his hand and shook it. 'I'm Wanda. Of course, come in.'

Inside, the small entry opened onto a living-dining room with a kitchen area visible through an archway. A large television in one corner was screening a soccer match. It all seemed pretty dismal, Tom thought. A vague smell of cigarette smoke and fried food lingered on the air.

The three occupants of the room looked up as they walked in.

A man half rose from the table, where he'd been reading a newspaper, stubbing out a cigarette as he did so. 'G'day, you must be Wanda's girl. I'm Don, Wanda's partner.' He looked Kate up and down, his gaze lingering over her breasts.

Tom's fists clenched.

'Don, this is Tom. Can you show him where the toilet is please?' Wanda moved into the living room.

Don nodded. 'Come this way, mate.'

As he left the room, Tom glanced back at the boy and girl sitting on an old couch. They hadn't moved, just observed Kate with curiosity.

'Brett, get up and say hello to your sister. You, too, Donna. And turn off the telly, Brett.'

Brett had the same pasty complexion and narrow face as Don, so Kate assumed Don was his father.

Reluctantly, Brett stood up, pressed the mute button on the remote and said, 'Hi,' in a surly tone.

'Nice to meet you,' Kate responded and turned to the girl. 'Hi, Donna. I suppose I'm a bit of a surprise to you.'

Donna nodded and mumbled. She looked like Wanda around the eyes, but she too had the same narrow face as Don, and the unhealthy complexion.

Silence descended, then Wanda asked them if they'd like a cup of tea. 'I expect you could do with one. What time did you leave? Donna, put the kettle on. Brett, let Celine, I mean Kate sit down,' she gabbled on nervously. Then when Tom came back into the room followed by Don, she added, 'sit down, Tom. How was the drive? Much traffic?'

'Not too bad.' Tom turned to Don, who'd sat back at the table and started to shuffle with a packet of cigarettes and a box of matches. 'That your Charger in the driveway, er Don?'

'Yeah, trying to do her up.'

Wanda broke in, 'So what are you doing now, Cel ... I mean, Kate? Have you left school?'

'Yes, I'm a hairdresser.'

Donna suddenly appeared in the kitchen doorway. 'So that's why your hair is so nice! And you've got Mum's hair. I got Dad's ...'

Kate had noticed Donna's lank mousy coloured hair as soon as she'd walked in. 'It just needs styling.' She smiled.

'Donna's only twelve, time enough for paying for a pricey hairdresser,' Don said.

Brett had started pressing buttons on his mobile phone.

'Put that phone away, Brett,' his mother said sharply. 'Where are your manners; we have visitors.'

'She's only my sister,' Brett muttered.

'Shut your effin' mouth and do as your mother says,' Don intervened.

Kate blinked, taken aback by Don's words.

Wanda's gaze darted from Kate to Don. She bit her lip. 'I'll make the tea,' she said. 'You all stay and chat.'

Kate felt like bursting into tears. This was not how she'd envisaged meeting her birth mother.

After a long silence, Tom spoke up. 'So you're a mechanic, Don?'

'Nah. Friend, who is, owes me a favour; he's going to come round one day and work on the old Charger.'

Tom nodded. 'Right.' He glanced at Kate, who sat motionless, then turned to Brett. 'So you still at school, Brett?'

'Yeah.'

'Ah. So what do you want to do when you leave?'

'Dunno.'

Tom took a deep breath. 'How about you, Donna?'

She looked up, and her eyes slid towards Kate. 'Think I'll go for hairdressing, like her.'

Kate brightened at that. 'That's a good idea,' she said. 'I left school when I was sixteen.' She swallowed, remembering that awful last day of school. 'I worked on Saturday mornings in a hairdressing salon before that, so I asked the owner if I could do an apprenticeship with her. You have to go to TAFE and study.'

Brett snorted. 'Dunno what you'd need to study for to cut someone's hair. I could cut yours for you, Donna, no probs.' He leered at his sister.

His mother walked in with two mugs of tea. 'Donna, fetch the milk, and there's a packet of biscuits, bring them, too. Oh, and the sugar.' She put the two mugs on the table, then returned to the kitchen, calling out over her shoulder, 'You want tea, Brett?'

Brett shrugged. 'Nah, but I'll have a biscuit.'

Wanda came back with another two mugs. 'Help yourselves to milk and sugar,' she said, looking at Kate.

Kate got up and went to the table. She turned to Tom, who sat perched on the edge of the couch. 'Tea, Tom?'

He nodded. 'I'll get it.'

They all sat silently eating their biscuits and drinking the tea. Kate didn't really want a biscuit, but took one, feeling that it would be rude not to. She could think of nothing to say. For the last two years, ever since finding out about her birth mother, she'd imagined scenarios where a beautiful woman would sweep her into her arms, crying, '*Oh, my long-lost daughter! At last my life is complete. Not a day has passed since you were stolen when I haven't thought about you.*' And she'd imagined a brother a bit like Tom and a sister a bit like herself, someone she could share with

...

Thomas shifted uncomfortably on the low couch, his long legs sticking out. 'So what's your line of work, Don?'

Don frowned and slurped his tea. 'Worked on the buildings, but hurt my back a few years ago.'

'Oh, sorry to hear that. Give you much pain?' Tom looked lost, as if he didn't know what else to say.

Wanda and the two children looked at Don, waiting for his reply.

'It's pretty bad, but I don't complain,' Don said self-righteously.

Brett snorted, earning a scowl from his father.

'If you had to put up with what I have to put up with, you'd know all about it,' Don growled.

Tom fell silent and glanced at Kate, but she just frowned at her cup of tea.

Wanda broke the silence. 'Well, isn't this nice, now? Catching up with your sister, Brett and Donna?' She asked brightly.

They muttered some reply.

'We should've probably chatted a bit more before meeting,' Wanda continued, 'but now we've broken the ice and you know where we live, perhaps you like to come and stay for a few days when you get some time off.'

Kate nodded. 'That would be nice, thank you.' She couldn't imagine anything worse.

Don suddenly came to life. 'So what was the story about the woman who stole you?' he asked.

His question stunned Kate. She opened her mouth, then closed it again.

Thomas came to her rescue. 'It's a very complicated story,' he said. 'Perhaps Kate can fill you in the next time you meet.'

'I reckon you should sue her, Wan,' Don said, taking a cigarette from the pack and tapping it on the packet. 'For all the years you've missed out with your child. Get in touch with that magazine again. Bit of money in it for you, Wan.'

Wanda blinked. 'I only ever wanted to know Celine was all right,' she said. 'Well cared for and happy.' She turned to Kate. 'Did you have a happy childhood?'

Kate let out a long breath, and nodded. She suddenly realised it was true. 'Yes.' She frowned and looked at Tom.

He took one look at Kate's face, stood up and put his mug on the table. 'Well, Wanda and Don, thank you for the tea, but we should probably be heading off now. It's been a long day; we left at five this morning. I'd like to get back before it's dark. If that's all right with you, Kate?'

She nodded, stood up and put her mug on the table. 'Thank you, Wanda. That was lovely.'

Don opened his packet of cigarettes. 'Smoke, Tom?'

'No, thanks, Don.'

Don lit up, took a drag and blew out a plume of smoke. 'Nice to meet Wanda's girl at last,' he said, then turned back to his newspaper.

Wanda walked to the door with them.

Kate looked back at Brett and Donna. 'Bye, guys,' she said, and Tom echoed her.

Brett didn't answer; he'd unmuted the television, and the noise drowned anything Donna might have said.

Outside the door, Wanda tentatively hugged Kate. 'We'll be in touch, dear.'

Kate nodded, unable to speak for a moment. Then she looked at Wanda and came out with the question she was burning to know. 'My father ...' she whispered, 'what was his name? What did he look like?'

Wanda frowned. 'Everyone called him Bazza,' she said, 'I didn't know his proper name. It was a commune, love. I wasn't there long ... What did he look like?' Her frown deepened. 'I guess he looked okay. It's a long time ago. I can't really remember.'

Kate closed her eyes, overcome by a wave of nausea.

Thomas put his arm around her and led her gently to the van. 'Bye, Wanda,' he called, opening the passenger door for Kate to get in.

She collapsed into the seat and fumbled with her seat belt. Tom leant over and fastened it for her. He gave her a hard look, then walked around to the driver's side, got in and started the engine. After a toot on the horn, he drove off, stopping around the corner to set the GPS on his phone to 'home'.

After half an hour driving along the freeway, he pulled into a rest area. 'You want to use the loo?'

'Thanks, Tom.'

'I need to stretch my legs.' He got out and sat on a bench.

Kate came back from the toilet and sat beside him. He put his arms around her, and she started to sob. 'Oh, Tom, that was awful.'

He kissed her forehead. 'Bound to be difficult, the first time,' he said. 'Be easier the next time.'

Kate stared at him. 'I don't know if I want there to be a next time. She couldn't even remember what my father looked like! Or his proper name.' She swallowed, took a deep breath, dried her eyes and blew her nose. 'Tom you were amazing. Thank you so much. Imagine if I'd got the train and had to stay there for a night! What a horrible man! And that Brett.'

'But Wanda is nice,' Tom said. 'I liked her. And at least Brett didn't pick his nose.'

Kate gave a teary laugh. 'You want me to drive for a bit? Give you a break?'

Tom smiled at her. 'No, I'm fine, you just relax. It's been a difficult day for you.'

***

Kate remained silent for most of the return journey. Tom glanced over at her a couple of times and eventually saw that she'd fallen asleep. He felt good. Kate said he'd been amazing, and he'd dared to kiss her. Even if it was only on the forehead.

At Kempsey, he pulled into a MacDonald's.

'Kate,' he whispered. 'Wake up. I'm starving and have to get petrol.'

Kate started and looked around in fright. 'Where are we?'

'Kempsey. Maccas.'

She shook herself awake, and struggled to get up. 'Wha ...?'

'I'm hungry; fancy a burger?'

'Er, no. Maybe.' She sat up and ran her fingers through her hair. 'Did I sleep?'

Tom grinned. 'You've been snoring since Wollongong.'

'Really?' Kate blinked and sat up. 'Okay, I think I can manage to eat something.'

Half an hour later they were back in the van. Tom started the engine. 'Feel better, Kate?'

'Dunno, Tom. I've been thinking. Imagine, if Jessica hadn't stolen me, I'd be living with that Don as a step-father.' She shuddered.

'Maybe not, Kate. He might not have hooked up with Wanda if she already had a baby with her.'

Kate considered this. 'Even so.'

'Anyway, from what Dad has told me, Jessica didn't steal you. He said a woman had left you on the train asking Jessica to mind you. Then she disappeared. Jessica didn't actually steal you.'

'Hmm.' Kate went quiet again.

Tom glanced at her from time to time. 'So I'll drop you back at Gladys's place, then, and see you maybe next week sometime?' he asked.

'Perhaps I should go and see Jessica, go home,' Kate said pensively.

Tom didn't know what to say. He didn't want to be the one to tell her that Jessica had moved to a retirement village and The Shack had been sold. He was afraid Kate would start crying. She seemed to turn on the waterworks for any reason. On the one hand he could see himself taking her into his arms and comforting her, but on the other, well, he'd have to be sure he had a clean handkerchief and while he was driving was not the most auspicious time. Was auspicious the right word? Anyway. Not the best time or place. She'd had enough shocks for one day. He resolved to tell her another time. 'Best go to Gladys's,' was all he said.

'Okay.'

'You know what, Tom?'

'What?'

'Jessica bought a tent one year. We went camping. Up the coast. It was awesome.'

'Sounds great,' Tom murmured, thinking that Rob had never taken them camping. It would have been fun to go with Jessica and Kate.

'Yeah. She was great really, Tom.'

'Mmmh.'

'Maybe I was a bit hard on her, Tom. What do you think?'

'Um... Dunno Kate.' He was in a bit of a dilemma. He didn't want to make Kate feel bad but then he really liked Jessica.

He stopped outside the cottage. 'You'll be okay, Kate?'

'Yeah. Thanks, Tom, for everything.' She leaned over and kissed his cheek, got out the van and walked slowly up the path. He waited until she was inside, touching his cheek where she had kissed it, before driving back to Sullivans.

***

The next day being Sunday, Kate slept late. It still felt strange not having Gladys there. The hospital was too far away for her to visit; she'd have to wait for Tom to drive her. But she was so tired. Yesterday had been an exhausting day. She thought of Tom, driving over seven hours down to Wollongong and then seven hours back. What would she do if she didn't have him? She sent him a text message, thanking him again. *You're the best, Tom.* She wrote. She didn't like to ask him to take her to see Gladys that afternoon, instead she'd ask him to take her the following Sunday.

She sent a text to Wanda: *Hi Wanda. It was so nice to meet you at last. Thanks for everything.*

A message came straight back: *Lovely to meet you after all this time, Kate. I still call you Celine in my mind. Love Wanda. Xxx*

Kate just couldn't think of Wanda as her mother. She kept thinking of Jessica and how different her life would've been if she'd had to live in that cramped house with that horrible Brett and even more horrible Don. How could Wanda stand living with Don? The way he'd looked at her, Kate, his eyes going up and down her body. She shuddered. Perhaps she'd been lucky that Jessica had taken her.

She couldn't get all these thoughts out of her head. Eventually she gave herself a mental shake and started to give the cottage a good clean. She'd ask Tom to take her to The Shack next week, after visiting Gladys in hospital.

CHAPTER 19

Rob was surprised to see Tom's van outside when he got up on Sunday morning; he hadn't heard him come in. He knew Kate had had contact with her birth mother and that they'd gone to meet her in Wollongong.

'Long way to drive from here, son,' he'd said when Tom had told him. 'Will you stay the night there?' He had visions of Tom and Kate checking into a motel together.

'Don't know. Depends.'

Clearly, they hadn't stayed overnight.

He quietly opened Tom's bedroom door and was relieved to see him sleeping soundly in his bed.

Later that afternoon, after visiting Jessica, he returned home to find Tom out in the yard checking the oil and water in his van.

'How did the visit go?' Rob asked as he got out of the ute.

Tom looked up, slammed the bonnet of the van and grimaced. 'Her mother's okay, and the sister seems okay, too,' he replied slowly. 'But the husband is pretty grim and the brother ...' He shrugged.

'So it didn't go off too well? How did Kate take it?'

'I think she was a bit disappointed. Think she'd imagined things differently.'

'You must have been tired last night, driving to Wollongong and back in one day.'

'Yeah, was a bit.'

'What's the next step?'

'Dunno. What's for dinner?'

They went into the house.

***

The following Sunday when Kate and Tom arrived at the hospital, they found that Gladys had been moved that morning to Oakley House, an aged-care home just outside town.

'I suppose Dorothy hasn't had time to let me know,' Kate said. 'Can we go there now, Tom?'

'Okay. I'll just get the directions.' He picked up his phone and typed Oakley House into his Google Maps app. 'About twenty minutes' drive,' he said.

When they arrived at the home—a big old house with a lot of extensions built onto it—Kate commented that the place didn't look too bad. 'Look, you can park over there.' She pointed to a small driveway leading to a parking area.

They walked up to the main doors which appeared to be locked; a sign read, *Please ring the bell.*

Kate frowned. 'I suppose that's to keep people from wandering in or out.'

When the door opened, a woman with an official-looking badge on a chain around her neck looked enquiringly at them.

'We're looking for Gladys White,' Kate said. 'She came in this morning.'

'Oh right.' She gestured them inside and indicated a small table in the entrance hall. 'Sign the visitor's book just here, please. Mrs

White's probably in the lounge; I think they're still preparing her room. Over there.' She pointed to a door.

Thomas and Kate walked towards it. Kate wrinkled her nose. 'Get that smell, Tom?' she whispered.

They opened the door and peered into the large lounge room. A few old people sat in wheelchairs, but most sat in armchairs arranged around the walls. A big television blared from one corner. Some of the old people appeared to be asleep, their chins sunk on their chests. One or two watched the TV screen avidly, while the others seemed focused on some point in the middle distance. Kate scanned the room and spotted Gladys sitting in a wheelchair near the window. She took Tom's arm. 'She's over there, looking out the window,' she said in a low voice.

They walked across the room, smiling at the other people, who seemed to wake up as they crossed their path.

'Gladys!' Kate called softly.

Gladys turned her head. 'Oh! It's you, dear,' she exclaimed. 'Please take me home, dear. I don't like it here. It's full of old people.'

Kate gave Gladys a quick hug, then crouched down beside her. 'How are you feeling now? You'll soon be up and about with your new hip.'

'What new hip?'

'You broke your hip, and you've been in hospital getting a new one.'

'Oh, of course. I knew that. But I don't like it here, dear. I want to go home. It's all old people.' She looked at Tom. 'Here's that nice young man. He'll take me home, won't you, dear?'

Tom opened his mouth, but it was a few seconds before he managed to say, 'if I can, Gladys. But we must wait until you can walk properly.'

'I don't like all these old people. And I didn't like what they gave me for lunch. I asked for a boiled egg, and they gave me some kind of meat with gravy. I couldn't eat it. Not like your cooking, dear.'

Kate took her hand. 'I think you might be going home next week, Gladys. Can you hang on for a few more days?' Knowing how Gladys forgot everything, she hoped she'd have forgotten that by next week.

'I've got a daughter. She might take me home.'

'I'm sure she will.' Kate glanced at Tom. 'I wonder if we can wheel her around outside in the garden for a bit of fresh air.'

'I'll go and ask,' he said, then hurried out the door. Five minutes later he returned, disturbing the television watchers yet again. 'Yes, we can wheel her out the back. There's a ramp leading into the garden.'

Kate said in a low tone to Gladys, 'We're just going to go for a walk with you.'

Gladys brightened. 'You're taking me home?'

Kate didn't answer as they passed through the room.

'Sorry, sorry again,' Tom said to the other occupants.

They wheeled Gladys along the path around a big lawn. 'It's nice here, Gladys,' Kate said, 'Look at all the roses.' She bent down and pointed them out, then heard a voice say, 'Tom! What are you doing here?' She looked up, turned around and was surprised to see Rob just behind them.

'Hi, Dad; we're just taking Gladys for a spin,' Tom replied. 'She was sent here today from the hospital. What are you doing here? Um, here's Kate.'

Kate was shocked at how old Rob looked since she'd seen him last—nearly two years ago. 'Hi, Rob; nice to see you.' Then she became aware of the wheelchair in front of him. It contained a woman, her body twisted in the wheelchair, one of her arms bent at an odd angle to the side. Kate frowned as a feeling of disbelief and horror came over her. It couldn't be ... no, surely not!

'Jessica is living here now,' Rob said.

Tom stared at Jessica. 'I didn't know she was in a home,' he stammered.

Kate gasped, her hand flying to her mouth. 'Mum!' Her body seemed to have a life of its own as it propelled her towards the wheelchair. 'Oh, Mum.' She kneeled down in front of Jessica and put her head in her lap. 'Oh, Mum, I'm so sorry,' she sobbed, tears streaming down her cheeks.

Jessica tried to speak, but only a mumble came out.

'What's happening?' A querulous voice came from Gladys's wheelchair. 'When are you taking me home?'

'Soon, Gladys, soon,' Tom said. He turned to his father. 'What do we do now, Dad?' he asked in a low voice, his brow creased with worry. 'We have a lot of explaining to do. Kate's in for a shock. Why didn't you tell me Jessica was in a home? I just thought she'd gone to a retirement village?'

'She didn't want anyone to know. And I think Kate's already had a big shock,' Rob replied drily. He looked back at the two women, both now crying and he took a breath. 'Perhaps it's best if you take Gladys inside and then come back here and we'll sort out what to do. Maybe bring Kate back to our place for tonight. She can sleep in Andrew's room.'

Tom nodded, looking relieved. 'Good idea. I'll take Gladys inside.' He turned to Gladys. 'Time for afternoon tea, Gladys. We have to go back in now.' He wheeled her towards the ramp leading inside the building. Her complaining voice faded into the distance.

Ten minutes later, he returned to the garden. 'Gladys started to kick up a dust, crying and stuff. She wants to go home. Had to find a carer to take over.'

'All these women crying,' Rob said, trying to smile, and then he turned to Kate. 'Kate, dear, Tom's going to take you back to our place. He'll stop on the way for you to get a few things. We need to have a talk.'

Kate closed her eyes, took a deep breath and nodded. 'Okay. Whatever.' She turned back to Jessica. 'I'm so sorry, Mum,' she whispered. 'I love you. I'll come again as soon as I can.'

Jessica's eyes filled with tears again. 'Love you, too,' she managed to say.

Kate gave her a hug. 'Forgive me, Mum.'

'You give me ...' Jessica slurred.

Tom took Kate's hand. 'Come on, Kate,' he said. 'Bye, Jessica, we'll see you again soon.' He led Kate away.

She said nothing while they drove back to Gladys's house.

Tom parked the van, then said, 'I'll wait outside while you get your stuff.'

Kate sniffed and nodded. 'Okay. Thanks, Tom.'

Once back in his van with an overnight bag, Kate said, 'Do you think we could call by The Shack, Tom? I'd like to go home.'

Tom grimaced, then took a deep breath and said in a low voice, 'Kate, The Shack has been sold. Jessica had to sell it. I thought she was moving into some kind of retirement home. I haven't seen her for ages. I didn't know she'd got so bad. Dad never said anything. I'm sorry, Kate.'

Kate stared at him, motionless. Tears filled her eyes and then overflowed down her cheeks. 'I can't bear it, Tom,' she sobbed, then looked up. 'Where's Lucky? What happened to Lucky?'

'Oh, Kate, Lucky was very old. One morning just after you left, she didn't wake up. It was very peaceful,' he added hurriedly.

This news caused Kate to sob even harder. 'I can't bear it, Tom. I can't take anymore.'

He put the seat belt around her, then started the engine. 'We'll go to our place,' he said.

***

The first thing Kate saw when they arrived at Sullivan's was the tangerine Holden van.

'What's Tangy doing here?' she asked.

'Your mum, I mean Jessica, wanted you to have it. I've been giving it a service.'

Kate burst into fresh tears. 'Where's all the stuff—Mum's furniture, paintings and books?'

'Dad packed them all up. They're in the back shed.'

'Oh God, I can't bear it.'

'Come, Kate.' Gently Tom took her hand. 'Come inside and sit down. You've had too many shocks lately. I'll make a cup of tea.'

She let herself be led into the house, then collapsed onto the couch just as they heard Rob's ute coming down the driveway.

He walked in, tiredness written all over his face, and looked anxiously at Kate. 'Hello, Kate,' he said softly, then he saw Tom boiling the kettle. 'Good man, Tom; we could all do with a cup of tea.'

'I think I need something stronger,' Kate muttered.

'You don't drink,' Tom pointed out.

'Oh, Rob,' Kate suddenly burst out. 'I've lost everything. I've no home, no-where to go. The Shack has been sold, and Dorothy is selling Gladys's house, and I've hurt and upset Mum, and I don't want to go and live with Wanda,' she moaned.

'Who's Wanda?' Rob turned to his son.

'Kate's birth mother,' Tom whispered. 'Sorry, forgot to mention that's her name.'

'I just want to die!' Kate wailed. 'I've been a liability ever since I was born!'

Tom looked alarmed. 'No! Don't even think such a thing!' he exclaimed.

Rob sat down at the kitchen table and put his head in his hands. 'Let's all have something to eat and get an early night. I'm stuffed,' he muttered.

'I don't think I'll be able to sleep.' Kate sniffed. 'And I'm not hungry.' She turned to Rob. 'How long has Mum been in that awful place? It smells! And it's all old people like Gladys there.'

'She's been in there over a year now. There's nowhere else around here. I've been looking. There's a place in Newcastle, but it's too far. I wouldn't be able to visit her.'

'I could look after her.'

Rob stared at her. 'Kate, you couldn't. She needs constant care. She has to be spoon fed, bathed and other stuff.'

'Oh, Rob, when you said she had that disease, whatever it was ...'

'Huntington's.'

'Yes, that thing; I didn't think it was like that. I dunno what I thought. Maybe arthritis or something, and then I thought she was a secret alcoholic. I never imagined it could be so awful.'

Rob looked up at her. 'It's a living death, Kate.'

'Oh, Rob!' she cried. 'And I've been so horrible to her.'

'Kate, you weren't to know, and you've had a basinful, too, but look how well you've coped. Jessica is proud of you! In fact, she told me once that you were the best thing that ever happened to her.'

Kate lifted her head. 'Really?' she whispered.

He nodded. 'Yes. Now, Kate, my love. Please go to bed and get some rest.'

She looked at him. 'You're tired, Rob. I owe you for all you've done for her.' She took a deep breath, then got up and gave him a hug. 'Thanks, Rob. You're the best.'

Next morning Tom got up early and called Kate through the door, 'Come on, Kate. I'll take you back to Gladys's house, and you can get ready for work.'

Only a muffled response came from Andrew's room. It sounded like Kate was crying.

'I've got breakfast for you.' He could just make out her saying she wasn't hungry.

Rob emerged from his bedroom. 'Kate!' he shouted 'Come on! Get up!'

Kate came out of the bedroom in her nightie, causing Tom to gulp and hastily avert his eyes.

'Now, Kate,' Rob said, 'it's no good going into hysterics and being a drama queen—'

'I'm not a drama queen!'

'I know,' he said more gently. 'What I mean is, you've had a rough trot the last couple of years, but so has Jessica. We just have to keep going and make the best of things. Now. You just go to work as usual. You still have Gladys's house to go to, and you know you can consider this your home, too. For now, though, Jessica is our first priority. Let's just focus on her.' He rubbed his eyes with his knuckles. 'Kate, we all love you,' he continued. 'We'll support you and be here for you always. Now, get ready for work.'

She disappeared back into the bedroom and emerged five minutes later fully dressed. 'Thanks, Rob. You're right. Thank you for everything and for looking after Mum; I mean Jessica.'

Chapter 20

Two months later, Gladys's house still hadn't sold.

'I know it's old and needs a lot of work done to it, and it's not in a nice part of town,' Dorothy remarked to Kate, 'but it's on a good-sized block.' She sighed. 'The real-estate agent said I should drop the price, and I think I will. It's all too much. I just want to get rid of it and pay the bond for Mum's aged-care place. But thank you, Kate, for taking such good care of it.'

Kate nodded. 'That's okay, Dorothy; it's suited me to be here.'

Dorothy nodded and handed her an envelope. 'Here's your money for caretaking the place.'

Kate shook her head. 'I won't take it, Dorothy. I should be paying you rent, instead.'

'Nonsense, dear. I appreciate how you've looked after the place and been so kind to Mum, and gone to see her.'

Later that day, Kate told Tom that Dorothy had dropped the price she wanted for the house. When he heard the new price, he went away thinking hard.

That night after their dinner, Tom studied his father. He looked so tired and drawn. 'Dad?'

'Hmm?'

'I've been thinking about Kate, and Gladys's house and the HJ ...'

Rob nodded. 'And?'

'Well, Dorothy has dropped the price, and well, I was thinking maybe if Kate sold the HJ, she could buy Gladys's house.'

Rob frowned. 'I don't think the old HJ would fetch that much, Tom.'

'Wait Dad, look at this website.' Tom got his iPad and showed his father the screen.

Rob's eyes widened. 'I can't believe it. There's one for $84,000!'

'Yes, and look, there's one for over $100,000. I was looking for spares for Kate's HJ and came across these.'

'That's great, son. I'm proud of you. I thought the HJ would be worth a bit, but not *that* much.'

'Well, it's in pretty good nick, and I'll work on it a bit more.' Tom paused. 'So I was thinking that if Kate sold it, she could buy a small car and with the rest put down a deposit on Gladys's house. It needs a lot of work done on it, but it's still liveable and I could help ...'

Rob's frown deepened. 'I think she'd need much more than that to get a mortgage. I don't suppose she earns a lot at the moment.'

Tom's shoulders slumped. 'Hmm. I didn't think of that.'

'Tell you what, I'm going to see Jessica on Saturday morning. How about I tell her. She might have some money left over from when she sold The Shack. I'm not sure how much she had to put down for the bond on the nursing home.' Rob finished his breakfast and stood up and looked at his watch. 'I'd better get going.'

'Kate asked me if I'd give her a lift on Sunday to visit Gladys and Jessica.' Tom sighed. 'She feels so bad, Dad.'

'Jessica understands Kate's reaction. She doesn't blame her.' Rob picked up his mug and plate.

'It's not fair, Dad.'

'No, son. Sometimes life isn't. Well, I'd better load the ute. I've got some chainsawing to do tomorrow.'

'Need a hand?'

Rob smiled. 'It's okay. But well done with your plan. Have you mentioned it to Kate?'

'No, I wanted to check with you first, to see if you thought it was a good idea.'

Rob paused. 'Actually, I was thinking of moving as well. I want to get something nearer to Jessica. I don't know how much longer she'll live. Maybe another two years, perhaps four. No one seems to know. But the time I spend with her means the less time I have to maintain this place. It needs a lot doing to it, and I'm not getting any younger.'

'Oh, Dad!'

Rob smiled sadly. 'And the place needs a family.' He looked down at Tom.

'Maybe Andrew would be interested?' Tom asked hopefully.

Rob gave a small laugh. 'Where would he get computing work around here? And when will he ever stick to one girlfriend? He has a different one every time he comes home! Don't worry, son. I'll work something out.'

***

When Rob saw Jessica the following Saturday, he took her out into the garden, as he usually did when he visited and the weather was favourable. He stopped the wheelchair under the shade of a tree facing a bench, then kissed Jessica and sat down.

'Jessica,' he began slowly. 'It seems that your Holden van is worth a lot of money.' He waited until it seemed Jessica had understood before continuing, 'Tom was thinking that if Kate sold it, she'd be able to buy a house. You've seen Gladys, who Kate was caring for. She's living here now. Well, her house is up for sale. It needs a lot doing to it, so it's going cheap.' When Jessica gave a tiny nod of her head, he continued, 'I know it's none of my business, but I was wondering if you had any money left from the sale of The Shack that she could have to help her buy her own place.' He stared down at his hands, then looked up at her.

She managed to say, 'No. No money.' She remained quiet for a bit, then said something that Rob figured was, 'Paintings. Sell paintings. Valuable.'

'Your mother's painting?'

'Yesh, she bought ... Valable now.'

He nodded. 'Right. So your mother bought some paintings, and you think they might be valuable as well as the ones she painted?'

'Yesh.'

'You'd be happy with that arrangement?'

'Yesh. Kate need a home.'

***

A week later, Tom waited outside Snippits for Kate to finish work. Eventually she emerged from the salon, saw his van and walked over.

'Hi, Tom,' she said, 'how nice of you to come for me. I'm very tired. Appreciate a lift.'

After she'd climbed in and clicked her seatbelt in place, he turned to her. 'Kate, I want to talk to you.'

'Right,' she said, surprised. 'Here? Or back at Gladys's'

'Back at number seven.'

'Okay.'

Once inside and in the kitchen, she put the kettle on. 'Sit down, Tom. Now what's this all about?'

'Well, I've been thinking. You see, when I was servicing your Holden, I was looking for parts and came across Holden Sandman vans for sale.'

'Right.' Kate got out two mugs and put tea bags in each one, scarcely listening. *If Tom's going to rabbit on about cars ...*

'And I was thinking about this house.'

'Oh?' That caught Kate's interest. She turned off the gas under the kettle.

'I think you could buy it. You'd be happy living here, wouldn't you?'

Kate gave a sardonic laugh. 'Yeah, I wouldn't mind staying here, but *buy* it! With what money?'

'That's the thing, Kate. Holden Sandman vans fetch a good price on the market at the moment, especially ones like yours. Get your iPad. I'll show you.'

'Oh my God,' Kate exclaimed five minutes later. 'That one is for sale for $84,000!'

'Yes, look, there are a few others around that price. One's even priced at $104,000'

Kate stared at him. 'No-one would pay that for an old car,' she scoffed. 'So what are you suggesting?'

'Well, I thought that if you sell the Holden, you could buy a small car. I'd find one for you, so you could go and see Jessica whenever you want, and you'd have enough money left over for a deposit on a house.'

She stared at him. 'But what about the mortgage?'

'Well, Dad spoke to Jessica about all this, and she said to sell her mother's paintings. It seems there might be some valuable ones that her mother bought when she went to galleries selling her own paintings. They were cheap then, but might be worth something now.' He stopped and looked at her, waiting for a response.

'I'll think about it,' she said after a pause.

'Would you like to come over to our place tomorrow and we can go through your mum's paintings. Perhaps put them on eBay.'

She nodded. 'Okay. And Tom?'

'Yes?'

'Would you sell the Holden for me?'

'Of course. So how about I come over tomorrow morning. I'll take you to see Jessica, and then we can go back to our place and look at the paintings.'

She nodded, frowning in thought.

Next day when Tom called round for her, she was waiting at the gate.

'Been thinking, Tom,' she said as she got in the passenger seat of his van.

'Hmm?'

'I don't want to buy Gladys's place. It's too big for me and needs too much doing to it. I was thinking that I could buy a little flat for a lot less money than this place.'

Tom looked at her. 'Gladys's place would be a great invest-ment.' He frowned. 'It needs some work done on it, painting, new kitchen and so on ...'

'But, Tom, I don't have the time or the inclination to do that, and if I can get a little car, I can go and see Jessica whenever I get a chance, so I wouldn't have time for do-it-yourself, even if I was any good at it.'

Tom frowned. 'Yeah, I can see your point, but I could help you.'

She put a hand on his thigh. 'I know. Thanks, Tom; you're the best of friends.'

He gripped the steering wheel and took a deep breath. 'Okay, well, we'll look at the paintings after visiting Jessica.'

They stayed with Jessica until Rob arrived, then drove back to Sullivans.

Tom took Kate to the back shed. 'All the stuff from The Shack is here,' he said as he opened the sliding door.

Kate gasped when she saw all the furniture and boxes.

'Dad and Jessica thought you might like some of the stuff, once you get your own place.'

Kate gulped. 'I don't know what to say.'

'I think the paintings are over here.' Tom led the way to the back of the shed and carefully removed a dust sheet.

Kate said nothing as she pulled out some of the stacked-up paintings. She found one of a man. 'I remember Mum saying this was her father,' she said slowly. 'I assumed it was my grandfather but now I think of it, she never used that word. Just said it was of her father and this one here,' she took out another one, 'is of her mother. I think I'd like to keep them. And this one of Mum when she was a little girl. But the others, well, let's try and sell them. We can sort through them all another day. Didn't Rob tell you that some were by other artists and might be valuable?'

She stopped and looked at all the furniture that Rob had carefully stored. Tears came to her eyes. 'My childhood is here,' she whispered.

Tom took her arm. 'I'll take you back to Gladys's place,' he said, afraid she'd burst into tears.

***

Rob suggested they get an art dealer to come and look at the paintings. 'I know nothing about art,' he said with a shrug.

Tom nodded. 'Yeah, and I'll put the HJ for sale online. Might take a while to sell. Kate doesn't want to buy Gladys's house. Says it's too big and too much to do on it. Wants to get a small flat or something similar.'

Rob sighed. 'You're disappointed, aren't you?'

'Yeah.' Tom nodded.

'We're a couple of sad cases, aren't we, Tom? You're in love with Kate, who hasn't noticed, and here's me with Jessica and it's too late.'

Startled, Tom looked up at his father. 'How did you guess? About Kate I mean.'

Rob laughed. 'Pretty obvious.'

Tom blushed. 'Dunno what to do; she thinks I'm like a brother to her.'

'She's had a lot to cope with in the past couple of years, and she's still young—what? Nearly nineteen?'

'Yeah, next month. And I'm twenty-three.'

Both men lapsed into silence as they ate, then Rob said, 'You're really keen on Gladys's house, aren't you?'

'I think it's a great investment.'

'Why don't *you* buy it, then? I could help you.'

'Really, Dad?' Tom's eyes widened. 'I've got a fair bit saved. I don't go out much, as you know, and all the money I get from the work I've been doing on neighbour's tractors and machinery, well, I've saved most of it ...'

'Okay, well, let's sit down later on and go over the money situation.'

Tom made an offer on Gladys's house a few days later.

***

The HJ sold and all Sybilla's paintings cleared at auction. The HJ hadn't realised as much as Kate had hoped, but the paintings had stunned them all. Some of them that Sybilla had bought back in the 1970's from then unknown artists had turned out to be quite valuable. Kate had enough to buy outright a one-bedroom flat on the side of town nearest to Oakley House, as well as a second-hand small car that Tom found for her. Rob and Tom helped her move some of the furniture that had been stored in the shed to her flat.

'What will I do with all these books, Rob?' Kate asked as she surveyed the stacks of boxes. 'I'm never going to read them all ...'

'Charity shop?' Rob suggested.

Kate nodded. 'Would you take them for me?'

He smiled. 'Of course.'

'Thanks, Rob; that's good of you.'

She turned to Tom, who'd had his offer for Gladys's house accepted and was waiting for the mortgage and paperwork to come through. 'Tom, you're welcome to any of the furniture I don't need. I can't fit everything into the flat.'

'Thanks, Kate. Dorothy asked me if I wanted any of Gladys's stuff, but to be honest, most of it was a bit past it, so I said no. She said she'd pay me and Dad to take it all to the tip, just keep anything I did fancy, like kitchen utensils and crockery.'

Kate grinned. 'Looks like we're all sorted! A new start for you. And for me.'

Tom nodded.

It didn't take Kate long to settle in. Her small flat had an open-plan kitchen and living area with a bathroom, laundry and one bedroom. There was also a parking space outside. She could drive to work and to Oakley House, so no longer depended on Tom to drive her places.

She was pleased to be able to spend more time with Jessica. She desperately wanted to help, to try and make up for her past actions.

She took massage oil and would kneel on the floor and massage Jessica's legs.

The first time Kate did this Jessica made an effort to speak. 'Father same mother,' she muttered.

Kate looked up. 'Your father did this for your mother?'

Jessica gave a small nod.

Kate tried to think of other ways to help. She thought of Gladys and how she loved being read to. The next time she went to Oakley House, she produced a book.

'Look, Mum, I've brought a book to read to you. I know you like History, so I brought this one by Charles Dickens. His books are all about the olden times. I thought you'd like 'The Tale of Two Cities.' She thought she saw Jessica's eyes light up.

Jessica managed to nod and smile.

***

'I guess you see more of Kate than I do,' Tom remarked to his father one day when Rob called in with a sign he'd made to put on the gate. It had 'Glad's Place' carved into an old fence paling.

'Well, Kate seems to be at Oakley House most times when I go there,' Rob replied. 'She does a lot, helping to feed Jessica, massaging her legs. Kate's matured a lot. Give her time, Tom.'

Tom didn't see Kate for several months. A text message broke the drought:

Hi Tom. My car needs servicing. Should I take it to Olly's?'

Kate X

Tom thought about the X and decided it probably didn't mean anything from her point of view. He sent a reply:

Bring the car round to me in the morning. I can drop you at Snippits and then take it to work, get it serviced and pick you up after work. That ok?

Tom X

When she brought her car round early the next morning, Kate peered at the sign and said, 'Glad's Place? Shouldn't it be Tom's Place? Sign's nice, though.'

Tom shrugged. 'Probably, but I think it's nice to remember Gladys. How is she by the way? And your mum? Sorry I haven't been to see them for ages; so much to do here.'

Kate studied the outside of the house. 'You're doing a great job, Tom. It all looks so bright and fresh.' She looked around with approval, then continued, 'Gladys is very frail now, crankier than ever. I've been doing hers and Mum's hair. In fact, doing the hair for a few of the old ladies there. It cheers them up.'

Tom looked at her in admiration. 'That's nice of you, Kate.'

'I don't mind.' Her eyes clouded. 'But Mum, well, she's getting worse. The doctor said that Huntington's is like having Alzheimer's, Parkinson's and Motor Neurone Disease all together.'

Tom frowned. 'What's Motor Neurone Disease?'

'Some kind of disease that wears away the nerve cells in your brain. I didn't know, either, so I asked the doctor. And her personality seems to have changed. She's in such pain with these terrible cramps that twist her legs. Sometimes she doesn't seem to know who I am, or Rob. Oh, Tom, it's cruel to see her. I feel so bad that I thought all the time that she had a drinking problem ... I was horrible to her.' Her eyes filled with tears.

'Kate! You weren't to know! Dad told me Jessica didn't want anyone to know. Especially you; she didn't want to worry you.'

The tears threatened to overflow.

Tom searched for some way to change the subject. 'Do you hear from Wanda at all?'

Kate shrugged. 'Sometimes. I don't know, we don't seem to have anything in common, and what with moving and seeing Mum and everything, I just haven't had time to think about her.'

'Did you ever contact that magazine and tell them you'd found her?'

'No. I was worried in case it all came to light and Jessica had to go to court and prison and stuff.'

Tom looked at his watch. 'We'd better make a move.'

'Do you ever get lonely here on your own, Tom?'

Startled, he stared at her. 'Not really; I've been too busy, spend every spare minute doing up this place.'

'Hmm. I'm busy, too, but sometimes in the evenings, I feel a bit lonely.'

'Well, you've never had a break, or a holiday.' He thought rapidly. 'Why don't you and I go away somewhere for a few days?' His heart started to thump. He looked at her anxiously.

'Hmm. Dunno. I don't like to leave Jessica. She might not be here much longer.'

Well, at least she didn't dismiss the idea outright. He smiled. 'It's my birthday next week, how about you and I go out to celebrate.'

'Oh, Tom, I'd forgotten! Yes, good idea. Your Dad as well?'

Tom's heart dropped. 'Well, I thought just you and me.'

'Okay. I'll book somewhere and treat you.' She smiled. 'You've been so good to me, Tom, and I've never said how much I appreciate it.'

Heat rushed to his face. He opened the passenger's door of her car for her. 'Hop in. I'll drop you off at Snippets and pick you up this evening.'

'Thanks, Tom.' Kate slid into the car and buckled her seat belt.

Tom adjusted the driver's seat, looked over at her and turned on the ignition.

The next day, Tom received a text message:

Hi Tom, booked The Thai House for Thursday 7pm. I'll pick you up about 6.45. My turn to drive you.

Kate X

Tom's heart jumped. He sent a text straight back:

Hi Kate.

That'll be great.

Thanks.

Tom X

On Thursday, Tom was ready by six o'clock for his first real date with Kate. When he heard her car stop outside, he took one quick look at his reflection in the hall mirror and walked out.

She was getting out of the car as he shut the front door.

'Wow, you look awesome, Kate!' She did, too. She'd grown her hair a bit, and the dark curls formed a halo round her pretty face. He plucked up courage and kissed her cheek.

'You're looking pretty good yourself, Tom! Didn't realise you'd scrub up so well!'

He blushed. 'Thanks, Kate. I um, well, okay,' he mumbled.

'And where are your glasses?' She frowned.

He shrugged. 'I got contact lenses.'

'I thought you looked different.' She laughed. 'Oh, it's so nice to be going out somewhere. We should do this more often.'

The Thai restaurant was like most Thai restaurants: a nice spicy smell; pictures of the King of Thailand on the walls; and elephant motifs.

They'd just started on Tom Yum soup when the door of the restaurant opened and a few seconds later, a girl's voice said, 'Well, if it isn't Tom! Yummy Tom! I mean Tom Yum.' She giggled.

Kate looked up to see an attractive girl with a tight, extremely low-cut dress leaning over Tom, thrusting her chest under his nose.

Tom made a choking noise.

Her boobs are going to fall out at any moment, Kate thought. *Into the soup!*

The girl turned to Kate, gave her a swift, appraising look, then turned back to Tom, who managed to say, 'Oh! Hi, Ruby; how's things?'

'Good thanks, Tom. Enjoy your meal! I'm just collecting take away. See you!' She kissed her fingers and put them on his lips.

Kate stared at Tom, who spluttered into his soup and muttered, 'She's in the office at work. Does the accounts.'

Kate frowned. She'd never thought about him having girl-friends, and that girl was certainly giving him the eye. She realised that she really knew very little about Tom's life since he'd moved to town.

He looked up and caught her staring at him. 'What's up, Kate? Food all right?'

'Yes,' she smiled. 'It's lovely.' Her mind was whirling. *What if Tom meets someone and gets married? This is his twenty-fourth birthday. He must've had girlfriends! But if there was anyone special, surely, he'd be celebrating his birthday with her.* 'Happy birthday, Tom.'

'Oh, thanks, Kate.'

'Um, any special girl in your life, Tom?'

He went red and waved his hand in front of his face. 'Phew, that soup's pretty hot ...'

Kate kept looking at him.

'Why? What about you, Kate?'

'Me?' She hesitated. 'No, no-one special.' She looked down at her plate.

When they'd finished eating, they both said, 'I'll pay.'

'No, Tom, please! I asked you.'

When they arrived back at Glad's Place, Tom asked her if she'd like to come in for a coffee.

Kate felt suddenly shy but she said, 'Okay, thanks.'

Inside, the atmosphere seemed charged, and Tom didn't appear to know what to do. 'Sit down,' he said to her, opening the door of the lounge room and indicating the couch. 'I'll make the coffee.'

'I'll help.' Kate followed him to the kitchen. She felt awkward and didn't want to sit primly waiting for her coffee. She sat at the kitchen table. 'What have you been doing since you moved into town, Tom?'

'Oh, well, working, doing up this place. Think I'm nearly there now. What do you think?' He waved his hand around the kitchen.

'It's lovely,' she said, her gaze following his hand. 'Great colours; who helped you choose them?'

'Um, no one ...' he stammered.

Kate frowned. Her eyes narrowed as she watched him grind beans in a machine and make coffee in a plunger. *A coffee grinder! A plunger! There has to be a girl behind all this!*

He opened a cupboard and took out a jar with coffee sugar in it. 'How do you like your coffee, Kate? With milk?'

She nodded. 'Yes, please.' She watched him pour milk into a small jug and heat it in the microwave, then he took nice china cups from a cupboard, added the hot milk to one and then coffee from the plunger. *Who showed him how to do that?* She'd been expecting instant coffee in a mug!

He placed a spoon on a saucer, the cup on the saucer, then put it in front of her and smiled. 'Hope that's okay for you, sugar's there.' He poured himself a black coffee and sat opposite her.

'Thanks, Tom.' Kate felt shaken. She didn't know this new Tom. She looked up and saw him watching her and quickly looked down. An awkward silence followed...

Tom cleared his throat. 'It's been a lovely evening,' he said. 'Thanks for the meal, Kate.'

'My pleasure.'

'Um, perhaps we could do it again some evening?'

Surprised, she smiled. 'That would be lovely, Tom.'

'Next week, then? I've got bush fire training on Thursday, how about Friday?'

'Great.'

'What about a movie?'

She nodded. 'Sounds good.' She sipped her coffee, unsure of what else to say.

Tom appeared to be the same; then he broke the silence, 'how's work?'

Kate managed to talk a bit about work, then stood and said she'd better go. 'Thanks for the coffee, Tom.'

He stood up. 'No probs. Thanks again, Kate, for the evening.' He walked her to the door.

She turned, reached up to him, and gave him a quick kiss. 'Night Tom,' she said, then headed down the path to her car.

Next morning when Kate checked her mobile, she found a message from Tom:

Hi Kate,

Thanks for dinner last night.

There's a movie at 7pm Friday night. Pick you up at 6.30? That OK?

Tom X

This must mean he had no girlfriend at the moment.

Hi Tom,

Great. What's the movie?

Kate X

A reply came back immediately:

Dunno, there's three on in different cinemas. Whichever one you like.

Tom X

***

On Sunday mornings when she went to Oakley House, Kate would kiss Jessica, then help give her breakfast. It took ages. Jessica had a problem with the food in her mouth. It seemed to go around from one side to the other and was hard for her to swallow, often causing her to choke. When this happened, Kate thought Jessica was about to die. Today, Kate lightly stroked Jessica's throat. That sometimes helped the food go down. Some foods Jessica simply could not swallow—it depended on the texture and type of food. Often Jessica got tired before the meal was finished, or she would have a choking fit. This time, after about half an hour, she closed her mouth when Kate put the spoon to her lips. Kate knew this meant she'd had enough.

Gently she wiped Jessica's mouth. 'Shall we go out in the garden, Mum?'

There was always something in bloom to which Kate could draw Jessica's attention. A high wall surrounded the pretty garden, sheltering it from the wind. Kate pushed the wheelchair out and along the path surrounding the neatly manicured lawn. Jessica was on medication to stop the chorea, or shaking of her limbs, but it had the unfortunate side effects of drowsiness and depression.

Kate pushed the wheelchair into a sunny spot. 'You need your Vitamin D from the sun, Mum,' she said. 'look, there's your favourite rose.' She pointed to a crimson bloom, then crouched down in front of the wheelchair. It seemed Jessica was trying to smile. Her eyes followed Kate.

'Mum, you remember Tom, Rob's son?' Kate could see Jessica making an effort to concentrate. Although she didn't know whether Jessica understood what she was saying, she kept on chatting to her as she usually did. She stood up. 'Well, it was Tom's birthday on Thursday and we went out for dinner.'

Jessica's expression didn't change.

'I hadn't seen him for ages, Mum, and then I realised something. He's a bit different. Well, I suppose he's grown up. Like me really.' Kate felt her mother wasn't listening—she seemed to be in a different world—but she kept chatting. 'So then we went back to Tom's place. It's where I was staying when I looked after Gladys. Which reminds me, I must go and see her a bit later. Maybe I could push your wheelchair to her room. I don't think she mixes much with the other residents—says they're all old people. She stays in her room most of the time watching TV. Anyway, as I was saying, I went round to Tom's place, where Gladys used to live. Tom has it all done up beautifully...' She bent down to look at Jessica, whose eyes were closed. She appeared to be asleep.

With a sigh, Kate stood up. 'What I was going to say was that I suddenly realised I loved Tom. I know I always kind of loved him like a brother but now, not seeing him for ages, I see him differently. He's not the skinny, awkward, boy anymore ... Oh,

Mum, I wish you could reply, tell me it's all okay; he's not my brother; it's ok to love him ...' She gave another sigh. 'Let's go and see Gladys. Anyway, Rob will be here this afternoon to see you.'

Kate thought Rob was amazing. He came every Saturday and Sunday afternoon to see Jessica. He didn't talk much, but just sat most of the time holding one of Jessica's hands. He'd stay until her dinner time and take over trying to feed her.

Friday came, and Kate took extra care with her appearance. She was ready half an hour too early and waited nervously for the sound of his van. She didn't hear it, so her doorbell ringing surprised her. She opened the door. 'Oh, Tom! I didn't hear you. Where's your van?'

Tom laughed and pointed across the road to a gleaming red car. 'She's there—got a new car, Kate. Well, it's ten years old, but in mint condition. Had it a few months now.' His face lit up with pride. Then he turned to her. 'Ready?'

They ended up watching a horror movie. It was the only one on at the time they arrived, and Kate thought it would do. She refused Tom's offer of popcorn or an ice-cream.

About ten minutes into the movie, Kate realised they'd made a bad choice of film. Tom seemed enthralled but at the first scary bit, Kate jumped and grabbed Tom's hand and kept holding it. During the next scary bit, she hid her face on his shoulder.

'It's okay, darling,' Tom whispered and stroked her hair, then shifted in his seat and gave a little cough.

Afterwards, coming out from the darkness into the sudden light, Kate stumbled.

Tom put his arm around her waist and didn't take it away. On their way to Tom's car they passed a restaurant with outdoor tables. Tom cleared his throat. 'Um Kate, what would you like to do now? Would you like something to eat? Or drink?'

'How about we go back to my place and I make you a coffee?'

Tom nodded. 'Sounds good.' He opened the passenger door of his car for her, then got into the driver's side and drove to Kate's flat.

'Come on in,' she said, leading the way. 'Nothing much has changed since you were here last. Ages ago.'

'Not since you moved in.' Tom looked around.

'Sit down, Tom.' Kate filled the kettle and turned it on. 'Sorry, I've only got instant.'

'That's okay.' Tom sat at the kitchen table.

Kate sat opposite him. 'Tom,' she said hesitantly, 'I have to know ...'

He looked at her, a puzzled expression on his face.

'Do you have a girl friend?'

Tom went red. 'Why?'

She gulped. 'We've always been friends. Well, you've always been my best friend ...' She twisted her hands and looked down at the table, then glanced up. 'I can't bear it if you have a girlfriend.'

Thomas frowned. 'Why?'

'Oh, Tom, you're making this so difficult for me!'

'Sorry,' he muttered, then, 'Kettle's boiled.' He stood. 'Shall I make the coffee?'

'Tom!' Kate raised her voice. 'Bugger the coffee! I have to know how you feel about me.'

'Um ...' He paused for a moment, then said, 'I think you're beautiful, and awesome and ...' His cheeks blazed.

Kate stood, went to him, took his face in her hands, brought his head down and kissed him.

CHAPTER 21

Thursday 5th December 2019: Kate's twentieth birthday. She woke early, hot and sweaty; unable to open any windows due to the smoke from the catastrophic fires which raged all that summer after the long-running drought. She'd hoped to be able to celebrate her birthday with Tom, but he was away fire-fighting. Both he and Rob had been in the local Rural Fire Service for years, attending the regular training sessions.

She worried about them. Rob had stored his most treasured possessions at Tom's place in town; his dog too. Kate had started going over every morning and evening to take Kelly for a walk and to make sure she was alright. She couldn't have a dog in her flat. Then Tom suggested she move in while he was away. 'Bit easier for you,' he'd remarked. Then proceeded to give her a list of instructions just in case the fires reached town. 'You should be safe at Glads,' he'd continued, taking her in his arms. 'I couldn't bear it if anything happened to you,' he'd murmured into her hair.

'I'll be fine,' she'd replied then, but now, as she looked out the window at the eerie red glow of the sun through the grey, smoke-filled, sky, she knew she wasn't. She was sick with worry. She showered and dressed, ate a hurried breakfast then took Kelly for a walk.

'My birthday today, Kelly,' she said, 'we won't go far, the smoke is too horrible.' As she walked, she thought about her birthday, it still hurt that Wanda hadn't been able to recall the exact date. *Not that it really matters. Unless I want my stars read...* 'Come on, Kelly, we'd better go back. I'll try and finish work early today to go and see Mum.'

***

Christmas was a sad occasion for Kate. Tom and Rob still away fighting the fires. She had text messages from Tom whenever he had a chance to contact her, saying he was fine but they were all very tired, and not to worry about them.

Kate went to Oakley House early on Christmas morning to help out. The nurses and carers had all tried to make the place look cheerful, most of them wore red pixie hats with white bobbles and decorations hung in the rooms.

'Happy Christmas, Kate,' one of the carers said, as she opened the front door. 'Your mum's in her room. You can give her breakfast if you like. It's nearly ready.'

'Thanks, Clarice, I'll get it now.'

'I think she misses Rob coming to visit,' Clarice continued. 'I told her he was fire-fighting, so she understands. At least I think she does.'

'Yes, the doctor told us that she probably understood more than we thought.'

'It's too smoky to take her outside, so best stay in her room with her for a while.'

'Okay, thanks Clarice.' Kate went to the kitchen. 'I've come for mum's breakfast,' she said after exchanging Christmas good wishes.

She spent Christmas day at Oakley House helping out. She looked wistfully at other residents who had family coming in to visit with presents for their elderly friends and relatives. Dorothy came over for a chat after spending some time with Gladys. 'How are you, dear?' she asked Kate. 'Your mum any better?' Not waiting for a reply, she continued, 'Mum's about the same, seems to be settled here now. Anyway, I'd better fly, my husband'll be waiting for his Christmas dinner!' With a wave of her hand she was gone.

***

They were only just over the fires when torrential rain caused floods. The ash that lay everywhere from the fires, turned into a grey sludge. What a start to the new year, Kate thought as she tried to clean the windows of her unit. When Rob and Tom returned from fire fighting, she'd moved back to her unit. Thank goodness Rob's place had been safe from the fires. He'd stayed with Tom for a few days and as soon as he was rested, went to see Jessica. Then took Kelly home. Kate missed her.

It seemed things were just settling back to normal when there was talk of a new virus. At first everyone was dismissive of the pandemic, but when each state started to impose restrictions, reality kicked in. Nursing homes only allowed two visitors at a time, and they had to maintain the new social distancing measures. Kate thought that was crazy. How could she and Rob help feed Jessica if they had to stay over a metre away? In the end, they just ignored it. The nursing home needed their help, and Kate was only working three days a week—hairdressers were able to stay open but were restricted to two or three clients at a time. People weren't driving much, so Tom was only working two days a week; few cars came in to be serviced.

But Tom was happy. He had Kate, and he still had a lot to do on his house. Building a new outside entertaining area took up most of his time.

At Easter Tom suggested Kate move in with him and let out her unit. 'You spend nearly every night here anyway,' he said.

She had to agree. It was so nice being with Tom all the time. She still remembered the fear that overtook her at the thought of Tom fighting fires. She wanted to have him in her sights ... she laughed at herself about that.

Rob seemed happy that she and Tom had at last got together. 'Thought you'd never see the light, Katie dear,' he'd said. 'There was Tom, languishing with unrequited love, and you not seeing what was in front of your nose.'

'I know.' Kate sighed. 'I guess I always loved Tom, just didn't realise that was what it was.'

Tom looked over at her. 'Nah.' He winked at her. 'She just loves my cooking ...'

Kate smiled at Rob. 'That's true.'

***

Mother's Day came on the second weekend in May. Kate and Tom got ready to visit Jessica. Kate had a big bunch of red roses to give her and hoped Jessica would like them.

When they got to Oakley House, Rob was already with Jessica in her room. Apparently, the carers had been busy elsewhere.

Rob smiled. 'Hello, love birds.'

'Hi, Rob, Mum.' Kate bent down to kiss Jessica and show her the flowers. She thought she saw her mother's eyes light up. 'Happy Mother's Day, Mum.'

Tom nodded at his father and said, 'Hi' to Jessica.

Then Kate went to Tom's side and nudged him.

Tom flushed bright red, and a huge grin spread across his face. 'Big news, guys.' He gulped. 'Dad, how do you fancy being a pop?'

'And you a grandmother, Mum?' Kate knelt in front of Jessica.

Rob stared at Kate and his son. 'You mean ...'

'Yes, dear Rob.' Kate smiled. 'There's a little Sullivan on its way.' She took one of Jessica's hands. 'Did you hear that, Mum? You're going to be a grandmother.'

Jessica's eyes filled with tears. 'Luvvy,' she managed to say, and tried to smile.

Kate started to cry.

***

Early one morning a few months later, the phone rang at Tom's place. He picked up the phone, glancing at Kate, hoping it hadn't woken her. She needed her sleep. He could see the bulge of her belly under the doona.

'Tom. It's Dad.' There was a gulping noise.

'What's wrong, Dad?' Tom sat up in the bed and fumbled for his glasses.

'Jessica died in the night. The hospital just rang me. Pneumonia, apparently. She's not been well since that choking fit a few days ago, and they think it's possible food got into her lungs. Anyway, can you tell Kate? Then bring her to Oakley House? I'm going there now. I'll see you there.'

'Okay, Dad.'

Tom gently shook the sleeping Kate. 'Kate, wake up. I'm afraid I have bad news.'

'Wha ...'

Tom put his arms around her. 'Kate, darling, Jessica passed away in the night.'

She stared at him, then her eyes filled with tears.

'Get dressed, we'll go there now.'

In a daze, she obeyed.

Rob was already in Jessica's room when they arrived. 'Apparently she died in her sleep,' he said when they walked in. 'The nurse found her this morning.' He took one of Jessica's hands. 'She looks so peaceful,' he whispered. 'She's out of pain now.' His voice broke and tears started to slide down his face.

'Oh, Mum!' Kate sobbed as she smoothed Jessica's hair. Tom brushed away tears from his eyes.

A nurse entered. 'The doctor's been. Perhaps after you've had a while with Jessica, you'd like to come into the office, and we can talk about arrangements.'

Rob nodded. 'I'll come with you.'

He got up and followed the nurse, closing the door quietly behind him. Tom took Kate in his arms and held her until her sobs ceased, then he took out a handkerchief and gently dried her tears.

'Dad's right,' he whispered. 'She's out of pain now.'

***

The post-mortem report showed that Jessica had died of aspiration pneumonia. They buried her next to her mother and father.

ACKNOWLEDGMENTS

I'd like to thank:

Dr Dimithu Gamage for his help in describing how a doctor would have been able to diagnose Huntington's Disease in the 1970's without the help of MRI and genetic tests.

My beta readers, Barbara Spence, Trish Behan and Shirley Gould for their patience and encouragement.

My editor, Tahlia Newland, without whose help this book would not have seen the light of day.

ALSO BY LYN BEHAN

The Men and the Medium – Based on a true story. When radio inventor and spiritualist, Leslie Carter meets the beautiful psychic healer, Lily Bancroft, he is immediately entranced and knows she's his soulmate and that he could love only her. But Lily is focused on becoming a healer and spiritualist medium. Through two world wars and three marriages, she struggles to fulfil her dreams. Leslie stands by her as each of her marriages fail. Will his love ever be returned?

Seeking Samuel Goldberg – In 1965, on the day of her beloved grandfather's funeral, Liesel discovers that she has Jewish heritage – a family secret held since the days of Nazi Germany – and learns of her grandfather's unfulfilled quest to find family members missing since the outbreak of World War Two. After an unfortunate love affair, Liesel takes on the task of locating her father's cousins, using the few clues her grandfather left. Her travels from Sydney to England and Germany bring her much more than she could ever have expected.

The Unpredictable Past – When a mysterious man, Will, moves into the house opposite hers, Elizabeth's quiet village life is turned upside down. Their friendship develops when Will helps with researching the involvement of one of her ancestors, Edward, in the last revolution in England. This friendship sets the neighbours gossiping and infuriates Elisabeth's daughter, who is convinced Will is a con man preying on her mother, thus raising doubts in Elizabeth's mind. Elizabeth and Will delve more into the past and attempt to solve the mystery surrounding the death of Edward's son, Edmund. How can Elizabeth find out the truth about Will? Is he who he seems?

A Note from the Author

Did you enjoy my book?

If so, I would be very grateful if you could write a review and publish it at your point of purchase. Your review, even a brief one, will help other readers to decide whether or not they'll enjoy my work. Goodreads has a review website.

QUESTIONS FOR BOOK CLUBS

1. Did you know about Huntington's disease before this book? Has the disease affected you personally?

2. Sybilla's intention to abort her baby. Did you find this distressing?

3. What happened to women seeking an abortion before it was legalised in Australia?

4. If you had been in Jessica's situation, after being left with the baby in the train, would you have made the decision to keep the baby?

5. Having made the decision to keep the baby was Jessica right to lie about Kate's birth in order to obtain a birth certificate?

6. Was Kate's reaction understandable after discovering Jessica was not her natural mother ?

7. Were you surprised at Kate's natural mother's home situation?

8. Did you sympathise with Tom in his love for Kate which never seemed to be returned?

9. Was Rob's love for Jessica believable?